UNDER THE
MOONS of MARS

UNDER THE MOONS of MARS

NEW ADVENTURES ON BARSOOM

EDITED BY
JOHN JOSEPH ADAMS

SIMON & SCHUSTER BFYR

New York London Toronto Sydney New Delhi

An imprint of Simon & Schuster Children's Publishing Division
1230 Avenue of the Americas, New York, New York 10020
This book is a work of fiction. Any references to historical events, real people, or real locales are used fictitiously. Other names, characters, places, and incidents are products of the author's imagination, and any resemblance to actual events or locales or persons, living or dead, is entirely coincidental.

Title page illustration copyright © 2012 by Mark Zug. • Foreword copyright © 2012 by Tamora Pierce. • Introduction and compilation copyright © 2012 by John Joseph Adams. • "The Metal Men of Mars" copyright © 2012 by Joe R. Lansdale. Illustration copyright © 2012 by Gregory Manchess. • "Three Deaths" copyright © 2012 by David Barr Kirtley. Illustration copyright © 2012 by Charles Vess. • "The Ape-Man of Mars" copyright © 2012 by Avicenna Development Corporation. Illustration copyright © 2012 by Jeremy A. Bastian. • "A Tinker of Warhoon" copyright © 2012 by Tobias S. Buckell. Illustration copyright © 2012 by Chrissie Zullo. • "Vengeance of Mars" copyright © 2012 by Robin Wasserman. Illustration copyright © 2012 by Misako Rocks! • "Woola's Song" copyright © 2012 by Theodora Goss. Illustration copyright © 2012 by Joe Sutphin. • "The River Gods of Mars" copyright © 2012 by Austin Grossman. Illustration copyright © 2012 by Meinert Hansen. • "The Bronze Man of Mars" copyright © 2012 by L. E. Modesitt, Jr. Illustration copyright © 2012 by Tom Daly. • "A Game of Mars" copyright © 2012 by Genevieve Valentine. Illustration copyright © 2012 by Molly Crabapple. • "A Sidekick of Mars" copyright © 2012 by Garth Nix. Illustration copyright © 2012 by Mike Cavallaro. • "The Ghost That Haunts the Superstition Mountains" copyright © 2012 by ClearMountain Creatives LLC. Illustration copyright © 2012 by John Picacio. • "The Jasoom Project" copyright © 2012 by S. M. Stirling. Illustration copyright © 2012 by Jeff Carlisle. • "Coming of Age on Barsoom" copyright © 2012 by Catherynne M. Valente. Illustration copyright © 2012 by Michael Wm Kaluta. • "The Death Song of Dwar Guntha" copyright © 2012 by Jonathan Maberry. Illustration copyright © 2012 by Daren Bader. • Appendix: A Barsoomian Gazetteer, or, Who's Who and What's What on Mars copyright © 2012 by Richard A. Lupoff. • Story Notes copyright © 2012 by John Joseph Adams and David Barr Kirtley.

All rights reserved, including the right of reproduction in whole or in part in any form.
SIMON & SCHUSTER BFYR is a trademark of Simon & Schuster, Inc.
For information about special discounts for bulk purchases, please contact Simon & Schuster Special Sales at 1-866-506-1949 or business@simonandschuster.com.
The Simon & Schuster Speakers Bureau can bring authors to your live event. For more information or to book an event, contact the Simon & Schuster Speakers Bureau at 1-866-248-3049 or visit our website at www.simonspeakers.com.
Book design by Tom Daly
The text for this book is set in Berthold Baskerville Book.
The illustrations for this book are rendered in various media.
Manufactured in the United States of America
2 4 6 8 10 9 7 5 3
Library of Congress Cataloging-in-Publication Data
Under the moons of Mars : new adventures on Barsoom / edited by John Joseph Adams.
   v. cm.
Summary: An anthology of original stories featuring the Edgar Rice Burroughs character John Carter, an Earthman who suddenly finds himself on a strange new world, Mars.
Contents: The metal men of Mars / by Joe R. Lansdale – Three deaths / by David Barr Kirtley – The ape-man of Mars / by Peter S. Beagle – A tinker of Warhoon / by Tobias S. Buckell – Vengeance of Mars / by Robin Wasserman – Woola's song / by Theodora Goss – The river gods of Mars / by Austin Grossman – The bronze man of Mars / by L. E. Modesitt, Jr. – A game of Mars / by Genevieve Valentine – A Sidekick of Mars / by Garth Nix – The ghost that haunts the Superstition Mountains / by Chris Claremont – The Jasoom project / by S. M. Stirling – Coming of age on Barsoom / by Catherynne M. Valente – The death song of Dwar Guntha / by Jonathan Maberry.
ISBN 978-1-4424-2029-8 (hardcover)
1. Carter, John (Fictitious character)–Juvenile fiction. 2. Mars (Planet)–Juvenile fiction. 3. Science fiction, American. 4. Short stories, American. [1. Mars (Planet)–Fiction. 2. Science fiction.] I. Adams, John Joseph. II. Burroughs, Edgar Rice, 1875-1950.
PZ5.U574 2012
[Fic]–dc23
2011034391
ISBN 978-1-4424-2031-1 (eBook)

For
Christie,
my Dejah Thoris,
and
Edgar Rice Burroughs,
Jeddak of Jeddaks

CONTENTS

Foreword by Tamora Pierce............... **ix**
Introduction by John Joseph Adams ... **xiii**

§ § §

§ § §

FOREWORD

BY TAMORA PIERCE

John Carter, Jeddak of Jeddaks, Warlord of Barsoom.

These words still raise goose bumps on my arms. Edgar Rice Burroughs's Mars books, with their dramatic landscapes and rich cast of characters, were my first experience of a complete, fully imagined setting like nothing in my family's *World Book Encyclopedia*. They were like nothing in the small coal town where I lived, like nothing I saw on television.

They were miraculous.

I was a kid when my father, tired of hearing my complaint that I had nothing to read, handed me *A Princess of Mars*. I then gorged on at least five of the books, one right after the other, before I moved on to Burroughs's other work. While I liked many of them, none of them had the same effect of reshaping my world as did the Barsoom titles. Burroughs's vivid world was easy for me to see in my head. From the moment John Carter awakens on Mars—from his description of the ochre moss to that of the native people—I had a clear view of an alien place. Every page introduced a new aspect of the culture, a different kind of interaction among the natives, or between the natives and John Carter, or a new beast. Different peoples ate, slept, and entertained themselves differently. I watched it all through the eyes of a man born before our American Civil War, and turned every aspect over in my thoughts long after I was supposed to have been asleep.

This was something Burroughs would always do for me, from Barsoom to the London and Africa of the Tarzan books, to the equally strange landscape of Venus, to the savage subterranean land of Pellucidar. He had that happy author's gift of painting entire pictures with only a few sentences, bringing alien horses, commanding princesses, and giant apes vividly to life. I wanted a calot–a Martian dog–like John Carter's, more than anything. (I was convinced they had to be available somewhere.) I wanted to be a telepath, so I would never have to deal with my lisp again. And from Burroughs, I first lit onto the idea that a single moon was not an absolute, that different moons were features of different worlds.

Burroughs did one thing more, something that has had a lifelong effect on my view of my own planet and on my career: Burroughs's women were *strong*. The women of the Tharks were weapons-makers and reserve troops who backed up their fighting men. Sola fights valiantly to defend Dejah Thoris, and Dejah herself was a leader of her people, willing to act in her realm's diplomatic interests even when it brought her into peril. In later books, the Red Woman Thuvia proves herself a willing fighter. The women of his other universes were the same, able to defend themselves and their families with weapons and tenacity. Burroughs probably didn't intend it, but he made the books deemed by my teachers to be fit for my age and gender lackluster and unsatisfying. For a very long time, I found women like his nowhere else in fiction, and I missed them. Deeply.

For years, I knew no one else who felt the same way about the Mars books that I did. Now I discover there are writers who also heard that thrilling call. Some of their stories are here. I hope you enjoy them, and that you, too, will come to dream of the ochre mosses, dangerous rivers, and heroic citizens of Barsoom.

INTRODUCTION

BY JOHN JOSEPH ADAMS

When Edgar Rice Burroughs published *A Princess of Mars* in 1912 (originally published as a serial in the magazine *All-Story*, as *Under the Moons of Mars*), he gave birth to the iconic character John Carter and his wondrous vision of Mars (or as the natives call it, Barsoom). With this setting and character, Burroughs created something that has enthralled generation after generation of readers. Now, a hundred years after the series first debuted in print, new generations of readers—thanks, in part, to the new Disney/Pixar film—are still finding and discovering the adventures of John Carter for the first time.

Edgar Rice Burroughs—who also authored the Tarzan and Pellucidar series, and dozens of other books—wrote only ten Barsoom novels (plus one collection of two stories). Yet anyone who's read the novels cannot help but imagine the plentiful adventures of John Carter and his ilk that were never cataloged by Burroughs. The last Barsoom story written by Burroughs ("Skeleton Men of Jupiter") was published in the magazine *Amazing Stories* in 1943, intended to be one of a series of short stories that would later be collected into book form. It was the last ever published by Burroughs, however, and legions of fans have been left waiting for the new adventures of John Carter ever since.

Until now.

This anthology depicts all-new adventures set in Edgar Rice Burroughs's fantastical world of Barsoom. Some of the stories in this volume, such as Joe R. Lansdale's "The Metal Men of Mars" and "The River Gods of Mars" by Austin Grossman, imagine the new or lost adventures of John Carter, while others focus on the other characters and niches not fully explored by Burroughs. So if you've ever wanted to find out what happens to the villainous Thark Sarkoja after her encounter with John Carter, Robin Wasserman's tale "Vengeance of Mars" delivers. Or if you've ever wanted to know more about John Carter's calot companion Woola, then Theodora Goss's "Woola's Song" fills in those gaps. Catherynne M. Valente's story "Coming of Age on Barsoom," unveils some hidden truths about the Green Men of Mars, and details how John Carter might not have understood their culture as well as he thought he did.

Some of the stories, meanwhile, deal with John Carter and Dejah Thoris's descendants . . . such as Genevieve Valentine's tale, "A Game of Mars," which has John Carter's daughter Tara playing Barsoom's deadliest game–Jetan! We also have two tales exploring the adventures of the children of Llana of Gathol and the Orovar Pan Dee Chee; L. E. Modesitt, Jr.'s, story, "The Bronze Man of Mars," has one of John Carter's great-grandsons returning to the ancient city of Horz, while S. M Stirling's story, "The Jasoom Project," has another great-grandson endeavoring to find a way to travel to Earth (Jasoom) via spaceship.

Authors David Barr Kirtley and Tobias S. Buckell deliver plenty of action and adventure in their tales; in "Three Deaths," after losing a duel with John Carter,

Kirtley's Warhoon warrior Ghar Han swears revenge, and in "A Tinker of Warhoon," Buckell presents us with a Green Martian like we have never seen—one whose greatest weapon is his brain, not his brawn.

Two of our stories examine what would happen should John Carter encounter new visitors from Earth on Barsoom. Peter S. Beagle's story, "The Ape-Man of Mars," speculates what might have happened if John Carter had encountered Tarzan, Burroughs's *other* most famous literary creation, in the sands of Barsoom. Garth Nix's tale, "A Sidekick of Mars," imagines the possibility that John Carter had an irascible sidekick throughout most of his adventures who was never mentioned in any of the write-ups of Carter's adventures published by Burroughs. Chris Claremont's story, "The Ghost That Haunts the Superstition Mountains," meanwhile, imagines John Carter, Dejah Thoris, and Tars Tarkas are instead transported to Earth, and there encounter not only the great Indian chief Cochise, but weapons of mysterious origin as well.

And then we have "The Death Song of Dwar Guntha," which shows us a distant future in which John Carter is poised to finally bring an end to the endless cycles of warfare that have rocked Barsoom . . . but gives us one last epic battle for the ages to remember it by.

Whether you're a longtime fan, or you're new to Barsoom, I hope you enjoy these all-new adventures of John Carter of Mars.

◆ ◆ ◆

In the novel *The Gods of Mars,* John Carter finds himself transported to the Valley Dor, which the Barsoomians believe to be a heavenly paradise, a place to which they willingly travel at the end of a long, full life. He finds instead that the place is a fiendish trap, and he is immediately set upon by hordes of monstrous plant-men—savage, faceless creatures who bound after their prey and strike with wicked tentacles. And this is hardly an isolated incident. Carter just seems to have a knack for stumbling upon hidden corners of Mars in which undreamt-of horrors lurk. Many of these horrors involve wondrous Martian technology, which is far advanced beyond what we know on Earth. The most visible examples of Martian technology are the fliers and airships of the Red Men of Mars, but more grotesque examples abound. Perhaps the most vivid example of Martian science occurs in the novel *The Master Mind of Mars,* in which we are introduced to the mad scientist Ras Thavas, who runs a business transplanting the brains of wealthy clients into healthy young bodies. In *Synthetic Men of Mars,* Carter visits Morbus, city of Ras Thavas, where the scientist is engaged in other strange experiments, such as growing men from a single cell. So it would seem that with Martian science, anything is possible. In the tale that follows, John Carter once again stumbles upon a secret realm, and finds himself face-to-face with some new technology that's visceral and terrifying even by Barsoomian standards.

◆ ◆ ◆

THE METAL MEN
OF MARS

BY JOE R. LANSDALE

I suppose some will think it unusual that mere boredom might lead a person on a quest where one's life can become at stake, but I am the sort of individual who prefers the sound of combat and the sight of blood to the peace of Helium's court and the finery of its decorations. Perhaps this is not something to be proud of, but it is in fact my nature, and I honestly admit it.

Certainly, as Jeddak of Helium, I have responsibilities at the court, but there are times when even my beloved and incomparable Dejah Thoris can sympathize with my restlessness, as she has been raised in a warrior culture and has been known to wield a sword herself. She knows when she needs to encourage me to venture forth and find adventure, lest my restlessness and boredom become like some kind of household plague.

Of course, she realizes I may be putting my life on the line, but then again, that is my nature. I am a fighting man. I find that from time to time I must seek out places where adventure still exists, and then, confronted by peril, I take my sword in hand. Of course, there are no guarantees of adventure, and even an adventurous journey may not involve swordplay, but on Barsoom it can be as readily anticipated as one might expect the regular rising and setting of the sun.

Such was the situation as I reclined on our bedroom couch and tried to look interested in what I was seeing out the open window, which was a flat blue, cloudless sky.

Dejah Thoris smiled at me, and that smile was almost enough to destroy my wanderlust, but not quite. She is beyond gorgeous; a raven-haired, red-skinned beauty whose perfectly oval face could belong to a goddess. Her lack of clothing, which is the Martian custom, seems as natural as the heat of the sun. For that matter, there are no clothes or ornaments that can enhance her shape. You can not improve perfection.

"Are you bored, my love?" she asked.

"No," I said. "I am fine."

"You are not," she said, and her lips became pouty. "You should know better than to lie to me."

I came to my feet, took hold of her, and pulled her to me and kissed her. "Of course. No one knows me better. Forgive me."

She studied me for a moment, kissed me and said, "For you to be better company, my prince, I suggest you put on your sword harness and take leave of the palace for a while. I will not take it personally. I know your nature. But I will expect you to come back sound and whole."

I hesitated, started to say that I was fine and secure where I was, that I didn't need to leave, to run about in search of adventure. That she was all I needed. But I knew it was useless. She knew me. And I knew myself.

She touched my chest with her hand.

"Just don't be gone too long," she said.

I arranged for a small two-seater flyer. Dressed in my weapons harness, which held a long needle sword that is common to Barsoom, as well as a slim dagger, I prepared for departure. Into the flyer I loaded a bit of provisions, including sleeping silks for long Martian nights. I kissed my love goodbye, and climbed on board the moored flyer as it floated outside the balcony where Dejah Thoris and I resided.

Dejah Thoris stood watching as I slipped into the seat at the controls of the flyer, and then smiling and waving to me as if I were about to depart for nothing more than a day's picnic, she turned and went down the stairs and into our quarters. Had she shown me one tear, I would have climbed out of the flyer and canceled my plans immediately. But since she had not, I loosed the mooring ropes from where the craft was docked to the balcony, and allowed it to float upward. Then I took to the controls and directed the ship toward the great Martian desert.

Soon I was flying over it, looking down at the yellow mosslike vegetation that runs on for miles. I had no real direction in mind, and decided to veer slightly to the east. Then I gave the flyer its full throttle and hoped something new and interesting lay before me.

I suppose I had been out from Helium for a Martian two weeks or so, and though I had been engaged in a few interesting activities, I hesitate to call any of them adventures. I had spent nights with the craft moored in the air, an anchor dropped to hold it to the ground, while it floated above like a magic carpet; it was a sensation I never failed to enjoy and marvel at. For mooring, I would try to pick a spot where the ground was low and I could be concealed to some degree by hills or desert valley walls. The flyer could be drawn to the ground, but this method of floating a hundred feet in the air, held fast to the ground by the anchor rope, was quite satisfying. The craft was small, but there was a sleeping cubicle, open to the sky. I removed my weapon harness, laid it beside me, and crawled under my sleeping silks and stretched out to sleep.

After two weeks my plan to find adventure had worn thin, and I was set to start back toward Helium and Dejah Thoris on the morning. As I closed my eyes, I thought of her, and was forming her features in my mind, when my flying craft was struck by a terrific impact.

The blow shook me out of my silks, and the next moment I was dangling in the air, clutching at whatever I could grab, as the flyer tilted on its side and began to gradually turn toward the ground. As I clung, the vessel flipped upside down, and I could hear a hissing sound that told me the flyer had lost its peculiar fuel and was about to crash to the desert with me under it.

The Martian atmosphere gave my Earthly muscles a strength not given to those born on the red planet, and it allowed me to swing my body far and free, as the flyer—now falling rapidly—crashed toward the sward. Still, it was a close call, and I was able to swing out from under the flyer only instants before it smashed the ground. As I tumbled along the desert soil beneath the two Martian moons, I glimpsed the flying machine cracking into a half dozen pieces, tossing debris—including my weapon harness—onto the mossy landscape.

Glancing upward, I saw that the author of the flyer's destruction had turned its attention toward me. It was a great golden bird, unlike anything I had ever seen. It was four times the size of my flyer. As I got a better look, its resemblance to a bird evaporated. It looked more like a huge winged dragon, its coating of scales glinting gold in the moonlight. From its tooth-filled mouth, and easing out from under its scales, came the hiss of steam. With a sound akin to that of a creaking door, it dove at top speed toward me.

❖ ❖ ❖

I practically galloped like a horse toward my weapon harness, and had just laid my hands on it and withdrawn my sword, when I glanced up and saw what I first thought was my reflection in the golden dragon's great black eyes.

But what I saw was not my reflection, but the moonlit silhouettes of figures behind those massive dark eyes. They were mere shapes, like shadows, and I realized in that moment that the golden dragon was not a creature at all: It was a flying machine, something I should have realized immediately as it had not flapped its wings once, but had been moving rapidly about the sky without any obvious means of locomotion.

It dove, and as it came toward me, I instinctively slashed at one of its massive black eyes. I had the satisfaction of hearing it crack just before I dropped to my belly on the sward, and I felt the air from the contraption as it passed above me like an ominous storm cloud, perhaps as close as six inches.

It doesn't suit me to lie facedown with a mouth full of dirt, as it hurts my pride. I sprang to my feet and wheeled to see that the flying machine was still low to the ground, cruising slowly, puffing steam from under its metal scales. I leapt at it, and the Martian gravity gave my Earthly muscles tremendous spring; it was almost like flying. I grabbed at the dragon's tail, which was in fact, a kind of rudder, and clung to it as it rose higher and wheeled, no doubt with an intent to turn back and find me.

I grinned as I imagined their surprise at my disappearance. I hugged the tail rudder with both arms without dropping my sword, and pulled. The dragon wobbled. I yanked at it, and a piece of the tail rudder came loose with a groan. I fell backward and hit the ground with tremendous impact; I wasn't that high up, but still, it was quite a fall.

As I lay on the ground, trying to regain the air that had been knocked out of me, I saw the craft was veering wildly.

It smacked the ground and threw up chunks of desert, then skidded, bounced skyward again, then came back down, nose first. It struck with tremendous impact. There was a rending sound, like a pot and pan salesman tumbling downhill with his wares, and then the dragon flipped nose over tail and slammed against the desert and came apart in an explosion of white steam and flying metal scales and clockwork innards.

Out of anger and pure chance, I had wrecked the great flying machine.

Crawling out of the debris were two of the most peculiar men I had ever seen. They, like the dragon, were golden in color and scaled. White vapor hissed from beneath their metallic scales, and from between their teeth and out of their nostrils. They were moving about on their knees, clanking like knights in armor, their swords dragging in their harnesses across the ground.

Gradually, one of them rose to his feet and looked in my direction; his face was a shiny shield of gold with a broad, unmoving mouth and a long nose that looked like a small piece of folded gold paper. Steam continued to hiss out of his face and from beneath his scales.

The other one crawled a few feet, rolled over on his back, and moved his legs and arms like a turtle turned onto its shell . . . and then ceased to move at all.

The one standing drew his sword, a heavy-looking thing, and with a burst of steam from his mouth and nose, came running in my direction. When confronted by an enemy with a sword, I do not allow myself to become overconfident. Anything can go wrong at anytime with anyone. But for the most part, when a warrior draws his sword to engage me, I can count on the fact that I will be the better duelist; this is not brag, this is the voice of experience. Not only am

I a skilled swordsman, but I have tremendously enhanced agility and strength on my side, all of it due to my Earthly muscles combined with the lighter Martian gravity.

On the armored warrior came, and within an instant we crossed swords. We flicked blades about, wove patterns that we were each able to parry or avoid. But now I understood his method. He was good, but I brought my unique speed and agility into play. An instant later, I was easily outdueling him, but even though my thin blade crisscrossed his armor, leaving scratch marks, I couldn't penetrate it. My opponent's armor was hard and light and durable. No matter what my skill, no matter how much of an advantage I had due to my Earthly muscles, eventually, if I couldn't wound him, he would tire me out.

He lunged and I ducked and put my shoulder into him as I rose up and knocked him back with such force that he hit on his head and flipped over backward. I was on him then, but he surprised me by rolling and coming to his feet, swinging his weapon. I parried his strike close to the hilt of my weapon, drew my short blade with my free hand at the same time, stepped in and stuck it into the eye slot in his helmet.

It was a quick lunge and a withdrawal. He stumbled back, and steam wheezed out of the eye slot and even more furiously from out of his mouth and nose, as well as from beneath his armor's scales. He wobbled and fell to the ground with a clatter.

No sooner had I delighted in my conquest than I realized there had been others in the wreckage, concealed, and I had made the amateur mistake of assuming there had been only two. They had obviously been trapped in the wreckage, and had freed themselves while I was preoccupied. I sensed them behind me and turned. Two were right on top of me and two more were crawling from the remains of the craft. I had only a quick glimpse, for the next thing I knew a sword hilt struck me on the forehead and I took a long leap into blackness.

I do not know how long I was out, but it was still night when I awoke. I was being carried on a piece of the flying dragon wreckage, a large scale. I was bound to it by stout rope and my weapon harness was gone. I did not open my eyes completely, but kept them hooded, and glancing toward my feet, saw that one of the armored men was walking before me, his arms held behind his back, clutching the wreckage I was strapped to as he walked. His scales breathed steam as he walked. It was easy to conclude another bearer was at my head, supporting that end, and I was being borne slowly across the Martian desert.

After a moment, I discarded all pretenses and opened my eyes fully to see that the other two were walking nearby. The fact they had not killed me when they had the chance, especially after I had been responsible for killing two of their own and destroying their craft, meant they had other ideas for me; I doubted they were pleasant.

The moonlight was bright enough that I could see that the landscape had changed, and that we were slowly and gradually descending into a valley. The foliage that grew on either side of the trail we were using was unlike any I had seen on Mars, though even in the moonlight, there was much I could not determine. But it was tall foliage for Mars, and some of it bore berries and fruit. I had the impression the growth was of many colors, though at night this was merely a guess made according to variation in shading.

Down we went, my captors jarring me along. I felt considerably low, not only due to my situation, but because I had allowed myself to fall into it. I might have defended myself adequately with my sword, but I had been so engaged with

the one warrior, I had not expected the others. I thought of
Dejah Thoris, and wondered if I would ever see her again.
Then that thought passed. I would have it no other way. All
that mattered was I was alive. As long as I was alive, there
was hope.

"I still live," I said to the heavens, and it startled my war-
dens enough that they stumbled, nearly dropping me.
We traveled like this for days, and the only time I was
released was to be watered and fed some unidentifiable gruel
and to make my toilet. Unarmed or not, I might have made
a good fight had the blow to my head not been so severe.
Fact was, I welcomed the moment when I was tied down
again and carried. Standing up for too long made me dizzy
and my head felt as if a herd of thoats were riding at full gallop across it.

I will dispense with the details of the days it took us to
arrive at our destination, but to sum it up, we kept slowly
descending into the valley, and as we did the vegetation
became thicker and more unique.

During the day we camped, and began our travels just
before night. I never saw my captors lie down and sleep, but
as morning came they would check to make sure I was well
secured. Then they would sit near the scale on which I was
bound, and rest, though I never thought of them as tired in
the normal manner, but more worn-down as if they were
short on fuel. For that matter, I never saw them eat or drink
water. After several hours, they seemed to have built up the
steam that was inside their armor, for it began to puff more
vigorously, and the steam itself became white as snowfall. I
tried speaking to them a few times, but it was useless. I might
as well have been speaking to a Yankee politician for all the
attention they paid.

After a few days, the valley changed. There was a great
overhang of rock, and beneath the overhang were shadows

so thick you could have shaved chunks out of them with a sword. Into the shadows we went. My captors, with their cat-like vision, or batlike radar, were easily capable of traversing the path that was unseen to me. Even time didn't allow my eyes to adjust. I could hear their armored feet on the trail, the hiss of steam that came from their bodies. I could feel the warmth of that steam in the air. I could tell that the trail was slanting, but as for sight, there was only darkness.

It seemed that we went like that for days, but there was no way to measure or even estimate time. Finally the shadows softened and we were inside a cavern that linked to other caverns, like vast rooms in the house of a god. It was lit up by illumination that came from a yellow moss that grew along the walls and coated the high rocky ceilings from which dangled stalactites. The light was soft and constant; a golden mist.

If that wasn't surprising enough, there was running water; something as rare on Mars as common sense is to all the creatures of the universe. It ran in creeks throughout the cavern and there was thick brush near the water and short, twisted, but vibrant trees flushed with green leaves. It was evident that the moss not only provided a kind of light, but other essentials to life, same as the sun. There was a cool wind lightly blowing and the leaves on the trees shook gently and made a sound like someone walking on crumpled paper.

Eventually, we came to our destination, and when we did I was lifted upright, like an insect pinned to a board, and carried that way by the two warriors gripping the back of the scale. The others followed. Then I saw something that made my eyes nearly pop from my head.

It was a city of rising gold spires and clockwork machines that caused ramps to run from one building to another. The ramps moved and switched to new locations with amazing timing; it all came about with clicking and clucking sounds of metal snapping together, unseen machinery winding and twisting and puffing out steam through all manner of shafts and man-made crevices. There were wagons on the ramps, puffing vapor, running by means of silent motors, gliding on smooth rolling wheels. There were armored warriors walking across the ramps, blowing white fog from their faces and from beneath their scales like teakettles about to boil. The wind I felt was made by enormous fans supported on pedestals.

The buildings and their spires rose up high, but not to the roof of the caverns, which I now realized were higher than I first thought. There were vast windows at the tops of the buildings; they were colored blue and yellow, orange and white, and gave the impression of not being made of glass, but of some transparent stone.

Dragon crafts, large and small, flittered about in the heights. It was a kind of fairy-tale place; a vast contrast from the desert world above.

The most spectacular construction was a compound, gold in color, tall and vast, surrounded by high walls and with higher spires inside. The gold gates that led into the compound were spread wide on either side. Steam rose out of the construction, giving it the appearance of something smoldering and soon to be on fire. Before the vast gates was a wide moat of water. The water was dark as sewage, and little crystalline things shaped like fish swam in it and rose up from time to time to show long, brown teeth.

A drawbridge lowered with a mild squeak, like a sleepy mouse having a bad dream. As it lowered, steam came from the gear work and filled the air to such an extent that I coughed. They carried me across the drawbridge and into the inner workings of the citadel, out of the fairy tale and into a house of horrors.

❖ ❖ ❖

For a moment we were on streets of gold stone. Then we veered left and came to a dark mouthlike opening in the ground. Steam gasped loudly from the opening, like an old man choking on cigar smoke. There was a ramp that descended into the gap, and my bearers carried me down it. The light in the hole was not bright. There was no glowing moss. Small lamps hung in spots along the wall and emitted heavy orange flames that provided little illumination; the light wrestled with the cotton-thick steam and neither was a clear winner.

In considerable contrast to above, with its near-silent clockwork and slight hissing, it was loud in the hole. There was banging and booming and screaming that made the hair on the back of my neck prick.

As we terminated the ramp and came to walk on firm ground, the sounds grew louder. We passed Red Martians, men and women, strapped to machines that were slowly stripping their flesh off in long, bloody bands. Other machines screwed the tops of their heads off like jar lids. This was followed by clawed devices that dipped into the skull cavity and snapped out the brain and dunked it into an oily blue liquid in a vat. Inside the vat the liquid spun about in fast whirls. The brains came apart like old cabbages left too long in the ground. More machines groaned and hissed and clawed and yanked the victim's bones loose. Viscera was removed. All of this was accompanied by the screams of the dying. When the sufferers were harvested of their bodily parts, a conveyer brought fresh meat along; Red Martians struggling in their straps, gliding inevitably toward their fate. And all the time, below them were the armored warriors, their steam-puffing faces lifted upward, holding long rods to assist the conveyer that was bringing the sufferers along, dangling above the metal men like ripe fruit ready for the picking.

◆ ◈ ◆

The cage where they put me was deep in the bowels of the caverns, below the machines. There were a large number of cages, and they were filled mostly with Red Martians, though there were also a few fifteen-foot-tall, four-armed, green-skinned Tharks, their boarlike tusks wet and shiny.

The armored warriors opened a cage, and the two gold warriors, who had followed my bearers, sprang forward and shoved those who tried to escape back inside. I was unbound and pushed in to join them. They slammed the barred gate and locked it with a key. Men and women in the cage grabbed at the bars and tried uselessly to pull them loose. They yelled foul epithets at our captors.

I wandered to the far side of our prison, which was a solid wall, and slid down to sit with my back to it. Though I was weak, and in pain, I tried to observe my circumstances, attempted to formulate a plan of escape.

One Red man came forward and stood over me. He said, "John Carter, Jeddak of Helium."

I looked up in surprise. "You know me?"

"I do, for I was once a soldier of Helium. My name is Farr Larvis."

I managed to stand, wobbling only slightly. I reached out and clasped his shoulder. "I regret I didn't recognize you, but I know your name. You are well respected in Helium."

"Was respected," he said.

"We wondered what happened to your patrol," I said. "We searched for days."

Farr Larvis was a name well-known in Helium: a general of some renown who had fought well for our great city. During one of our many conflicts with the Green Men of Mars, he and a clutch of warriors had been sent to protect citizens on the outskirts of the city from Thark invaders. The invaders had been driven back, Farr Larvis and his men pursuing on their thoats. After that, they had not been heard of again. Search parties were sent out, and for weeks they were sought, without so much as a trace.

"We chased the Tharks," Farr Larvis said, "and finally met them in final combat. We lost many men, but in the end prevailed. Those of us who remained prepared to return to Helium. But one night we made our camp and the gold ones came in their great winged beasts. They came to us silently and dropped nets, and before we could put up a fight, hoisted us up inside the bellies of their beasts. We were brought here. I regret to inform you, John Carter, that of my soldiers, I and two others are all that remain. The rest have become one with the machine."

He pointed the survivors out to me in the crowd.

I clasped his shoulder again. "I know you fought well. I am weak. I must sit."

We both sat and talked while the other Red Martians wandered about the cell, some moaning and crying, others merely standing like cattle waiting their turn in the slaughter-house line. Farr Larvis's two soldiers sat against the bars, not moving, waiting. If they were frightened, it didn't show in their eyes.

"The gold men, they are not men at all," Farr Larvis told me.

"Machines?" I said.

"You would think, but no. They are neither man nor machine, but both. They are made up of body parts and cogs and wheels and puffs of steam. And most importantly, the very spirits of the living. Odar Rukk is responsible."

"And who and what is he?" I asked.

"His ancestors are from the far north, the rare area where there is ice and snow. They were a wicked race, according to Odar Rukk, fueled by the needs of the flesh. They were warlike, destroying every tribe within their range."

"Odar Rukk told you this personally?"

"He speaks to us all," said Farr Larvis. "There are constant messages spilled out over speakers. They tell his history, they tell his plans. They explain our fate, and how we are supposed to accept it. According to him, in one night there came a great melting in the north, and the snow and much of the ice collapsed. Their race was lost, except for those driven underground. These were people who found a chamber that led down into the earth. It was warmer there, and they survived because the walls were covered in moss that gave heat and light. There were wild plants and wild animals, and the melting ice and snow leaked down into the world and formed lakes and creeks and rivers. In time these people populated all of the underground. They found gold. They discovered hissing vats of volcanic release; it's the power source for most of what occurs here. They built this city.

"But in time, the time of Odar Rukk, the people began to return to their old ways. The ways that led to their destruction by the gods. And Odar Rukk, a scientist who helped devise the way this city works, decided, along with idealistic volunteers, that there was a need for a new and better world. Gradually, he changed these volunteers into these gold warriors, and then they captured the others and changed them. The goal was to eliminate the needs of people, and to make them machinelike."

"All of them under his control?" I said.

"Correct," Farr Larvis said. "Ah, here comes the voice."

And so it came: Odar Rukk's voice floating out from wall speakers and filling the chambers like water. It was a thin voice, but clear, and he spoke for hours and hours, explained how we were all part of a new future, that we should submit, and that soon all our needs, all our desires for greed and romance and success and war, would be behind us. We would be blended in blood and bone and spirit. We would be collectively part of the greatest race that Barsoom had ever known. And soon the gold ones would spread out far and wide, crunching all Martians beneath their steampowered plans.

I do not know how long we waited there in the cell, but every day the gold ones came and brought us food, which was more of the gruel. They gave us water and we made our toilet where we could. And then came the day when the speakers did not speak. Odar Rukk's voice did not drone. There was only silence, except for the moaning and crying from the captives.

"The gold ones come today," Farr Larvis said. "On the day of Complete Silence. They take the people away and they do not come back."

"I suggest, then, that we do not let them take us easily," I said. "We must fight. And if they should carry us away, we should fight still."

"If it is at all possible," Farr Larvis said, "I will fight to the bitter end. I will fight until the machines take me apart."

"It is all we can do," I said. "And sometimes, that is enough."

True to Farr Larvis's word, they came. There were many of them, and they marched in time in single file. They brought a gold key and snicked it in the cell lock. They entered the cell, and the moans and cries of the Red Martians rose up.

"Silence," Farr Larvis yelled. "Do not give them the satisfaction."

But they did not go silent.

The gold ones came in with short little sticks that gave off shocks. I fought them, because I knew nothing other than to fight. They came and I knocked them down with my fist, their armor crunching beneath my Earthly strength. There were too many, however, and finally I went down beneath their shocks. My hands were bound quickly with rope in front of me, and I was lifted up.

Farr Larvis fought well, and so did his two men, but they took them, and all the others, and carried them away.

Along the narrow path between the cells we went, in their clutches, and then a curious thing happened. The half a dozen gold ones carrying me, giving me intermittent shocks with their stinging rods, veered off and took me away from the mass being driven toward the Meat Rooms, as Farr Larvis called them: the place of annihilation.

I was being separated from the others, carried toward some separate fate.

Farr Larvis called out: "Good-bye, John Carter."

"Remember," I said back. "We still live."

They hauled me into a colossal room which was really a cavern. The walls sweated gooey liquid gold, thick as glowing honey. There were clear tubes running along the ceiling and they were full of the yellow liquid. In spots the tubes leaked, and the fluid dripped from the leaks and fell in splotches like golden bird droppings to the ground. The air in the room was heavily misted with gold. It gave the illusion that we were like flies struggling through amber. There was a cool wet wind flowing through the cavern, its temperature just short of being cold.

I was carried forward to where a domed building could be seen at the peak of a pyramid of steps. On the top of the dome was an immense orb made of transparent stone, and it was full of the golden elixir. It popped and bubbled and splattered against the globe. Up we went, and finally, after giving me a series of shocks to make sure my resistance was lowered, they laid me on the ground and stood around me, waited, looked up at the dome and globe.

A part of the dome's wall lowered with the expected hiss of steam. A multi-wheeled machine rolled out, and in it sat an obese, naked, red-skinned man with a mis-shapen skull. The skull was bare except for a few strands of gray hair that floated above it in the gold-tinted wind, wriggling like albino roach antennae. The eyes in the skull were dark and beady and rheumy; one of them had a mind of its own, wandering first up, and then down, then left to right. His massive belly looked ready to pop, like an overripe pomegranate. He was without legs. In fact, from his lower torso on, he was machine. Hoses and wires ran from the wheeled conveyance to the back of his head, and when he breathed, steam issued from his mouth and nose like a snorting dragon. His long, skeletal fingers rested on the arms of the chair, in easy reach of a series of buttons and switches and levers and dials. Off of the chair trailed transparent tubes pulsing with the gold fluid, and red and blue and green and yellow wires. All of this twisted back behind him, along the ramp, and into the dome, and I could see where the wires and horses curled upward toward the globe. All of this ran out from the globe and into the wall behind it.

Having recovered somewhat from the electrical shocks, I slowly stood up. Two of the gold men moved toward me.

"Leave him," said the man, who I knew to be Odar Rukk. I had heard his voice many times over the speakers in the walls. "Leave him be."

He fixed his good eye on me. "Your name?"

I pushed out my chest and stuck out my chin. "John Carter, Warlord of Mars."

"Ah, that obviously means something to you, but it means nothing to me. Do you know who I am?"

"A madman named Odar Rukk."

He smiled, and the smile was a glint of metal teeth and

hissing steam. "Yes, I am Odar Rukk, and I may be the only sane man on Barsoom."

"I would not put that up for a vote," I said.

"Oh, I don't know. My golden army would agree."

"They neither agree or disagree," I said. "They blindly obey."

"As do all armies."

"Armies and men fight for beliefs and for purpose."

"Oh. You titled yourself Warlord of Mars. Do you not enjoy battle? War?"

I said nothing. He had spoken the truth. It was not all about ideals.

"I brought you here because my golden warriors have been recording in their memory cells all that they saw you do. They know you single-handedly brought down my flying machine, destroyed one of their kind in the crash, another with your swordsmanship. Those events they recorded in their heads and now those events are in my head."

Odar Rukk paused to tap his skull with the tip of his index finger.

"They brought those images to me, and with but a twist of a dial and the flick of a switch, they come into my head and I see what they have seen. They showed me a man who could do extraordinary things. Before I take those things from you, tell me, John Carter, Warlord of Mars, why are you so different?"

"I am from Earth. The gravity is heavier there. It makes me stronger here. And most importantly, I do what I do because I am who I am. John Carter, formerly of a place called Virginia."

"You, John Carter, will be my personal fuel. I will suck out your spirit and your abilities and into me directly they will go."

"You will still be you. Not me."

"I do not wish to be you, John Carter. I wish to take away your spirit, your powers. I will use them to live longer yet. I will use them to change this planet for the better. Soon, I will spread our empire. I will take away the insignificant needs of men and women. I will eliminate hunger and fear and war, all the negative aspects."

"Except for yourself," I said. "You remain very manlike."

Odar Rukk smiled that steamy, gleaming smile again. "Someone must rule. Someone must control. There must be one mind that oversees and does not merely respond. That is my burden."

"What you have done here is nothing more than an exercise in vanity," I said.

"Have it your way," he said. "But soon your strength, your will, shall be contained inside of me, and I will be stronger than before. When I saw what you could do, your uniqueness, I decided it would be all mine. Not spread out among the others. But all mine."

"Being unique somewhat spoils your vision of everyone and everything being alike, does it not?"

"I have no need to argue, John Carter," he said. "I have the power here, not you. And in moments, when you are strapped in and sucked out and all those abilities are pumped into me, you will cease to exist, and I will be stronger."

The shocks had worn off, and the ropes they had tied me with had loosened. They had not been tied that well to begin with, but still, they were sufficient to hold me. No matter. I had decided I would give my life dearly before I let this monster take away my spirit, my abilities, my blood and bones and flesh.

And then, when I was on the verge of hurling myself at Odar Rukk, knocking him out of his chair with my body, with the intent of trying to bite his throat out, there was an unexpected change of situation.

◆ ◈ ◆

There was a noise beyond our cavern, a noise that echoed into our huge chamber and clamored about the walls like a series of great metal butterflies clanging against the walls. It was the sound of conflict from beyond our cavern. Somehow, I knew it was Farr Larvis and his two warriors. They were managing to put up a last hard fight.

In that moment, with Odar Rukk's head twisting about, trying to find the source of the sound, the gold ones having turned their attention to the back of the cave, I jumped toward the nearest gold one, grabbed his sword with my bound hands, and pulled it from its sheath. I sliced at him, catching him beneath the helmet and slicing his head off his shoulders. There was a spurt of gold liquid from his neck, a spark from a batch of severed wires, and he went down.

I managed to twist the sword in my hand and cut my rope and free my hands. Then I turned as they came at me. I wove my sword like a tapestry of steel. Poking through eye slots, slicing under the helmets, taking off heads, chopping legs and arms free at joint connections where the armor was thinnest.

I spun about for a look, saw Odar Rukk had wheeled his machine about and was darting up the ramp, back into the dome. Already the ramp was rising. Soon he would be safe inside. I leapt. My Earthly muscles saved me again, for the horde of gold men were about to be on me, thick as a cluster of grapes, and even with all my skill, I could not have fought them all. I landed on the ramp. It was continuing to lift, and it unsettled my footing. I started to slide after Odar Rukk, who had already driven himself inside the dome.

When the door clamped shut, I was in a large room with Odar Rukk. He had turned himself about in the chair, the hoses and wires fastened to the back of it twisted with him. I saw at a glance that the walls were lined with darkened bodies, both Red folk and Green Men. They hung like flies in webs, but the webs were wires and hoses and metal clamps. This was undoubtedly Odar Rukk's power source, something he had planned for me to become a part of.

"This is your day of reckoning, Odar Rukk," I said.

From somewhere he produced a pistol and fired. The handguns of Barsoom are notoriously inaccurate, as well as few and far between, but the shot had been a close one. I leapt away. The gun blasted again, and its beam came closer still. I threw my sword and had the satisfaction of seeing it go deep into his shoulder. His gun hand wavered.

Leaping again, I drove both my feet in front of me. I hit Odar Rukk in the chest with tremendous impact. The blow knocked him and his attached machine chair backward, tipping it over. Odar Rukk skidded across the floor. The part of him that was machine threw up sparks. Hoses came unclamped, spewed gold fluid. Wires came loose and popped with electric current. Odar Rukk screamed.

I hustled to my feet and sprang toward him to administer a death blow, but it was unnecessary. The hoses and wires had been his arteries, his life force, and now they were undone. Odar Rukk's body came free of the chair connection with a snick, and he slipped from it, revealing the bottom of his torso, a scarred and cauterized mess with wire and hose connections, now severed. The fat belly burst open and revealed not only blood and organs, but gears and wheels and tangles of wires and hoses. His flesh went dark and fell from his skull and his eyes sank in his head like fishing sinkers. A moment later, he was nothing more than a piece of fragmented machine and rotten flesh and yellow bones.

I recovered his firearm, cut some of the wire from the machine-man loose with my sword, used it to make a belt, and stuck the pistol between it and my flesh. I recovered my sword.

Outside of the locked dome, I could hear the clatter of battle. Farr Tharvis had been more successful than I expected. But even if he had put together an army, the metal men would soon make short work of them.

I looked up at the pulsing globe that rose through the top of the dome. I jumped and grabbed the side of the dome, in a place where my hands could best take purchase, and clambered up rapidly to the globe, my sword in my teeth.

Finally I came to the rim below the globe. There was a metal rim there, and it was wide enough for me to stand on it. I took hold of my sword, and with all my strength, I struck.

The blow was hard, but the structure, which I was now certain was some form of transparent stone, withstood it. I withdrew the pistol and fired. The blast needled a hole in the dome and a spurt of gold liquid nearly hit me in the face. I moved to the side and it gushed out at a tremendous rate. I fired again. Another hole appeared and more of the gold goo leapt free. The globe cracked slightly, then terrifically, generating a web of cracks throughout. Then it exploded and the fluid blew out of it like a massive ocean wave. It washed me away, slamming me into the far wall. I went under, losing the pistol and sword. I tried my best to swim. Something, perhaps a fragment of the globe, struck my head and I went out.

When I awoke, I was outside the dome, which had collapsed like wet paper. I was lying on my back, my head being lifted up by a smiling Farr Larvis.

"When you broke the globe, it caused the gold men to collapse. It was their life source."

"And Odar Rukk's," I said.

"It was a good thing," Farr Larvis said. "The revolt I led was not doing too well. It was exactly at the right moment,

John Carter. Though we were nearly all washed away. Including you."

I grinned at him. "We still live."

There isn't much left to tell.

Simply put, all of us who had survived gathered up weapons and started out as the machinery that Odar Rukk had invented gradually ceased to work. The drawbridge was down. All the gates throughout the underground city had sprung open, and had hissed out the last of their steam. The gold ones were lying about like uneven pavement stones.

We found water containers and filled them. We tore moss from the walls and used it for light, made our way up the long path out. After much time, we came to the surface. We gathered up fruit and such things as we thought we could eat on our journey, and then we climbed higher out of the green valley until we stood happily on the warm desert sand.

It was a long trip home, and there were minor adventures, but nothing worth mentioning. Eventually we came within sight of Helium, and I paused and stood before the group, which was of significant size, and swore allegiance to them as Jeddak of Helium, and in return they swore the same to me.

Then we started the last leg of our journey, and as we went, I thought of Dejah Thoris, and how so very soon she would be in my arms again.

✦ ✦ ✦

Here on Earth you can basically expect that any large animal you see is going to have four limbs. How dull! Fauna on Barsoom is much more colorful, with a profusion of limbs everywhere you look. The Barsoomian lion, called the banth, has ten legs, and the Barsoomian horse, a reptilian creature known as a thoat, has eight. The Barsoomian dogs, called calots, have six legs. (John Carter's faithful pet Woola was one of these.) There are also the four-armed white apes who haunt the abandoned cities. Burroughs never specifies how many legs the ratlike ulsios have, nor how many are possessed by the elephantine zitidars, but it seems likely that both have more than four. (Many artists have depicted them with six.) And of course, most notably of all, the Green Men have six limbs—four arms and two legs. For those of us who grew up on Earth, it usually seems that four limbs is plenty, and we look upon the many-legged beasts of Barsoom as exotic oddities, but of course the denizens of that world would surely regard our own planet as strange, particularly with regard to Earth's parsimonious distribution of appendages. Our next story explores the idea that having two hands can seem like a terrible burden when you've lived your whole life with four.

✦ ✦ ✦

THREE DEATHS

BY DAVID BARR KIRTLEY

This is a tale of Mars, which the Martians call Barsoom— a dying planet that clings to life only through the striving of its most civilized inhabitants, the Red Men, who maintain its grand canals and atmosphere plant.

This is a tale of the wild Green Men of Mars, four-armed giants who roam in great hordes across the dead sea bottoms and who dwell amid the ruins of ancient cities.

This is a tale of three deaths.

Our story begins on the day that a small band of Warhoon scouts crossed paths with John Carter of Virginia, and Ghar Han, one of the greatest warriors of the Green Men, challenged the Earthman to single combat. By all the laws of Mars such a challenge may not be refused, and the man so challenged must choose a weapon that is no better than that wielded by his adversary.

Ghar Han held swords in each of his four hands, and the skulls of half a dozen great warriors rattled upon his harness, for he had won many battles, and added the names of many a vanquished foe to his own. He towered over his opponent, and gazed with contempt upon the Earthman, who held but

a single blade, and who seemed small and freakish with his strange pale flesh and black hair. Around them stood a ring of Green Men, including two young warriors, the arrogant Harkan Thul and the sly Sutarat. Nearby, the mounts of the Green Men, the eight-legged reptilian thoats, grazed upon the yellow grass that stretched away in all directions.

Ghar Han attacked, now stabbing with his upper right hand, now slashing with his lower left, his four blades a whirlwind of steel, glinting in the sun. John Carter backed away, ducking from side to side, parrying strike after strike. When the Earthman had been backed against the spectators and had no more room to retreat, Ghar Han employed his favorite attack, a devastating overhand chop with his upper right sword, a move which had cleft many an opponent nearly in two.

The sword buried itself in the sand as John Carter spun away and came around with a double-handed blow aimed at Ghar Han's exposed right shoulder. The Green Man raised his lower right sword to block, but the Earthman's blade knocked the weapon aside and sank deep into Ghar Han's flesh.

Ghar Han stumbled back, feeling a terrible wrenching as the Earthman's blade was ripped free. Ghar Han's upper right sword fell from his nerveless fingers, and his upper right arm now hung from his shoulder like a pennon. That arm, his strongest, would never fully heal, he knew.

John Carter pressed the attack, and Ghar Han reeled, dazed. The Earthman's blade was everywhere, and Ghar Han hurled up sword after sword to deflect the blows, but three swords were not enough. He needed a fourth sword, a fifth, a sixth, to fend off the relentless attacks.

A crushing stroke swept the upper left sword from his grasp and sent it spinning into the crowd, and then the tip of John Carter's blade lanced through Ghar Han's lower right forearm, causing him to drop that sword as well. Blood streaked the Green Man's side. Dizzy, half-blind with pain and fear, he sank to one knee, feebly holding up his last remaining sword.

John Carter kicked him in the chest, and Ghar Han sprawled, sliding backward through the sand.

He lifted his head. The sun was in his eyes, and all he could see was a dark form wreathed in blinding light. The shadow raised its sword and brought it down.

Ghar Han, one of the greatest warriors of the Green Men, felt his lower left arm part, and fall away.

He awoke, which surprised him, since duels among the Green Men are fought to the death. He was in his tent, lying on a mat, and it was night. He went to rub his eyes with his upper right hand, but nothing happened. He glanced at his shoulder, and saw bandages there soaked in blood. More bandages bound his abdomen.

"We were forced to remove the upper right arm," came a woman's voice. "And the lower left was—"

"Where is John Carter?" said Ghar Han.

"Gone. The others brought you here."

"Get out."

"I—"

"Get out!" he said, sitting up. The woman fled.

Ghar Han fell back, writhing. Phantom pains lanced up and down his missing limbs. He cursed the cruelty of the Earthman, for not striking a killing blow. He cursed the potent medicine of the Green women. He was a freak now, a cripple. Two arms only remained to him—two arms, like any of the lesser races of men.

For days he did not leave his tent. He drifted in and out of sleep, haunted by strange, vivid dreams. In one he was running and fighting, stabbing and slashing, and he realized that he had four arms again, and felt elation. It was only a dream, he thought, only a dream that I had lost them. Then he woke in the tent again and moaned, despairing.

In another dream he'd lost all his limbs, even his legs, and he lay helpless on his back like a worm, staring up at the stars, and the twin moons, and Earth. From the darkness around him came the growls of circling banths, and somewhere above him echoed the cruel laughter of John Carter. It was a dream he would have many more times.

When he was awake, he replayed the duel over and over in his mind.

How was it possible, he thought, that he should have been defeated by such a small and wretched man? Not through skill, that was certain. No, rather this John Carter had come from another world, a world whose heavy gravity had given him muscles unmatched on Barsoom. It was treacherous, thought Ghar Han, to use Earthly muscles here. The more he thought about it, the greater grew his sense of outrage. John Carter did not belong here. John Carter had caught him off guard. John Carter had cheated!

We will meet again, Earthman, he thought. *And next time I'll be ready.*

Finally he strapped on four swords—one at each hip and two crossed across his back—and strode out into the harsh light of day. As he moved through the camp, the Warhoon regarded him with disdain. Harkan Thul and Sutarat emerged from behind a tent and stopped to stare. Normally they would never have the nerve to mock Ghar Han to his face, but now that he'd been shamed and crippled they jeered.

"Look!" cried Harkan Thul. "An intruder in our camp! What manner of creature is it, Sutarat?"

"I know not," said Sutarat, with a grin. "It almost seems to be one of us, but of course we have four arms, and this strange creature has only two."

31

"Perhaps it is the Earthman John Carter," said Harkan Thul. "And he has smeared himself with green paint in order to infiltrate our ranks."

Sutarat laughed.

Ghar Han scowled and walked on past. He sought out the tent of Xan Malus, Jeddak of the Warhoon, and was shown into the presence of the great lord, a cold, imperious man who clutched a spiked scepter and sat upon a jeweled throne.

"Kaor, Ghar Han," said Xan Malus. "It pleases us to see that you are up and useful to us once more."

"Kaor, Excellency," said Ghar Han, crossing his two arms and bowing his head. "Thank you."

"Now tell us," said the Jeddak, "why have you come?"

"Excellency," said Ghar Han, "if it please you, I should like to pursue the Earthman John Carter, and challenge him once again to—"

"No, no," said Xan Malus impatiently. "It does *not* please us. John Carter's death is nothing to me, and in any event you would not succeed. I relinquish no asset, however small. I will not sacrifice one of my warriors, even a cripple, to no end."

"Excellency, I—"

"I know, I know," said the Jeddak, with a wave. "You would prefer an honorable death to your present humiliation. But what care I for your honor, Ghar Han? I am Jeddak, and you are mine, and so long as I breathe you shall be deployed to my ends, not yours. Tomorrow we strike camp and journey to retrieve the eggs of our offspring, and I desire that every able warrior be on hand to guard them. You know our wishes. Go."

Ghar Han bowed again, and departed.

He was not accustomed to being treated with such contempt, but in the days that followed he became quite practiced at it. Many of the younger warriors seemed never to tire of mocking him for his missing arms, and Harkan Thul and Sutarat remained the worst of his tormentors. Once, he would have simply challenged the two of them to duels, but without the use of his strongest arm he was no longer confident of victory, and besides, spilling their blood would not erase his shame. Only the death of John Carter could do that. Ghar Han's only hope now was that fate would deliver John Carter to him once again. In his dreams he slew the Earthman a hundred times.

As the months passed, he found that his feelings about his people had begun to change. From his lofty vantage as a fearsome warrior, the ways of the Warhoon had always seemed fair to him. Harsh, yes, for Barsoom was a harsh world that required a harsh people. But fair. Now though, he was not so sure. More and more the ways of the Warhoon seemed to him pointlessly cruel. Why should he, who had suffered a misfortune that might befall anyone, be so scorned? Did such ruthlessness make them stronger as a tribe, or weaker?

One day he was walking through camp and turned a corner into a shaded area between two tents, and came upon Harkan Thul and Sutarat and some of the others. They'd surrounded a young woman, who'd been knocked to her knees, and they were taunting her and laughing.

Without thinking, Ghar Han stepped forward. "Leave her alone."

Harkan Thul turned to regard him with contempt. "Oh, leave us be, two-arm. You're not wanted here."

"Don't call me that," warned Ghar Han, and the others laughed.

For an instant he considered walking away. Then he took a deep breath, collected himself, and said calmly, "I said leave her alone."

Sutarat exchanged glances with some of the others, and they moved away from the girl and slowly closed in on Ghar Han, their faces dark.

Harkan Thul sighed. "Oh, what has become of you, Ghar Han? Not only do you *look* like one of the lesser races, now it seems you have one of their soft hearts as well. You don't belong here. You are not one of us. Go."

Ghar Han didn't move.

Harkan Thul reached for his swords. "Do you lust for suffering, Ghar Han? This will go worse for you than the day you faced John Carter."

"And how would you know?" Ghar Han said sharply.

Harkan Thul paused, caught off guard.

"How would *you* know what it's like to face John Carter? You never have. Only I have." Ghar Han's voice rose, his fury pouring out of him. "The Earthman was here among us. I fought him, and then he departed, and none of you raised a sword to stop him. Because you were afraid!"

Harkan Thul drew his swords. "Call me a coward? I will kill you."

"Oh, so brave!" cried Ghar Han. "To fight a cripple. But where were you when John Carter was among us?" He pounded his fist against his chest. "Only Ghar Han had the courage to face him then."

Harkan Thul was silent. Finally he sheathed his swords.

"It's true," he said, "spilling your blood would be too easy. Bring me a real challenge. Bring any man of this world or another and I will face him. I am not afraid."

"We'll see," said Ghar Han. "Someday the Earthman will cross our paths again, and then we'll see who's not afraid."

Harkan Thul sneered and turned away. "Come on," he said to the others. "Let's go."

When they were gone, Ghar Han offered his hand to the girl.

"Here," he said, "let me—"

"Do not touch me, cripple," she said, furious, climbing to her feet.

Years passed, and Ghar Han grew ever more isolated and withdrawn, watching grimly as Harkan Thul and Sutarat amassed power and status. Harkan Thul attained the rank of jed and became leader of their scouting party, with Sutarat as his second-in-command.

One day the scouting party rode up over the crest of a hill and looked out on the valley below. Before them lay an ancient ghost town, a lonely place of stairways and minarets and white marble. Then the Green Men noticed, off in the distance, a lone figure trudging across the sand toward the village.

Sutarat said, "Who is that, who dares invade our territory?"

"Let's find out," said Harkan Thul, urging his thoat to a gallop.

As the beasts thundered down the hill, the stranger broke into a run, racing toward the village. Then, as the Green Men watched, astonished, he took a great flying leap, hurtling through the air. In two bounds he'd reached the outlying buildings, and then he sprang to a third-story window and disappeared.

Ghar Han's heart beat faster. John Carter! It must be, for only the unnatural muscles of an Earthman could propel such wondrous leaps. After all these years they would meet again. At last had come his chance for redemption, or perhaps an honorable death.

When the Green Men reached the city gates, Harkan Thul wheeled his mount and cried, "Circle the village, all of you! Make sure he doesn't sneak off! I will enter and challenge him to a duel. Sutarat will be my second. Come."

"No!" said Ghar Han, riding forward. "John Carter is mine!"

Harkan Thul glared. "I am jed here, not you, and I say—"

"No!" yelled one of the warriors. "Ghar Han should face John Carter. If he dares."

"Yes," said another. "He was crippled and shamed by the Earthman. Let him fight."

Others muttered agreement, and Harkan Thul saw that he risked mutiny if he tried to press the issue.

"All right," he said at last. "Ghar Han will have his chance. But if he fails, I will not. Come on."

As the others fanned out around the village, Ghar Han, Harkan Thul, and Sutarat rode through the gates. They tied their thoats to a hitching post, then proceeded on foot through the narrow streets, swords in their hands.

Ghar Han heard footfalls on a nearby rooftop, and glanced up just as a dark form catapulted across the sky, leaping from building to building. An instant later it was gone, but not before Ghar Han had seen that this Earthman had yellow hair.

Yellow, not black like John Carter.

"Come on!" said Harkan Thul. "After him!"

They pursued the figure, and Ghar Han's mind raced. What if this was not John Carter?

If not, then Ghar Han would not be able to exact vengeance upon the man who'd shamed him, but he found that this no longer moved him the way it once had. What disturbed him more was the idea of more than one Earthman on Barsoom. Bad enough that John Carter had found his way here through some arcane means, but now it seemed there might be two, and if two then why not three, or four, or ten? Any one of them a match for even the strongest native warrior. And suddenly Ghar Han imagined the Earthmen building great fleets, imagined those ships soaring across the void and landing here, disgorging armies.

As the Green Men burst into a courtyard, Harkan Thul cried "There!" and pointed.

Ghar Han wheeled, and regarded the shadowed third-story window of a palatial manse.

Harkan Thul shouted to Sutarat, "Go! Down the alley! Make sure he doesn't slip out the back." Sutarat took off running.

Harkan Thul turned to Ghar Han. "I'll watch this side. Now enter, find the Earthman, and slay him. And do not forget the favor I've done you this day, and do not dishonor us."

Ghar Han nodded. He leapt through the open doors, then passed through an antechamber and made his way up a spiral stair. He glanced into the room where the Earthman had been, but it was empty.

"Earthman!" he cried. "Show yourself! I am Ghar Han. I dare you to face me."

He explored room after room, all of them empty. He moved cautiously, holding his swords before him, picturing the Earthman crouched in some shadowed nook, just waiting to fall upon him. Finally he grew exhausted. It seemed he'd explored every corner, and still there was no sign of the Earthman.

He glanced out a window into the courtyard. Harkan Thul was nowhere in sight.

"Harkan Thul!" he shouted. "Sutarat!"

Silence.

He felt a chill. Could they have fallen to the Earthman? Or had the Earthman fled, and they'd gone chasing after him? But surely Ghar Han would have heard the commotion.

Then he knew.

It was a trick. The Earthman had never been here at all.

Ghar Han dashed out into the courtyard, cursing himself. He strained to hear, but heard nothing, so he picked a direction at random and began to run.

It was near sundown, and shadows filled the streets and alleys. In the empty silence of that dead city, he could almost imagine that he was the only living thing on all of Barsoom, and everywhere the black windows seemed to watch him like the eyes of skulls. He hurried down block after block, certain that he would miss whatever was about to happen.

But luck was with him. As he passed an ancient fountain, he heard a voice upon the air, and pursued it. He peeked around a corner.

In the center of a broad avenue stood Harkan Thul, facing one of the dwellings that lined the street. "This is your last chance, Earthman!" he called. "I know you're in there! My warriors have this village surrounded, and I have come, alone, to challenge you. If you defeat me, you will be permitted to depart in peace."

More lies, thought Ghar Han. The others would not allow the Earthman to escape. And where was Sutarat?

There. Down the street a ways, crouched at the base of a statue. And in his hand he held a radium pistol.

No! thought Ghar Han. Surely not. For to challenge a man to duel with swords and then ambush him with a pistol was the most heinous crime that could be dreamt of on Barsoom.

The Earthman appeared in the doorway.

A woman.

She was tall, for her kind, and long-limbed, and stern, her pale hair cut short, and she held a sword. She regarded Harkan Thul coldly as she emerged from the building. "All right," she said. "All right."

Sutarat leaned out from behind the statue and took aim at her back.

"Look out!" Ghar Han yelled.

The woman spun, and spotted Sutarat, who opened fire. Harkan Thul leapt to the ground as the woman fled, shots bursting all around her. She dove into an alley and disappeared.

As Ghar Han strode forward, Harkan Thul stood and screamed, "What are you doing?"

"What are *you* doing?" said Ghar Han. "This is shameful! Are you afraid to face the Earthman fairly?"

"No fight with an Earthman is fair," said Harkan Thul. "They *cheat* by coming here, from a world with such heavy gravity."

I once thought as he does, Ghar Han realized. And now he saw how petulant and contemptible he'd been.

"Listen, Harkan Thul," he said. "The Earthmen are stronger than us. That's a hard truth, but one we must face. With honor."

Sutarat approached, and leveled his pistol at Ghar Han's chest.

"So," said Ghar Han, "now you fear a fair fight with *me* as well?"

"Yes, put it away," said Harkan Thul. "Save it for the Earthman."

Sutarat tucked the pistol in his belt and drew four swords.

Harkan Thul raised his own swords as well. "Long have we despised you, Ghar Han, but it pleased us to mock you, so we suffered you to live. But no longer."

The two of them advanced, their eyes full of hate, and Ghar Han backed away, drawing his own weapons, knowing he stood no chance against both of them.

"I challenge Sutarat to single combat," he said.

"No, you'll fight us both," said Harkan Thul, grinning. "Two opponents, one for each of your arms. It seems fitting."

Sutarat laughed.

Then suddenly the Earth woman was back, rushing Harkan Thul, slashing at him.

He spun, cursing, just barely in time to bring a sword around to block hers. As the two of them fought, Harkan Thul shouted, "Get him! I'll deal with her."

Sutarat leapt at Ghar Han, striking with sword after sword, and Ghar Han fell back before the onslaught, ducking and parrying as the blows fell. For an instant he despaired that his two arms could possibly prevail against Sutarat's four.

Then he remembered the day he'd faced John Carter, the way the Earthman had cut him to pieces. It was a battle Ghar Han had replayed in his mind a thousand times.

The next time Sutarat attacked with an overhand chop, Ghar Han spun aside and hacked the man's shoulder, causing him to drop a sword, and then Ghar Han battered another of the man's blades, knocking it from his hand. Then it was two swords against two.

Ghar Han smiled. What came next felt almost inevitable.

When Sutarat attacked again, Ghar Han skewered him through the forearm, then kicked him in the chest, knocking him onto his back.

Sutarat groaned, fumbling at his belt, grasping the radium pistol, raising it. Ghar Han brought his sword screaming down, and both pistol and hand fell away, and the blade plunged deep into Sutarat's chest, killing him.

Panting, Ghar Han glanced back over his shoulder.

Harkan Thul was standing over the woman. She lay in the street, reaching for her blade, which had fallen just out of reach.

As Harkan Thul raised his swords to deliver a killing blow, Ghar Han snatched up the radium pistol and shot him in the back.

◆ ◆ ◆

On the streets of a ghost town, beneath the twin moons, a Green Man knelt, staring at the pistol in his hand. Two corpses lay nearby.

The Earth woman came and stood beside him. "Hello."

He was silent.

"Who are you?" she said.

His voice was soft. "I don't know."

After a moment, he added, "We take the names of those we slay in battle. I am no longer worthy of those names. I have broken every law. . . ."

"You did what you had to," she said. "You had no choice."

"I had a choice," he said, and fell silent again.

A bit later, the woman said, "My name is Suzanne. Suzanne Meyers. Of Earth."

"Earth," he echoed. "Tell me, Suzanne, how did you come to Barsoom?"

"I don't know," she said. "I just . . . woke up, and I was here."

"Do you know John Carter? Of Virginia?"

"No," she said. "I'm from New York. Who's John Carter?"

"Someone I met once," said the Green Man. "Long ago."

They were silent for a time.

The woman said, "Thank you for saving my life. I owe you. I mean, if there's any way I can help you . . ."

The Green Man said, "If you would do me one favor, it is this: I foresee a time when Earthmen will come to this world, not one by one, but by the thousands. Do what you can to ensure that, when that day comes, my people will not be utterly wiped away."

"You have my word," she said. "For what it's worth."

"Who are you, on your world?" he asked. "A great warlord? A princess?"

"No," she said. "I . . . I'm nobody, really."

"I understand," said the Green Man. "I am also nobody."

"Two nobodies," she said.

After a moment, she added, "Maybe we should stick together, then. It would be fitting."

He raised his head and looked at her.

And why not? he thought. He could never return to his own people. Not now.

"Come on," she said, offering him her hand.

They stole through the quiet streets, to the place where the thoats were tied, and took two of them, and galloped away through the gates. Under cover of darkness they slipped the cordon of Warhoon scouts, though the warriors heard them, and pursued them.

When the two of them reached the hills, the Earthwoman said, "Follow me. I came this way before." And she urged her mount up a narrow trail, near-invisible in the dark, and the Green Man followed.

Hours later, as dawn broke, they saw that they'd escaped. Then they paused atop a ridge and looked out toward the horizon, knowing that all the weird and wondrous land-scapes of Barsoom lay spread before them.

"Where shall we go?" she said.

"Wherever we want," he replied.

"And what shall I call you?" she asked.

He reflected on this. Finally he said, "Call me Var Dalan. It means 'two-arm.'"

And that concludes our story, a story of three deaths.

The first death was that of the sly Sutarat, killed in single combat.

The second death was that of the arrogant Harkan Thul, shot in the back with a radium pistol.

And the third death was that of the fierce and terrible

warrior Ghar Han, reborn now as he gallops his thoat across the yellow hills beneath a purple sky, a two-armed man who rides with a two-armed woman at his side. For the man that he was, who served the cruel whims of the Jeddak, and who longed for the approbation of his people, and who was ashamed of the wounds he bore, and who lived for nothing but to take vengeance on John Carter, that man is dead now, dead as the dead sea bottoms of Mars.

John Carter's creator, Edgar Rice Burroughs, is best known for his character Tarzan, an English boy raised by apes in Africa. Tarzan travels to England and inherits the title Lord Greystoke, only to abandon civilization and return to a life of adventure. Tarzan is a formidable fighter who has wrestled pythons, crocodiles, sharks, tigers, rhinos, a man-sized seahorse, and even dinosaurs. His favored outfit is a knife and loincloth, he prefers to sleep nestled on the branch of a tree, and his favorite food is raw meat, preferably from an animal he's killed himself. (He's also in the habit of burying his raw meat in the ground for a week or so to soften it up a bit.) Though films have often depicted him as speaking only in fragments ("Me Tarzan, you Jane"), in Burroughs's novels Tarzan is an incredible intellect who speaks over a dozen languages, both human and animal. Tarzan is one of the best-known and best-loved characters in literature, and has inspired countless adaptations and imitations. (As a girl, Jane Goodall was so inspired by the stories of Tarzan that she later traveled to Africa to study chimpanzees, where she made ground-breaking discoveries in primate behavior.) Burroughs's two series heroes, Tarzan and John Carter, share many similarities. Both are handsome men with black hair and gray eyes. Both are noble, forthright, and chivalrous. And of course, both are peerless combatants. Our next tale explores what happens when these two legendary personalities collide.

THE APE-MAN OF MARS

BY PETER S. BEAGLE

The ape-man was restless. Even on a night as warmly tranquil as this, here in the West African jungle that was far more his heart's home than the House of Lords—where, as John Clayton, Viscount Greystoke, he was entitled to sit among its members anytime he wanted to—he could find no sleep in any of his favorite tree crotches or hollows. Nor did the pleasure of exhuming a week-buried haunch of antelope or lesser kudu provide anything more than a satisfactory belch and a good scratch. For the very first time in a life constantly adventurous from his birth, Tarzan was bored.

Looking longingly up at Goro, the red, gibbous moon, he thought, "What a night this would be to dance the Dum-Dum with a few of the old gang!" But of the Mangani, the great apes who had raised him from his infancy, few yet survived; and their descendants tended to avoid him, wary of his smell—human, yet *not*-human . . . Tarzan sighed and stretched his mighty arms up toward the star-sown jungle sky . . . and especially toward the brilliant red dot low in the west, stubbornly refusing to be rendered invisible by the moonlight. *Mars, god of war—the Warrior Planet! Perhaps it has always drawn me because I was born a warrior, and had to remain so to survive. Mars . . . Mars . . .*

In a strangely detached manner, he felt the soul being drawn out of his body, taking flight toward the glow above . . . *beyond* the glow. He clutched the knife that dangled on the rawhide cord at his throat, and felt it seemingly dissolve in his hands—then there was only intense cold—then: nothing . . .

Tarzan came to consciousness sprawled naked on dry, hot sand: somewhat dazed and disoriented, but apparently entirely himself in his own body, and in no least doubt of where he had been transmigrated to. *This is Mars,* he knew, just as surely as he had no slightest grasp on the means or purpose of his unbidden transport. The sky overhead was of a pale, Earthlike blue, but with a curious transparency about it, as though one could almost see through it to the pure blackness of deepest space beyond. There were two moons in this sky, brightly visible even in daylight, and both moving, as he stared, distinctly more swiftly than the satellite he knew. Of all the lost worlds and colonies that Tarzan had discovered on—and even within—his own planet, none had ever made him feel so lonely as he felt now.

His wide reading in several languages had prepared the ape-man for the low gravity and lighter air pressure on Mars; but all the same, the movement involved merely in rising to his feet almost took him off the ground, and his very first step caused him literally to bounce two or three feet into the air, and then to fall on his face with the second step. Practice, and a good deal of falling down, eventually allowed him to evolve a method of cautious, slogging progression, punctuated by sudden inadvertent kangaroo hops of as much as nine or ten feet straight up. It was at the zenith of one such hop that he discerned the curious glass-roofed structure over the low hills to his right. This being the only suggestion of habitation of any sort, Tarzan determined to make his way to it.

While the distance was not great, achieving his goal took him well over an hour, since the bounces he was only slowly learning to control frequently took him off in one undesired direction or another. Finally arriving at the building, he recognized it as a kind of giant incubator, containing, as best he could enumerate them, several hundred eggs, all between two and three feet across. Tarzan had seen—and eaten—ostrich eggs from time to time; any one of these would have fed a family of Mangani for over a week.

Tarzan dropped onto his haunches and scratched his head. A hundred million miles from Big Ben, his only clock was his stomach, and that organ was informing him that interplanetary travel—however long it had actually taken him—was a hungry business. Those eggs undoubtedly belonged to someone, but Tarzan's stomach belonged to him, and the moral issue was never really up for discussion. He pried open the entrance to the incubator—of glass, like the roof—selected the nearest egg, brought it back outside, and, with his mouth watering in anticipation, used the haft of his knife to crack it open.

Unfortunately the embryo curled inside the egg was far too developed—and infinitely too ugly—for even a ravenous ape-man to consider eating. It looked to him rather like a cross between an Earth vulture chick and a dinosaur out of Pal-ul-don or Pellucidar. Tarzan found it so revolting that he promptly buried it in the sand, as deeply as he could. His stomach was just going to have to wait for better times. Tarzan of the Apes had gone hungry before.

Sleep, however . . . sleep was another matter, easier to deal with. Without hesitation—and having some notion of how cold Martian nights must be—the ape-man reentered the incubator and dug down into the soft, warm reddish soil that cushioned the great eggs. Food would be something to consider when he awakened. Snug in his shallow burrow, the ape-man matter-of-factly closed his eyes and went to dreamless sleep.

He awakened abruptly, guardian senses detecting the presence of enemies even down through the sands of Mars. He had clearly slept through the night, for the sun was just above the horizon and there was still a morning chill in the air. He blinked his eyes, not to clear his vision—Tarzan of the Apes always woke with all his jungle-trained senses completely alert—but because he perceived that the incubator was now surrounded by such beings as he had not seen since he encountered the Ant-Men of Minunia, who had briefly enslaved him and reduced him to their own size. But these creatures were the complete opposite of the Minunians, standing anywhere from twelve to fifteen feet high and very nearly as naked as he. Their skins were all various shades of dark green; each had an additional pair of arms, set approximately at waist level, and their red-eyed, expressionless faces were each furnished with a set of hoglike tusks jutting upward from the lower jaw. Their mounts were almost as formidable: Some ten feet high themselves, they had four legs on each side, which gave them something of the air of carnivorous caterpillars, since their enormous mouths seemed to stretch all the way to the back of their heads. The great green riders' air of menace was distinctly heightened by the lances and projectile weapons of some sort that each carried—and that were all trained on him as he rose, breathed deeply, and left the incubator to stand before them, certain and unafraid.

Only two figures stood out among the twenty or so of

this outlandish crew, by virtue of their relatively small size and their human features. One, though clad like the gigantic Martians, was obviously an Earthman: tall, dark-haired, and gray-eyed, like Tarzan himself, with a certain arrogance of bearing that made the ape-man dislike and distrust him on sight. The second . . . the second, red-skinned or no, was the loveliest woman Tarzan had ever seen, and he had known beauties from the highest English society to American movie sets to the mines and palaces of Opar. He had never considered allegiance to any woman other than his Jane Porter, never broken faith even in his imagination. But this one, from her cloud of black hair to her delicate feet, with her expression a blend of pride and wonder, of serenity and innocence . . .

Tarzan shook his head, conscious of his nakedness for the first time since his arrival in this strange world. The Earthman riding beside the red woman dismounted and strode toward Tarzan, plainly more at ease than he in the low Martian gravity. Halting some yards before the ape-man, he asked, speaking with an unmistakable Tidewater accent, "Do you speak English, sir?"

"I do," the ape-man replied evenly. "And French, and German, Arabic and Swahili and the tongues of the Mangani and the pithecanthropi of Pal-ul-don . . ." He was just starting to enumerate the several dialects of Pellucidar when the Earthman waved him impatiently to silence, saying, "English will do. I am John Carter, of the Virginia Carters. This"—he gestured toward the red-skinned woman—"is my wife, the Princess Dejah Thoris of Helium."

His wife . . . Tarzan drew himself erect and bowed formally to both of them. "I am Tarzan of the Mangani." As Dejah Thoris appeared puzzled by the appellation, he added, "Tarzan of the Apes. I also speak some Russian, though with a rather coarse Siberian accent, I'm afraid—"

"You're English," John Carter said flatly. Tarzan bowed again, without answering. John Carter said, "You people were supposed to aid the South in the War."

"We thought better of it." The ape-man kept his voice level, his manner courteous.

"We lost the War because of your treachery." John Carter's growl might have been that of Kerchak, king of the apes among which Tarzan had been raised, regarding a rash upstart—and, in time, Tarzan himself. The ape-man could feel the old red scar on his brow beginning to throb dangerously—*I killed Kerchak, broke his neck*—but he controlled himself still, answering only, "I was in Africa, myself, during that regrettable confrontation. Perhaps civilized people may agree to disagree on that point. As we do in the House of Lords."

"The House of Lords?" The unexpected phrase clearly brought John Carter up short, but he rallied quickly, with a dry chuckle. "Well, you're not in any House of Lords here, Mr. Tarzan of the Apes. You're facing a squad of Tharks—friends of mine, if they're friends of anyone, even each other—and they're very upset to see that you've broken into their nursery, what with their newest generation being so near to hatching. I don't mind telling you that if you weren't a fellow Earthman, and if you weren't our guest, I'd as soon—"

"But he *is*!" Dejah Thoris's voice was as quiet and steady as her eyes. "He *is* our guest, my lord—and plainly your countryman." She continued to regard Tarzan as she spoke, and the ape-man bowed his head in acknowledgment of her courtesy. This time, when he raised his head, he stared back boldly, until it was she who looked away.

John Carter noticed none of this silent exchange. He was musing, "Remarkable, how after one person transmigrates, suddenly everyone starts doing it. Your body's up in a tree in Africa somewhere, I suppose? Mine's in a cave in Arizona, with a bunch of Indians outside, waiting for me to come out." His laugh was no more than a quick, short bark. "They'll be very old Indians by the time I do."

"I have no idea where my body is," Tarzan admitted candidly. "Is this not my real body? It certainly feels like my body."

"What you're standing up in—that's your *astral* body," John Carter informed him. "The astral body can go anywhere, once you know how to project it—to the outer planets, to the stars! Mine"—he placed a possessive arm around the slight shoulders of Dejah Thoris—"is staying right here on Barsoom. As we Martians call it." Turning briefly, he gestured toward the tusked riders ranged in a semicircle behind him. "The Princess and I were accompanying our green friends on a quick inspection of the hatchery before we start home to Helium. You'd best come along with us—I don't imagine you'd last long among the Tharks. They're fighters, not tree-climbers. And *they* keep their promises."

The last words set the ape-man's scar burning once again, but Jane Porter had spent a long time sweetly and lovingly domesticating the wild creature he knew himself to be. With some trepidation—and the aid of a large boulder as a mounting block—he got up behind one of the Tharks ("When a thoat gets to know you, he'll kneel down for you to get on," John Carter told him), although straddling the beast's spine stretched his mighty quadriceps painfully. But the eight-legged stride, much like that of the pacers he sometimes bet on when in England, was surprisingly smooth—perhaps because the thoat's well-padded feet absorbed the jolt of the Martian desert surface easily—and Tarzan quickly grew accustomed to the rolling rhythm.

John Carter, with Princess Dejah Thoris riding behind him, kept pace with the ape-man's mount, keeping up conversation with a tone that made Tarzan's mighty teeth hurt.

"Odd, you fetching up at exactly the same place where I arrived. Might be some sort of harbor for transmigrating astral bodies, eh?"

"Perhaps." Tarzan kept his own tone noncommittal. "I have seen stranger things."

"From up in your tree, chattering and scratching with your monkey friends?" John Carter chuckled again. "I'll tell you what would have been strange—seeing a few British warships sailing into Charleston Bay, Mobile Bay. Seeing the British standing up like men, instead of howling away across the ocean like a flock of monkeys—*that* would have been strange, don't you think?" He slanted his glance sideways at Tarzan, his contemptuous chuckle continuing.

Tarzan of the Apes, Lord of the Jungle, would have flown at his throat well before now, merely for the look of his eyes, ignoring his words. John Clayton, Viscount Greystoke, alone, friendless, weaponless, and naked on Mars, kept his temper, replying simply, "We desired your cotton, certainly, but the price was too high. England has done well enough without slave labor for some while now."

John Carter's Virginia accent grew more pronounced; his skin seemed to grow taut with anger. "Wasn't long ago that our cotton was good enough for you, no matter where it came from. Now suddenly you're all heart-bleeding hypocrites." He spat, narrowly missing Tarzan's bare foot.

"I was a slave myself once," the ape-man mused aloud. "Never liked it much."

"The War was never about slavery!" John Carter jabbed his forefinger at Tarzan as though it were a sword blade, or the barrel of a pistol. "The War was about states' rights to refuse to be told how to live, what to think, what to grow, how to grow it . . ." His face was flushed, and he was literally spluttering with furious disgust. "It was a second American Revolution, is what it was, and our Cause was just as honorable as theirs! Deny *that*, Sir House-of-Lords, and—" He checked himself abruptly, and his voice slowed and quieted to a menacing drawl. "Deny that, and we might quarrel."

It was Dejah Thoris who hastily changed the subject, describing the magnificence of the old city to which the ape-man was being escorted, so that by the time the caravanserai arrived there, toward evening, he was well prepared for the long, low marble buildings, brilliantly illuminated by the two Martian moons—both shockingly near, from an Earthman's perspective—and for the wide streets, now filling with the tusked green natives who spilled out into them to welcome their countrymen (and especially the great John Carter) back from their expedition into the barren wasteland.

Tarzan's mighty lip curled slightly to watch the Virginian visibly swelling under their praise, but he had to admit that the Tharks' previous experience with one Earthman made it a good bit easier for him to move around freely among the Martians—though every so often, he was waylaid and, with gestures toward John Carter, requested to *sak*, like his compatriot. Once it finally penetrated his comprehension that *sakking* meant bouncing straight up to fully the height of a Thark, he complied vigorously, and was eventually left alone, free to wander the city: no prisoner, but merely a visiting diplomat of some sort. He was well aware that he owed this privilege to John Carter's intervention, which pleased him not at all; but it amused him greatly, all the same, to feel snug around his bare shoulders the fur cloak that Princess Dejah Thoris had tossed to him off her own back against the cold of the Martian night—and to recall the look that John Carter had thrown him with it. Smiling to himself, he strolled toward the deserted-looking building that crouched at the end of the street in the brilliant shadows cast by the Martian moons.

For someone who habitually slept curled up in the fork of a jungle tree, or stretched out along a branch like Sheeta the leopard, the ape-man took a serious interest in architecture. The structures he had seen so far looked so much beyond the conception of any of the Tharks he had met so far that he desired to prowl for clues to their original creators: perhaps the extinct race that had once dwelled therein, when the empty Martian seas were full and high, and teeming with life. *They couldn't have built all this. They can't even build furniture.* . . .

He was halfway crouched, examining the unusual configuration of some broken steps plainly never made for Thark feet, when all his jungle-trained senses suddenly had him off his own feet and rolling to the side, so that the creature silently dropping on him from above missed him almost entirely. Coming instantly erect, Tarzan gaped in amazement at the beast facing him. It stood as tall as any Thark he had yet encountered, and seemed equally as firm on its hind legs—but it was an ape, beyond any possible doubt, for all that it looked more like a hairless gorilla than a Thark, and even more, to Tarzan's eyes, like a being from Earth, six arms or no. With a scream like that of a leopard that has just made a kill, the thing rushed upon the ape-man, hands reaching out to clutch and strangle and rend.

Tarzan met it with his ancient war cry of *"Kreegahh!"* which, to his great surprise, momentarily stopped the creature in its tracks. Then it came on again, but with a certain air of puzzlement, which allowed the ape-man to sidestep the crushing sweep of its four upper arms, all muscled to shame Bolgani, the gorilla. The white ape wheeled and came at him again, but Tarzan, taking full advantage of his new Martian agility, leapt over its head and came down behind it, striving for the full-Nelson hold with which he had more than once conquered Numa the lion. He was still having difficulty in learning to land correctly, however, and when he slipped and fell on his back, the ape was at him with a roar, two hands closing on his throat, another pair of arms encircling his chest and squeezing far more powerfully than he himself could have done. Desperately Tarzan struck out wildly with his mighty fists, but his hardest blow seemed to make no impression on the thick, bald hide or the gorilla features. The Martian moonlight was swimming before the ape-man's eyes, when the creature suddenly eased its grip on his throat, stared into his face, and growled, with a distinct questioning lilt at the end, *"Kreegahh?"*

Almost as bewildered as he was grateful to be alive, Tarzan indicated that he wanted to sit up, and the white ape—again to his amazement—released him and moved warily back from him. Struggling for both air and coherence, Tarzan inquired hoarsely in Mangani, *"Speak?"*

The white ape shook its head . . . but its reply, while hardly up to the linguistic standards of the tribe of Kerchak, was perfectly comprehensible to Tarzan. *"Speak not now. Lost."*

"You used to speak Mangani," the ape-man whispered. "Here, on Mars . . . Barsoom. How can that be . . . ?" He repeated the question in the tongue he had first spoken himself, and the white ape blinked blankly, and then made a gesture that was almost a shrug, while pointing indiscriminately at the heavens—to the stars and the two moons—and the Earth, dim on a far corner of the horizon . . .

Tarzan's own slow nod turned into a bow of wonder. "Why should transmigration only be one-way," he muttered aloud. "Why should it be limited to humans?" Abruptly, he pointed in turn to the building behind them, and to the other vast marble structures visible in the moonlight. In Mangani, he asked, forming the words carefully, *"Made these? You?"*

The white ape stared back at him for a long moment, and it seemed to Tarzan that he saw the shadow of an immense sorrow in the beast's black eyes. *"Not us now. Us . . ."* and it made a sort of pushing gesture with both hands, as though rolling away time. Again it said, *"Not us now . . ."*

"Your ancestors," the ape-man said softly. "Your distant ancestors . . . all this was their doing. . . ." He began to smile wryly, thinking back himself. "If Kerchak had been your size, with extra arms . . ."

The white ape stared uncomprehendingly. Tarzan suddenly clapped his hands. "Dum-Dum! Under two moons, with these new cousins of mine? Of course!" Again speaking Mangani with extreme precision, he asked, *"Dum-Dum? Dance Dum-Dum? You?"*

It seemed to him that a certain look of vague remembrance flickered in the creature's eyes. *"Dum-Dum,"* it repeated several times, but nothing further.

"Dum-Dum!" The ape-man was up now, beginning to shift his weight rhythmically from one bare foot to the other. *"Dum-Dum!"* leaping now in the lighter Martian gravity, coming down hard enough to make a slapping sound in the street. *"Dum-Dum!"* with his head thrown back and his mouth open, as though he were drinking the moonlight. *"Dum-Dum!"*

When he looked over at the white ape, it too was on its feet, clumsily mimicking his side-to-side steps, its huge feet creating pounding echoes between the marble buildings. *"Dum-Dum! Dum-Dum!"* Other white figures were emerging from the shadows, joining in the dance of the Mangani . . . their ancestors' dance. *"Dum-Dum! Dum-Dum!"* In Tarzan's jungle, there would have been a hollow log to beat out the rhythm on, but here in this street, on a far-distant world, there was no need. *"Dum-Dum! Dum-Dum!"*

So intoxicated with the ancient dance to the moon was

the ape-man that it took him a moment to focus his eyes on the small, slender figure standing apart, her hands clasped before her, and her own eyes wide with marveling. Then he stopped, on the instant, and went quickly to take the hands of the Princess Dejah Thoris and lead her away from the growing horde of the dancing white apes, so caught up in the Dum-Dum themselves that none noticed his leaving. "You should not be here," he told her, his voice harsher than he meant it to sound. "I have set something loose among them. I don't know what it is, or what it will come to, but it could be dangerous. I think it *is* dangerous."

"But it was wonderful!" Dejah Thoris whispered. "I never saw anything so wonderful. I wish my lord could have seen it!" Then she caught herself and shook her head. "No, I do not wish that. He views the white apes as the Tharks do—as evil, murderous vermin that must be hunted down and wiped out altogether . . . of course, the Tharks feel that way about almost all other peoples. . . ." Her voice trailed away as she gazed up at Tarzan in helpless perplexity. "You think this is not so?"

"All I know, Princess," the ape-man responded gravely, "is that they are not vermin. In some way they are distantly related to my own people, the great apes of Africa, who raised me as one of their own. For good or ill, I could never raise a hand against them ever again."

Dejah Thoris stepped closer, peering up at him, as though into the highest branches of a great tree. "You are as tall as my lord," she mused, "and your eyes are as gray as his. But you are a very strange sort of Earthman, are you not, Tarzan of the Apes?"

"I believe I am an ape in my deepest heart," Tarzan replied, "nothing more than an ape of Kerchak's tribe. But when I look at you, Princess Dejah Thoris of Helium, I cannot but remember that I am also a man."

That was how Tarzan of the Apes learned that a Red Martian can indeed blush. One quick, shaky smile that the ape-man took with him to his grave; then Dejah Thoris, without speaking further, fled ahead of him toward the building where he and John Carter and she were to spend the night. Finding the quarters assigned to him, Tarzan dropped into the pile of furs and silks waiting there, and fell asleep with Princess Dejah Thoris's cloak still around his shoulders.

In the morning, after an excellent breakfast of items that Tarzan was quite happy not to have identified, he helped John Carter, Dejah Thoris, and their several Red Martian servants pack their belongings onto borrowed thoats, and assumed that they would be setting out shortly for distant Helium. He was getting acquainted with his own thoat, practicing mounting and dismounting, when John Carter suddenly said, "Hear you had a tussle with a few maggots last night." Tarzan blinked in puzzlement. "The white apes," John Carter explained, "That's what I call them, because they're white like maggots, and because there's not a thing to be done with them except kill them. Until there aren't any more." He was toying with a Thark pistol, a cut-down version of one of the rifles Tarzan had learned were powered by radium. "Show me where the struggle took place, Sir House-of-Lords."

"You won't find them out in daylight," Tarzan warned him. "And the Princess is clearly anxious to start home." In fact, Dejah Thoris had hardly spoken all morning.

"Sir Englishman," John Carter said without expression, "don't you ever presume to tell me whether or not my wife is *anxious*. . . ." He broke open his weapon, casually inspected the load, and snapped it shut again. "I told you, I want to see last night's battlefield. No one's going anywhere until I do."

If it is not this place, it will be some other. As well have it over with. The ape-man stood up. He said, "I will show you, and then we will get on our way."

"Absolutely," John Carter agreed. "Just indulge an old Johnny Reb, if you would." Dejah Thoris said nothing, but the fear in her eyes angered Tarzan in a way that he had not thought possible. He strode ahead, and John Carter followed close on his heels.

Nearing the deserted building where he had been attacked, Tarzan pointed ahead, saying, "There. One of them ambushed me, but I fought him off and he ran away. There was nothing more to it than that."

"Really?" John Carter was still toying with his pistol—then, to Tarzan's alarm, he suddenly lifted it. "Would that be the fellow, do you suppose?"

A moment of whiteness—a flash of a great hunched body trying to pass an empty window without being seen. John Carter's finger was already squeezing the trigger when Tarzan struck his arm up, so that the strange bullet whined harmlessly off the wall of the building in a flurry of marble chips. And John Carter struck Tarzan in the face with the butt of the revolver, so that the ape-man reeled backward and sat down hard in the Martian street.

"Been wanting to do that from the first sight," John Carter said flatly. "I don't like you, Sir House-of-Lords. You're no better than a damn Yankee—worse, in some ways. And I don't like the way you look at my wife. Not one whit."

The ape-man was on his feet now, smiling blood. He said simply, "Thank you for doing that."

"You're the challenged party—the choice of weapons is up to you." John Carter was smiling genially himself. "I've got a couple of Thark swords, or we can make it pistols. Up to you."

Tarzan shook his head. He said nothing, but simply beckoned John Carter in toward him. For the first time, the

Virginian looked slightly uneasy, but he tossed the pistol aside, said, "Come and get it, then," and contradicted himself by taking a fifteen-foot spring straight at the ape-man, knocking him down again. The battle was on.

As against the white ape, Tarzan realized that he was fighting for his life—and perhaps against a less reasonable opponent. John Carter was a peerlessly brave man, and he came at the ape-man with a fury that had only partly to do with Tarzan himself, and more to do with a lost war in which Tarzan had taken no part. Forced onto the defensive at the start of the combat, the ape-man warded off blow after blow as best he could, enduring as much punishment as he had ever taken in his youth from Bolgani or Kerchak. Momentarily dazed, he kept John Carter's hands from closing forever on his throat only by butting his head desperately into the Virginian's face, or doubling his legs to push him away, like Sheeta the leopard eviscerating a foe. He was vaguely aware of a growing crowd of noisy Tharks, as always happy to see someone, anyone, being beaten. He could not see Dejah Thoris anywhere.

Slowly, however, the battle began to turn. John Carter was a splendid fighter under any circumstances, as he had proven on two planets; but most of his victories over Martians had been achieved with the aid of weapons, low gravity, and the fact that Tharks are less muscular than they appear, and far less quick than a reasonably fit human. Strong and fast as he was, nothing in his oddly doubled life had prepared him for an opponent who had taken down lions and gorillas bare-handed, and who could run all the day unwinded across the great African veldt. Against the ape-man his one advantage was familiarity with Martian conditions, and once his measure was taken, that knowledge was not enough. For every blow he struck, he received three, as Tarzan hit him from all sides and all angles, employing not just his jungle-trained fists, but his elbows and knees, his head, and sweeping kicks that shook the Virginian like thunderbolts. But for all the battering, for all the blood, John Carter would not go down, nor would he surrender, not even when the ape-man stood back, letting go of his killer animal instincts, holding up his open hands and whispering "Please . . . please fall, please stop . . ." as the Virginian stumbled blindly toward him. John Carter was still coming on at the end, muttering to himself . . . sinking to one knee . . . rising again . . . surely about to fall face forward at last at Tarzan's feet . . .

It was then that Dejah Thoris picked up the Martian pistol and hit Tarzan over the head with it.

The ape-man went down without a sound. Dejah Thoris looked at the two fallen men, glanced at the grinning, cheering Tharks with utter contempt—quickly bent and kissed the ape-man's cheek, and then turned her attention to her fallen husband. She did not look back at Tarzan again.

The Lord of the Jungle smelled Africa before he opened his eyes. He was draped, highly uncomfortably, over the crotch of a tree, like the remains of a leopard's meal, which was exactly the way he felt. His skull thundered, his lower lip was split, and his entire body felt as bewildered as his head. Yet he was grateful for the pain, because it proved everything that had happened to him real, and he could not have borne to have dreamed Dejah Thoris. He smiled slightly at the memory, then winced as his lip started bleeding again.

Did I vanish there when I awoke here? Am I dead on Mars—Barsoom—and alive on Earth, or is my spirit alive in both worlds? And which, if either, is real? What will happen to my relatives up there, the white apes—can they ever be safe?

. . . Will she ever think of me?

At last he simply lay back again on the branch and looked up through the softly shivering leaves at the stars. At the farthest edge of the horizon the red planet still shone dimly, flickering in the haze like a candle flame about to fail. For all the calling of his heart he could not turn his gaze to it.

♦ ♦ ♦

In *A Princess of Mars*, John Carter escapes the Green Men of the Warhoon horde only to find himself lost and starving in the desert. He seeks aid at a giant building, four miles square and two hundred feet high, and is allowed inside by a wizened old man. Carter is able to read the man's mind, though the man has no inkling of this. The man tells Carter that the building is an atmosphere plant that supplies air to all of Barsoom, and that the doors can be opened only through the use of a secret code, and that this code is revealed to only two men on Barsoom at any given time. At this point Carter reads the man's mind and learns the code. As the two of them say good night, Carter again reads the man's mind and learns that the man intends to murder him in his sleep, since the man now suspects that Carter has learned too much. Carter escapes the building, and much later, when the atmosphere plant fails, he's able to use his knowledge of the secret code to spring the doors and save all of Barsoom. Our next tale shows us this key event in Barsoomian history from an entirely different point of view—that of a very unusual and talented young member of the Warhoon.

♦ ♦ ♦

A TINKER OF WARHOON

BY TOBIAS S. BUCKELL

"**G**et up!" snarled three-armed Gar Kofan, silhouetted against the light of Barsoom's two moons.

Kaz slowly rose, brushing sand off his gun belt. "It is foolish to stand when someone is shooting at you," he said sullenly.

"They weren't shooting *at* you," Gar Kofan said, cuffing him lightly on the side of the head. "It was a warning shot. We've found the Jedwar's party."

Kaz looked back toward their wagon. He'd rather be back inside, poring over the insides of an electric range finder.

His people, the Warhoons, were unpredictable and violent, Kaz had always felt. Even more violent than their mortal enemies, the Tharks. They'd spent the last few days watching men fight to the death in the arena in the ruins of what had once been some glorious city. And now they were moving across the wastes once more, looking for new victims and plunder.

Kaz hated this. He'd rather be back in Warhoon.

He'd rather be fixing things.

Machines didn't trick you. Machines didn't have an inscrutable warrior code that always seemed to end with bloodshed. Machines didn't attack you for accidentally bumping into them.

Or yell at you for ducking when bullets flew.

They could cuff him as much as they wanted, or call him coward. He wasn't about to stand still and be shot.

Any other young runt of a Warhoon with a single name like Kaz would have been killed long ago for thinking this way. But unlike any of his kind, Kaz could fix things—weapons in particular—and so he was tolerated by his tribe.

But more importantly, he was tolerated by *Gar Kofan*.

Gar Kofan did that mostly because he couldn't give up his only apprentice. Gar Kofan was old, and one of his eyes was milky white and blind, from an old duel. He stood hunched over, and he was missing an entire arm, leaving him with only three. His remaining hands now shook whenever he tried to fix small machines, and it was difficult for him to see small things, even when they were right in front of him.

Kaz knew that Gar Kofan needed him more than he needed Gar Kofan. Gar Kofan was really a warrior, not a tinker, and the machines often frustrated and stumped him and left him cursing and throwing them against the wall. Kaz was the far better tinker, because he understood the machines.

With Gar Kofan's past reputation as a fighter and his skill (he had taken the name of Kofan in the usual manner: by killing a Kofan Jedwar), they had built a good life in Warhoon. And so, although Gar Kofan had only three arms and was going blind, Gar Kofan would cheerfully kill anyone who threatened Kaz.

Gar Kofan had turned to tinkering with machines and fixing the electric range finders on rifles after he'd lost his arm. He had taught Kaz all he knew, since the day two years ago when he found Kaz loitering around his wagon and asking questions about how everything worked.

At first, Gar Kofan had thrown him out of the wagon and told him to go away. But when Kaz showed a knack for fixing things, Gar Kofan took him on as an apprentice.

Soon Kaz had gained a spot in the back of the wagon to sleep on, a knife and pistol of his own, and food.

And life was . . . acceptable, Kaz thought.

At least when people weren't shooting at him.

The Jedwar, Aav Kanan, had designs on becoming a jed, if possible. He was always roaming the wastes, looking for new conquests, or new ways to raise his stature. One day, everyone knew, Aav Kanan would challenge a jed and kill him to take his position.

"Gar Kofan?" Kaz asked, as he followed behind. "Aav Kanan never comes out here to the northwest. It's filled with Zodangan or Helium scouts who would strike at us from the air."

Gar Kofan glanced up. "Then there must be something important enough to bring him out here."

And that was all he would say about that.

In the rocks among an outcropping nearby, a small council had gathered around Aav Kanan, who gestured at them to approach. "Hurry up, cripple," he snarled at Gar Kofan. "We don't have much time before the attack."

Kaz climbed up the ridge behind Gar Kofan and Aav Kanan, struggling to keep up. Even infirm and half blind, Gar Kofan's days as a warrior left him energetic and strong enough to outpace him. When Kaz managed to catch up, Aav Kanan was pointing in the distance at a canal and the high trees that ran along its sides.

And at the massive building that squatted there.

Two hundred feet high and dominating the landscape for miles, it was a building that brought a smile to Kaz's

lips. Unlike the city of Warhoon—stripped down, crumbling, reused by a people who had no idea how it had even been built—this building gleamed with purpose. It had been built and it had been maintained, and whoever *had* built it . . . their craft, their *purpose* seemed to call out to Kaz.

"The Red Men don't want us out here, near this . . . thing," Aav Kanan said. "Which means there must be great riches inside. Look at how massive it is."

They all stared for a long, silent moment.

"There was only one doorway in, that I can perceive," Aav Kanan said mildly, breaking the silence.

"Do you want us to try and tinker the doorway open?" Gar Kofan asked.

Kaz saw straightaway this was not Aav Kanan's intent. Not if he was planning to attack so soon.

"I want you to set the detonator for a very large explosion that will disable the doors," Aav Kanan said. "You will throw it inside that structure when the doors open. There is a guard or a keeper, who comes out once in a great while. The next time he does, we will be nearby to throw the bomb inside, thus wrecking the door's closing mechanism, and we will storm it and take our plunder and be gone before the next flier comes overhead. The Red warriors might be able to fly, but their stupidity is that they keep regular schedules."

Gar Kofan snorted, along with all the other warriors, but Kaz remained silent. Schedules, he thought, were perfectly sensible things. He had to admit, however, if you were guarding something valuable, it was foolish to be predictable.

The Red warriors—if indeed they had built this great building—had assumed the impenetrable walls were all the protection they needed. The flier patrols were an afterthought.

One the Warhoons would exploit.

Aav Kanan's men were nervous about using explosives. They, like most Green Men, were uniformly excellent marksmen with a rifle, but preferred fighting hand-to-hand with swords. "Real weapons for real warriors," they said.

Back in the wagon, Gar Kofan and Kaz set to building a powerful explosive and fitting a timer to it, while Aav Kanan paced around muttering about time.

If time was of such essence, Kaz thought, then maybe Aav Kanan shouldn't have sent for them at the last minute.

But it was not in the nature of Warhoons to plan too far ahead.

A strange warrior once fought a great fight in the arena when Kaz was just out of the egg. Kaz thought about him often, and was thinking about him as he worked on the bomb. The man had been neither Green nor Red, but almost colorless. Someone had said the stranger called himself Jan Kahrtr, an odd enough sounding name.

Normally Kaz paid no attention to the bloodshed out in the arena. He had too many rifles to fix. But seeing this oddly colored stranger, who must have traveled from some far corner of Barsoom, had set Kaz's imagination ablaze. How big was Barsoom? What other people roamed its surface, traversed the great canals that stretched forever over the horizon?

What other great, ruined cities lay littered under the two moons? And what secrets might they give Kaz?

He thought about that a lot.

It was a shame the Kahrtr man had died from the blade of a Zodangan. Kaz had hoped the man might live, so that he could visit his cell and ask him where he came from.

There was a rumor that Kahrtr was now a Prince of Helium, and had been the one who led the Thark attack on the Zodangans, but who knew if that was true?

◆ ◆ ◆

Kaz showed the timer mechanism to one of Aav Kanan's bolder warriors, and gave him the ball-shaped explosive. "It will roll without harming the timer," Kaz said. He'd buried the timer into the heart of the explosive, and wrapped it all in husk leaves shaped into a ball.

The bomb was crudely made of Zodangan explosives, probably stolen by Tharks and traded northward. Kaz always questioned anyone who traded things to him, trying to ascertain where they came from. It was a shame, he thought, that Warhoon couldn't make explosives of their own. They could use them to divert canals, blow open ancient tunnels, and explore old ruins, or just help fight enemy clans . . . but Warhoons were uninterested in science and building things. So there was no chance of it.

Aav Kanan's warrior slowly crawled along the ground and hid behind a bush. And waited.

And waited.

The night wore on, and Kaz found himself wanting to drift off and sleep. But he wanted to see what was coming, and no one had cuffed him and ordered him back to the wagon, so he forced himself to stay alert.

And then it happened: A crack of light broke out from a cut in the wall as a door slowly opened. In the light, a frail, old Red warrior slowly walked out. He looked up at the moons and bowed to them, and then took in a deep breath of air with what looked like great satisfaction.

The moment the Red turned his back, the hiding warrior sprinted forward. As he threw the bomb, the old man half-turned, saw him, and moved to run back inside.

That was when a rope Kaz hadn't noticed on the ground leapt up, the noose catching the old man by the foot. On the other end of the rope, Warhoon warriors pulled quickly and dragged the old man away from the building.

The door began shutting automatically, an emergency reaction, but the bomb made it inside just before it snapped shut.

Nothing happened for a long moment. Then, just as Aav Kanan turned toward Kaz, fury on his face, a distant thud indicated that it had worked. A faint trickle of smoke leaked out from around the door, and the Warhoons cheered.

But that cheer died soon enough as they approached the door and tried to force it open.

Kaz swallowed nervously. This was not good.

The old man on the ground laughed. "There is no explosion on Barsoom that could break that door, or even those walls. You fools."

Aav Kanan's attention flicked away from Kaz, and Kaz felt a surge of relief. Very carefully, and so as not to draw attention, he stepped back as Aav Kanan stalked over to the old man.

"How do we get it inside?" Aav Kanan demanded.

"You can't," was the reply. "I'm the keeper of the plant, and I will not let the likes of you in." He spat.

Aav Kanan hit him, and Kaz heard the man's brittle old ribs crack. He screamed in pain. They always did. But Aav Kanan was just getting started.

The beating continued, and Kaz wondered how the old man was able to take so much of it.

"What is inside?" Aav Kanan finally asked, bent close to the old man's crumpled face.

"The most precious thing you can imagine," the keeper of the complex said. And he laughed.

Aav Kanan snarled and struck him with a tremendous punch to the side of his head. The old man lay still on the ground.

The warriors left him there and returned to the door. But nothing would budge it.

◆ ◆ ◆

"Fliers are approaching," Aav Kanan said, and ordered that
the old man to be thrown in the wagon with Gar Kofan and
Kaz. "At least your services will be of some use. When the
old man awakes, interrogate him. We must find a way in."

They fled for the hills where the valleys and caves could
hide them from eyes in the sky.

At midday, the old man woke up, groaning. Kaz sat
with him, as he thought it best to keep himself hidden in the
wagon, away from Aav Kanan's fury.

Kaz gave the Red Man sustenance, as they had stopped
by several mantalia and milked the plants. The old man
thanked him, and then Kaz asked him how they could get
inside the building.

"You cannot," the man said. "The doors will sense duress
from any of us if you force us to open them. It is a safety
protocol."

"But what is inside?" Kaz asked, dreaming of amazing,
magical things.

"The most precious thing in all Barsoom," the old man
insisted. "Air."

He had, Kaz concluded, obviously been hit on the head
too hard.

When they'd found shelter from the fliers, Kaz's fears became
realized as Aav Kanan pulled him out of the wagon and threw
him out into the center of a circle of many warriors.

"Your bomb failed," he said. "I do not tolerate failure."

Kaz looked up at him. The bomb had been the most
powerful anyone in Warhoon could have built, better than
anything Gar Kofan could have built.

That's why Gar Kofan hadn't tried to do this. Because
he couldn't do it; only he, Kaz, possessed the necessary
skills. Yet now his master stood quietly in the circle, saying

nothing in Kaz's defense. Aav Kanan was either going to beat him unconscious for failure or kill him.

Kaz wasn't sure which to hope for.

"Wait," Kaz said, thinking quickly. "He said 'us' when he woke up."

Aav Kanan hesitated. "What do you mean?"

"Perhaps he has an apprentice, as I am apprenticed to Gar Kofan. Still in the building, or maybe elsewhere. The more of them we can capture, the more we can find out. Maybe the apprentice will tell us something the old one won't."

Gar Kofan, nervous about having his name dragged into the matter at hand, glared at Kaz. But Aav Kanan thought about it, and then nodded and lowered his four hands.

"We will get the old man to tell us where his others are," he said. "And then see what they will tell us."

Kaz let out a deep breath.

He'd escaped something horrible. For now.

Kaz's suggestion set into motion more beatings of the old man, who eventually confessed to having an apprentice living near Helium.

So Aav Kanan had left them with the old man, who Gar Kofan said was dying from his beatings. There was nothing they could do for him but proceed slowly and carefully on their journey back to Warhoon. This way, they would get out of Aav Kanan's way, and hopefully he would soon forget his wrath as Gar Kofan and Kaz hid in the ruins of Warhoon and in the crowds of the arena.

"If we are lucky," Gar Kofan said, "the Red warriors will spot him and kill him and we'll be rid of him."

Kaz did not reply, but secretly agreed.

On the fourth day of the journey Kaz found the old man playing with a piece of machinery he'd kept hidden away, holding it up and frowning. "Is your wagon airtight?" the old man asked.

"No." Kaz pointed at all the grilles and openings throughout.

"Then we are in great danger! All of Barsoom!"

"What do you mean? What danger?" Kas Jalat asked.

"I am the keeper of the atmosphere plant that you abducted me from," said the old man slowly. Kaz feared that he was further along toward death than life. "It has been my life's work. I have guarded it zealously, but in my old age, I grew too fond of walking outside to remind myself how beautiful it was to stand outside and taste the world. It is my own fault. I have grown weak in my old age, and should have retired long ago.

"You know Barsoom is a dying world. The great city-makers left us long ago. We are fewer in number and we've forgotten much of our history and technology.

"Our atmosphere is dying as well. But this plant pumps enough air into the crosswinds out here in the northwest to circulate around the world, and it lets us keep living. Without it, we will slowly suffocate and die. And now my instruments tell me the quality of air has dropped slightly. Your savage warriors, who threw that bomb inside after kidnapping me, have destroyed one of the great machines inside. I must get back there to fix it. Do you understand?"

Gar Kofan and Kaz argued about it for an entire day. Gar Kofan even insisted on seeing the device, and forced the dying keeper to explain everything about it, looking on as the keeper tested the air.

Still, he was suspicious.

"Let us think about this," Kaz told him. "Why would he lie, only to be taken back to a treasure-hold, if he is dying? He seems scared. And that device . . ."

"It could be anything," Gar Kofan sniffed.

"But what if he is right?" Kaz insisted.

"But what if he is lying?"

Kaz held out his hands. "If we are right, and he is lying, than it only costs us something small to change our course, and go check. If he is right, then we may as well all die right now."

"We're already well into our journey," Gar Kofan protested.

Kaz further considered the matter then said, "Suppose he is wrong, and is hiding a treasure. If we go with him and he takes us into a treasure-hold, then we will succeed in gaining the plunder. If he speaks the truth, then we will save all Barsoom. If he lies and we continue to Warhoon, then we lose another chance at the treasure. If he speaks true and we continue down this path, we may lose the very air we breathe."

Gar Kofan grumbled, but finally saw the wisdom in Kaz's argument and turned them around.

Kaz wanted them to hurry, but Gar Kofan could only drive the thoats to pull the wagon so fast.

He took a deep breath.

Did it seem less filling? He wasn't sure. He could just be imagining it, driven to fear by the ravings of an old man who was dying from the beating Aav Kanan gave him.

The keeper died when they were within sight of the canal's tall trees. As his last breath rattled from his lips, Kaz groaned. They'd been so close!

"Our only hope now is that Aav Kanan has the apprentice, and that maybe he can help us," Gar Kofan said.

They buried the keeper in the shadow of the structure he had spent most of his life guarding, and then hid from the flier patrols in the nearby hills.

"We'll wait for Aav Kanan to come back and try the doors again," Gar Kofan said.

Kaz noticed the old warrior taking deeper breaths. How long did they have before the bad air would overcome them? He wished he knew more about machines than he did; he wished he knew more about everything.

They spent the next days in a cave, quietly waiting and doing something Kaz never thought he'd do: hoping for Aav Kanan to return.

Three days after the death of the old man, with no sign yet of Aav Kanan, the fliers that had been circling overhead descended from the skies in a panic. Scouts surrounded the building, and more fliers than Kaz had even realized existed flocked nearby and then landed along the sides of the canal.

"They know something's wrong," Kaz told Gar Kofan. And by now, even Gar Kofan had to admit there was something wrong with the air. They were both breathing more heavily, and not just because they were climbing around so much.

There was something wrong with the very air of Barsoom itself.

The old man had been right.

"I did this," Kaz whispered sadly to Gar Kofan. "This is all my fault. I used those Zodangan explosives. They must have broken something inside the atmosphere plant."

In the end, he thought, all of Barsoom would be a ruin because of him.

"Aav Kanan would have killed you had you refused. And then I would have built the bomb," Gar Kofan said.

But, Kaz thought, Gar Kofan wouldn't have made one as powerful as his. And maybe the atmosphere factory would still be working.

Aav Kanan returned after another four days in a foul mood, having evaded the Red warriors of Helium and tracked across the sacked city of Zodanga. They'd moved so quickly they had left exhausted and dying thoats in their wake.

"The apprentice?" Kaz asked.

"He was of no use," Aav Kanan said. "We could torture no useful information out of him, so we threw him into the pits beneath his own home."

Kaz slumped. "You fool!" he said, before he realized the words were out of his mouth.

Aav Kanan hit Kaz so hard he was knocked off his feet and sent flying backward, and when Kaz looked up, the Jedwar had his sword out and was ready to kill him. But Gar Kofan suddenly leapt in front of Aav Kanan, and the Jedwar's blade struck Gar Kofan, who grabbed hold of it. "Listen to Kaz, Jedwar," he gasped. "You must listen."

And as Gar Kofan kneeled before Aav Kanan, slowly dying but never letting go of the sword with his three hands, Kaz told Aav Kanan everything the keeper had told him.

But the Jedwar only laughed and jerked his sword out of Gar Kofan's stomach, leaving him to die on the ground. "You are the fool, tinker, if you think I'll believe something is wrong with the air. It is *air*, little one. The air always *has been*. It will *always be*."

Kaz bit his lip as Aav Kanan walked away. Did the Jedwar not use his mind? Didn't he understand the consequences if he was wrong?

He wished he were strong enough to stand, to fight Aav Kanan. But Kaz well knew what the consequences would be if he tried.

Aav Kanan would skewer him even faster than he had Gar Kofan.

❖ ❖ ❖

Aav Kanan was studying the collection of Red warriors that had grown around the building. They kept arriving by fliers, and soon a crowd of them gathered around the door.

One of Aav Kanan's warriors had forced Kaz to watch the Reds. "What are they doing? They're trying to get in, aren't they?"

"Yes," Kaz said. "But don't you think it's strange that they can't? Maybe this place is as important as the keeper claimed—" He would have said more, but he was knocked back with a solid punch.

"Stop your mewling, idiot," Aav Kanan snarled. "There is something more important in there. Get out of here. Get your wagon and go back to Warhoon. You are of no use. Go, before I change my mind and kill you."

No use? Kaz thought, stumbling out of the camp. *No use?*

Who fixed their guns? Who made sure their electric range finders worked? Who fixed the grips on their swords? They came to him when their things were broken, but they despised him because he didn't share their bloodthirst, their desire for plunder, and their hatred of outsiders. They made fun of his curiosity. They cuffed him for his questions.

No use.

Gar Kofan was dead. At Aav Kanan's own hands.

And now they sent Kaz away, too. How many other tinkers were there in Warhoon? Not enough to keep the broken equipment the warriors depended on going. Without the likes of Kaz, eventually Aav Kanan and his kind would have nothing but sharpened sticks and stones to kill one another with, and then the Tharks or some other tribe would sweep in and destroy the Warhoons. They'd be cutting their own throats if they kicked Kaz out.

They'd be cutting all of Barsoom's throats, he thought.

◆ ◆ ◆

Kaz did not prod the thoats into snorting and pulling the wagon back to Warhoon. He sat inside, still, just like one of the old statues lying on its back in the ruins of Warhoon.

The Red Men had fliers, and good weapons, but Aav Kanan and his men were furious fighters. If they overwhelmed the Reds, who might be there to fix the atmosphere plant, then all of Barsoom would all die for sure.

And since they didn't even realize they were being watched, they were vulnerable. Kaz was a tinker, but even he knew the effect a surprise attack would have on the men gathered around the plant: They'd be overcome. Maybe slaughtered.

Kaz looked over at one of Gar Kofan's long, wicked swords, which he kept mounted over his workbench.

If there was to be a future, the men who could build machines, the men who could create things, must triumph. And those who gathered unawares by the atmosphere plant needed all the help they could get if they were to survive Aav Kanan's onslaught.

Kaz had to hurry. Already he could feel that the air was stale, and getting worse.

In addition to arming himself, he would need something else. An edge only he could create.

The warrior party spread apart as Kaz appeared, one of his repaired rifles in hand, pointed at the sky.

"Why are you holding a rifle?" Aav Kanan hissed. "And what is that thing around your neck?"

He pointed to the hose dangling from a canister that Kaz had welded together.

"I'm here one last time to talk you out of this," Kaz said, not answering his question. "Can you not feel the air getting harder to breathe? Like a small, crowded room on a hot day?"

Some of Aav Kanan's warriors shifted. Yes, they *had* noticed it, but the lure of plunder was too great. And as Aav Kanan had insisted, air had always been. How could people affect that? It was a Red warrior trick, that was all.

"Talk," Aav Kanan said. "And why the rifle?"

"Because I'm going to shoot you if you try to attack them," Kaz said calmly. "And by firing, I will warn the technicians trying to get into the building. And if you shoot me, right now, that will also warn them."

Aav Kanan blinked, working out the logic. He pulled his sword free, and Kaz lowered the rifle to aim at him.

"You aim a rifle at me?" Aav Kanan spat. "When I hold a sword? This is why you are no real warrior, little one. You are a disgrace. Drop the rifle and truly face me. With a blade."

"No," Kaz said. "There is something more important at stake."

They remained frozen, Kaz trembling slightly inside as he kept the gun aimed at Aav Kanan, until the Jedwar lowered his sword. "You are dead, tinker," he told Kaz.

"You killed us all when you ordered me to throw that bomb inside the plant," Kaz said. "So it matters not to me whether I die now or die later."

Already the air was thin enough that he found it hard to take in sufficient breath to speak a full sentence. How was Aav Kanan ignoring this?

"If the air fades, then it was meant to be," Aav Kanan said softly. "Maybe it isn't our place to meddle with such things. We are here to live as we are here to live. Is that not enough?"

Out of the corner of his eye, Kaz noticed two warriors were edging away from Aav Kanan, and Kaz realized that they were slowly surrounding him.

"No, it isn't," Kaz said. "There is more than that. There—"

One of the warriors moved too close, and Kaz swung the rifle to warn him back.

The moment he did, Aav Kanan leapt at him with startling speed. Kaz couldn't swing the rifle back to shoot at him, and the Jedwar smacked into him so hard that Kaz couldn't see anything for a second.

He was dead. He knew it with such certainty that he relaxed and waited for it to happen.

But it didn't. Kaz opened his eyes and found Aav Kanan pushing himself up onto all his arms and feet, coughing and gasping for air.

Kaz kicked him in the ribs and crawled back away. As he did so he grabbed the hose and put it in his mouth. The machine he'd built worked: air compressed and stored inside the canister now flooded his lungs. Kaz's head cleared, and he could stand easily now.

The two other warriors watched, not interfering. A duel, after all, was a duel.

Aav Kanan focused on the fight again, his mighty leap still leaving him gasping for air, but Kaz had gotten clear and stood again. He fumbled for the rifle, looking to fire it and warn the Red warriors, but Aav Kanan knocked it free. Even struggling to breathe he was still stronger than Kaz.

He raised his sword with an unsteady hand.

This gave Kaz time to free his own sword, one of Gar Kofan's keepsakes. He blocked Aav Kanan's weak strike and the two slowly fumbled around, Aav gasping for air and trying to gain the strength to strike, and Kaz doing his best to stay free of the wicked blade.

With each sword thrust, they both weakened. For Aav it was the air getting thinner and thinner. For Kaz, it was the heavy sword and his small stature. The warriors no longer stood in a circle around them: they'd started to sit down, out of breath and dizzy.

Aav Kanan raised his sword with two hands over his head, and began laughing. "It was just air," he said. "Worthless, useless, air."

When he swung, Kaz hit him on the head with his sword handle, and the confused Jedwar stumbled, tripped, and fell onto the point of his own sword. He cried out, and then lay on his side, holding the wound and falling silent.

The canister of air gasped and whistled, and gave out. There was nothing to breathe but the thinning atmosphere now. But his ability to build things had saved him. Without the strength of real air to breathe from his device, he would have died instantly at Aav Kanan's many hands.

Kaz staggered to the top of their hiding place and watched the atmosphere plant with what he thought were his last breaths. He watched as a flier hastily landed. He watched as a strange warrior with no color ran to the doors. It was Jan Kahrtr himself. The rumors were true, he wasn't dead, he had escaped Warhoon somehow, and allied himself with the Red warriors.

He opened the doors—how, Kaz couldn't tell—and the half-dead technicians ran inside.

And then Kaz passed out.

When Kaz awoke, it was to the sweet taste of fresh air. The Warhoons walked up to his resting place. "Kaz Kanan!" they called out, as they offered him all Aav Kanan's possessions. By the right of combat, Kaz was Jedwar now.

Him, Kaz, a Jedwar, by right of battle! Who could have imagined such a thing? *Kaz Kanan,* he repeated to himself, *a Jedwar of Barsoom.*

He looked around. That meant that these Warhoons were his to lead. What great things could he do as a leader when he returned to Warhoon? There were parts of the city that could be rebuilt. There were ruins that he could command be explored. He could turn Warhoon into a great city. A more powerful one, even.

But every warrior who wanted to prove himself would challenge him to a duel to the death to take the title of Jedwar from him. No, Kaz realized, they would not take his orders happily. Because his orders would have nothing to do with blood, and fighting, and conquest. And if he helped his people become even more powerful, what would they do with that power?

There would be more spilled blood and fighting. And it would steal him away from being able to tinker, to think, and to hunt for answers. No good would come of it, he realized.

So he left the Warhoons, confused, with Aav Kanan's body and possessions, as he led the thoats and the wagon away from the canal and the atmosphere plant.

There was more in Barsoom than just the city of Warhoon and its warriors, Kaz thought. More than bloodsport in the arena, or the challenge of battles. And for him, maybe there could be more than just repairing rifles. Rumors said Tharks moved about in the city of Helium. Perhaps Kaz could pass as a Thark, and learn the technologies of the Red warriors.

Or maybe he would travel farther than just Helium.

He didn't know. But the air had never tasted sweeter, and the morning had never held more promise.

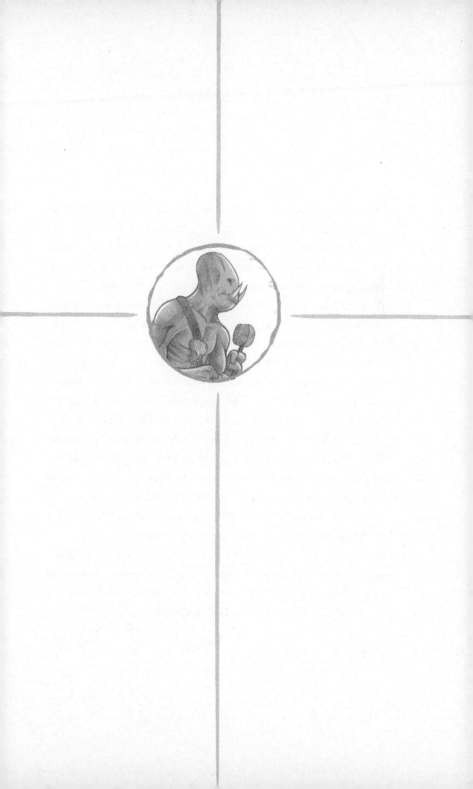

When John Carter first arrived on Barsoom, he was captured by the Tharks, one of the tribes of giant, green, four-armed men who roam the dead sea bottoms and who dwell amid the ruins of ancient cities. Carter soon learned that these strange alien warriors are hatched from eggs and that they possess limited telepathic abilities. Carter's strength at arms earned him the respect of the Tharks, and also earned him a position of authority among them, but he soon ran afoul of Sarkoja, an old woman who had positioned herself as the most fervent proponent of the cruel morality of the Tharks, a code that forbids all affection. When Carter witnessed Sarkoja's mistreatment of the prisoner Dejah Thoris, the lovely red-skinned princess who would later become his wife, he threatened to kill Sarkoja, thus earning the woman's eternal enmity. Carter then befriended Sola, whose kindly heart made her an aberration among her people, and soon learned her secret—that she was a product of a forbidden love between the great warrior Tars Tarkas and a sweet and loving woman named Gozava, who had been tortured by Sarkoja but who had died rather than reveal the name of her lover or the identity of her daughter. Tars Tarkas did not know that Sola was his daughter, and when the truth was revealed to him, he warned Sarkoja to leave and never come back. Our next tale explores what happens next in the life of the bitter, vindictive Sarkoja.

VENGEANCE OF MARS

BY ROBIN WASSERMAN

These are the things she knows: blood and pain, dust and rock.

Hunger.

Hate.

The man from elsewhere is a smudge on the horizon, but she will not close the distance. Not yet.

Patience. She knows this, too. All too well. Eight years she has waited. Amassed her forces and nurtured their hate. Watched the man from afar, noted his habits, his weaknesses, his desires.

Weakness and desire: She knows these to be the same.

She desires his blood flowing through her fingers, staining the desert floor. She craves his moans of agony, the last gasps of his puny lungs, the slackness of death as his soul escapes his body and takes its last voyage. Surely not to the Valley Dor, for there can be no eternal berth in paradise for one like him, for one who has brought such hell down upon her and her world. She desires the longsword in her hand, the swift and sure strike, the final blow that will send him home.

But she is stronger than her desires. She has waited. And

now she will wait one more sundown and one more sunrise, and then he will die.

Tomorrow, Sarkoja will kill John Carter, the madman monster of Barsoom, and all will hallow her name.

Vengeance. This she knows above all. And tomorrow, the man John Carter will know it, too.

They expected her to die. A warning, Tars Tarkas called it, allowing her a chance to flee before he took his final revenge. This supposed mercy was nothing but another sign of his disease, the infection that John Carter had brought to her world. That Tars Tarkas, the mightiest of all the Tharks in all Barsoom, should show mercy—it was an abomination.

She had saved him once from corruption, from the so-called *love* for that female. It had been disgusting, their secret rendezvous, their cooing passion, the soft spots he exposed to her and loved in her, their shared ecstasies of weakness—for what was attachment, what was so-called love but the worst kind of weakness, the fault-line of civilization, the flaw that had been eradicated all those generations ago? The female was an atavism, a parasite, and Tars Tarkas her prey. Sarkoja had rescued him from his sorry fate and cauterized the wound: Once the female was gone, Tars Tarkas returned to his natural state of glory. It was not in the nature of the Tharks to deceive, but she had allowed herself one small lie of omission, and behaved as if she knew nothing of his crimes. This sacrifice she had made for him, and for their people, so he could someday rule. He had made adequate use of the gift. For many years, there was no Thark harder, stronger, truer to the spirit of the Green Martians.

And then came the man John Carter, and he was worse than the female, because his venom spread. As it was in the wild, so it was among the Tharks: The weakest was first to fall.

Sola's betrayal was no surprise. But for Tars Tarkas, of all Tharks, to succumb to the man John Carter's lies, this was unthinkable. For Tars Tarkas to cast her out, though she had been his most loyal female, his most dogged servant, this too was unthinkable. But for him to do so as an act of mercy, to consign her to a coward's death, this was *intolerable*.

He had offered her a weakling's way out, and she had taken it, for it seemed even she was not immune to the poison, the diseased emotions coursing through her tribe. She had successfully walled herself away from the most obvious enemies, those cancers of love, friendship, guilt, kindness. But she had discovered in herself a will to live that exceeded her will for honor and battle glory, and for this, she had the man John Carter to blame.

He would *pay*.

Three weeks she had passed roaming the dead seas, the sun rising and setting without incident. She had begun to believe she would live—refusing to ask herself, live for what, live with whom, live how, when her tribe had turned its backs to her and when all reputation and glory were lost.

She was eating the last of her supplies, a tasteless handful of stale nuts, when the first blow fell. A troupe of Warhoon scouts. They asked no questions, solicited no alliance or intel, only struck at her with their short-blades, one blow after another, and this was right, this was the true way, and for the first time since Tars Tarkas had offered her his diseased mercy, she felt her burdens lift, and laughed at the glee of slashing and bashing and killing, even as their daggers skinned the flesh from her bones and ripped jagged gashes in her face, her arms, her chest. War was life, life was war, and it was only in battle that she truly came alive, whirling and dancing on her sturdy limbs, hurling one of the larger males off his feet and stomping his face as she targeted his brother.

Three of them fell to her hand, and when the others left her for dead, it was these bodies that kept her alive, one mouthful at a time.

When the white apes approached, she buried herself beneath the dirt and soft yellow moss, carving a small tunnel in the earth through which to breathe. They roamed through the gnawed bones of the dead, sensing her presence, frustrated by her camouflage. She listened to them padding above her, and knew that if a thick white paw plunged through the shallow mound of dirt, she would be unable to defend herself. She was weak, bloodstained—finished. And as she lay there, as she waited for the River Iss to beckon, she let her mind play over the past, and wonder. For perhaps all she knew was wrong, and Tars Tarkas was right. Perhaps the man John Carter had brought truth to Barsoom; perhaps the brutal, cold life of kill after kill was less than necessary; perhaps there was another way. Perhaps it was so, because somewhere the man John Carter walked the earth, stupidly happy with his weak female, and somewhere the betrayer Tars Tarkas and the defective Sola embraced and delighted in their perverse and unnatural bond, while Sarkoja lay desiccated and disintegrating, food for the white apes.

Even Barsoom could not be so unjust. The gods would not allow it.

And so, if she fell and John Carter rose, perhaps that was as it should be.

This she allowed herself to believe, for the long moment of silence after the white apes padded away, leaving her intact and alive. It would be easier, she thought, to stay beneath the earth in her cool and shallow grave, and let Barsoom reclaim her.

Then came the wind.

A great wind, sweeping the yellow plains.

An invisible hand, lifting the dirt from her broken body.

She opened her eyes, and she saw sky.

From that moment, she never questioned again. Barsoom wanted her to live.

And that could only mean Barsoom wanted John Carter to die.

She walked.

When she could no longer walk, she crawled.

Through valleys, over shallow hills, across dry riverbeds that carved ribbons through the endless yellow plains.

Through heat that scorched her throat and set her empty belly on fire.

Through cold that numbed her limbs and frosted her open wounds.

There was no more food; no more water. There was no destination, except forward. No thought, except *forward*.

She would go on until she could go on no longer.

The structure before her was low and made of a gleaming glass. Within, carefully arranged, the eggs waited. Rows and rows of eggs, their shells thinning, their hidden creatures stirring, limbs creaking and stretching, their time nearing, the outside world calling.

Sarkoja did not see the incubator. She saw nothing of the world before her. Legs carried her forward. Arms clawed the dirt. Mechanically, she slurped from the miracle, the thin fountain of water that trickled from a weak underground spring, her body drawn to the moisture like a thoat to a trough, but she knew none of this. She saw only the visions of her fevered brain, visions of a wrathful army, their weapons raised in might and right. She saw Sola broken on the ground; she saw John Carter, his dumb, zitidar-like eyes wide in fear as her army mowed him down. She saw Tars Tarkas rise again, purged of all poison, and saw herself at his side. She tasted blood, and tasted joy.

For two days, she dreamed of death. And when she awoke, when the gray curtain lifted from her eyes and she took in the eggs, each hard shell protecting a life as yet untainted by flaw or failure, she knew that the fever dreams had not been dreams at all, but visions of a future she could now make manifest.

She knew where she would find her army.

Every night, she tells them stories. She has always told them stories.

Days are spent on training: How to use a longsword, how to wield a spear and aim a rifle, how to disable an enemy in hand-to-hand combat, how to live off the land, how to scavenge food and track water, how to hide from white apes and banths, how to ambush vulnerable travelers and take what is needed, how to survive and how to kill and why the two are inseparable. But it is the nights that matter. It is the stories that keep her going, and it is the stories that make these children, her children, an army.

"The man was a stranger to us, as we were strangers to him, and yet he did not hesitate to interfere. He curried favor with his strange powers, and he slaughtered those who would not bend to his will. This man—"

"John Carter," they say, in unison. This is their role, and they relish it.

"—was unlike all who dwell on Barsoom, for this man had it in his power and will to lie. To close off his mind and cache his whims. He was a deceiver, and he brought this corruption to the heart of the Tharks. He claimed to come from another world."

"Lies."

"He claimed to offer his allegiance to Lorquas Ptomel and Tars Tarkas."

"Lies."

"He claimed that Sarkoja had betrayed her people and her leader."

"Lies!"

"He claims to be strong."

"But he is weak."

"He claims to be noble and true."

"But he is hollow."

"He claims to love this world."

"But he loves only himself."

Sarkoja does not believe in love. What she feels for her children is far greater. They are a part of her, powerful limbs that respond to her every will. Their thoughts are her thoughts; no part of them has not been molded by her. She has given them an identical dream and for six years they have pursued it with identical single-mindedness; they circle her and listen to the stories with identically rapt gazes.

But she must admit, they are not identical. Projal is clumsy with his dagger, while Biquas is too easily distracted—by sudden noises, by tricks of the light, by, more than once, one of his four arms, flickering at the edge of his field of vision.

And then there is Rok, who has no equal with the sword and no rival to his strength or purity of will. Rok, who was the first to contribute to the telling of the stories, whose booming responses inspired the others to join him. Rok, who was the first to learn to speak, and as soon as he did, pestered her nonstop with questions about John Carter, whose name had been his first word, as it was for them all. Had she believed in such a thing as love, Rok would have been the most deserving of it. But fortunately for them both, she believes only in strength, and that she has given him instead.

"He killed many of the males and females who gave you life," she says, for the last time, because after tomorrow, there will be no more need for stories, after tomorrow they will have only one story to tell: the story of their triumph and John Carter's death. "But his crimes are far more grave. He killed the spirit of the Tharks. He ripped out its heart and stomped on it with his puny feet. He stole your legacy and corrupted your brothers and sisters, who now look to him as a god. He is power-mad and bloodthirsty and knows nothing of nobility or custom. He believes that people should do as they *feel* and not as they *must*. He believes the good of the one—the only one mattering to *him*—is worth the slaughter of the many. The slaughter of our people, and our way. There is only one hope for cleansing Barsoom of his taint. He claims to be our savior, but there is only one thing he can do to save us."

"He can die," they chant, and chant again, until their voices merge with the wild howls of the plains and it as if the night itself calls for John Carter's blood.

They are not all Green Martians. There are those among them with two arms rather than four; those who toddle on spindly legs at half the height of a grown Thark. Those who were once tended, as babes, by the weak Red Men who dwelt in cities and pretended to a civility and superiority they had not earned. There are those who, in another life, would have been her enemies.

But they are all her children.

The city of Zodanga was filled with orphans. She did not intend to steal them. Not at first.

She crept into the city in search of food and weaponry. She had sent the children into the broken skyline, warning them to stay close to one another and not be intimidated by the Red Men. She had taught them how to disappear into shadows and how to kill in silence, and Zodanga was nearly in ruins–John Carter and his army had seen to that. She had no doubt they would escape detection and return to camp with what was needed. Still, she kept Rok by her side. Of all of them, he was the one she could least afford to lose.

The first Red child came upon them as they were pawing through a burned-out weapons cache, piling rifles and ammunition into Rok's large sack. The child's skin was smeared with ash; long waves of black hair nearly obscured her face. She stood frozen in a crumbling doorway, mouth slack, eyes taking in the sight of the two plundering Tharks. Sarkoja knew that to the child, she must look like a monster, large and hungry, and that she could not risk the child's scream. She raised her pistol.

But Rok stayed her hand.

And because he was Rok, she allowed it.

"Who are you?" the child asked. She held her hands behind her back and her head down. "What more can you take from us that you have not already stolen?"

Sarkoja realized that the child had mistaken her for one of the army that had stormed, looted, and finally razed the city. "I have stolen nothing," she said. "I take only what I need, to avenge what was stolen from me, by the man John Carter."

The girl tossed her hair from her face, revealing a gaze that rivaled the sun for heat and fury. "John Carter killed my father," she said. "Slit his throat while he was sleeping, when his only crime was doing his job, guarding a threshold John Carter saw fit to pass. I watched from the shadows, and I saw the knife cut his throat and the blood slide out. I waited for John Carter to pass, and then I threw myself on my father, I pressed the torn flaps of flesh together between my hands, tried to force the torn skin back together, but the blood flowed through my fingers. I sat in a pool of my father's blood, and as his life leaked away, I watched the city burn."

"And your mother?" Sarkoja asked.

"Dead," the child said. "She would have died of grief and hunger, surely, but John Carter's men did not give her that chance. He is from a different world, they say. He had no quarrel with us, nor we with him. And yet we are ruined. While he continues to breathe. They say he is loved."

"Not by me," Rok said, his voice a growl.

"Nor by me," Sarkoja said.

"I will kill him," the girl said, and showed them her hands. In her tiny, tight fist, she clenched a long, silver blade. "Someday. I will find a way."

Sarkoja laughed, and when the child did not recoil from the harsh sound, so painful to Red ears, the sound that all Barsoom knew to mean carnage, she knew her suspicions were right. "Perhaps," she told the child, "you have found one."

The child was Zana Lor, and she was the first. There were many other children who had lost their parents to John Carter's orgy of destruction, but Sarkoja chose carefully. She found the children who spared no time for weeping or bemoaning their fate, the children who fixed their sight on what must be done. She looked for the familiar—the hate that blazed in her own heart, the physical need for justice. And when she found these children, she took them.

They came willingly, as did the women—for someone needed to care for the children, who were far more helpless than the young Tharks. There were plenty of women too, for John Carter had been an effective widow-maker, cutting a swath of death through the city's husbands, fathers, and sons. Again, she selected only those women who hungered for his blood, who lost no time mourning the fallen but instead devoted themselves to vengeance.

She followed only one rule: Never did she take a woman

with child. There was attachment there, and attachment was weakness, distraction. She had no use for mothers. Thus the women she did choose had no use for children.

So the young ones were fed and bathed, but they were not mothered; they were molded by no one but Sarkoja, and they listened to her stories as attentively as the women, as attentively as the Tharks. They learned to fight with the same weapons and though they were smaller and weaker, they were all the more determined, because they did not need to rely on stories. They knew why John Carter needed to die without Sarkoja telling them, and they had capacity for more anger than she had ever imagined their fragile bodies could contain.

None of them could match Zana Lor for white-hot anger. The girl glowed bright with fury. She was destined for great things, Sarkoja knew, and Rok saw it as well. Night after night, Zana and Rok trained together, her swift, sure movements matching his as they sliced their swords through the night air. She was like no Red Man Sarkoja had ever known.

She rarely slept, and when she did, she screamed.

Tomorrow.

She has waited eight years.

She has watched her children grow, and grow strong.

Two days ago, John Carter set off with Tars Tarkas and two Red Men of Helium on a ride through the desert, in search of adventure or solitude or more souls to kill; this she does not know, nor does she care. He sets off on such a course once every six months, and this time, the unexpected awaits him.

Two days ago, her army took off in pursuit, keeping enough distance between themselves and their prey that they will not be detected, not until they lay the trap and strike, and then it will be too late.

Two days ago, she saw Rok and Zana together, their

heads bent so close that their foreheads kissed, Red girl and Green man in solemn communion, and though it is not natural, and though Rok has of late been keeping his distance so as to keep his thoughts close, and though she has misgivings, because she has seen this posture, this tenderness before, she ignores it. Because they have all waited eight years, and now, tomorrow, comes the reckoning.

It is a strange time for all, so she tells herself.

It is nothing.

"He will see a girl lying in the desert."

They gather as she speaks, as they always do, for hers is the only voice that matters, and it is their beacon in the darkness.

"She will be wounded, innocent, beautiful."

They knew from the stories that John Carter was powerless against a beautiful female. All others, he destroyed without thought, but these women he believed it was his duty to save.

"He will dismount, and call his fellows to dismount, and they will tend to her wounds and offer her sustenance and service. That is when we will strike."

There were nervous murmurs of assent, a single cheer. The night was electric with anticipation. The stars themselves seemed eager.

"Zana," she says. "You will bait the trap. It will be your honor."

There is a silence. Heads are bowed. It is an honor indeed, one she knows they all crave. But it must be Zana.

"But she will not survive it!" Rok is not at the fore of the group, close enough to receive her embrace, as he always was in his youth. He speaks from the very back, but he speaks loudly, and there can be no mistaking his words.

"It is her honor," Sarkoja says, and this should be enough.

Rok persists. "You propose to leave her injured and alone. Defenseless—what if a banth should happen on her before John Carter appears?"

"Then this will offer him even more to save her from," Sarkoja says, "and all the more distraction from the real threat."

"And when the trap is sprung, and we attack, who will save her then?" Rok shouts. "She will fall, if not by our hands, then by his."

"Then that is how it will be," Sarkoja says. She fixes her gaze on Zana, who meets it, unflinching. The child, no longer a child, says nothing.

Sarkoja nods. "The plan is good. Many of us may not live to see another sunset, and this, too, is good, because we will die knowing we have saved our world. Tomorrow . . ."

"John Carter will die," her children say.

But not Rok. Rok says nothing.

Not until the others have retreated into sleep. He comes to her in the night; he comes to beg for the girl's life.

"Forego the ambush," he tells her. "We will challenge him to battle, as equals, as custom demands. We will face him on even ground, not sneak and skulk like cowards. This is the Thark way, as you have taught us."

"John Carter is not our equal!" she roars.

He bears the wrath. He was never one to be afraid.

"He is not our equal," she repeats, with steely calm. "And we, I fear, are not his, not on the battlefield. The man John Carter has powers that no living creature should possess. He has the strength of ten Tharks, and if he is to die, we must allow ourselves to violate custom, in service of ending his greater violation. It is the only way."

"Then choose someone else," he tells her. "Choose anyone."

"It cannot be anyone; it must be her."

"Why?"

Zana is the bravest, Zana is the strongest, Zana is the angriest. This is the only reason. This and no other. She does not speak this aloud. He can read it within her. He should not have to. It is truth; it should live within him already.

"To punish me," he says. "Because I need her alive, you consign her to death."

Sarkoja does not ask what it means, this need. Perhaps she would rather not know.

"She is only a young girl," he says. "She deserves a better life."

"I did not teach you to speak like that," Sarkoja says. "I did not teach you to *think* like that. Her life is no more or less precious than yours, than Yezqe's, than Libor's, than mine. It derives its value from its use to us, her people. It is worth only as much to her as it is worth to our cause. Zana knows that. All my children know that. But you—"

"She is only a young girl," he says. "Please."

"This is beneath you." She can feel his raw need, and it disgusts her. She has let him get too close to the girl. It is not natural, for a Thark and a Red girl to share so much. The girl has corrupted him. It is her fault for allowing it, Sarkoja knows. For being lenient and ignoring what she knows to be true.

No longer.

"Begging for the life of a female, as if she cannot choose for herself. You speak like the man John Carter," she tells Rok. He does not flinch from the insult.

"She chose nothing," Rok says. "You chose for her. You chose for us all."

The dagger is cold in her hand.

It is shameful, to strike an enemy while he sleeps. It is cowardly.

And Rok is not her enemy. Rok is her child.

But they are all her children, and the strong cannot survive the depredations of the weak. This is why only the most perfect of eggs are allowed to endure. Even the hardest stone, if riven with faults, will shatter with a single blow. So it is for the Tharks; so it is for her family. Aberrations, defects, weaklings cannot be tolerated. Sacrifices must be made.

Rok has proven himself weak. And so, the sacrifice.

He moans softly in his sleep.

He has always done this, since he was newly hatched, lacking the words to express his needs, lacking even the needs themselves. She gave him both. She gave him everything.

There had once been another hatchling, a single Thark who should have died so that the Tharks could flourish. It had been Sarkoja's duty to dispatch the child, and she had failed. All that followed could have been prevented, had she struck that fatal blow. But the child slipped away; the child lived, and grew up to be Sola, and saved the life of the man John Carter, and blamed Sarkoja for all her miseries, and brought ruin to the world.

A sharp blade brought down with the right velocity, at the right angle, would kill him instantly. There would be no struggle and no pain.

But again, she fails. And this time, it is a failure of will.

The excitement of tomorrow, the anticipation, the culmination of a lifetime of training and rage: He is, surely, not thinking clearly. Perhaps, neither is she. Tomorrow, she will speak with him again. She will explain the facts of their lives, and she will brook no argument. Either he will accept his duty, or he will die—not like an animal, slaughtered in his sleep, but like a Thark, on his feet, girded for battle.

It will not come to that, she assures herself. He is Rok, and he has never disappointed her. He deserves the chance he has fought and longed for, the chance to stand by her side when the moment comes. Tomorrow, they will slay and triumph, as it should be, together.

But when the sun rises on tomorrow, he is gone.

It goes perfectly, exactly as planned. Zana lies in the desert, a gash in her leg, her limbs artfully splayed, her face tear-stained, her lips ruby red. Sarkoja and her warriors have secreted themselves behind the jagged rocks that jut from the desert floor. They watch John Carter steer his thoat toward the girl. Sarkoja silently rejoices: He is *alone*. Her army, thirty strong, against his one. It will be over nearly before they have time to savor their victory.

The man John Carter dismounts. He is even smaller than she remembers him. Uglier, too. It is unthinkable that this creature should have caused so much damage. But his reign of ruin nears an end. Sarkoja raises a hand and gives her soldiers the signal. John Carter walks slowly to the girl, kneels by her side. The warriors raise their weapons. They take aim.

"Sarkoja!" Libor shouts, then there is the sharp report of a radium rifle, and he is down.

Sarkoja whirls around. John Carter's men are everywhere, Red Men and Tharks alike, swarming over her army, their rifles firing, their swords slashing. Their ambush has been ambushed.

A Thark knocks her to the ground. Sarkoja smashes the hilt of her sword into his leg, then, as he stumbles, flicks it around and draws blood. She stabs him once, twice, then uses his lifeless body as a shield to block the slashing long-sword of an advancing Red Man. He is even more easily dispatched. A kick to the gut, a blade to the throat, and he folds into himself, spurting fountains of red. The enemy surrounds her, but they are no match for her fury. She kills one, then another, working her way through the thrashing crowd, desperate to reach John Carter—but as a space opens before her, she stops, transfixed.

For there is Zana, still on the ground. The man John Carter has disappeared into the thick of battle. Another figure has replaced him by Zana's side: Rok. Sarkoja is close enough to hear his final words. "For you," he says. "To save you."

He has betrayed them all to John Carter; he has betrayed them all to love.

Sarkoja cannot move.

Zana bares her teeth, and gazes up at him as fiercely as she did the day they met, when visions of death and destruction danced in her eyes and Sarkoja promised to make her fondest wish come true. She says nothing. Her only response is the knife, the same knife she held in her tiny fist that first day, the same knife around which her small body has curled while she slept, night after night, while she ate and breathed and lived for a single purpose that Rok has stolen away. Zana is wounded, but the knife is sharp, her aim sure. Rok cannot block it, or perhaps will not. He is dead before his head cracks to the ground.

"I gave you a chance," says a voice behind her, and still, Sarkoja cannot move. She is too heavy with shame. Zana, the Red girl, found the strength to do what Sarkoja could not. And because of her failure, her children are falling; her children are screaming. A radium shell tears into Zana and blows a hole through her midsection. Her body goes limp. The knife falls from her hand.

The battlefield is littered with Sarkoja's lifeless children. Libor has fallen. Projal has fallen.

"You should not have come back," says the voice.

Yezque has fallen. Biquas has fallen.

"Turn around," says the voice. "I will not strike you from behind."

She turns to face Tars Tarkas.

"I have hoped for this moment," he says. Sarkoja raises her longsword. But the great warrior is too quick. His blade slices cleanly through her shoulder; the sword and the arm that grips it drop to the ground.

Sarkoja staggers. She throws her weight against Tars Tarkas, pummeling him with her remaining fists. The ground is slippery beneath her, slippery with her own blood. His longsword dances. She is too slow for him, and slower with each gash and wound. The blood is leaving her, carrying with it her strength. Hers is the only fight that still continues; her army has fallen.

"It was for you," she tells Tars Tarkas, choking on the blood that fills her throat. "To save you."

He laughs.

And then Sarkoja is on the ground, her strength fled, her life fleeing in its wake. Through blurry, bloodshot eyes she sees John Carter summon his men and congratulate them on their victory. She sees John Carter and Tars Tarkas embrace. She sees them check Rok's body for signs of life; she sees their sorrow that this new friend, this *hero*, has sacrificed himself for their survival.

This is too much.

There is strength in her yet, strength in her rage, and she rises to her knees, then to her feet, drags herself toward the monster, muscles through his pathetic defenders, she will not be stopped, she will push on, push forward, until John Carter's neck is between her hands. She squeezes the life from his fragile body, snaps his brittle bones; she sees his empty eyes roll back in his head; she sees his face go slack; she sees his spirit depart.

She sees what she wants to see.

She sees the dreams behind her lids, as she lies in the dirt with blood pooling around her shuddering body. She sees nothing of the real, of John Carter approaching her body, smiling because she writhes in pain.

She can feel John Carter's neck in her grip, but her hands clutch empty air. And then they drop to her sides, and she lies still.

She dies believing she has done the world a great service. That someday all will be grateful. All will hallow the name of Sarkoja, warrior of justice.

She dies a hero in her own heart. She dies a victor.

She dies, and they set her body afire, and soon the apes and the ulsios will come and pick through the ashes and gnaw at her smoldering remains.

She dies, and she will not be mourned, and she will not be remembered.

She dies, and John Carter lives.

She will not be avenged.

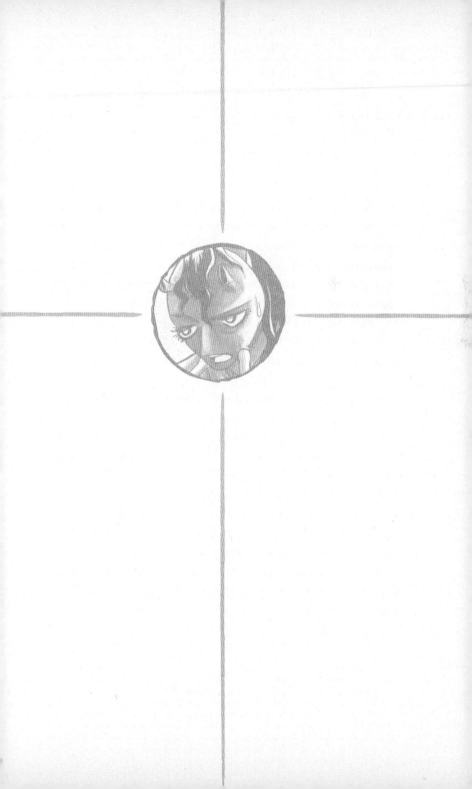

◆ ◆ ◆

The first race on Barsoom was the Orovars, white-skinned men and women with blond or auburn hair. A million years before John Carter's arrival, the Orovars built the great cities of Korad, Aaanothor, and Horz, and they controlled an empire that stretched from pole to pole. However, as the oceans dried up, this empire began to fray, and the Orovars foresaw that their race did not possess the hardy constitution necessary to thrive on a dying planet, and so they bred the Red Men to be their successors, and by the time of John Carter's arrival the Orovars were generally believed to be extinct. Of course, John Carter knew nothing of this at first. Barsoom to him was a strange and hostile place. But he did manage to make a few friends in those early days, including his trusty pet Woola, a doglike species known as a calot, which possess eight legs and a pair of long tusks. Woola was initially ordered to guard John Carter and keep him from wandering off and falling afoul of the four-armed white apes who haunt the abandoned cities of Barsoom. Carter once petted Woola the way one would scratch any hound, and the beast, who had known only the cruelty of life among the Tharks, afterward became ever-loyal. Our next tale is told from the point of view of Woola, and fills us in on some of the amazing adventures of that faithful beast that John Carter was not around to witness.

◆ ◆ ◆

WOOLA'S SONG

BY THEODORA GOSS

isten, my clutchmates. Listen as I tell you how I met my master, John Carter. How we fought the ilthurs, how we fled from the Tharks into the mountains and valleys of this land, where I lost my master. How I came at last to the lost valley of our songs, where water flows and the trees give pleasant shade, and met the others of our kind. Where I learned—

But let me begin as I ought to, with praise for our mother, Awala, the fierce, the many-tusked, protector of her clutch. She longed to raise her children in freedom, so when her time came, she hid from the Tharks in one of the buildings of this city, which once belonged to the Orovars of our songs but now belongs to the Tharks, whose slaves we are.

There she sang her birthing song and laid us, seven eggs in a hollow she had dug in the dirt, where the floor tiles had long ago cracked. The warm earth held us as we grew, learning her songs even as we lay curled in our eggs, learning to sing with our minds, together as a clutch, my brothers and sisters.

Alas the day that an ilthur found her, curled on her clutch, crooning to us! How she fought! Praise to our mother, to the fierce Awala, who wounded the ilthur, who thrust her tusks into its throat so that it died, its white fur soaked with blood. Praise her and mourn her, our mother who died when the hands of the ilthur, in its death-agony, crushed her throat. As long as we live, we shall remember her and sing her praises, who died so that we might hatch and feel the cool air and warm sun, and sing together as she had taught us.

Listen, my clutchmates. You remember how we hatched out of our shells in that chamber, how for seven days we ate nothing but that ilthur, gnawing it although our teeth were still soft. How we would not eat our mother, even though we were starving because we had no mother to hunt for us. After seven days we were found by Sola of the Tharks, who brought us to her master, Tas Tharvas. There we were raised as our kind are raised, as slaves to the Tharks.

Sola was kind to us. She fed us well and crooned to us with her mind, almost as our mother would have, although she could not hear our songs. Remember how we tumbled over the floor and each other, chasing a ball. Wala lying on her back, her legs flailing. Awol falling on his nose in his eagerness. Lawala and Oola bumping into each other, Alool singing a song of triumph when at last he cornered it. Olawa stealing it from him. Those were good days, with food and song, my brothers and sisters.

But soon enough, we were trained as our kind is among the Tharks. We were given food enough for five, and made to fight one another for it. We were taught to fight ulsios, thules, bakaras, all to prepare us for when we were adults and would fight in the arena for the amusements of the Tharks. What saved us then, my brothers and sisters? What kept us from wounding one another more than we had to, working together to defeat the mindless animals that the Tharks sent against us? It was the song we shared, mind to mind, as I am singing to you now.

And so we grew in the house of Tas Tharvas, trained to

be fierce, trained as our mother had been to use our tusks to kill. Who showed us tenderness? Only Sola, who would stoke our ridges, who would bring us food when Tas Tharvas had ordered us to be starved, to make us more bloodthirsty. Only Sola wept when we were separated, I to remain with Tas Tharvas, you to be sent to the houses of other Tharks or to the arena. Only Sola put her arms around me while I howled and rattled my chains. At last, weary, I lay down beside her and wept with her, my clutchmates!

One day Sola came into the chamber where I was kept, her eyes brighter and her steps lighter than usual. I could hear the song in her mind: Tas Tharvas was dead, struck by a strange visitor whose skin was as pale and ugly as an ilthur's, but who was as strong as the strongest of the Tharks. "Come, Woola," she said. I followed her down the corridors and into a chamber where I saw him, John Carter as I was later to learn. He was indeed as ugly as an ilthur, although hairless. Not green like the Tharks or one of our kind.

"You must make certain that he does not leave this chamber," she said to me. And so I guarded the door.

That was how I met my prisoner, for John Carter was my prisoner before he was my master. Twice he tried to escape from me. Once, I followed him to the border of the city, where the buildings are unoccupied. It was close to where we had hatched, my brothers and sisters, and I remembered our mother, Awala, and praised and mourned her in my mind. I tried to warn him, tried to drive him back, but like the Tharks, he could not hear my mindsongs, and my motions meant nothing to him.

He went into one of those buildings, and just as he was looking at the curious paintings on the walls, paintings left by the Orovars of our songs, an ilthur sprang upon him. It had the branch of a bodi tree in its hand, and it would have killed him with it, had I not thrown myself at its throat. I fought as our mother had fought, biting the ilthur through the shoulder so that it dropped the branch, but it clutched my throat and I thought I was surely going to die in that room. "I'm coming to you, Awala my mother," I sang. "Wait for me in that valley we sing of, where our kind live together, and where no Thark has ever set foot."

But John Carter picked up the branch of the bodi tree and with one blow, he crushed the head of the ilthur. And then we heard a roar. It was the mate of the ilthur, who had come into the room and seen its mate lying dead upon the floor. It lay dead, I lay dying, and John Carter turned to the window, about to leap outside and so make his escape. But he looked back and saw me lying there, at the mercy of the ilthur.

What would a Thark have done, my clutchmates? I had lost my fight, and a Thark would have left me there to die. But John Carter did not leave me to die. He threw the branch of the bodi tree at the ilthur, striking it on the head. The ilthur fell to the floor, and then John Carter struck it again and again, until it lay dead.

Then both of us heard laughter. There at the door stood Sola and several Tharks. She had noticed our absence and led them to us. It was they who were laughing, having witnessed and enjoyed our struggle with the ilthurs. One of them said, with a broad smile on his face, "Let the calot be killed," and another took out his weapon. He pointed it at me, but John Carter struck his hand so that the projectile hit the wall. And then he knelt beside me and said, "Follow me, Woola." So I rose and followed him, grateful to be alive, grateful to my new master for having saved me twice in one day from certain death.

That day, for only the second time in my life, I felt affection toward someone other than you, my clutchmates. I had loved Sola because of her kindness to us. Now I learned to love John Carter, not only because he had saved my life, but also because he treated me with a kindness to which I was not accustomed among the Tharks. He would sit with me, talking about the place he had come from, and about Dejah Thoris, the granddaughter of the Jeddak of Helium, whose airship had been captured by the Tharks. I could not hear his mindsong as clearly as I could hear those of the Tharks, but I could hear his tenderness toward her, his desire to rescue her from certain death.

At last, one day, he decided that an attempt at rescue should be made. I was determined not to be left behind, although I could hear in his mind that he was planning to leave me because he believed I belonged among the Tharks. But I had no desire to remain among them. I would rather leave the city of my birth, leave you, my brothers and sisters, than remain a slave.

He had hidden his thoats in one of the buildings at the edge of the city, close to where we had fought the ilthurs. He was planning to bring Sola and Dejah Thoris to our chamber, and then flee with them before the sun rose in the sky. Before he left, he put his arms around me and said, "You're a good dog, Woola. Take care of yourself, all right?"

I lay in our chamber, waiting until I knew he was gone. I was going to follow him stealthily, creeping through the back alleys of the city. I was not going to allow him to leave me behind.

But soon after he left, two Thark warriors came to his chamber.

"They will throw him to the wild calots," said one, "but only after he is forced to watch Dejah Thoris suffer at the hands of Tal Hajus."

The other laughed, as though anticipating such as spectacle with pleasure, and then said, "What about the calot?"

"Tie it up for the night. We will take it to Tal Hajus tomorrow."

113

I thought about fighting, my clutchmates. But both of them had projectile weapons, and they would have killed me. Then what good would I be to myself, or my master? No, I allowed them to tie me with a rope. A rope, I thought, I can bite through that! But it took all night for me to gnaw through it, all night in that silent room, not knowing whether or not my master had been captured, whether or not he was even now enduring the tortures of the Tharks.

After the warriors left, I rose and ran, as swiftly as I was able, to the building where I knew John Carter had left the thoats. They were gone. But I could follow their scent, so I ran even more swiftly than I had thought possible through the city, and when I had left the city buildings behind, over the plains to the north, where our songs say the first calots were laid and hatched by our Great Mother, Lal. It was with joy that I felt the warmth of the sun on my body. I coursed swiftly over the plain, knowing that my master was ahead of me. I smelled nothing but his thoats, so I knew he had not been followed. The wind over the plains tasted of freedom.

When the sun was already high in the sky, I saw them, resting beneath the shade of the thoats. How joyful John Carter was to see me! And Dejah Thoris herself embraced me and said, "I'm so glad to see you, Woola," before she kissed my snout.

But our journey that day did not go well. One of the thoats became sick and could not carry a rider, so we left it. John Carter and Sola walked, which slowed us down considerably. And when the sun was beginning to descend, Dejah Thoris cried, "I see Tharks—or warriors of some other green tribe!"

We turned, and there they were, hundreds of warriors ranged along the horizon. We saw a flash of light, and heard a distant shout—one of them had seen us with his field glasses. Suddenly, hundreds of warriors were moving toward us over the plain.

John Carter turned to us. "Sola, take Dejah Thoris and ride into the mountains. I'll stay behind and fight. Go, now!"

"No, my chieftain," said Dejah Thoris. "I will stay and fight beside the man I love."

If I had ever been jealous of the favor in which John Carter held her, and I admit that I had at times felt such jealousy, it melted at that moment. She was as brave as a calot.

"I could not fight them as well, Dejah Thoris, if I knew you were in danger," said John Carter. "Ride for the mountains, and I will at least slow them down. Go, my Princess!"

Reluctantly, Sola and Dejah Thoris mounted the thoat. I stood beside John Carter, ready to give my life to protect him. But he knelt beside me, took my head in his hands, and said, "Woola, you must protect my Princess. Can I trust you to do that?"

I growled, unwilling to leave him. But I could hear his mindsong, asking me to go with her, to protect her. So, with Sola and Dejah Thoris upon the thoat, and me loping beside them, we made for the mountains, where we could lose the warriors among the ravines and defiles.

Only once did I look back at my master. He was battling Green warriors—not Tharks but Warhoons, by their ornaments—jumping like one of the litvak of the mountains, attempting to avoid them. But there were too many of them, and as I looked, they swarmed over him and he was taken captive. In sorrow I turned and followed the thoat, certain that I would never see my master again. My duty was now to protect Sola and Dejah Thoris.

That night we slept in one of the ravines, trying to conceal ourselves as best we could, lighting no fire. Sola gathered sap from an ighur plant, and she brought some for Dejah Thoris to eat. I ate some as well, and it assuaged both my hunger and thirst, for there was no water anywhere. She and Dejah Thoris had not seen John Carter fall to the Green warriors, and I was glad—let them hope, at least for a little while. But I was sunk in sorrow, and as I lay upon the ground, watching the moons rise, I began to compose his song of lament and praise.

The next day, we made our way through the canyons, trying to stay where we hoped we would not be seen. We were hungry and thirsty, for there were few ighur plants in that area, and Sola had given much of what she had gathered to the thoat. But on we went, Sola and Dejah Thoris riding, and I loping at their side, in the direction of the highest peak. From that peak, we would be able to see the country around, and find a canal—which would lead us to Helium.

By late afternoon, we had almost reached it. It would be a steep climb, but I was relieved to be able to rest for a while in the shade of a large boulder. As we were resting there, we heard a shout. Quickly, Dejah Thoris rose and drew her weapon. Sola was just behind her. I, too, looked around, but could see and smell nothing. Then another shout, and suddenly a Red warrior was running down the side of a gorge toward us. Sola shot and he fell, but he was followed by another, and then another, and then an entire army of Red warriors running toward us and shouting.

In a moment they were upon us. Dejah Thoris was captured at once. Sola fought valiantly, but she too was captured. I wounded many of them with my tusks before they were able to capture me and tie my snout, so I could no longer gore or bite. Dejah Thoris's and Sola's hands were tied as well.

Then one of the Red warriors, a jed by his ornaments, strode up to Dejah Thoris and said, "I recognize you, Princess of Helium. I traveled with our ambassador to your grandfather's court, when he refused our offer of peace between Zodanga and Helium. He will regret that decision.

You are now a prisoner of Zodanga. Than Kosis will be so pleased to have you in his dungeon, he might just promote me to his personal guard. And you, Green warrior, and that hideous beast, will all come with me to Zodanga, where you will meet your deaths."

"My grandfather would never purchase peace at that price!" said Dejah Thoris. "Helium is a free city. We will never submit to Zodanga!"

"Speak those brave words to Than Kosis himself, and see how quickly he cuts out your tongue, Princess!" said the Red warrior. "Now, march!"

Thereafter, even Dejah Thoris marched in silence. We followed the Red warriors, Sola and Dejah Thoris walking, for the Zodangans had taken the thoat as their own, until the first moon rose and we rested among the canyons.

That night, we were fed by the Zodangans, and I realized what I had never thought possible: that it is better to be free and starving than a captive and well-fed. But I ate the flat portions of ghram they gave us because I knew that whatever happened, I would need my strength.

As I was eating, the Jed who had captured us passed by me, no doubt checking on his prisoners. Another Red warrior walked beside him, and to that warrior he said, "We will be well-rewarded by Than Kosis when we reach Zodanga. The Princess of Helium will fetch a fine ransom, and I have no doubt that the Green warrior and the thoat can both be put to work in the palace. They look strong and healthy. But the calot is too wild and will have to be killed. I wonder if Than Kosis will allow me to take its skin for a rug?"

So I was to be killed! As if I were of no more use than a litvak or an ulsio! The Zodangans prided themselves on being more civilized than the Tharks, but even a Thark would not kill a calot unless he were wounded, or in battle.

What to do now was a conundrum to me, my clutchmates. I had promised John Carter that I would stay with Sola and Dejah Thoris, but I would be of no use to them in Zodanga as a rug on a Red jed's floor. While the second moon rose, still not knowing what I should do, I rubbed the rope that tied my snout against a rock until it snapped, and went to where Sola and Dejah Thoris were lying upon the ground. The Zodangans were asleep, and the guards did not see me. They were concerned with intruders from the outside, for earlier that day one of them had seen a Warhoon in the distance.

Sola was asleep, but Dejah Thoris sat up as I came near her. Her hands were bound, but she put her face next to my snout and said, "Dear Woola. You always know the right thing to do. Listen well: You must escape from this camp and find John Carter. Do you understand, Woola? You must find him and bring him to us. He will save us from the Zodangans."

I had no way of telling her that John Carter had fallen, and was either dead or a captive among the Warhoons. But she was right, without his aid, we had no hope among the Zodangans. Her command released me from his—I would go find my master and if he still lived, I would help him in any way I could.

I growled deep in my throat, nuzzled her cheek (too roughly perhaps, because I almost sent her tumbling backward), and then turned and crept, silently, through two rows of guards. Just as I had reached the edge of their line, one of them spotted me and shouted, "Stop!" So I rose and ran as swiftly as I could through the boulder-strewn ravine where we had camped. I heard shots, and once I felt a pain in one of my legs. But I did not stop running until I was deep into the shadows of the canyon walls. There, by the light of the moons I saw a small cave, and deep into it I crept, to sleep until morning.

When the light of the sun woke me, I crept outside and looked around me. Where was I? I had paid no attention to where I was going in my flight, and now I was lost.

Before me, I saw a valley ringed by mountains. I had come from dry gullies and ravines, but here there were ighur plants, even small bushes and trees growing over the valley floor and up the sides of the mountains. And in the distance I saw—could it be possible? Sunlight glinting on what looked like a lake in the middle of the valley.

I stared in amazement. Where had I come to? And how had I gotten here?

"In the name of Lal, who are you, stranger?"

I heard the voice in my head. It was low, melodious, like no voice I had ever heard before, except perhaps when our mother sang us lullabies, my clutchmates.

I looked around. There, standing by a bush with red leaves, were three—were they calots? They looked like me, and yet they were smaller, their hides not bare but covered with fur of various colors. One was orange, one brown, and one a sort of pale cream. The orange one was striped, and the brown one had patches of lighter brown. They had no tusks.

"I am Woola, son of Awala," I sang. "I fled from Thark but was captured by the Zodangans. Again I fled, and was wounded by their projectiles. By moonlight, I crawled into a cave in the side of the mountain. When I crawled out again, I found myself here. By Lal, since you know our Great Mother, tell me where I am. What is this place?"

"I am Azorn, son of Razd," sang the orange one. "Come with us, Woola. We will take you to Orda, who will tell you what this place is. It has been a long time since we have seen one of our kind from beyond the mountains. Orda will want to know what is happening in the world outside. You are injured and hungry, so we will tend to you and feed you, for that is the way of our kind. Follow me."

Bewildered, I followed, slowly because of the pain in my leg. The projectile of the Red Warrior had wounded me more severely than I had realized. Azorn and the brown one, who I learned was called Har, son of Hoorda, walked ahead, while the cream-colored one walked beside me.

"I am Lilla, daughter of Tal," she sang. Her mindsong was the most melodious I had ever heard. "Do you realize what this place is, Woola?"

"I cannot imagine," I responded. "Unless this is the Valley Lal, about which my mother Awala sang to us, when we were still in the egg."

I heard a high tinkling, as though bells were ringing all together, and realized that Lilla was laughing. "This is indeed the Valley Lal, where our Great Mother laid the first egg. Woola, you have come home."

I walked beside her in stunned silence, scarcely knowing whether to believe her. But the plants around me, their red and purple leaves swaying in the sunshine, and the fresh, scented air I was breathing–these could not be dreams.

"You crawled into a cave and fell asleep, you told Azorn. You must have woken and crawled the other way, to the cave's other entrance. There are several caves that go right through the mountain walls, where they are narrow. Once, they were used to communicate with the outside world, but they have not been used for a thousand years."

"Then, you have lived here all your life?" I asked her. For the first time I remember, I felt shy and awkward. She was like no calot I had ever seen, soft of fur rather than hard of hide, and her tusklessness made her seem even more gentle. I had never seen such a beautiful creature.

She asked me about Thark, and I told her our story, my clutchmates. She was shocked at the cruelty of the Tharks, and when I told her how we had been separated, so that we could no longer sing together, she almost wept.

"You must tell this story to Orda," she sang. "We did not know that the children of Lal were so cruelly treated.

Orda will know how to act, what we must do. We are not thoats or ulsios, to be treated in such a way by the Green warriors."

By this time we had come to a place where there were many dens dug into the sides of small hills, within sight of the lake. And I saw something, my brothers and sisters, that gave me a pain in my chest, around the region of my hearts. I saw clutchmates playing together, rolling in the dirt in mock battles, then lying together in the sun. Together, as we should have been.

So many of them gathered around me and greeted me, wanting to hear my story, that Azorn told them to follow us to my meeting with Orda—although I still did not know who or what that might be.

But I soon learned. We came to the largest den of all, dug into the side of a hill. Sitting before it was the oldest calot I had ever seen. Her hair was entirely white, and so thin that I could see her hide, which was white also.

"Greetings, Woola," she said as we approached.

I wondered how she knew me, but she sang, "Even as you slept in that cave, I heard your mindsong. It was I who confused you so that you went the wrong way, into our valley rather than back into the hands of the Zodangans. I hope you can forgive me for reaching into your mind, causing you to come to us. But in your mind I saw such images! Calots enslaved, separated from their clutchmates, forced to kill and die in the arena. We did not know that our brothers and sisters outside this valley had fallen into such a state! I am old, and I can hear your mindsong in a way the others cannot. Tell them, Woola. Tell them your story so they can hear how calots live in the world outside."

I told them then—my story and our story, my brothers and sisters. As I told them, I could hear from their own minds sounds of wonder and sorrow. I concluded, "I am glad you brought me here, Orda. I never imagined that the valley of our mindsongs was real, or that I would see calots living in such a way—and looking so different from calots among the Tharks."

"Once, all calots looked like us," sang Orda. "Do you know the story of the calots, Woola? I hear in your mind that you do not. In this valley, we have always lived as you see, since the first clutch was laid by Lal. But long ago, when the Orovars built their cities and sailed the seas, calots were their companions. They could hear our mindsongs, and we traveled with them to distant lands, or hunted with them and guarded their houses. We sat beside their chairs and lay at the foot of their beds, participating in their lives. But as the seas dried up and the Orovars died out, they created the Red and Green warriors, who could not hear our mindsongs. We could not be companions to them. The Red warriors left us alone, but the Green warriors still used us for hunting and guarding. I see from your mind that over a thousand years, since we last heard from the outside world, the Green warriors have grown more savage, and they have treated our kind with the same savagery. And worse, I see from your hide and your tusks, which can gore an ilthur, that the Green warriors have changed the calots, breeding them for fierceness, to become fighters. This cannot continue."

"Orda," I sang, "if you have heard my mindsong, you have also heard of John Carter. In his mind, I found the story of a great war, a war for freedom that was fought in the place where he comes from. Can we not fight for the freedom of the calots?"

"We can, Woola," she sang. "But I have no wish to see calots die, even for freedom. No, what I wish is for the calots of Thark and Warhoon and Torquas, and the other cities that once belonged to the Orovars, to learn of this valley and plan for escape. Let them come here to study our history and our ways. And then, if they choose, let them go back into the world again, but as free calots. If they must fight, let them fight. But let them first learn what they are fighting for. My children," she sang to the calots seated around us, "will you help with this plan? Will you welcome calots from the outside world into this valley, so they can learn and grow strong, so they can free themselves?"

I could hear their minds together: one clear, ringing song of affirmation.

"Then I will go back, Orda," I sang. "I will spread this story to every calot, and it will spread through song so that all calots will come to know that the Valley Lal is real, and will welcome them. But before I can do so, I must find my master, John Carter, if indeed he is still alive, and help him to rescue Sola and Dejah Thoris."

"First you must rest, Woola," she answered. "You are tired and hungry, and you must heal before you can return to the outside world." And so for many days I rested in the Valley Lal, learning from the calots there, allowing my wound to heal. I saw how loving their clutches were, heard what songs they sang as the moons rose. I ate my fill and swam in the lake with the other calots. And Lilla became my friend.

"Come back to me, Woola," she sang when I had recovered my strength and was ready to return, to begin on the mission Orda had given me. "I would like to see what strange-looking calots hatch from our clutch! Will they have fur, do you think? Or tusks? Or both?"

I purred deep in my throat. That night we lay side by side, fur to hide, in a hollow we had dug in the earth by the shore of the lake. The next morning I bade her farewell and crept back through the cave in the mountain. I felt sad to be leaving the Valley Lal, but also hopeful that my mission would succeed, and I would come back to see Lilla again.

I had not forgotten my promise to Dejah Thoris, so I headed toward Warhoon, hoping that I would find John Carter alive. It was a long journey, and I was hungry and thirsty again by the time I saw, by the light of the first moon, a gar fighting—was it a Red warrior? No, it was John Carter! At last, I had once again found my master. I fought the gar and drove my tusk through its throat. Afterward, I sat beside John Carter, sharing food and drink, and I thought that he was not truly my master, but my companion, as the calots once were to the Orovars. Perhaps, with time and patience, I could teach him to hear my mindsong.

Would that he could hear it now!

I do not know where he is, my clutchmates. At the edge of the city of Zodanga, he bade me return to Thark, and although I wished to go with him to rescue Sola and Deja Thoris, I obeyed. So here I am, fulfilling Orda's mission. I am singing you the song of the Valley Lal. Go and sing it to the other calots who are held here in captivity, and tell them to sing it to their clutchmates and the other clutches, so that the song spreads, calot to calot. Let all calots know that there is a day when we shall be free.

Will I see John Carter again? Will he have rescued Sola and Dejah Thoris? I do not know. We do not know our fates, although we must fulfill them. My task now is to spread this story among you. Spread it to the calots of Thark, and then begin to disappear. Calot by calot, one by one, go across the desert to the north, toward the star we call Ird. There you will find a mountain with two jagged peaks. The calots of the Valley Lal will be waiting for you, singing. Follow their songs, and you will find our ancient home. There, learn and plan, so that one day all calots may be free. And the blessings of Lal go with you.

❖ ❖ ❖

One fact of life on Barsoom is that any form of organized religion usually turns out to be a cruel hoax. When they reach the age of a thousand, most Martians float down the sacred River Iss, believing they'll arrive in a heavenly paradise called the Valley Dor. What they find instead is a nightmarish deathtrap full of hideous monsters and ruled over by a clan of cannibalistic priests. In *The Master Mind of Mars*, Earthman Ulysses Paxton encounters the people of Phundahl, who worship the god Tur. Their absurd rituals include bumping their heads against the floor and crawling madly in a circle. They also have two chants, "Tur is Tur" and "Tur is Tur." When Paxton observes that these two chants are in fact identical, he's accused of having a lack of faith for being unable to appreciate the important differences between the two. Burroughs was an atheist who often expressed dislike for churches and who wrote a newspaper article in defense of schoolteacher John Scopes (when Scopes was put on trial in Tennessee for teaching evolution), but Burroughs also believed that an author's first responsibility was to entertain, and he felt that some of his contemporaries, such as Sinclair Lewis, had gone too far in promoting their own anti-religious views. Though organized religion on Barsoom is always a dodgy proposition, the world is nevertheless suffused with a powerful sense of wonder and mystery, which our next tale explores to great effect.

❖ ❖ ❖

THE RIVER GODS OF MARS

BY AUSTIN GROSSMAN

I walked through the night beneath the twin tumbling moons of Barsoom, gaining on my deadly pursuers even as I led them farther and farther out onto the dead sea Korus and closer to my goal, the spiral towers of the accursed city of Pra-Ohn. Kai-Wen and his ragged band of Warhoons followed me doggedly, though I had twice mauled them in previous encounters only to retreat in the face of superior numbers. In the still air of the Martian midwinter the remainder of his barbarian crew would have no trouble following the prints I left in the smoothly piled sands, which even by moonlight sparkled dully with a mineral unknown to terrestrial science.

I had lost my supplies in the first encounter, and since then I had journeyed for a day and a half with little rest under a cloudless sky. I was nearly dead of thirst when I beheld at last the starlit azure spires and ivory domes of Pra-Ohn, once the greatest port on the mightiest ocean on the face of the red planet, before Barsoom's southern ocean receded into who knew what dark areological cavity.

It stood on a granite cliff next to what was once the titanic waterfall where the river En-Kah-Do, sacred to the deity of

that name, tumbled into the sea after its thousand-mile journey from the Mountains of Zont. I climbed from rock to rock up the dry cascade, then stood on the docks looking out over the dead sea. The beached hulls of antique watercraft lay scattered across the sand like chips of bark, double-hulled pleasure-barges and Martian ships of the line bristling with cannon. Immense skeletons of cetaceans whose half-buried ribs arched forty feet into the air and whose spines stretched the length of a football field, greater than any Earthly whale.

For a quarter million years Pra-Ohn had stood empty and abandoned, shunned alike by the Red, Green, and Yellow races of Barsoom. It remained to be seen whether the Warhoons would follow me into that accursed place, or if superstition would keep them at bay. I contemplated laying a trap for the dozen or so warriors behind me, but pressed on instead for fear of taking a disabling wound. I had perhaps two hours' grace before they reached me and took their long-postponed vengeance, and I could not stop moving for an instant.

The Warhoons were not my true concern. It was a full week since Dejah Thoris, princess paramount of Helium, had vanished together with her father and seven red Martian loyal attendants, so it was there I would go, though all the spirits of ancient Mars forbade it. I had thought of little else since my latest arrival on this planet.

The planet Barsoom knows gods of every possible description, and no one has named them all. They inhabit mountains, lakes, caverns, rivers, sizable rocks. They are worshiped through idols, carved symbols, cities, seasonal winds, and masked pretenders. There are hundreds, but all agree that the greatest of all were the ones the ancient White Martians worshipped: gods of radiation and healing, of trivia, of tides, of mystery.

I paused in my march, just to smell the dry Barsoomian air and revel in the feeling of having returned to my spiritual home. Mars again! The transfers happened an average of about once per decade, but there was a great deal of variation. The shortest interval was a mere two weeks. Once, it took twenty-eight years—a whole quarter-century spent standing outside each night in supplication before the red star, before I was again caught up and carried away in the ineluctable Barsoomian rapture.

I have long, long outlived my close contemporaries, my nieces and nephews and their children, and anyone with whom I could plausibly claim kinship. I fought in the War Between the States and the wars that followed, each time anticipating it would be my end. I have come to know psychoanalysts, hedge funds, napalm, and John Updike. I have learned French and Russian and Arabic, seen Henry Ford's production lines, pepperoni pizza, Bruce Lee films, and failure.

The only constant figures in my life have been Dejah Thoris, princess of Mars; her father; Tars Tarkas, chieftain of the Tharks; my son, Carthoris and daughter, Tara; and all the host of Martians. And always, always, there is the red planet called Ares, called Al-Qahira, called Labou, called Nirgal, called Mars, called Barsoom.

This time it took four years, eight months, and six days for me to return, transferred spectrally across the intervening void in the year nineteen hundred and seventy-one. When I arrived, I was found naked and snoring outside the city gates. As I hastened to don Martian garb, the people of Helium explained: Dejah Thoris and her father were on a scientific expedition to learn all they could of a moving light in the sky that flared and died. According to ancient writings, such lights were predictors of terrible changes, perhaps disaster, so she and her father set out along the line of its descent into the southern hemisphere.

I followed, of course. Dejah Thoris had lately read much

of the ancient texts, so I could not guess what she hoped to find there. I knew only that she was ahead of me and I would find her. A few years ago I saw an analyst who spoke at length about the curious dynamics of our relationship—pursuer and pursued, maiden and rescuer. Was she trying to communicate with me? Did she, perhaps, "need a little space"?

I have little time for such reflections. Simply another mystery of Mars! I stalked the streets of Pra-Ohn for almost a full day, sword in hand, happy simply to be alive and hunting. I found no trace of my beloved, but I was strangely drawn to the structure at the city's heart; its walls were deeply incised with chiseled runes but whether it was palace or fortress or temple I could not say.

All the while, I knew, a deadly enemy was closing in behind me, and still there was no sign of my beloved. As the day waned I gave in to impulse. The broad stone steps were dusted with sand blown in from the desert. Enormous bronze doors inlaid with lapis lazuli hung loose on their hinges, and in the dry air I caught an unexpected whiff of that most precious substance—water! I drew my curved blade and entered.

Less than two thirds of Barsoom has been explored by the Red Martians. The remainder is a wasteland of dead cities, drained oceans, salt flats, inaccessible mountains, forests infested by blue plant-men, apt-riddled cave complexes, accursed river valleys, golden cliffs, Thark-menaced plainlands, psychic heads, pretend deities, enclaves of the elder Martians, Rovers, Therns, Lotharians, and Martians, Yellow, Black, and White. And then there are the Kangaroo Men.

The space within rivaled the Earthly Hagia Sophia in Istanbul for splendor; the vaulted ceiling was almost lost in the gray dimness; pillars were topped with grotesque carvings of Red, Green, and Yellow Martians, white apes, and things stranger still. Golden light, somehow both thinner and more illuminating than its Earthly equivalent, poured through tall vertical slits in the walls. The floor was tiled with a complex mosaic in blue and peach, not unlike the Roman mosaics recovered at Pompeii, displaying fantastical beasts from Barsoom's distant past, so that I seemed to stride over ancient oceans. Murals on either side showed an Arcadian landscape of green grasses, canals, collonades, humanoids in pastoral attitudes—all the joys of long-lost water-rich Mars.

Archway after archway receded before me toward a distant altar where, at the limits of vision, a struggle seemed to be taking place. I ran forward as only an Earth-born man on Mars can run, and as I grew closer I saw in the swirl of wrestling bodies first the face of a hooded Yellow man of Mars, and next the full lustrous raven hair of my own, my beloved, Dejah Thoris. The Yellow Martian held a long dagger gripped overhand. The princess held fast to his wrist; his other hand held her hair. Between them, unconscious or dead, lay her father, Jeddak of Helium. In the concentration of battle her lip quivered, and her eyes were huge. I saw her take her opponent in an Asiatic wrestling hold I had shown her, but before I could see the outcome, a Warhoon, a terrible Green Man of Mars, enemy of the Tharks, rose up before me.

The Warhoon's eyes, placed on either side of his head, scanned the room from a height of fifteen feet. The Green Martians are the most alien of Mars's sentient life. They are hexapods, with two legs, a pair of arms, and a stronger intermediate pair of limbs in between. He wore a complex harness ornamented with jewels where its straps met in front and back, and long bronze daggers hanging at waist level. He gripped two silvered longswords in an orthodox two-handed fighting stance familiar to me from countless duels for status and survival, the right-hand sword raised and the left extended, and he waited, bug-eyed and determined.

I don't remember the first Earthman I killed, it was too long ago, perhaps in the War Between the States. I remember the first Green Martian, though—I did it bare-handed and without realizing it. I was a captive of the Tharks and he pulled me roughly to my feet, so I struck him with my fist and he fell to the ground. It was only days later I learned that I had killed him, and that his name was Dotar. I inherited his clothes, weapons, and women, and in some contexts I am still addressed by his name. Since that time I have learned that the weaker gravity here allows the Martians to grow to enormous height but leaves them comparatively weak.

Hand-to-hand combat with a Green Martian is rather like fighting a tree in high winds. The trunk and limbs bend and whip around in fast motion, and the swords follow in terrible rapid slashing arcs and land with tremendous force. I gave ground, parrying desperately and hoping for a moment of opportunity. Our swords clashed and for many minutes the ancient temple rang with sound like a factory floor.

When I sensed the temple wall close behind me, I shoulder-rolled under a backhand swing and struck an overhand blow. My opponent anticipated me; he had already whirled around and met the assault with crossed swords, but nonetheless he staggered. The Martian now knew who he was fighting. He showed no visible apprehension, but he gave off the distinctive floral reek of Green Martian sweat.

Over my many sojourns on Barsoom I have lost some of the Terran muscle tone that made me an unbeatable force in countless battles, but I am still far stronger than any indigenous Martian, and far more experienced than when I first arrived in this place. The defect of the Warhoonish Orthodox is that it is designed for fighting fellow Green Men, or for hewing off the heads of hapless Red Martians in brief engagements such as happen in a pitched battle. In a prolonged duel against a human opponent, the unarmed lower limb tends to be neglected and open to attack (of course, such duels are seldom prolonged, as the Warhoons are surpassingly deadly). I have left more than one three-handed corpse on the Martian sands, and this was to be no exception. He took two slashes, the first taking off a nailless Martian finger, the next taking the limb off nearly to the forearm. My opponent shuddered, but no Green Martian knows fear and so he sprang at me again and fought until he was too weak to continue.

Blood covered the tiled floor by the time it was over. Blood coated me as well; it had got into my nose and mouth, a coppery taste. I hastened to the altar, but by then the robed man lay dead, and Dejah Thoris and her father were gone.

Every female animal and sentient being on Mars is oviparous. The woman I have given my heart to was born from an egg, as were both of my children. Mars knows no mammal but myself.

When I gained the top of the dais I could not comprehend how Dejah Thoris had escaped me. An enormous stone idol stood seemingly carved entirely from jade into the shape of a four-armed ape, its mouth open, frozen in a shriek of fury. I stood before it, then abruptly felt the stone slab tilt and fall away beneath me. Martian gravity pulled me down a glassy tube, down and down through absolute darkness, the stone growing colder until it gave way to empty air. I thrashed in black space a full four seconds before I hit the water. Salt! I spluttered and tasted for the first time the cold, bitter seas that lie beneath the Martian desert.

I swam blindly and soon I detected the sound of waves crashing ahead of me. I hastened my strokes until my hand found a smooth stone surface and I pulled myself, gasping, onto a shore which lay at the edge of a cavernous space.

A row of canoes woven from the dry reeds of Mars stood before me, and I saw by the light of phosphorescent fungal ridges that I stood near the cave's outlet, a swift, massy tongue of water disappearing down into further depths.

A splash and a clatter of wooden oars against stone turned my head, and I again caught a glimpse of my dear, my only, Dejah Thoris, a flash of coppery shoulder and painted nails as the current bore her from me, down into the swirling cascade and away.

I don't know what I am. No one knows how or why I come to Barsoom, or what it means. It could be a dream; or perhaps Earth is the dream. It could be a psychotic episode, or the last feverish hallucination of a man dying in an Arizona cave. Barsoom has divided my life at the root, and I'll never know the person I would have been if I hadn't become a prince of this lush alien planet. A weaker man, maybe, but one with more capacity for reflection. A man I might despise, or admire. The man who stayed home.

The tunnel swept me along, south by my reckoning, with no need to paddle. After a long interval, an hour perhaps, I began to hear the bass roar of a subterranean cataract ahead of me. The river was descending to a lower level, some deeper subterranean pocket. As I was swept along, I glimpsed a torchlit dock, a stone stairway ascending from the river, and Dejah Thoris standing on the topmost step watching me pass. A moment of parted lips, clear golden eyes, pupils wide in the darkness, and then gone. Or had she winked at me?

The white noise of the Martian waterfall grew louder and louder. I could see only forty feet in front of me, but the water around me deepened and the wind blew harder against my face. The stone tunnel was smooth on either side of me; I paddled against the current but it was useless even for me. I passed two more landing areas but too fast to do anything about it. I passed a place where the walls and ceiling of the cave had been carved to form a giant's face with an open mouth, its eyes faceted jewels of incalculable worth. In the end I sat in the bow and waited as the water grew green and translucent and white, and then in an instant I was over the falls and falling through a cavern whose far wall was invisible. To my left I saw a titanic castle carved into the stone, and a strange flying vehicle hanging aloft in the subterranean air, a hooded figure at the controls. For a moment I was excruciatingly conscious that this must be the last moment of my unnaturally extended life.

It's not impossible that when I come to Mars I travel in time as well as space, deep into the past, so that everything I do here is to present-day Earth, as the deeds of the ancient Martians are to me. Or—and I have not confided this even to Dejah Thoris, my heart's other half—it is possible I travel into a future Mars, to a time when my own Earth is a desert wasteland or ball of ice. The Martians, so proficient in medicine and aeronautics, have not developed a telescope powerful enough to scrutinize the Earth's surface, but scholarly texts from millennia past describe flashes of light that began and ended over a period of days. When I looked through the lenses in Erem Prianus's laboratory I seemed to see mist, blue water, and a single massive continent like a blind eye.

I awoke with the sun hot on my face, my back resting in dry sand. I assumed my violent loss of consciousness had triggered a return to Earth, but when my eyes opened I saw the smaller, paler sun of Mars, and rolling to my side I saw the nailless green toes of a Green Martian. Finally, I heard the guttural bass voice of my oldest friend on Mars, Tars Tarkas, call out, "He's awake!"

Again I had escaped! I bounced lightly to my feet, fearing to show any weakness before the savage Tharks, who were as like as not to execute the wounded or infirm. The Tharks were camped in the desert, and bore the signs of a recent fight.

Tars Tarkas rubbed his bald skull, and grinned toothily. "My friend! How came you here? We found you lying in the shallows of a river that cascades from the mountain range that borders the southern desert."

"Tars Tarkas, I might ask the same of you," I added.

"We journey south in response to the strange phenomenon we witnessed in the sky," he replied, "a light that streaked toward the southern lands and then vanished. The spoken traditions of our people reach back millennia and they predicted at this time a portent of great change, and perhaps great danger as well. They bid us find its cause and make it our own, no matter the cost."

"For my part I care nothing for any lights or portents," I responded, "But Dejah Thoris and her father have set out in search of this thing as well, and you know I go where my princess goes."

Tars Tarkas folded his median limbs and considered me before speaking. "Aye, it was ever thus. John Carter, I tell you plainly we may yet become enemies despite the many years we have fought side by side, for no Red Martian lays claim to what we hold sacred. And I know, fool that you are, you will side with your queen even against the Tharks who first welcomed you to Barsoom."

"I fear it is so, old friend, though I fight out of loyalty, not rancor."

This left us with an awkward hitch in the conversation, such as I had not known since our first encounter before I had learned the common language of Barsoom. I sought for eye contact but a Green Martian's eyes are on either side of his head. We waited while the distant sun peeked out from behind a rare cloud. With an upper hand he scratched his nub of a Martian nose, a poor try at distracting me from a lower limb inching toward the gilded pistol he wore strapped to his thigh.

Even as he drew it in a flash of emerald motion, I sprang and landed a hundred feet across the sand. I heard him fire, but the shot went hopelessly wide and before the startled Tharks could begin to move I was in one of their fliers. My hands blurred automatically through the activation sequence, grappling with a control scheme built for a four-armed pilot. By luck, I was in Tars Tarkas's personal vehicle, one which I knew well and that could outdistance its fellows. I taxied across the flat sands, scattering warriors before me, and then I was aloft, trailing a spatter of misdirected fire. The buzz of its semimystical engine filled my ears and thrummed between my knees. I circled the camp, twice waggled my wings, and was away. South.

If I could resurrect and speak to any person no longer living it would be the ancient woman whose body I discovered in the Arizona cave from which I was first translated to Barsoom. I returned to find her desiccated remains propped before a copper brazier containing a curious green residue. I now own three hundred square miles of desert in that region, but I never found it again.

There were other bodies hanging there—previous travelers? Suppliants found unworthy? Sacrifices? When I discovered her body, my mind was still occupied with the slow strangulation of Barsoom's entire population as the atmosphere failed and Therns, Tharks, and Black Martians were all dying together. It was years before I learned the truth, that I had saved them all.

Barsoom by air is a stirring sight. The land that at ground level seems like an endless expanse of red-orange dust from the air reveals itself in bands and shadings and swirls of red, white, gray. Canyons, mountains, and plains are like a map of Mars's forgotten waterways, and you can almost see the world that used to exist.

The natives say that Barsoom began to die a long, long time ago, and no one knows why. Where so many Earthly mythologies speak of a flood, Barsoom's defining catastrophe was a great desiccation, a dry apocalypse. The White Martians were seafarers, and when the waters receded they changed, interbred with less civilized races. They became hard, warlike, and short-lived; they lost the qualities of friendship, empathy, and mercy. The old secrets were lost (except to a few scattered, degenerate conclaves), but the contemporary Martians have built a new one, a technology of strange rays, miraculous healing, and telepathy, the new science of a dry, fallen world.

Barsoom's southern hemisphere is sparsely settled. Over half the day passed as I flew slowly toward the pole, scanning the terrain below me for a sign of my beloved, and with nothing but wind and pale sky around me I fell into a contemplative, semihypnotic state. In the end my target was not hard to find. The impact crater was large enough to see without difficulty although the winds were already blurring its outline. A cluster of fliers had already settled nearby. I landed my flier next to them, and descended to join the small group standing at the edge of the hemispherical depression.

There at last stood the Jeddak of Helium, and by his side was my wife, Dejah Thoris, clad only in silver-linked chains that held a crimson cape in place. She greeted me formally, hiding any emotion she might be feeling, as is her way. I behaved the same. The gray-bearded mathematician Erem Prianus stood a short way away, and five or six attendants. No one spoke.

Courtly Martian speech is highly formalized and complex beyond my ability, but I haltingly broke the silence.

"What new mystery is this?" I inquired.

"I know not, my prince," answered Dejah Thoris, "Nor has the wisest scholar of our people has been able to say."

A gust of wind announced the arrival of another flier, this one less welcome. Tars Tarkas and an attendant Thark climbed slowly out; each aimed twin pistols in our direction. Seeing we had brought no weapons, they lowered theirs. I knew they would kill us at their leisure without hesitation should logic or custom dictate.

There was nothing I could do. I ignored them and leapt lightly down into the crater, stumbling only a little on the sand, to inspect the object that had fallen to the Barsoomian surface. The others crowded to the crater rim. The two Tharks approached behind them, craning over the Red Martians, lost in wonderment, an expression foreign to their savage physiognomies. "By the ninth ray!" I heard someone breathe, but did not turn to see who.

The eighth Barsoomian ray is propulsion, the seventh is disintegration; the fifth, revivification; the third, time.

The thing lay half buried in the sand on the shores of a dead sea. It was a rough spheroid, ridged and finned, its body four feet across, composed of a white metal badly carbonized during its descent. It had four cup-shaped triangular fins a few feet across which projected on metal rods. Two of them had broken off. The exterior had cracked, revealing an interior space and a tiny wheeled cart like a child's toy, like an unborn chick in a monstrous egg.

There were raised characters molded on the inside edge of one ring circling the shattered sphere. Unfamiliar at first, but gradually I began to know them. I served in the occupation of Berlin in the weeks after the second world war, and I puzzled out the Cyrillic script as far as MARS 2 LANDER and a string of numbers. They'd done it now, and there would be more. Whatever happened, Mars would never be the same. I had never before realized quite how much I prized the mysteries of Barsoom, and how much I stood to lose. I turned away from Dejah Thoris to hide ridiculous tears I did not understand, that came suddenly, and then racking sobs bent me over, dripping, heaving, streaming down my face, the deep unforeseen, unexplained waters of Mars. I bent over until my forehead rested in the sand.

I could hear the others shuffling, muttering, but I couldn't look up at them. I felt as if waking from a nonsensical dream, and they were just bizarre, naked strangers now. What was I doing here? It was minutes before I could even straighten up. Erem Prianus cleared his throat in the silence.

Dejah Thoris approached. "What ails you, my prince?" she asked, puzzled.

"I . . . I know not, for it seems–I seem to see–oh, damn it. Oh, god damn." I could barely form the words in Martian.

"Is it a device of our enemies? Sent to bedevil us?" She put her hand on my arm, but I shook it off.

She tried again. "Is it Olovarian make, or perhaps Zodangan?"

After a long time, I replied with an effort. "Aye, it may well be."

"Is this the return of our deadliest foe?"

" . . . Nay. Best leave the thing for the Green Men to do with as they will. The less we see of it, the better."

"But–"

"It is theirs now, and for whatever time remains to this planet. Leave it be, my love." I told her, "Let's away to the north, and pleasanter pursuits."

We led our party back to the fliers without opposition, leaving the broken artifact behind us. Tars Tarkas watched us go with a knowing inscrutable gaze, then turned and gave orders to his barbaric cohort. They began to dig.

It can be found frozen on the snowy mountains of the poles and as morning dew in the temperate forests. The northern lands are silvered with canals and rivers, and the fetid jungles of the equatorial lands are like steam-baths. In truth, water is not so rare on Mars.

One night, years ago while in lethal pursuit of Matai Shang, Father of the Therns, I was walking in the far northern region late into the night, bleary-eyed, recent wounds scabbing over, near collapse. All of a sudden I saw a darker mass against the dunes, its mountainous bulk bigger than any Martian beast. I crept closer and it obscured the stars. It was so large I had difficulty deciding how far away it was and I ran up against it by mistake, catching my breath and scraping my knuckles on the cool, rough stone.

I stepped back to see it fully, and knew what it was. It was a Barsoomian sphinx, a statue with the long body of a crouching Banth, with its five legs on either side, and the bald and tusked and bug-eyed head of a Green Martian. Nameless, it stood astride a small canal that might once have fed a small farming community. The ancient Martians knew much that has been lost, and the sphinx meant something to them—a mystic, profane union of Barsoomian opposites. I spent the rest of the night asleep between its forepaws, and in the morning I ran on.

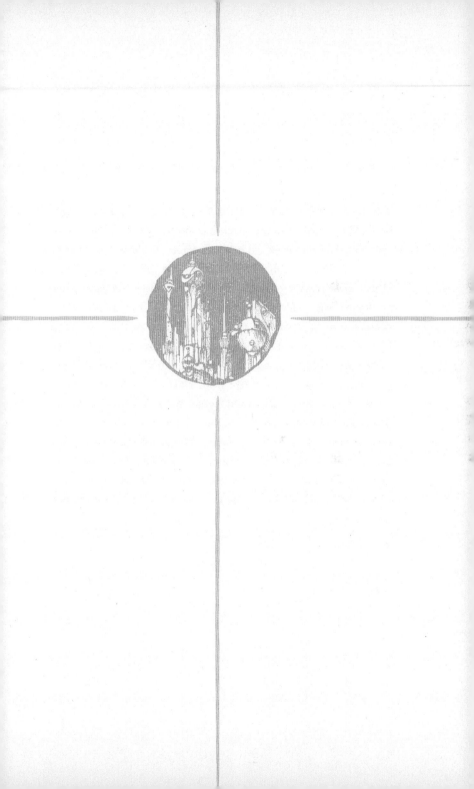

The book *Llana of Gathol* collects four Barsoom stories that were originally published in the magazine *Amazing Stories*. Those stories are "The Ancient Dead," "The Black Pirates of Barsoom," "Escape on Mars," and "Invisible Men of Mars." In "The Ancient Dead," John Carter travels to Horz, capital of a vanished empire, where he discovers a small community of surviving Orovars (the white-skinned race of Barsoom). Carter rescues one of them, Pan Dan Chee, from a group of attacking Green Men, thus earning Pan Dan Chee's friendship, but Carter is then captured by other Orovars and sentenced to death, a fate from which he narrowly escapes. He soon encounters his granddaughter Llana (daughter of Gahan of Gathol and John Carter's daughter Tara), who explains that she was abducted by the nefarious Jeddak Hin Abtol. Carter and Llana flee the city, along with their new comrade Pan Dan Chee. Our next tale picks up many years later, when the bold young son of Llana and Pan Dan Chee returns to seek adventure in the haunted byways of Horz.

THE BRONZE MAN OF MARS

BY L. E. MODESITT, JR.

It's a terrible thing to be the son born of a great love story, perhaps the greatest in the recent history of Gathol—to be the son of Pan Dan Chee, the only Orovar to leave the hidden sanctuary of ancient Horz in hundreds of thousands of years, who offered his sword to my mother at first glance, and then fought his way across the rugged terrain of Barsoom. After protecting her honor the entire way, he arrived just in time to break the siege of Gathol, which was under attack by millions of the frozen men of Panar. If that were not enough of a burden, it is even more terrible to be the great-grandson of the most famous warrior of Barsoom. Yes, my mother was Llana of Gathol, the granddaughter of the Jeddak of Jeddaks, John Carter, whose accomplishments and legends are so vast as to be beyond enumerating . . . as well as unbelievable to those who do not know him.

Those accomplishments were the reason I now stood in the ancient city of Horz, listening, in the darkness, to the shuffling feet of the creatures that scurried within. I had heard that the ulsios of Horz were far larger than the knee-high creatures that frequented the depths and declivities of most cities. I turned slowly, torch in one hand, sword in the other, searching for the first sign of one of the repulsive needle-toothed rodents.

I barely managed to get my blade up in time to slash-block the leap of the creature that had suddenly leapt at me—an ulsio almost twice the size of any I'd ever seen in my explorations of the depths beneath Gathol. My quick defense barely deflected the beast, however, and it took another series of cut-and-thrusts to leave it gasping for life on the ancient stone pavement, missing three of its six legs by the time it finally expired. Leaving me no time to celebrate, another leapt forward out of the gloom. I dispatched it quickly with a slash to the neck, removing its head with one clean strike. The sight of me removing its head was apparently sufficient to quell any further attack, for, although another followed at a distance, it clearly decided that feasting on its own kind was preferable to the risk I posed.

And how, you might wonder, did I come to be prowling the pits of Horz, whose dark depths had been unprobed (except by my father and great-grandfather) in hundreds of thousands of years? Horz—once heralded as the greatest of the now-dead cities of Barsoom, and the queen city and most magnificent port on the vanished Throxeus—had been built downward over the eons—to follow the dwindling ocean—then largely abandoned.

My journey to Horz was inevitable, for from the moment I left the egg it was clear I did not look like either of my parents. My mother possessed the fair-skinned redness and red hair of a princess of Barsoom, while my father had the white skin and blond hair of an Orovar. I, meanwhile, appeared before my mother with golden bronze skin and reddish bronze hair. There had been, in the long history of Barsoom, white men, yellow men, black men, green men, and even plant men . . . but never, until my birth, a *bronze* man. Add to that the gray eyes of my great-grandfather, and

I possessed an appearance unlike anyone in Gathol—at least until my brother left the egg some ten years later, but he'll have to tell his own tale.

When my father saw me, he swallowed . . . and then began to teach me everything he knew about swords. He had others teach me to fight with nothing but my body, a skill at which he was less adept . . . for he was an Orovar, and his weapon was the blade—though he was expert with the radium rifle as well. My parents would not let me leave the palace until they were convinced that I was a match for all but the finest of swordsmen. That training that took years and years, naturally, because all too many of the men of Barsoom are indeed accomplished with the blade.

That did not mean I had no adventures as a youth—for the palace of Gathol is vast indeed, and some of those deep chambers had seen no man for centuries before I entered them. In those depths and darknesses I found *some* adventure; I fought off ulsios, and feral calots, and once even a banth that had found an ancient tunnel and made its way through haads of underground passages to the palace. Vanquishing a banth would have given me some small stature . . . but, alas, I had no proof, for, as I ran it through, it had thrashed about, and then rolled backward into a shaft that descended into such depths that I never heard the impact of its fall. Had I told anyone that tale, I would have been the laughingstock of all Gathol.

On an unusually warm morning, prior to my journey to Horz, I had stepped into the small side courtyard of the palace where I made a practice of exercising, only to find the lovely Jasras Kan sitting on one of the ersite benches.

"Kaor, Jasras."

"The same to you, Dan Lan Chee."

"You are most beauteous this morning, as you are every morning and evening. . . ."

"Words . . . polished words, and words alone are but sounds and flattery. . . ." Like her mother, Rojas, Jasras said what she meant, if less politely.

"I would flatter you, for you deserve it," I said.

"Without deeds behind the words, those words are like the wind. What have you done in your life, Dan Lan Chee? You are among the best Jetan players in Gathol, but that is but a game of mental skill. You have illustrious ancestors, but you have never even left Gathol. . . ."

Strictly speaking, her words were not true. I had taken my personal flier hundreds of haads from Gathol, even into the frigid lands of the last remaining Panars. I'd served under my father when he led a force against the Yellow Men of Barsoom, but I had not distinguished myself individually. For all the skill required to move padwars and princesses across the squares of the gameboard, Jetan did not hazard the body. While I had heard that in times long before Jeddaks had played Jetan with real warriors on a life-size courtyard gameboard, I myself had never partaken of such a game, although I had heard stories about my grandmother Tara having been forced into playing as a live piece in one.

Those quiet words of Jasras Kan had bitten deep into my mind, much as I would have liked to dismiss them. For Jasras was a worthy prize, a woman of wit and beauty, if of a wit sometimes too sharp. She was also the daughter of Rojas, once a princess of the invisible people, and of Garis Kan, an odwar of Hastor, who had won the heart, or at least the mind and body, of Rojas after she had returned to Gathol with my mother. Rojas had aided my mother's return from her abduction by Hin Abtol, as had my father and greatgrandfather, but none of them would ever speak of it, only her rescue and adventurous return.

What else could I do? That very afternoon, I stocked my flier and set out for Horz, seeking to establish some honor by doing something my father had not: recovering the ancient and wondrous devices used by the near-immortal and evil Lum Tar O, who had preserved warriors for tens of thousands of years, creating food and sustenance from nothing, while surviving for untold generations in the depths beneath Horz. Hundreds upon hundreds of my ancestors had distinguished themselves by their blades, and Jasras was not a woman to be impressed by mere feats of arms; I was determined to do more than that. I had to.

For days, I flew north and west, my directional compass holding my flier on course while I slept, over haads and haads of ochre moss that grew on the lands that had once held oceans, seeing not a soul in all that time. Late on the fifth day, I beheld Horz, a sweep of buildings at the west end of a vast plateau. As I neared the city, despite the tales I had heard, I was awed at its size, and at the buildings and towers, magnificent still in their partial ruin. Following what I recalled of the little my father had said—and what he had demanded that I tell no one, on my honor as his son—I took care to circle the uppermost level of ancient Horz, avoiding the great courtyard that was doubtless still watched by the remaining Orovars, for they would put to death any outsiders for fear that others would come to take their secrets—especially, no doubt, their secret of creating food and water from nearly nothing.

I landed the flier on the flat roof of a small building on the far side of the great citadel, as close as I could to a narrow way leading to it, for, as my father had once revealed, the only known entrance to the pits of Horz was near that ancient citadel. Deep in those pits was where I determined to find Lum Tar O's secrets. Not for me the mere baubles of ancient golden harnesses and endless jewels; of what value were those to Jasras Kan, a princess who was the daughter of a princess?

There was no obvious access to the rooftop, only a covered staircase off a side alley in this deserted quarter of the ruins, affording a measure of security to the flier. I locked the controls, slipped the master key into a hidden space in my harness, and made my way down to street level, blade in one hand, a torch of the kind used by my ancestors in the other.

Yet I saw no one, heard no one, on my way to the small windowless building set to the rear of the citadel. The massive gates had no locks, but they were so corroded that it took all my strength to move one enough to squeeze through and then move it back so that any Orovar who chanced to come that way would see nothing obviously amiss.

As I walked toward the wide stone ramp that led away from the citadel and into the depths, I eased the cover off the torch. When the air struck its central core, a cold bluish light issued forth. I kept the light low, just bright enough to see by, and continued downward.

I had not even reached the first of the ancient dungeon chambers when the first ulsio had darted from the darkness of a dungeon chamber and attacked. Even after disposing of two, a third followed me for another hundred ods or so before it slipped back into the darkness.

Only after dispatching the vile creatures did I glance into the dungeon chambers from whence they came. The first held little besides ancient chains and bones and dust. The second held two carved, metal-bound chests. The first of these was filled with golden harnesses and jewels. Outside of a handsome dagger that fit on my harness, I left the jewels and moved to the second chest, some seven ods long; it was empty.

With my torch in hand, I returned to the main corridor and proceeded onward through the darkness that retreated before my torch and closed in behind me. At each dungeon chamber I checked to see what lay within. Most held little but dust and chains unused in eons. Occasionally I found a chest like the others, chests that had once held bodies, according to my father, bodies embalmed in the ancient past by Lee Um Lo—embalmed so well that the dead did not know that they were dead when they were infused by the will of the maniacal Lum Tar O. They had all died a final time and turned to dust when my grandfather had slain the mad scientist who had almost taken over his very mind.

I was not looking for treasure—although there was plenty to be found—but for the amazing devices of Lum Tar O that would bring me accolades—and the hand of Jasras Kan.

Before long, certainly no more than a zode, I came upon a particular chamber, the very one I had sought. It was large and filled with all manner of items: a simple couch, a bench, a table, a stove of a design eons old, bookshelves filled with ancient tomes, and a reservoir of water. There was also a pile of dust, and beside it lay a dagger. Several empty chests with their lids set askew or detached and beside them lined the walls.

I had found the lair of Lum Tar O. Yet, there was no hint of the devices I sought. I walked to the wall opposite the doorway through which I had entered and examined it with care. Nothing. Nor did the wall adjacent to that reveal anything. On the third wall, I found a square slightly different in shade to the rest of the wall, and when I touched it, it flaked away to reveal the symbol of an armed warrior—a panthan by its appearance—in jet, inlaid into the stone.

Knowing not what else to do, I pressed upon the figure. A rumbling, creaking noise followed, to no immediately obvious effect. It was only when I turned, holding the torch, that I saw the corner of the wall had recessed, leaving a narrow opening. I hurried toward it, uncapping the torch more to better see what I had uncovered.

I beheld a set of stone stairs leading downward, with a door below, set perhaps ten ods from the bottommost step. I stepped through the opening and descended until I stood in a small square room facing the door. There was a massive bronze lever on the dark iron door, but no hole for a key. Nor was there a circular dial with numbers upon it, in the fashion of locks on Jasoom. Instead, there was a depiction of a game of Jetan, half-played, if not more, with the profile of each piece in either jet black or gold.

The lever did not budge, even when I exerted all my strength—which is not inconsiderable.

I examined closely the Jetan game before me. The pieces were displayed in outline, all except one: the gold princess. While her likeness was small, it showed an exquisite golden-skinned face, with jet-black hair and piercing green eyes. It would have been defilement to touch that figure, and so I did not. Instead, I studied the game, recognizing that the position of the pieces represented one of the timeless puzzles of Jetan, the beginning of the end game where every move but two led to disaster.

The problem was simple. I could not tell whether the next move belonged to jet or to gold, and there were very different outcomes to the game depending on whether that move was by the jet or by the gold. Gold or jet? Jet or gold? Finally, as much by my sense as by logic, I looked again at the tiny perfection of the gold princess and touched the gold chief and then the square to which I would move him.

For several tals, nothing happened. Then the door shuddered and the very stone beneath my feet trembled. But the door did not open, and nothing else occurred.

I pulled down on the massive lever. Still, it did not move. I tried lifting it then, and suddenly the door slid sideways—not open toward me, but out and across the wall—revealing a larger room containing two upright chests, each on a pedestal and identical to those I had found in the other dungeon chambers. Behind them was another door, unlike any I had ever beheld, hexagonal in shape, and made not of iron, but of a greenish metal.

I had no more time to devote to pondering the door, for the top of the first chest suddenly dropped away, revealing a well-muscled man with the harness of a panthan who darted forward, blade flashing toward my gut. Both his harness and his sword were jet black. He was half a head taller than me, and quick. I barely managed to slide his blade and jump sideways. Thinking that the dark might benefit me, as I moved back, I capped the torch, only to discover that a faint greenish radiance issued forth from the chest he had vacated—and that the lid of the second chest was now moving as well.

The jet panthan's blade flashed like black lightning, and almost as swiftly, yet I managed to parry it and then slashed back with a rising twist-cut that ripped his biceps, causing his blade to fall from his hand and strike the stone floor with a muted clang. Yet he—relentless—pulled a dagger from the sheath on his harness and attacked again. I could not help but admire his persistence, but when I saw another panthan emerging from the second chest, I had to end things quickly and so thrust my blade through the jet panthan's neck, jerking it out just in time to block the thrust of the gold panthan that now approached me.

Unlike the first warrior, this one held his blade in his left hand, and—strangely—his moves seemed to be mirror-images of those of the first. But that is where the opposite-mirroring ended, for our encounter ended in exactly the same way—with the panthan dead on my blade.

For several moments, I simply stood there, breathing heavily. As I watched, the bodies of both panthans crumbled into dust before my eyes, leaving behind only their har-nesses, daggers, and blades. Then the green luminescence also vanished, leaving me in pitch darkness.

I quickly uncapped the torch and stepped toward the green metal hexagonal door. It had no lever, only another depiction of a Jetan board, this one with the pieces displayed in red and green.

The puzzle was one with which I was unfamiliar. So I had to work through the possibilities, visualizing each potential move . . . and where each would lead. Finally, I touched the red odwar and the square to which I would move him . . . unsure if the move I was making was the cor-rect one, for the move was actually a sacrifice.

The stone trembled beneath my feet before the door split and each half recessed into the wall. So perfect had the seam been between the two halves that I'd had no inkling that the door had been in two sections. Beyond the green metal door was a far smaller chamber, with yet another chest in the center, one of gleaming bronze resting flat on a low pedestal made of the same green metal as the door. A shimmering gold and black cable ran from one end of the chest into a green metal pedestal and through a bronze fitting.

I stepped forward to the chest. There were three Jetan boards inlaid in the metal on the top of the chest. Below the center of each board was a jet-black square, and a different piece was circled by a gold ring on each board. It took but a tal for me to grasp that the puzzle posed was to determine which move on which board represented the correct one.

A faint grinding sound began to build. I glanced around. The green metal door had closed behind me! No sooner did I realize this than a faint shower of dust drifted down past me, and I looked up to see the ceiling descending! There appeared to be a recess in that solid slab of stone that matched the chest and pedestal. Clearly if I didn't solve the puzzle—and soon—I would be flattened by the inexorably descending stone.

I examined the first Jetan board, but the move shown would lead to defeat by the jet pieces. The same was true for the second board—and the third!

What was I missing?

The stone ceiling was pressing down now, less than an od above my head.

I decided . . . and pressed black squares on all three of the boards, one after the other, as quickly as I could, in the order in which the games would end, beginning with the one that had the shortest number of moves remaining.

The grinding stopped, and the ceiling halted its progress toward me, but did not return to its former position.

The top of the chest before me suddenly swung back, revealing a young woman whose skin was the same gold as that of the Jetan pieces, and whose hair was as black as jet. Her eyes were closed, but I could see her breathing . . . or had she just begun to breathe? And was there the faintest tinge of green on that perfect skin? It had been her likeness, I realized, on the princess piece on the first Jetan board! Lying beside her in the chest was a sword, shorter than mine, made entirely of black metal, except for gold traceries on the hilt. The same was true of her harness: black with traceries of gold.

Her eyes flicked open.

For long moments, we looked at each other. Her forehead wrinkled, but the frown vanished after a moment, and she sat up in the chest, that single movement creating a shower of greenish dust, leaving her bare skin unblemished gold.

"What manner of man are you?" Her words were clear, although it took me a moment to understand, for the way in which she spoke was somehow . . . different.

"I am Dan Lan Chee of Gathol. And you?"

"Gathol? I have never heard of it, and I have heard of all the cities of Barsoom. Are all who live there bronze?" She frowned.

"No. Most are red." I waited.

She continued to study me. Finally, she said, " I am . . . Cynthara Dulchis . . . of high Horz, of course, but you should know that."

"Perhaps I should, but high Horz has vanished. All but a tiny part of the city is abandoned, and the once mighty ocean Throxeus is no more." Even as I said those words, I wondered if she would protest, as my father had said the fading survivors of Lum Tar O did before they had turned to dust. Would Cynthara do the same?

"I might doubt your words, but let us go see." With that she stepped from the chest, retrieving her black blade and sliding it into the scabbard on her harness.

"Before we go," I said quickly, "is there anything that will reveal the secrets of this chamber and the devices that have kept you alive for all these eons?"

Another frown followed my question. "I can only have been here a few years, a few hundred at most, while my family's enemies were vanquished."

"I fear they were not, Princess Cynthara."

"Princess? I am . . ." She broke off and laughed, softly and bitterly. "I suppose that title is as good as any other. Your very presence indicates an unpleasant truth. How unpleasant . . . well, let us see."

I looked at the platform below the chest. "How did this all come to be?"

"From my father, Emperor of Jeddaks, and his workshops adjacent to this chamber."

"And how might we enter them?"

"In the same fashion as you entered this one," replied Cynthara.

Rather than argue that point, I gestured toward the closed green metal doorway. "Shall we?"

For the first time since she awakened, Cynthara looked puzzled.

I found that momentary lapse of attention most attractive, though I must admit that she was already the most beautiful woman I'd ever beheld.

"That door . . . it wasn't there before. You came through it?"

"I had to solve two Jetan puzzles and evade a few traps to get through it."

The side of the door facing us remained featureless as we neared it. There were no Jetan boards, just a black and a gold square at shoulder height.

"Touch the gold one," I suggested, because she represented the gold princess on the Jetan boards.

She did, and the door split and slid back into the recesses, revealing the chamber that held the two empty chests and the weapons and harnesses of the two panthans.

"My guardians . . ." Her eyes took in the dust and harnesses left behind.

"They tried to kill me."

"And you vanquished them?"

"I had little choice."

She walked through the square arch and studied the levered door, her eyes drawn to the inlaid Jetan board. "This was not here when I last stood in this room, but the work has the mark of my father."

She glanced around, as if searching for something, before walking to the wall and, using a small knife—jet-black—that she pulled from her harness, she scraped away a small section of the wall's surface. After several tals, her scraping cleared away the surface to reveal a golden square edged in black.

She pressed it. The wall began to shake. I pulled Cynthara back as the very stones of the wall collapsed away with a roar. We waited until the dust of ages and sundered stone dissipated. Beyond the irregular gap in the wall were the remains of machines of black and jet. The curves and swirled tubes of those strange devices threatened to twist my eyes and mind—even though they had already been wrecked and smashed in places.

"No . . . it cannot be . . ." Cynthara's words were barely above a whisper. She turned to me. "How long has it been . . . ?"

"So many years that no one knows how long."

From out of the mass of half-untouched, half-wrecked machinery emerged a huge silver-skinned calot—more than twice the size of any I'd ever seen, larger and more fearsome than even the largest of banths, with shining silver teeth and eyes like red coals. How had it survived in a place where there was so little food? For that matter, how had the ulsios that had attacked me earlier?

"That is the destroyer of warriors," said Cynthara. "My grandsire imprisoned it beneath the city hundreds of years before I was born. It took all of his skills and the deaths of a hundred panthans to capture it."

A dagger arrowed from the red eyes of that calot toward Cynthara, a missile of the beast's mind accompanied by a feeling of hatred and vengeance so palpable that it felt more deadly than the missile it accompanied. Somehow, my blade moved quickly enough to slice through the dagger—and both halves changed into smaller darts that arced toward me. I concentrated on trying to block those missiles with my thoughts, even as my blade wove in and out and across their path, finally blocking and destroying them, only to find that the silver calot was now almost on top of Cynthara. Her black blade was a blur, yet she was retreating, not quite able to hold her ground against it, its claws like shimmering knives, its teeth like short, sharp blades.

I struck at the calot's right shoulder with all the force I could bring to bear, cleaving a wide and deep wound. The calot turned. As its mouth opened wider, I could see that gaping wound begin to close, healing instantly.

What kind of beast was this silver calot? Could it heal itself through its thoughts, such as they were? My father's tales ran through my mind . . . about how the ruler of the last Orovars could create warriors and even food through his thoughts alone . . . but I had no more time to ponder, for the calot was almost upon me.

I slashed away a paw—only to see it regrow.

A cut across the beast's eyes blinded it, but for only a few tals.

In desperation, as I kept my blade between myself and the creature, I thought of the calot's death, of corruption of the wounds I had dealt it, of the futility of besting my blade, and followed this with thoughts of futility, ancient dust, and despair.

The animal offered a terrible scream—yet one that echoed only in my thoughts—before slumping to the stone floor, its wounds festering into corruption. In moments, it was a bloody heap of silver.

Then it was gone.

Cynthara looked at me, wide-eyed, if but for a moment. "No single warrior has ever bested the hunter of hunters."

"No single warrior did now. It took both of us."

"You are kind, Dan Lan Chee, but my blows scarcely slowed the destroyer of warriors."

"Without your blows, it would not have died."

"It wished me dead, as if it held me an enemy."

"Perhaps it recognized you as the granddaughter of its ancient foe."

I gestured toward the twisted tubes and strange machinery. "What do you know of that?"

"Everything." She smiled proudly. "I helped my father build all of it."

"Could you rebuild it, then?"

"I could . . . with time," she said. "I even know the secrets of the genetor."

I glanced around. The walls seemed to press in upon me. "The genetor . . . what is that?" I asked.

"It creates things from the ether itself."

From the ether itself? What ether? I wondered.

She looked toward the ancient machinery. "The genetor looks untouched. The other machines? In time, perhaps. If the materials even exist, but they require Ur-radium to power them."

My heart sank. The ancient tomes in the lower library of Gathol mentioned Ur-radium, but only as an element that vanished eons before.

Cynthara's face suddenly took on a look of concern. She pointed at the gap in the wall. "Look!"

The twisted metal beyond the wall had begun to glow.

"We must flee. Now!" The urgency in her voice was palpable and commanding. "Before we are destroyed!"

Quickly, we retraced our steps back to the hidden stairs and up into the chamber of Lum Tar O.

Cynthara glanced around, then shook her head. "We must be farther away. The energies within the very metals are being released. Nothing will remain for haads and haads." Her face was a mask of despair.

"Come!" I fully uncapped my torch, letting it blaze forth.

We began to run back along the passageway, then up

the ramp. I was breathing hard, and my heart was straining when we reached those corroded gates. Still, it took but a moment to push them open enough for us to step through and into the way beyond.

Cynthara looked around. "Where are the people?"

"As I said, all but a tiny handful have gone. The city died over the ages."

"That cannot be. How could it—"

"Those who remain survive by their minds and wits." I had never quite believed my father's tales of how the Jeddak of Horz, if that was what he was, could create armies and food with his thoughts—except Cynthara had mentioned a genetor that accomplished the same thing. Had the Jeddak—and Lum Tar O—somehow drawn on that ancient machine without even knowing it?

A yell echoed down the walled avenue I had thought deserted. Two Orovars came charging around the corner, likely from the larger square on the other side of the structure that afforded access to the pits of Horz. Behind them were several others of their kind.

"Who are they?" asked Cynthara, bringing up her blade.

"The Orovars . . . they must have come here after your time." I could say no more because the first Orovar sprinted toward me, his blade out and ready. He was no match for me, and in three quick passes, his blade lay on the stones, and he clutched his shoulder, staggering back.

The second man gaped—he even turned pale—as he beheld Cynthara, but that didn't stop him from attacking. That was a mistake, because Cynthara ran him through with her jet blade that looked so delicate. That allowed me a moment to beat down the guard of the third man and deliver a deep cut to his sword arm, so hard that he dropped his blade.

"This way!" I called.

Cynthara disarmed another Orovar. Her blade was almost as quick as mine. In fact, much as it pained me, she was faster, although she could not deliver quite the force behind her point or edge. While the other Orovars paused, we turned and hurried down the narrow way that led to where I had concealed my airship.

We had almost reached that small building when the padding of sandals on stones alerted me, and we swiftly turned—to face four other Orovars wearing the harnesses of panthans. So quick was our turn that I managed a gut thrust to the leading Orovar. In turn, that allowed Cynthara a crippling blow to the calf of the second man.

None of us got in another blow, however, because the very stones beneath our feet started shaking violently.

"This way!" I grasped Cynthara's wrist, wondering as I did so if she would turn to dust like those ancient Horzians my father had met. But her wrist was firm, with strong tendons.

In only a few tals we had cut down the side alley and up the narrow staircase to where my airship remained. Cynthara hesitated, and I half-pulled, half-dragged her onto the main desk, extracting the control key from my harness.

"What manner of vessel is this that rests on a rooftop?" she asked in that accent I found both so charming and alluring.

"One that sails the skies as ships once sailed the Throxeus," I replied.

She did open her mouth for a moment, then grasped the railing as the building beneath us shuddered. I concentrated on getting us airborne, and then headed away from the center of Horz . . . and then down over the descending series of structures that the ancients had built to follow the Throxeous ocean as it dwindled away.

"Look!" Cynthara touched my arm, and the warmth of

her touch, as much as her voice, caused me to glance back.

A column of dust had shot upward, a column almost half a haad wide, and stones spewed out from it. Could there be anything left at the center of old Horz? Somehow, I doubted it. Another spewing of stone and dust erupted, and towers and buildings shook and then wavered . . . and many toppled before my eyes.

Slowly, I turned my airship back toward Gathol, giving the city of Horz a wide berth.

Cynthara continued to watch while the city that had once been hers so long before disappeared behind us. In turn, I watched her, realizing that while my quest had begun to impress Jasras Kan, I had found much more than strange devices or riches. I had found someone who offered far more than the lovely face and sharp and polished words of Jasras Kan. Yet I did not know what Cynthara might feel.

Finally, she turned and stepped forward, beside me.

"The Horz I knew is gone, so far in the past that not even legends remain. So are my people. Is that not true, Dan Lan Chee?"

"It is."

"You did not soothe me with pleasant falsehoods."

"No."

"Nor did you attempt to take advantage of me."

"I doubt any man would have much success in that." I could not help but smile at her words.

"You respect me."

I nodded. How could I not? Could I have awakened after eons with strange machines keeping me uncorrupted and acted as decisively as she had?

Abruptly, she knelt and laid that deadly black blade at my feet. I'd never seen a woman do that. In my Barsoom, only men offered their blades and lifetime loyalty. I could not reject the gesture . . . and yet. . . . Quickly, I unbuckled my own blade and scabbard and laid it at her feet.

"You mock me. . . ." Her green eyes flashed.

"I would never mock you, Cynthara Dulchis. But I cannot accept what you offer, unless you accept what I offer in return."

The smile on her face was confirmation enough that I had found a great treasure in Horz . . . if not exactly the one I had sought. But this treasure was not one I could have bought with devices and riches, just as my father could not have bought my mother with such. And so we stood together, at the beginning of another journey.

The Chessmen of Mars tells the story of Tara, daughter of John Carter and Dejah Thoris. In the beginning of the novel, Tara meets a young prince named Gahan of Gathol, and is thoroughly unimpressed with him. Later she is out in her flier (a small craft kept aloft by advanced Barsoomian technology) and a storm sweeps her off course. Upon landing, she is captured by the grotesque Kaldanes, who resemble large heads with crablike legs. The Kaldanes have bred Rykors, headless human bodies, and the Kaldanes are able to mount the Rykors, becoming their heads and steering them like a vehicle. Meanwhile Gahan, who has fallen in love with Tara, sets out after her, and falls victim to the same storm. He comes upon Bantoom, land of the Kaldanes, and manages to rescue Tara, although initially she doesn't recognize him due to his haggard, disheveled appearance. They arrive at the city of Manator, and Gahan ventures inside, seeking food and water, but he and Tara are captured and forced to participate in a sadistic spectacle—a game of Jetan (similar to chess) in which living prisoners are used as pieces. Tara and Gahan ultimately fall in love and escape the city. Upon returning home, they learn that Tara's betrothed, Djor Kantos, believing her dead, has married another. Tara marries Gahan, and together they have a daughter named Llana, focus of the novel *Llana of Gathol*. Our next tales sees Tara return to the blood-drenched sands of Manator.

A GAME OF MARS

BY GENEVIEVE VALENTINE

> "The Princess may not move onto a threatened
> square, nor may she take an opposing piece."
> —*The Chessmen of Mars*

When Tara stepped from her flier, she was surprised her brother was not there to greet her.

Djor Kantos was.

Djor Kantos, a noble of the city. Djor Kantos, who had been her intended husband, until the morning a year ago that she discovered he cared for another.

That was the morning she'd taken her flier into a storm and ended up a prisoner of the Kaldanes, a living player in a gladiatorial game of Jetan.

Much had changed since then.

"Princess," he greeted. "Your mother, Dejah Thoris, has bid me make you welcome."

It was a formal speech—too formal for old friends—and he didn't look her quite in the eye.

(Too much had changed.)

"You're kind," she said. "Where is Carthoris?"

"Your brother and his wife should be here shortly," Djor said, frowned. "Do you mind my greeting you?"

"No," she said too quickly, and when he held out his hand she took it without looking him in the eye.

(Her husband was waiting at home in Gathol. Djor Kantos had not been hers for a year, and she had not loved Djor Kantos to distraction then; why was it so hard to meet him now?)

They walked to the audience hall in a silence that made it hard to breathe.

They had grown up together; he'd been her dance partner, her sparring partner. (They each tested skills against her brother, Carthoris, and the ongoing tally of wins had been the biggest argument she and Djor Kantos ever had. Both of them hated to lose.)

How quickly two people can grow to be strangers, she thought.

Then they were at the door, and Tara was face-to-face with her mother.

"Greetings, Dejah Thoris," said Tara in the formal manner, but a moment later Tara was caught in an embrace, their arm-bangles clanging, as her mother said, "How I've been expecting you!"

Tara grinned. "I still have a whole speech our advisors wrote for me—a list of your best qualities. Apparently, that's very good for trade. Should I recite it now or wait for Carthoris?"

Dejah Thoris laughed, and Tara even caught the ghost of a smile on the face of Djor Kantos.

Then a messenger burst into the hall.

He was followed by two sword-wielding guards, but the messenger looked so terrified that Tara knew it couldn't just be the guards that worried him.

Something else, something worse, was wrong.

As soon as the messenger saw them he cried, "I request the audience of Dejah Thoris!"

"You have it," she said. "Speak."

He fell to one knee, his eyes fixed on the floor.

"Princess," the messenger gasped, "your son's ship has been destroyed—in the Bantoom desert outside Manator!"

Tara went cold.

Manator was the city of the Kaldanes.

But even as Dejah Thoris gripped the arms of her throne in terror and demanded the messenger explain, Tara knew what the messenger would tell them next.

There were no bodies.

Kaldanes took their captives alive, and saved them for the Game.

Djor Kantos was standing at her mother's side, asking the messenger for information he wouldn't have, and Tara felt as though it was all at a great distance, as if that horrific city was already dragging her back across the burning sand.

(*For my brother's sake,* she thought, her heart pounding. *My brother!*)

Without thinking, Tara was running for the armory, then for her flier, her favorite shortsword in her hand.

It was a shame, she thought, to leave Helium again so soon. Gathol was still not her city, and she had been so looking forward to coming home again.

But she had no choice. By the time her mother had spoken to her advisors, had made plans, had dispatched soldiers enough to overpower the Kaldanes, Carthoris and Thuvia would be dead.

In Manator, Jetan was played to the death, and Kaldanes did not delay their pleasures. They would be pulled onto the board before they had time to strategize, because a hasty Game meant better fighting.

Tara had survived the Game as a Princess, forbidden to fight, fought over—but she had watched, and learned.

Now it was time to show what sort of pupil she was.

(To go alone might well be suicide, but there was no time to wait—there was no *time*.)

Her flier was standing open on the landing pad, and she was already in the cockpit when she heard echoing footfalls from the palace.

"Where are you going?" Djor shouted.

She said, "To Manator."

Tara expected him to tell her how her mother needed her, or that she had other considerations that should keep her home, or that there was nothing she could do.

But he only glanced back at the palace and squared his jaw, as if he was deciding something.

"Then I go too," he said, turning back to her.

She bristled—she had been very headstrong about small things, not long ago—but there was not enough time left, not even to be proud.

"Come, then," she said, starting the engine, "and close the door behind you. We have to reach the Bantoom desert before dark, or we'll be too late."

"For what?"

She smiled, all teeth. "For the Game."

Tara knew better this time how to navigate the ravine and the vicious storm between Helium and Manator, though the winds battered them until her hands were white-knuckled on the controls.

Behind her, Djor braced himself as best he could. Her flier was meant only for one, and he spent the journey kneeling beside her with one hand on her chair for balance, like a sprinter about to hear the starting horn.

She was almost glad for the storm, as it kept her from wondering why he had come with her.

(He was as loyal to Carthoris as she was; it didn't need to be more than that. Aid was aid.)

Whenever she dared take a breath, she tried to explain what he could expect once they were inside the walls.

She described the Kaldanes—parasites, jarred brains that used tentacles to attach themselves to senseless headless bodies, as most Barsoomians put on and discarded coats—and he gripped the chair until his fingers shook.

"They are ruthless and cruel," she said, "though one of them, Ghek, was kind to me when I was imprisoned."

"Not kind enough to free you," Djor said.

But Tara knew some things were out of a soldier's power, and she said, "He helped me prepare for Jetan, and I will always be grateful."

After they were safely around the next bend, he ventured, "Tell me the Game. I haven't seen it since I was a boy. I remember orange and black squares, and the Chief and the Princess on each side, and that each side had two flier-shaped pieces that didn't look anything like fliers I'd seen."

"Fliers aren't on the living board," she said. "Bad luck for our escape. It's just two more terrified men fighting for their lives in the arena."

He glanced at her, didn't answer.

She explained the rules of Jetan; panthan mercenary pieces that formed the first expendable line of defense, staid Captains and Lieutenants who moved in only one direction, Warriors who had more flexible paths, Thoat-mounted fighters who could jump intervening pieces.

"We won't know what to expect until they're already on the board," said Tara. "Often a Chief can choose his own pieces, but sometimes the Kaldanes assign them from within the prisons."

"Is that where your brother will be?"

"Thuvia will be kept in a tower," she said. "Carthoris underground. It's a maze of cells. There won't be time to look there. We'll have to wait until they're on the board before we strike, and hope Carthoris is Chief—he won't be in danger right away, and we'll have some time."

"And Thuvia?"

"Thuvia will be safe until after the Game," Tara said.

Djor raised his eyebrows. "But this Game is played to the death. How can you know she'll be safe?"

"The Princess does not fight," said Tara darkly. "She is preserved, as a prize for the Kaldane that wins."

He frowned. Then, after a moment, he said, "I'm sorry for what you've seen."

"Don't be," she said. "What I've seen might save Carthoris's life."

Still, it was good to hear; it gave her an idea why he had been so uneasy around her this last year, and why he had insisted on sharing this danger now.

After that there was a companionable silence—the most comfortable she'd felt with him since the morning she'd realized he loved someone else. It felt familiar, and it steadied her for the fight ahead.

Her course was bold, and her piloting sure, and she made it nearly to the Bantoom desert in one piece.

Then the clouds thickened, and she overcorrected, and the edge of one wing caught the wall of the ravine.

It was barely a scrape—on a calm morning she would have righted and not given it a thought until she landed back home.

But in winds as tangled as these, deep in shadows not even the moons could reach, it was a death sentence.

The flier ricocheted off the ravine and broadsided the opposing wall of stone. Tara and Djor were thrown against the ceiling amid a cracking and crunching Tara prayed was not bone.

The flier careened out of control, and with her last moments Tara thought, *If we must die, may this flier kill even one Kaldane when it lands.*

Then there was a sharp fall, and darkness claimed her.

When Tara woke, it was to pain and a sandy, claustrophobic darkness that nearly drove her to panic.

But she steadied herself, and after a few breaths she realized the crash had driven her underneath one of the consoles of her flier. She remembered her brother's danger, and Djor, and their ruined flight.

But if they had crashed, how was she not already in the towers of Manator? Had they been hidden from view? Were they miraculously safe?

No knowing in hiding. Tara steeled her nerves, untangled herself from the mess of wires, and crawled out into the cabin of the flier.

The first thing she saw was the dawn light glinting through the windshield; at least this was not a tomb.

The second thing was that Djor was gone.

It wasn't a mystery that took long to solve. The entry hatch of the ship was standing open, and the floor bore the marks of someone being dragged out fighting.

Djor had been taken by the Kaldanes, and they hadn't looked for others because her flier sat only one.

Poor Djor Kantos, she thought. To have come so far and be taken this way.

But not for nothing; if she could fight for two, she could fight for three.

She wrenched her hair into a knot, tightened her scabbard, and climbed out of her ship.

The city of Manator rose from the sand at the edge of the horizon, jagged and hopeless behind its walls. The sun was just rising over the lower buildings—the high towers and the flier-landing pad were thrown into silhouette, long shadows that warned her back where she had come.

Too late for that, she thought with a shudder, and started walking.

By the time she reached the gate of Manator it was morning, and she was almost out of time.

A guard, bemused, asked her name and business.

"Thora," she lied. "I'm a panthan. I am here to play Jetan."

The guard said, "You seem a bit young to be throwing your life away, but who can understand the decisions of the lesser-minded," and inside the glass his brain swiveled to indicate where she should go for her work.

She found she could walk alone through the streets, and though there was no time to waste, there was still enough time for her to note the streets and alleyways, and to see that the flier platforms were guarded by only a few Kaldanes, who seemed more interested in watching the streets below than in guarding their charges.

She prayed the novelty of the crowd would not have worn off by the time she came back this way.

(*If* she came back this way. She had seen Jetan before; it was not a game with many survivors.)

It was enough of a novelty for a young woman to play the Game that the two competing Kaldanes (whose names slimed past her in a single guttural laugh) offered her a choice of teams.

"Come," said one, and the arm of the headless body was held out to her in a mockery of a gentleman. "They are taking the field."

She stood in the gateway at the edge of the arena, watching black-armored panthans and thoats take their places along the first line, as the orange side did the same in the marked-out squares on their side of the arena.

Tara held her breath until she saw a tall, confident figure she recognized instantly, even from so far away.

"The black army," she said.

The two Kaldanes immediately launched into a fight with each other over her choice. A guard ran to stand between them and force them to their separate sides.

Tara paused a moment in the gateway, glanced at the wall beside her, and let something fall.

Then she was running across the arena as fast as her feet could carry her.

She didn't call her brother's name (he was too clever to use his own), but still he turned and saw her before she would have thought possible, and for a moment his entire face was suffused with joy.

It wouldn't last—there was too much danger for joy to last—but she understood; she smiled even as she ran.

When she skidded to a stop she didn't dare reach for him, and he crossed his arms as if trying to keep himself from embracing her.

"I should have known," he said finally. "You always did love games you knew you could win."

"Let's hope that holds, for your sake." Then her smile faded. "Make me a Warrior—they have the most flexibility, and at the end of the Game you and Thuvia—"

But here Carthoris's face fell.

The black Princess emerged from the shadows of the holding cell, trying bravely not to cry.

She was a stranger.

"Carthoris," Tara breathed, "where's Thuvia?"

He didn't answer.

In horror, Tara turned to look where the last of the orange pieces were emerging.

There was Thuvia, in an orange robe, taking her place as the prize.

Beside her, the Chief of the orange pieces was already in place, staring at them, horrified.

It was Djor Kantos.

Tara held her breath; her fingertips went numb.

Then a voice cried, "Let the Game begin!"

The Game was well-matched—too well-matched—and each side lost panthans at a staggering rate until only the trickier pieces remained.

Tara did not notice this (though she should have); she was thinking only of the gate.

The gate had but one guard, and he had not yet noticed that she had dropped one of her thick golden bangles to keep the ground-bolt from sliding home.

That was their escape. Her brother already knew her plan (whispered in the moments before the pieces were ordered to take their places), and as soon as Thuvia and Djor came within hearing, she'd make good on their escape. With all four of them armed, it would be easy enough to overpower the guards and steal a flier home.

(All the while, her stomach was churning as she snuck glances at Thuvia and Djor across the board, waiting for their turn to be played.)

However, when Tara saw that all the spaces to her right had emptied, she realized how clever the Kaldane controlling the black team must be. He had sacrificed so many panthans to give his stronger pieces room to cross the board. The thoat before her marched to battle, and she watched the last orange panthan die under its feet.

Then her square was being called.

With a glance at her brother, his hands fisted at his sides and his eyes fixed on her, she advanced.

The flier who slid forward gave her a pitying smile. She saw his hands shaking; he knew this Game was his last.

"Be brave," he said, as if to himself.

"Die with honor," she said.

A few moves later, he did, and Tara stood in the square, beside his body, breathing heavily and looking at the board ahead.

The Kaldane playing orange must have been angry with her for throwing his expectations; the next thing he moved was a thoat, pawing at the ground and straining against the reins of its rider. It had been inching toward one of their fliers, but apparently the Kaldane had lost his patience, and its course was now fixed on her.

A screech of laughter floated through the crowd as the black-side Kaldane ordered her to take the square.

Tara trembled, and stepped forward.

She remembered sparring with Carthoris and Djor, when they could still barely lift their swords.

"Watch here," said her brother to Djor, brushing his hand along the back of Tara's arm. "It cannot be defended, and incapacitates. Every creature has these. Find them, and use them."

(The soft spot of a thoat is just behind the front legs, in the space usually protected by the elbow.)

When the thoat crashed to the sand, it trapped the rider waist-high beneath it. He struggled to reach his weapon, but it was pinned beneath the beast.

He looked up at Tara in terror.

Tara lifted her sword, hesitated.

("There is a line between bravery and cruelty," her brother told her. "Find that, too.")

She stepped back, lowered her sword, and called, "I will not kill him."

There was a murmur from the stands, and a moment

later two of the slavemasters were flanking the board.

"I am a volunteer," she told them. "You have no power here. I cry mercy for this man—the Gamemaster decides."

Softly, from behind her, she heard her brother whisper, "Careful."

But she offered them neither abuse nor apologies, and after a moment they got some signal and moved to remove the thoat and walk the warrior off the board. (He cast a grateful glance over his shoulder, and she nodded back.)

She was still focused on the victory, and it took her a moment to realize how much closer she had moved to the ranks of the orange.

Thuvia was looking across the board at her husband, shaking her head in terror. Djor Cantos was looking straight at Tara with an expression that could cut marble.

Then she realized what the orange Kaldane had had in mind when he'd arranged the move.

It was a trap.

If she took two more squares, she was going to challenge the Chief.

The game moved on, but Tara was frozen, staring into the face of an old friend with whom she had just become comfortable again, after a painful absence.

Djor had looked away and now stood watching the board, frozen with dread. Beside him, Thuvia reached out a sympathetic hand.

"The Black Chief is challenged!" Tara heard.

She turned. Though the first challenge to a Chief was usually to test his skill rather than to take the board, she knew this Game had gotten ugly when she saw that the orange had sent a dwar, a captain, for the fight.

This was for the kill.

Tara knew Carthoris would win—the only person who

outclassed him with a blade was their father—but she could not think even of his being wounded, and she watched the battle with a sour stomach, fearing at any moment to hear the Captain's blade slicing home.

When the Captain fell to the ground, Tara let out a breath she didn't know she'd been holding, and it was so loud that Carthoris looked up from the body and smiled at her, so quickly no one else could see.

Then the Gamemaster called, "Warrior challenges Chief!"

Tara spun to look at Djor Kantos, who was moving forward as if his feet were in lead sandals.

"No!" cried Carthoris from behind her.

She stepped forward too, her sword at the ready.

Djor's face was stony, and she wondered if he had planned some hero's suicide for himself while he'd been waiting.

Not now, she thought; *don't you dare give up now that we're friends again at last.*

He stepped close, and raised his sword.

Then he murmured, "I hope you have an escape planned, or your brother is going to be very upset with me."

Relief flooded her, so sharp it was like pain.

"He'll be the least of your problems once I'm done with you," she said, and took a fighting stance.

Then they began.

It looked to the Kaldanes like a battle between two equals of skill; only Carthoris would know that it was their old dexterity figures, which looked dangerous but never struck.

(It felt, for a moment, like home.)

When they were pressed shoulder to shoulder, swords locked, Tara whispered quickly about the gate, and the fliers' tower.

"When?" he asked, over the clang of metal.

Even as he asked it, she realized.

"Now," she said. "It has to be now."

"All right," Djor said.

And the next moment, he had spun away from her, and the sword was flying out of his hand.

It struck one of the slavemasters and pinned him to the sand like an insect. Beside him, his fellow staggered backward with a squeal.

Even before the outcry rose from the Kaldanes in the arena, Tara was running for her brother.

"Here," she said, shoving her sword into the hands of the black Princess. "If you're fighting, fight."

The Princess blinked, but took a grip on the sword that looked passable.

Carthoris was shaking his head, but already his sword was in Tara's hands, and they were halfway to the gate.

"Those who would be free must fight!" Carthoris called.

Nearly all the remaining pieces shouldered their weapons and bolted.

Ahead of her, Thuvia and Djor were already at the gate, dragging it aside. The guard vanished under Djor's sword, and Thuvia braced herself at the other side against any oncomers.

Beside Tara, Carthoris was keeping pace, and they were nearly at the gate and free.

Then she crashed to the ground.

There was a searing pain in her right leg, and she knew at once that she had been struck—a knife, or a simple blade-disc.

Carthoris was already turning back.

"No!" she shouted.

But because he was her brother, he didn't listen; because he was her brother, he would risk death for her, too.

She heard the whistling of other blades as they seemed to bloom from the sand, and she knew that before he could get hold of her, he'd be struck.

Then, from behind her, she heard the clang of metal against metal.

The thoat-rider she had spared was standing over her.

"They'll be sending soldiers soon," he said without taking his eyes off the edge of the arena. "Go!"

Carthoris hauled her up by the ribs, and the two of them staggered together for the safety of the gate.

"Are they safe?" Tara gasped between breaths.

"They have made it out of the gateway, at least," Carthoris said. "If you hurry, we might not even die."

Tara could have hit him; instead, she ran faster.

Behind them came the cry of a wounded man.

Die with honor, Tara thought, with a pang of loss that was worse than the wound.

But her legs had not given out on her entirely; she ran against her brother with one blood-slicked foot, and then ahead of them was the gate, and the tunnel to the street, and then, if they lived, the fliers home.

The streets were full of panic, but not of swords, and they made good time, Tara slipping once or twice as her bloody heel skidded on the pavement.

By the time they reached the flier platform, the battle was struck in earnest. The Kaldanes had sent troops to reinforce the platform. Thuvia was farthest ahead, darting toward one of the fliers. The jetan-men in black and orange had fallen back, and were fighting side by side against the monstrous bodies of Kaldane troops, and from the side of the platform that was flush against the city, reinforcements were already coming.

Djor had hung back, and when he saw them coming, he reached for Tara to help ease her brother's burden.

"Help Thuvia!" Djor called, and Carthoris disappeared into the melee.

Djor surveyed the oncoming soldiers. "This will be an ugly fight," he said.

Tara grimaced. "Then put me somewhere, and give me a sword."

"I'll put you at my back," he said, "and we'll see if we can take some of the fight out of them."

A shortsword appeared in her hand, and she braced herself as best she could.

"And if we die today," said Djor, "know that it did me good to be your friend again."

Tara could think of nothing to say—she could not say "Die with honor," not to him—and instead she only raised her sword and prepared to fight.

One of the Kaldanes caught sight of her and began the charge along the edges of the platform, skirting the battle to reach her faster.

Warrior challenges the Chief, she thought.

Then there was the roar of engines, and the screams of the Kaldanes from below, and Tara looked up and saw a flier descending, bearing the crest of Dejah Thoris, come to take them home.

As soon as Tara was home and out from under the doctor's stitches, she sent for her husband, Gahan.

"Tell him nothing of what has happened," she told the messenger. "Let it wait until I can tell it."

That night, she lay on a chaise in her quarters, with Carthoris and Thuvia and Djor beside her.

Djor was his old self, open and easy, and Carthoris as he always was, and Tara thought it would have been worth the danger just to have Djor as her friend again. (To have a brother back was something that needed no words.)

"The Kaldanes have blades either rusted or poisoned,"

said Tara. "My whole leg burned when it struck me."

"Their blades might be trying harder to kill you," Carthoris pointed out. "You've triumphed over them so many times it has made them angry."

"I can triumph over you, too," she said. "I am advised not to stand; that doesn't mean I cannot fight."

A messenger interrupted–Gahan had arrived.

Thuvia smiled and stood. "I will greet him," she said. "Do not test yourself. Your will is greater than your need."

"It would never be the reverse," Carthoris said, and Djor nodded once in agreement.

Tara had no ready answer for the praise of a brother and a near-brother.

Behind them the sun was setting, and the warm light of the Barsoom sun bathed the room around them in just the way she'd grown up with.

Though she would have to leave Helium soon and return to her husband's city, this was the way she would always consider the light to be most beautiful.

Some things, maybe, did not have to change after all.

"Tara?" Carthoris cut in. "Is everything all right? How do you feel?"

She smiled and said, "At home."

In the first book in the Barsoom series, *A Princess of Mars*, we are introduced to John Carter as he's prospecting for gold in Arizona. When he runs afoul of a local tribe of Apache Indians, he seeks refuge in a cave, where he collapses from exhaustion. Upon awakening he finds himself paralyzed, unable to turn and glimpse the haunting presence that he senses in the cave with him. (The Indians flee in terror from this apparition.) Later, Carter finds himself staring down at his lifeless body. He wanders outside and stares up at the night sky, and finds himself drawn across outer space to Mars. And Carter's not the only Earthman to have this strange experience. In *The Master Mind of Mars*, a World War I soldier named Ulysses Paxton awakens on Barsoom after being mortally wounded. Our next tale tells of yet another Earthman who finds himself on Barsoom, though he's a very different sort from the gentlemanly John Carter of Virginia. *A Princess of Mars* begins in the Wild West, and in many ways Barsoom is a colorful echo of the West, with its tribes of hostile natives galloping about. Of course, on Barsoom the hostile natives have four arms, and their mounts have eight legs, but the flavor is much the same, and this next tale emphasizes that Western flavor to its utmost, with an irascible narrator who don't take no guff from anyone.

A SIDEKICK OF MARS

BY GARTH NIX

I'd guess you, like what seems to be most of the world these days, have read about John Carter, and his adventures and whatnot on the red planet we call Mars and the locals there call Barsoom. But I bet you've never read nothing about one Lamentation of Wordly Sin Jones, who was right there by J. C.'s side for more than a sixth of the time by my calculation but don't get a mention at all in any of the write-ups. Not even under the name by which Carter knew me, which wasn't the full moniker my god-fearin' parents dished up but the shorter, easier to get your mouth around Lam Jones.

See? I bet you're castin' your mind back through all those books and not remembering any Lam Jones, which is a downright insult, being as I was there, as I said, some eighteen percent of the time, only to get left out when Carter got back to Earth and decided to tell his tales to that nephew of his.

Not that Carter told it all, oh no, he was right reticent on a couple of matters. He could be downright *closemouthed* when it suited him, and probably still is, since for all I know he's living yet, me not having seen him for some considerable time due to him being back on Barsoom and me being back here on this green Earth. Where I hopes I will stay, come to think of it, though how long that will be is anyone's guess, there not being anyone alive who knows what in God's name that buffalo hide scroll I took off the body of that Indian did to me, aside from wrestling me right out of my flesh and flinging me off to the red planet and back again like a damn hot chestnut juggled between two hands.

Let me tell you how I first met up with Captain John Carter . . . but I s'pose I'm getting ahead of myself. As I was saying, Lam Jones is what I been known by since I was going on fourteen, except for a period in the Union Army when I was called Private Jones and then Corporal Jones and finally Quartermaster-Sergeant Jones, but as soon as the war was done with, not so long after my nineteenth birthday, I got back to being plain old Lam Jones again.

Me fighting for the North probably was the first thing that put Carter off me, him being a rebel and all. Or maybe like a lot of hot-blooded, rip-roaring cavalry types, he just hated quartermasters. There must have been a dozen or more occasions when I had to face down some shouting colonel or major who wanted something that I either just didn't have in the stores, or couldn't give them without a paper signed by the appropriate officer, not just any jumped up Brigadier-General. Why, sometimes what they wanted had to be approved by General Meigs himself, and it was a marvel to me that these officers couldn't understand a simple procedure and put their request through the proper channels in an approved fashion.

Now I'm getting behind. Suffice to say that at the end of the war, there I was, plain old Lam Jones again, left by the tide of battle (though not the sharp end of it) in a three-saloon town, with a meager bounty from a grateful government, that being I got to keep my Spencer carbine, a rusty old saber I'd never used, and two hundred and two dollars in back pay, most of it paper money which passed at a discount in favor of gold.

Gold! Like a lot of folks around then, I was mad for the yellow metal, and I'd set my sights on getting a whole lot more of it than the three Miss Liberty coins I had in my poke. That's why I went west as soon as I could, and sure enough I struck it lucky right away in Arizona, when I met a fellow called Nine-Tenths Noah, an old-time miner, who reckoned he knew a prime spot for a strike, only he needed a partner and a stake on account of him being a vagrant drunk.

To cut a long story down to size, we did well in our gold-diggings. Despite Nine-Tenths Noah being a soak of the first degree, being pretty much permanently pickled (as the nine-tenths referred), he knew his business and he provided the brains of the operation, while I provided the stake and then the digging power. I guess I ain't mentioned that short as I am from foot to crown, I am nearly as wide as tall, and all of it muscle. Some folks even tried calling me The Block, on account of my physique, back in the regiment, until I showed 'em I was against it.

That might well be another reason Carter misliked mentioning me in his stories. Sure, he was taller and had the looks and all, but I was stronger. He could jump farther, having the better balance, but when it came to grip and lift, I left him in the red dust. We had a thoat-lifting contest once (I 'spect you know a thoat is a Martian horse-thing) when we were both sozzled on the stuff that passes for whiskey on Barsoom. I lifted my thoat clear above my head, and he only got his to shoulder-height. It kicked him when he threw it down too, and he was kind of upset about the whole thing the next day, and blamed me for it, though it had been his idea all along. He wasn't a drinker, in a usual way, so maybe his wife, that Dejah Thoris, gave him a scold when he staggered back to the palace.

Anyways, that was much later. Back on Earth, Old Noah's nose had led us right, and I was digging out a lot of gold. All through the winter of 1866 we kept at it, and it was only when spring had started to come over and the snow melt begun that we realized that we were down to the final nasty-looking hunk of salt beef, there was but one sack of flour left, and Noah was having to dive headfirst into his puncheon of snakebite whiskey to dip his cup. We'd left it kind of late to resupply, which might surprise you what with me being a former quartermaster and all. It was the gold that did it. As long as more of it kept coming out of the mine, neither of us could bear to stop.

The nearest town was four days away, walking. I don't hold much with riding, being as I said, more square than rectangular in shape. I had to shorten stirrups so high as to provoke ridicule, and there weren't many horses that liked my weight none, either. So leading three mules, I left Noah behind to guard the mine, on account of him being incapable of walking any considerable distance. There was even a chance he might sober up while I was gone. He couldn't ever ration his drinking and there was only six gallons left.

Only I never did make it back in the nine days I'd reckoned, which was four to walk out, a day's business and four days back. In fact, I hardly got a mile from the mine.

It was Indians that done this, leastways one particular Indian. We hadn't seen any Indians at all over the winter, though we knew we were on Apache land. The mine was in a narrow mountain canyon, with few trees or foliage, and no hunting to speak of, so I suppose it wasn't worth a visit. I didn't know much about the Apache myself, or Indians in general, having been raised in Pennsylvania and never being in the West before. Noah had taught me a few signs to get along, but I hoped I'd never get close enough to need 'em, nor my Sharps carbine or the Colt Army .44 I had stuck in my pants neither.

I wasn't thinking about Indians, or much else neither, 'cept the slap-up meal I was going to have in town, when I just about tripped over the legs of a fellow, lying straight across the narrow path that was the only way out of the eastern end of the canyon. I jumped back into my lead mule, who protested at this kind of unexpected treatment. It let out a bray that echoed down the canyon walls and that didn't help me none as I was scrabbling to get my Colt out, it having slipped down a piece and the hammer getting stuck under my waistband.

With the gun in my hand I steadied a little, maybe also because the fellow wasn't moving at all. His bare legs were across the trail, but the top half of him were stuck in a little cave mouth I'd never noticed before, in the almost sheer canyon side. I called out to him, but he never moved. So I bent down and dragged him out, and had to jump back again as a huge snake come out with him, sounding its damn rattle as it lunged at me. I fired at once, and blasted it in half, the gunshot and the snake rattlin' and writhing about, making my lead mule decide to push past me and take off, with the others at its heels.

I was knocked back by the mules, and had a bad dance with the front half of that rattler, who still wasn't done till I stomped on its head, put my full weight on it, and screwed my heel around a few times.

After I'd calmed down a piece, I turned the Indian over. He was naked, save for a breechclout, and his head was pretty swole, with six or mebbe seven snake-bites across of his face and down his neck. I was a mite surprised that an Apache had stuck his head into that little cave, but I s'pose anyone can get caught out by a rattler if it's sitting quiet.

The dead man had a roll of some kind of parchment, probably scraped buffalo hide, clutched in his hand. I muttered an apology to him, in case of ghosts, and made the sign that I thought meant *It's a pity things is the way they are but what can you do,* and pulled the scroll out of his closed fingers, which took some doing, because he sure had a right death grip on it. Then I wandered on a few yards to get away from that hole and maybe more rattlers, and sat down on a boulder and put my back against the canyon wall. I knew the mules would be along all right, when they regained their senses, and I figured I'd take a look at that parchment while I waited.

I started to unroll it, and saw the beginnings of a picture. To this day I can't say what it was a picture of, or what the colors were, or nothing like that. As soon as my eyes set on it, I felt mighty strange. I got cold and stiff all over, like I was becoming part of the rock I leaned against, and then I got awfully tired. I tried to look away from that cursed drawing, but my eyes wouldn't move, and I couldn't stop my eyelids drifting south.

When I woke up, I was standing 'bout ten yards farther along the path. I glanced back to where I'd been sitting and had the terrible shock of seeing myself a-sitting there, still as a statue!

I rushed over, and reached out to my own shoulder, thinking perhaps I could shake myself awake. But my hand was like a ghost's, and for the first time in my life I couldn't get a hold of anything.

Then I figured I must have gone and died without knowing it. Maybe another rattler had got me, quick and quiet, while I was setting down. Or my heart had give out, like what happened to Sergeant Ducas that day in the mess hall, raising his spoon one second and dead the next.

Only I didn't feel dead and for sure I wasn't in heaven,

or hell, neither, as my parents always said I would end up. I felt fine, save for a kind of itchy yearning at the back of my neck, that made me want to crick it back and look up. Which eventually I did, seeing there was no reason not to.

I looked up along the narrow walls of the canyon, up to the sky above, which was a lot darker than I expected, with the stars already coming out. It was already night, so I guess I'd slept the day away.

One star caught my eye. A red star, that grew brighter, and brighter still. With nary a thought from me, my arms reached up toward that star, as if I might somehow drag it down, or be lifted up toward it.

I remember thinking very clearly *This ain't right,* then everything went red, as if I was passing through a fire, a huge fire that filled up the world, but a cold fire, 'cause I never felt it burn.

The next thing I knows, I was facedown in a tidy parcel of dust. I pushed myself up, noticing that once again I could feel the earth below me. I felt greatly relieved that I had been restored to my flesh, and now all would be well, that the strangeness would be over and done with.

Only I was mistaken about that. The first thing I saw when I stood up was the strangest figure of . . . a man, I guess . . . only he was some fifteen feet high, with two pairs of arms atop a pair of mighty legs, and an overall color reminiscent of a green tree frog, which is not exactly green but a kind of yellow greenness. He had a harness of leather and metal on his upper body and in each of his topmost hands he bore a long straight blade of some whitish metal. To top off this nightmarish aspect, his great head was riven by a mouth that bore enormous tusks, and his eyes were an evil red.

Naturally I reached for my weapons, only to discover that not only did I have neither Colt nor knife, I was barebuck naked in the bargain! The green warrior, correctly judging that motion of mine, raised both blades and swung them down. Seeking to dodge, I lunged forward, and was surprised to find myself projected into the midriff of the creature as if shot from a cannon! Despite his great size, my impact knocked him down and he did not immediately rise. I gripped his huge hand and twisted, planning simply to disarm him and take one of the blades to defend myself. But under my grip, bones cracked and flesh tore, so I fair messed up that hand before I got hold of his sword.

The green man tried to rise, and lift his other three blades. But before he could do so, I raised up the sword I had taken and plunged it deep into his chest. Again, my new strength surprised me, the blade driving through flesh and bone and into the ground beneath, so far that I could not easily withdraw it, particularly not when balanced upon a green giant undergoing the pangs and tremors of death.

But with a great exertion I did pull the blade free. Disturbed by my nakedness, I also cut away a broad swathe of leather from the creature's trappings and quickly tied it around my waist to make a makeshift garment like a Scotchman's kilt. Then I jumped, only to find myself hurtling high through the air once more, to land not next to the man as I'd thought, but dozens of yards away!

Given a moment's respite from fighting the big green fellow, I looked around and saw that while I was indeed in a canyon of sorts, it was not the canyon I'd been in moments ago. It was shallower, and wider, and the rock wasn't bare, but covered in some sort of moss or maybe lichen. The sun wasn't right neither, being smaller and punier than it should have been.

But I only glanced at the strange, distant sun, because beyond the green man I had killed, only a few hundred yards along the canyon or valley, there was a whole damn regiment of those green four-armed men, only they was

sittin' atop those thoat things I mentioned, what were like horses but with eight legs.

Unlike John Carter, the first thought in my head when spotting a right army of huge green warriors is not to wander over and beat up on the general and maybe the staff as well, just to make sure of the matter. The thought that was jumping to attention in my brainbox was: How I was going to get the heck out of there? Only no answer occurred as the green men lowered their spears and their eight-legged mounts began to charge toward me.

There was nowhere to hide, and nowhere to run, and the enemy was coming on at a rush. My head almost turned completely around on my neck as I tried to find some way out, but it were all for naught. Within a minute or two, I would be ridden down, speared, and trampled to death.

Then I saw that between me and the green man I had killed, there was a perfectly round pattern in the dusty ground, like the hatch to a cellar, too regular to be natural. I jumped toward it but even though I'd held back on my full strength, I overshot my mark. Then, trying to run back, I kept bouncing up into the air, as if the very force of gravity that bound me to the Earth had lessened—and it had, as I would later confirm.

But I managed to get back to that circular depression and, using the green man's sword, swept the red dust aside. There *was* a cellar hatch there, a round door of metal. But there was no handle, ring, or lever with which to open it. Reversing my blade, I banged on the strange door with the hilt, but there was no response, save the distant clang resulting from my blows.

Things was about as desprit as they get then, for the green cavalry was almost upon me. I turned to face them, a thousand thoughts of all the things left undone in my life racing through my mind, but chief among them was regret-tin' all that gold I'd never get to spend.

Then, as the thunder of the charging thoats filled the canyon, and the green giants and their spear-points were only yards away, I was suddenly lifted into the air from behind and yanked up into the sky like a fish jerked out of the water by a long-handled gaff.

Which ain't poetical talk, but a true saying, save that I'm no fish, and it was a boat of the sky that had lifted me aboard, the hook employed being very skillfully thrust through the back of my makeshift kilt, so that I had only a quarter-inch deep cut across one buttock to show for it and no more blood lost than a canteen might hold.

Later on I learned that John Carter himself had swung the hook, which was all to the good. Any normal fellow would probably have taken my head off. When it came to wielding a sword, gun, or even a hook, Carter really was the best. I often wondered how he might fare against Wild Bill Hickok, who was a wonder with a pistol. I met Hickok much later in what you might call my career, not on Mars, you understand. But even against Hickok, I reckon Carter might have had the edge.

So there I was, splayed and bleeding on the floor of this flying machine which was accelerating mightily toward the rim of the canyon, while an ordinary-looking fellow with a regular Earth-size number of arms and legs fired a long-barreled rifle of unfamiliar design over the stern. I was also relieved to see someone I at first took to be an Indian on account of him having the red skin that Indians was sup-posed to have (but didn't in actual fact), was directing the craft from a half cockpit forr'ard.

Sharp explosions sounded behind us in rapid succession, sending up clouds of dust where they struck the ground, obscuring our rapid retreat. The Earthman fired a few more rounds, then lowered his strange rifle and turned about. He jabbered something at the red man, who laughed, before he turned his attention to me, removing the hook from my belt without paying much attention to the blood that was flowing readily down my leg. Then he jabbered some more, at me this time, in a language I could not even begin to recognize.

"I fear I do not—" I started to reply.

This obviously surprised him greatly. Carter—for of course it was he—was never one to show much emotion in his face, but in this case both his eyebrows lifted for an instant, and a spark flashed across his steel-gray eyes.

"You speak English?" he interrupted. "Or have you learned it this moment from my mind?"

"I cain't read minds," I replied. "I've always spoken English, and a little Dutch and German, on account of being raised in Berks County, Pennsylvania."

"You're an Earthman!" exclaimed Carter. "I took you for some kind of White Dwarf Martian, emerged from the subterranean fastness back there."

"I ain't a dwarf, Martian or otherwise," I replied stiffly. "And I don't let no man call me one, neither. The name is Lam Jones, Arizonee miner, late quartermaster in the headquarters of General Sheridan."

"A Union man," said Carter, his manner immediately less friendly. "Allow me to introduce myself, Mister Jones. I am Captain John Carter of Virginia, and a Prince of Helium, here on Barsoom."

"Pleased to meet you, Captain . . . that is to say . . . Prince," I said weakly. I didn't want to look, but I could feel the blood trickling down my leg, and it felt like there was a lot of it. "The War being over and all. Uh, where might Barsoom be, your honor?"

"It is the fourth planet of this solar system," said Carter. "You would call it Mars."

"Mars?" I asked. "I'm on *Mars*?"

"Yes," said Carter. There was still a mighty chill in his voice. "You are only the second Earthman to come here, as far as it is known."

I kind of got the message then that he liked it better when there was only the one Earthman on Mars.

"Mars," I repeated, looked down, saw my own blood spreading across the deck, and fainted.

When I awoke, I found myself on a kind of padded shelf of silk, with my ass bandaged up and a fur robe loosely tied around me, the kind of fur robe that would have cost more than a hundred dollars from one of the finest stores in Philadelphia, like I was going to buy with my gold. The whole store, I mean, not the fur robe.

Apart from my buttock wound, I felt refreshed, so with only a little difficulty in the sitting-up department, I swung myself off that shelf and took stock of my surroundings. I could see from the tall arched window opposite that I was in some kind of tower room, a room straight out of the color plates in the book of Araby that Captain O'Hoolihan of the New York Zouaves had lent me once, in return for three more hogs over his company's allowance. It was all silk curtains and suchlike, that room, and more cushions than a madam's fancy-house.

No sooner had I got down than a woman rose up out of those cushions, a mighty fine-looking woman, with that real red skin like the fellow who'd been driving the flying boat. She bent her head and then looked straight at me, her eyes seeming to bore into my head, and I felt something twitch and give inside my brain, right behind my eyes.

Suddenly I knew her name: Kala. It was just there, as if I'd a-knowed it all along. Prancing along behind, straight into my head, came some other words, and before I really caught on what was happening I was answering back to her, without either of us uttering a word.

That's how I got started with that Martian mindtalkin' business, though I never got as good as Carter. I could talk with folks, but I couldn't read their minds. He could, right enough, except for mine. I used to think up some pretty insulting thoughts sometimes, about Johnny Reb and all, but he never caught on.

I was stuck in that tower for nigh on a week before Carter showed up to see how I was going. I guess he'd been off slaughtering some of the Warhoon greens or similar activities of which he was right fond.

Straight away he wanted to know how I'd got to Barsoom, though he never told me nothing about his own journey. I read it years later, like everyone else, and wondered why he'd kept it secret. He wanted to know if I was an immortal too, or couldn't remember my childhood. I reckon he was pleased to find out I was no one special in that regard.

'Course, I'd met quite a few folk along the way who couldn't remember their childhoods, like old Noah for one, but I never suggested to Carter that it might be whiskey that done in his memory. I knew right early he wasn't a man to trifle with. He killed too easily, and had it all sorted within himself. Just like my ma and pa. They would have whipped me to death over the smallest thing and said it was all for the best, just the way God intended.

Only Carter had his honor, instead of God, and that honor only had room for Virginian gentlemen and Martian princesses. Everyone else was pretty much window-dressing, providing a pretty frame for him and his lady to stand in the sunlight.

I asked him as soon as I might how I could get back to Earth and my gold (only I never mentioned that, and I never knew he was a miner too, neither) as polite as anything, well larded with "Sirs" and "Highnesses" and "Your Majestic-ness" and all. But either he didn't know—which he didn't, as it turned out—or he wouldn't tell me. Besides, since he didn't want to go back himself, he found it sort of peculiar that I wanted to. By this stage he'd sort of adopted me, not exactly as the First Earthman to the Second Earthman, but more like he might pick up a pet. I reckon I ranked somewhat lower than his foul dog-thing Woola.

He also put me to work. Though expressing the opin-ion that a Union quartermaster was only worth the mer-est part of a good Virginian quartermaster, or at a pinch an Alabaman, he still considered that a cut above the Martian variety. I was given a Martian assistant, and with Kala to help translate, was assigned the task of putting in order the stores and armories of Helium, the city which Carter's old man-in-law was the mayor of or the governor or whatever Jeddak signified.

I didn't mind the work, for to tell the truth, those Mar-tians already had things pretty well sorted. It was just Carter wanted things done the way he was used to, and him being such a hero to all of them Heliumites, they was happy to oblige.

I didn't mind the living either, once I worked out that Kala wasn't just provided to teach me the lingo but was happy to warm me up on that silk shelf as well. She wasn't a princess, but a princess wouldn't have suited me anyhow. If it wasn't for my gold waiting for me I s'pose I could have got used to the quiet life as a quartermaster in Helium.

So the weeks went past, and then months. I might be there still if John Carter hadn't got it into his head that a fel-low Earthman like himself must be pining for the excitements he got into every day, speeding about in flyers, shooting up green folks from miles away with a radium rifle, engaging in desperate hand-to-hand combat with a critter eight times his size, and all them larks.

"I've been thinking about that subterranean lair you found where we picked you up, Lam," he says to me one day, suddenly turning up as I was quietly counting bandoliers in a nice little corner armory where hardly no one ever visited. "You said you noticed a round trapdoor or some such, I think?"

"Yes, sir," I replied enthusiastically, before I let my face fall. "Only I'd never find it now, all that red dust and moss looks the same to me."

"Not to me," says Carter. "I have a complete recollection of the area. We'll pick up Kantos Kan and go and take a look. I've been wondering what's under there and there's nothing much else on at the moment."

Kantos Kan, I should have said, was the fellow who'd been driving the air boat when I was rescued. He was Carter's best friend and as mad a cavalry type as he was. Kind of an equivalent to General Custer, inasmuch as he'd do something crazy as heck just because he could, everyone would follow, and he'd come out the other side smiling even if most of the followers didn't. Only that don't always work, as Custer found out on the Greasy Grass. Kan had better luck than Custer all round, but I reckon he probably got ten times as many Heliumite soldiers killed in his time than Custer managed with the Seventh Cavalry.

"You and Kantos have fun, then, sir," I said, turning back to my bandoliers. Intentionally misunderstanding him, you see. Only Carter could play that game one better, for he really *didn't* understand why anyone would not want to go out on some crazy expedition with him.

"You have to come!" he laughed, clapping me on the back hard enough to kill a Thark. "Satisfy your curiosity, man!"

I muttered something about not having any damned curiosity, but not too loud. Like I said, I never wanted to push Carter too far.

We left that night in a three-man flyer, Kantos Kan naturally leapin' at the opportunity to stick his nose in somewhere dangerous. He laughed at me as I found it difficult to sit on what passed for a seat in them Martian flyers, but it wasn't because of the buttock wound. (That had healed up right nicely.) I just was a little awkward what with my three radium pistols, sword, knife, water bottle, and haversack, all of it worn over a fur robe 'cause I felt the cold. Carter and Kan, as per usual, were wearing outfits that would have got them arrested just about anywhere civilized, just a few leather straps, a pouch over the unmentionables, and some bits of metal stuck on here and there that Carter told me in his case meant much the same as Grant's three stars.

The valley where they'd found me was quite some distance away. I forget how far in Martian haads or karads, but it was nine hundred miles, give or take, about six hours' flight. Shame we ain't got those flyers here on Earth, cause they beat the railroad hollow for speed, and you don't get covered in soot, neither.

We arrived soon after the Martian dawn, and sure enough, Carter knew almost exactly where to go. Kantos Kan dropped the flyer down where Carter pointed, and then the three of us took no more than ten minutes looking about before we found that circular hatch.

As before, there weren't no way of opening the thing, but this didn't put Carter off. He knelt down by it, and just *thought* at it for a while, while I fidgeted about nearby and Kantos Kan went back and leant on his flier.

Even knowin' what I did about Carter being able to read Martian minds and all, I was still taken aback more than a bit when that trapdoor started to turn about, making a noise like a railroad engine straining for grip on a greasy rail. Then the whole dang thing rose up out of the ground, turning as it came, till there was a cylinder some ten foot high and six feet in diameter sticking up out of the dust.

Carter rapped on the side of it with his knuckle, and a door slid open. There was a whitish-kind of Martian standing there, dressed up in the kind of driving outfit folks wear here nowadays, with the long leather coat and the goggles and all. I guess I was staring like a fool, while Carter had stepped a little to the side—he always was in the right place—so when the Martian suddenly raised up this bellows thing and blew a cloud of green gas it went straight at me, and afore I knew it, I'd sucked it into my chest.

I don't know what was in that gas, but as soon as I breathed it down, I was stuck fast where I was, unable to move a muscle. I watched Carter lean in and stick the goggle-wearing Martian with his sword, then haul him out by his coat and throw him a good dozen yards away to die in the dust. Then he came back to me, and I saw his mouth moving, but I couldn't hear any words, and my eyes were already closing, being as I was unexpectedly come over weary.

I think he was saying summat along the lines of "Why did you stand there, idiot?" which fair sums up our dialogue, then and later. I reckon he thought I was willfully stupid, which was why he was always having to push me out of the way, or rescue me and all. Not that he ever complained when it was Dejah Thoris who needed rescuin', which happened a damn sight more to her than anyone might expect. I guess I was never much of a hero, but at least I weren't kidnapping-prone like Miss Dejah Thoris.

She never liked me, neither. Maybe because of the time I was checking over Carter's accounts and couldn't make them balance, though I never said a thing about it being kind of peculiar that her new jeweled doo-dah cost the same as the missing money.

That was much later, anyhow. After I sucked that gas and was knocked out or put to sleep, the next time I opened my eyes I was no longer on Mars! I was back in my own body, sitting in the canyon mouth, with my back against the wall. There was a kind of lean-to built over my head, and dry-stone walls up to near my waist, and sitting alongside of me in a rocking chair was my partner, Nine-Tenths Noah.

"You awake, then?" he said pausing in his rockin' to take a gulp of what had to be water, on account of I couldn't smell it.

"Reckon I am," I said, wonderingly. "How long has it been?"

"Five months and a week," replied Noah.

I slowly stood up, marveling that all my muscles and faculties worked as they should. I flexed my fingers, and right then noticed that I was no longer holding the Indian painting or whatever it was.

Noah saw me looking at my empty hand.

"Real bad medicine," he said. "I threw it back in that there cave it come from, where it should have stayed."

I looked at him properly, taking in his unusually bright eyes and pink skin. Forcible laying off the whiskey had done him good service it seemed, but I was kind of puzzled how come he was still alive.

"What you been eatin' while I was out of my head, Noah?"

"Mules," he replied. "You up to walkin'?"

"Yep," I replied. I felt fine, and mighty relieved to be back where I belonged. For good, or so I thought at the time, little knowing that I'd be back on Mars within the year, once again running along behind John Carter, and wishing I wasn't.

"We gotta go spend some gold," said Noah. "Where you been, anyhow? I seed you was spirit-walking."

"Mars," I said. "It ain't all it's cracked up to be."

"Mars," mused Noah, an odd, faraway expression passing across his face. "They got any gold up there?"

Anyhows, that's how I first met up with the all high-and-mighty John Carter of Mars, even if he don't care to recollect it himself, what with him being Warlord and Jeddak of Jeddaks and all that stuff. Or maybe he was still cantankerous about the South losing the War and all. He always did get all maudlin when he was back on Earth, whining about missing Dejah Thoris, and reminiscin' something horrid about what went wrong at Chancellorsville and suchlike.

I tried to tell my old general, Phil Sheridan, that the folks in Washington ought to keep an eye on Mars, because there was a Johnny Reb up there itching to start over if he could figure a ways of getting his army alongside of Earth. But then I disappeared back to Barsoom myself, and by the time I returned, Phil was dead.

I guess if J. C. does decide to attack the United States, I'll probably be there with him, dang it. I don't know how it's worked out like this, but I just can't get rid of the fellow, at least not permanent-like.

Or maybe it's that he can't rid of *me*?

◆ ◆ ◆

Whereas *A Princess of Mars* concerns the adventures of an Earthman on Mars, our next tale inverts the formula and presents the adventures of Barsoomians on Earth. The Superstition Mountains are a real mountain range in southern Arizona, and some Apaches believe that a hidden cave there leads down into another world. Many of the characters in this story are real historical figures. Cochise was a chief of the Chiricahua Apache who led a decade-long guerilla campaign against the U.S. Army and white settlers encroaching on Apache lands. In one famous incident, Cochise was lured to the tent of Lieutenant George Bascom, who mistakenly believed that Cochise was responsible for a recent raid. When Bascom attempted to arrest Cochise, the Apache drew a knife and cut his way free. Cochise's only white friend, a U.S. Army scout named Tom Jeffords, eventually brokered a peace agreement between Cochise and General Oliver O. Howard, called "The Christian General" because he tried to base all policy decisions on scripture. (He later founded Howard University to promote higher education for freed slaves.) Cochise, Jeffords, and Howard appear as characters in the 1950 film *Broken Arrow*, notable as the first major Western of its era to present a sympathetic view of American Indians.

◆ ◆ ◆

THE GHOST THAT HAUNTS THE SUPERSTITION MOUNTAINS

BY CHRIS CLAREMONT

CHAPTER 11

The days are warmer here in Arizona than their counterparts on Barsoom, but the nights there, on the planet that we of Earth call Mars, are much colder. I have always found it surprising how little the people of my adopted homeworld wear to protect themselves from the elements. I suspect that nature has cast the Red Martian race of somewhat firmer stuff than we.

I must confess I feel strange to be clad once more in the attire of my native planet, to be astride a horse instead of an eight-legged thoat. In the great scheme of things, very little time has passed since I first made the journey out across the heavens—and yet, now that I have returned, it is this place where I was born that seems alien to me. Heart and soul, I have embraced my adopted world as my home, as I have the Princess whom I love.

But fate—no doubt with a laugh of outright glee—has cast me along a different road.

And not alone, either. Beside me on the trail rides my wife, though her mount carries but the riding blanket of the Apache, plus a sheath for her long gun, whereas mine is laden down with saddle and gear and a Henry rifle.

On Barsoom, Dejah Thoris rides naked—as do all her people, male and female, young and old—her sole adornments being decorative jewelry of breathtaking beauty, and, of course, weapons. Here, such a presentation would guarantee to cause trouble, and so she has dressed herself in a leather riding skirt and knee-high soft-skinned boots of the Apache style. She wears a blouse common to Chiricahua women and over that a leather horse jacket more akin to what a frontiersman might favor. At first glance, aside from her own Henry repeater in its rifle scabbard, she seems to ride without weapons. She is, of course, a dead shot. Beyond that, scattered about her person, are an assortment of knives in sheathes that are mostly hidden to the easy eye. She prefers blades to pistols, she says they provide more variety of practical use—asking with a smile if anyone's ever tried carving up a piece of wood, or the day's meal, with a pistol barrel? Whoever looks on her as easy prey will find themselves with a very nasty surprise.

Her clothes are as well worn as mine, though she finds the wearing of them almost barbaric. Among her people, the body—indeed, life itself—is a gift to be celebrated, and to them that cannot be done by hiding it away. More importantly, the clothes my people wear here on Earth she sees as a significant detriment in a fight, an encumbrance that no proper warrior can afford—especially given the adversaries he, or she, is likely to face on Barsoom.

But, as she herself is the first to admit—as we have both discovered during our travels and adventures across the face of her ancient world—different people have different customs. When one is a visitor, it's always best to show those people, and their ways, an appropriate measure of respect.

"There were times," she notes quietly, and with a smile, as she reins in her animal and dismounts with practiced ease, "these past months, when I thought we'd never see these mountains again."

"The Superstitions are well-named," I concede, following suit and taking the reins from my Princess to secure our mounts to a convenient tree. "No one—among both my people and the Apaches—has properly explored them; there are just too many stories of travelers disappearing or falling prey to hideous monsters."

"Like a monstrous tall, green-skinned, four-armed Thark," she suggests. I respond with a nod, but truthfully my mind is suddenly wandering elsewhere.

"Make a wrong turn, and find yourself on Barsoom," she suggests idly. She is teasing—a little—but I take her words seriously.

"I did," is my reply. "Alternately," I continue as she nods, conceding the point, "an apt or a banth might find themselves transported here." The one is an arctic predator, the other Mars's equivalent of a terrestrial lion. Both are formidable hunters but the banth is truly fearsome in battle. "The question is, how quickly and how well a beast, a predator, of Barsoom might adapt to the environment here?"

"I did," says my beloved, simply and factually, tossing my words back at me.

"As did I," echoes a new voice, from farther up the deeply shadowed slope and as well better than a dozen feet above our heads.

211

Before us, striding into the starlight's clear view comes Tars Tarkas, Jeddak of Thark—and my very best friend. By any stretch, he is an imposing—if not outright terrifying—creature, standing double the height of a tall man.

His physique is similar to ours, in a general sense; he walks on two extremely powerful legs that have adapted well to the heavier gravity of this larger world. But from his torso reach a double pair of arms. His skull encloses a brain as sharp and gifted as our own, his face holds a pair of eyes. His nose is flat; it does not protrude like its human counterpart, or those of my beloved's people. And while his mouth bears a full stock of teeth, what dominates the lower jaw are a pair of upward-curving fangs, reaching to his forehead, bespeaking an ancestry so fierce that I don't care to think about what his race must have looked like back when it began.

He stands downwind of us and stays mostly in the shadows, amongst the trees, his emerald skin blending quite nicely with the local foliage. Our mounts sense that *something* is there but they also sense no threat and so remain quite calm.

"From what I've been hearing in town," I note, striding upslope to join him, "you've been creating a rather impressive legend for yourself up here, my friend. They're calling you the Ghost that haunts the Superstition Mountains."

"Not just among the settlers," agrees my Princess. "There are tales being told among the Chiricahua, as well."

"Perhaps, at night," concedes the Thark, "when I look up at the sky and toward my home, I let my emotions get the better of me."

"Not—singing," I cannot hide my horror. Few things sound as primal and as terrifying as a Green Martian crooning to himself. It is something common only to the males; thankfully, the females of their species are gifted with more taste. Yet even as we exchange our small bits of humor, my mind races along a different trail.

Dejah Thoris senses this and asks me, "What?"

"A thought," is my reply as I recall all that I've learned of her world and her people. At the same time, I stroll back and forth across the mouth of the cavern, wishing I had one of the artificial lights utilized by her people. Its beam would illuminate the cavern before us as brightly as the midday sun. Part of my mind reassures me that this is simply a cavern, nothing whatever to fear. And yet, another part, that I respect more because it's served me well in battle and adventures both, cautions that not all here is as it seems.

I shake my head, very much aware of my gun-hand perching itself close beside the Colt pistol on my belt. My left hand has already released the lanyard slung over the hammer to keep the weapon from falling free of the holster. "We make fun of what's happened here with Tars Tarkas," I tell her, "but I heard similar stories when I first came to Tucson, before I got transported to Barsoom. And among the Chiricahua, these tales of ghosts and monsters go back as far as those people can remember."

"So?"

"Your kind live a thousand years," I say, trying not to think of that primal difference between us: If I lived longer than any man known, I would still pass from the world before my beloved had breathed even a decent fraction of her allotted span. "Suppose, in ages past, another of your people crossed from Barsoom to Earth—and perhaps become the source of all these legends?"

"That is a thought, John Carter—but if so, then where is he? Or she? In our time here, we've seen no evidence of another like us."

"True," I concede with a shrug. "It was just a thought." Yet even as I say this, I realize that my pistol still hangs untethered in its holster, ready to be quickly drawn if needed. Whatever I may tell myself, that the night around us is quiet and peaceful, my body has a mind of its own—and that mind is very much on edge. My conscious thoughts may not yet be aware of it, but instinct is telling me to be careful here. Something is—not right.

I turn toward Tars Tarkas to ask, "Is the cave still clear?" It is a matter of no small concern, given the difference in our size.

"It is now as when we arrived, my friend," he assures me but there's a tenor to his voice that catches my attention.

"What's wrong?" I ask.

"I'm thinking, much like you, that this all seems so easy, we just walk through this entrance to the cave and—somehow emerge back home on Barsoom."

"It happened in reverse to bring us here," notes Dejah Thoris.

"And our lives have been chaos ever since." This is from me, as I recall our wild adventures, as Earth's greater gravity and air pressure brought down both my companions, very nearly stripping them of their lives over those first terrible nights. I could do nothing really for Tars Tarkas, I had to leave him in a desperate attempt to save my wife, trusting that his significantly more formidable physique would sustain him. Dejah Thoris's survival came about thanks to the intervention of Cochise, leader of the Chiricahua, and his blood brother Tom Jeffords, who manages the Pony Express riders coming in and out of Tucson.

Now, at long last, we have a chance to return home.

"If, as you surmise," notes our green comrade, "another of Barsoom made the transition to Earth in time past, why did he never return?"

"Simple misadventure," suggests Dejah Thoris. "Remember what almost happened to me?" I'd rather not, thank you, but I could not help but recall a frantic chase through mountains and desert after she'd been taken by a band of rogue French cavalry who'd crossed the Rio Grande from Mexico, only to fall into the hands of equally villainous Apaches. More than once, she'd faced death, and far worse.

"I don't know what will happen, my friend," I tell Tars Tarkas, gesturing toward the mouth of the cave, "but our work here is done. With the arrival of General Howard, there's a decent chance for a lasting peace between the Chiricahua and the settlers. And in truth there's no guarantee that whatever power brought us here will act in reverse. It could be exactly as you say: We walk in here, we walk out back home. Or not. I'm afraid there's but one way to find out for sure." To my own surprise, I have no doubt of what will happen: Whatever mysterious force brought us here will be considerate enough to return us safely to Barsoom.

And yet—and *yet*—something about all this doesn't feel quite right. Which is why my gun-hand refuses to stray too far from the hilt of my Colt.

I sigh at that feeling, mostly to myself. I should know by now, things are never as easy as they appear.

I hear a noise from Tars Tarkas, as my friend rises to his mostimpressive full height and turns partially toward the ridge, his stance one of intense concentration. I follow his lead but see nothing but the mountain. Good as my senses are, I know the Thark's are much keener.

"What do you sense?" asks Dejah Thoris.

"Humans" is his reply. "I believe"—slight pause, a shallow sniff, as he gathers more information from the scents—"there are two groups, one mounted." He doesn't sound happy. "The riders are approaching along the gorge but I suspect the others have been here awhile. The wind has shifted, that's why I'm catching their scents now."

"Ambush," I wonder aloud and from both his and

Dejah's stance in the moonlight, I know we have all jumped to that same conclusion.

Hurrying back to my horse, I draw my Henry repeater; Dejah does the same. From there, it's a quick scramble across the ridge-crest, taking care as we go to make no sound, until we achieve a respectable view of the scene below.

Even as we approach, the night silence is shattered by a volley of gunfire, followed by the shriek of terrified horses as startled riders jerk on the reins or, worse, the mounts themselves are struck. There are outcries as well, some expressions of alarm and rage, intermingled with sharp-spoken commands. The cries are those of Indians, which means the targets are likely a band of Apache. In the Superstitions, that means Chiricahua, which means people loyal to Cochise—which means those in peril below are quite likely known to us, if not outright friends.

Yet all those thoughts mean nothing because of what happens a moment later—as we behold a distinctive flash from among the attackers, followed an instant later by a vicious explosion in the midst of the targets.

"John Carter, did you see—?" cries my beloved.

"Impossible" is my reply.

Then, the sniper unleashes a second projectile, with as fearsome an impact as his first—and with that shot, the reality before us can no longer be ignored, or denied.

"A radium round," says Tars Tarkas. "Someone down there is firing a radium rifle."

"We have to draw their fire," I tell my companions, knowing full well the risk of what I ask.

"First blood to me, then!" Tars Tarkas draws up a longbow of his own design and construction. We all came to Earth as I had come to Barsoom—stripped of clothes and possessions. In the time since, we have all adapted to the world around us, but the tools and weapons of the human

race are simply too small for this Thark. During our time here, he's coped by simply making his own—leaving me to wonder, assuming all goes well and we manage to return home, what people in times to come will make of these artifacts. Knives the size of a man's arm, a curved sword as long as I stand tall, and arrows of similar length.

Quickly, and with practiced efficiency, I check my rifle and the Colt revolvers at my belt. On Barsoom, among my beloved's people, the preference is for bladed weapons. The warriors of Helium have firearms of immense power aboard their flying vessels, but they see little honor in such things. Their preference is to finish a fight hand-to-hand. The Green Martians are not so idealistic; for them, what matters is victory, and the variety of their weapons has to be seen to be believed. All of them, I might add, are lethal.

That said, the Thark gives Dejah Thoris and myself a few heartbeats to begin our descent before he lets fly his first arrow. His aim is flawless, the consequence lethal; amidst the gunfire and the outcries of the combatants, his target goes down without a sound. Within moments, the first is joined by a second. This one, regrettably, is noticed, which in turn prompts immediate outcries of alarm.

Even as these marauders start yelling, a third of their number is dispatched to join his two companions. An instant later, the slope erupts once more with noise as rifles and pistols unleash a barrage in what these marauders hope is the general direction of their new assailant.

These bushwhackers are so intent on Tars Tarkas they don't notice Dejah Thoris and me. As we move closer, I spare a glance farther down the slope, to see how their initial targets are faring. It isn't a comforting vision. The scene below is a mangled mixture of horror and slaughter; the radium rounds have taken a deadly toll of the Apaches.

And now, that weapon is turned on Tars Tarkas.

I hear the distinctive sound of the rifle being fired, followed quickly by the shock of impact.

The noise of weapons, even the radium rifle, is nothing compared to the monstrous, inhuman bellow that erupts from behind me up the slope. I know for a fact it is like nothing ever before heard on this world. I also know from experience how terribly effective it is on men in battle, especially when that single outcry is echoed by a hundred more. It is the war cry of the Green Martians, capable of striking fear into the hearts of even the bravest of Helium's warriors.

Men can resist the impulses of nature when confronted by that sound, but it is supremely difficult. They can choose to stand their ground, and more often than not pay for such arrogance with their lives. Their mounts react on a far more basic level. Somehow, even Earthly animals instinctively know what the roar means and respond accordingly. They scream and rear and kick and tear at their reins, until they can break free from where they're tethered and run for their lives. Any fool who tries to stop them, they simply trample to the ground.

Another arrow strikes, but only a tree trunk this time. In return, the radium rifle disgorges a fresh shot of its own. The rounds it fires are of similar size to the balls carried by the Kentucky rifles of my grandfather's era. The difference is that a rifle ball on Earth is little more than a shaped rock. The damage to its target comes solely from the force of impact, as forged iron punches through flesh and bone. Its radium counterparts are far more lethal; they explode on impact, with a titanic force far beyond any explosive on this world. A radium round does not merely wound. At best, it maims; most often, it simply blasts its target to bits.

I have to admit, this wretch is good. Give him a proper target, that may well be the end of things.

Amidst the clamor, none of them notices Dejah Thoris's first shot as she drops one of the attackers. I am not quite so fortunate. As I strike my target, a profane outcry draws the weapons of those nearest him around to unleash a staggered volley in my direction, forcing me to dive for cover. This is when I realize the men we're facing know their business; they've clearly been tested by service in the late War between North and South.

I return a hearty fire with my Henry rifle and drop another of our foes. A moment later I'm diving for my life as I perceive a distinctive flash I know only too well and hear a scrambling hiss through the air dangerously close beside me as the radium shell rockets past. The projectile strikes home on a nearby boulder and the air around me literally erupts with shock and fury. I find myself swept up by the fearsome shockwave and pitched head over heels, my Henry wrenched from my grasp.

Fortunately, if such a word can be applied to a horrific moment like this, the gunman significantly underestimates the raw power of the weapon he wields. Perhaps he should have paid closer attention to the shells he fired at the Apaches below? Perhaps he doesn't take time to think, he simply reacts—as if he holds an ordinary rifle? Whatever the rationale, the consequences are stunning.

Trees rock wildly from the shockwave and more than a few actually snap, trunks crashing down with terrifying force as the air fills with splinters. Men find themselves staggered where they stand, and not a few of them are actually knocked back off their feet.

I'm used to this, having fought far more than my share of battles on the Red Planet. I hit the ground hard but I still manage to hold fast to my wits. From there, in that moment of confusion where the attackers try to regain their bearings, many of them astonished to find themselves alive and substantially unharmed, I am upon them. I grab a Colt from its holster and start shooting.

This is why I prefer blades. So long as I hold a sword in my hand, I can defend myself. After six shots, my pistol is useless, save as a club.

And that is how I proceed to use it. I reverse my grip on the Colt and strike the wretch closest to me with a backhand across the jaw. I sense another, coming at me from my blind-side. As I spin to face him, I know that I'll be too late to stop him or avoid his bullet—only to see him drop as his legs are scythed out from under him.

The man recovers even as he strikes the ground, twisting to his feet and slashing forward with his knife—but not at me. Rather, at his attacker, who confronts him: Dejah Thoris.

The man lunges; my Princess catches him by the wrist and yanks him forward, once more slashing her legs across his—this time from the front—to pitch him onto his face; at the same time, she lands beside him on her back, twisting in the other direction with such force that her adversary both cries out in surprised pain and releases his hold on the knife.

Dejah Thoris lets forth a powerful kick but the man is strongly made. He withstands the impact and responds with a powerful punch to my beloved's jaw, forcing her to let him go. Worse, as this happens, he grabs hold of the pistol at his waist. Up it comes in his hand, his thumb cocking the hammer as he brings it to bear on my wife.

But at the same moment, she catches hold of his knife and lets it fly with all her strength. It strikes him in the base of the throat and just like that, his life is done.

To tell the tale takes time; to see it happen isn't even a matter of heartbeats. In truth, by the time I realize it is Dejah Thoris who's come to my rescue, the battle before me is done.

The next few minutes are a kind of madness, as we fight our way through to victory. Many is the time I have thought I was born to be a warrior. I love nothing so much as the ultimate test of a man facing seemingly hopeless odds; the triumph that follows such a struggle is unlike anything I have ever known, a sweetness of the soul that comes to a very few men and seems like both a blessing and a curse.

And yet, when the battle is done, and I survey the field, taking stock of the dead, the maimed and the bloody, I cannot help but feel an abiding sense of sorrow. So many lives cut short, so many dreams that will never be realized. True, there are some against whom a stand must be taken—but there are far too many battles where it is the innocents who pay the ultimate price. I have seen it here on Earth, and I have seen it on Barsoom.

I feel this way now because I have found someone who has become more important to me than my sword. Someone for whom my courage is needed not to level some fortress or defeat a villainous adversary but simply to hold her close and exchange a kiss.

I have never truly known loneliness until I met her. And now—I cannot bear for us to be apart. Thank God she feels the same.

Dejah Thoris is my Princess. She is my true love. She has been cast to Earth with me and with my best friend, and I am determined to bring them both safely home.

The grunts of a fierce struggle draw me back to the carnage. I sense more than see movement up ahead that shifts into focus as Dejah Thoris and I both hurry closer to reveal Cochise, chief of the Chiricahua Apaches, in mortal combat with another of our attackers. No guns for these two; they struggle with their bodies, and with knives. The renegade switches hands with surprising speed and lunges forward, Cochise pivoting so the blade cuts only his shirt. In the same movement, he grabs hold of the attacking hand and pivots, pitching his assailant up and over his shoulder, to come crashing down onto the sand-strewn rock with terrible force.

The man is stunned; chances are his back was broken by the impact, but the Chiricahua takes no chances. His knife comes down to bury itself to the hilt in the other's chest, right through the heart.

Around us, the scene is ugly. Bodies are strewn everywhere, most felled by the radium shells, but others in the struggle that followed. Out of the shadows emerge a pair of men. One of them—a comparatively young man, and handsome, with a beard, and only one arm—wears the uniform of a cavalry general. The other man helps the General along, and as the two of them come closer I see that it is none other than Cochise's friend—and mine—Tom Jeffords.

My focus, however, is not on these two but on the man who confronts them—and us: The last of our attackers now stands before us, holding the radium rifle.

The man seems to know his business. He wears a Colt at his waist, holster reversed as is the custom for the Cavalry, to allow for an easier draw of the weapon when on horseback, but he leaves his pistol be. The rifle, he knows, is a far more effective killing machine. At this range, he doesn't need the shell's explosives, impact alone will punch the round right through a living body. If the weapon's magazine is full and the man knows his business, Cochise and Dejah Thoris and I will all be dead before we can even take a step against him. I could certainly do that; prudence demands I treat this man with as much respect, even in the dark.

"You killed my friends," he snarls.

"You had the same intent for us" is my reply. The surrounding bodies are mute proof of that.

"Yeah." He smiles, proud of what he's done. "An' it looks like I win."

"You think," wonders a new voice, from above and behind. "I have to say, I see things somewhat—differently."

The gunman doesn't even try to turn. He knows he's

likely finished, so he simply pulls the trigger. At that same moment, the figure behind him reaches out with lightning speed to grasp the barrel and yank it away, so the radium shell goes spiraling up toward the stratosphere.

Now the man grabs for his pistol, only to discover that it's no longer there. Another hand has snatched it away. Before he can do anything more, a third hand and a fourth reach down from above to grasp him around the shoulders and scoop him up better than ten feet above the ground.

I don't have to look at Cochise or the other two to know that none of them can believe what they're seeing. My wife, however, chuckles with delight.

Cochise murmurs in Apache; now even I can't help a smile.

"This is indeed," I tell him, nodding, "the fabled Ghost of the Superstition Mountains."

Tars Tarkas quirks me a look sideways, his mouth twisting in disdain. We've known each other long enough for him to become used to my sense of humor, but that doesn't mean he always likes it.

"Well," chimes in my wife, "perhaps not quite dead."

Mind you, the man held snugly in his grasp may not be quite so sanguine, dangling as he is in uncomfortably close proximity to those terrifying fangs and the fearsome face they frame. To give him credit, despite whatever fear he may be feeling, he does not utter a sound. Villain he may be, but he faces his captor with no lack of courage.

Cochise does not seem overly impressed by my words.

"I have heard all the stories of these mountains," he notes dryly, "from my own people and the Navajo—as well as the Hopi, the Yaki, the Zuni—but never in the wildest of tales have I been told of a spirit resembling this one."

"The difference, perhaps," I suggest quietly, "between stories and reality."

"Bless my soul." This comes from the General, Oliver Howard, newly appointed by President Grant to bring peace to the southwest. The word on him is that he is a man of honor, a warrior who is also a man of peace. Jeffords trusts him, and that's enough for me—and also, it seems, for Cochise. Presumably, Jeffords has led him out here to meet with Cochise, to try to negotiate a peace treaty for this land.

Dejah Thoris turns to Jeffords with a question: "Are there any other survivors?"

Tom shakes his head. It seems we are the only ones who still live.

"You kill the General," he says, "you kill Cochise, it'd be like firing off a cap inside a pile of dry tinder. This country'd drown in blood, natives, and settlers."

"This is *our* land," the gunman cries with a snarl. "First we get rid of the Apaches, then we start in on you blue-bellies. And we won't stop till our country's free."

"Appomattox settled that," I counter. "Enough blood was shed, by both sides. It was time for the war to end."

"A mistake Lincoln paid for with his life." His reference is to the president's assassination at the hands of John Wilkes Booth. That had been a hard day for me. True, he'd been my enemy, but when I heard the news I truly thought my heart would break. It was in large part why I rode for the Southwest; I wanted a new land, with new hope and opportunity, where a man could start fresh and build something of value, untainted by the mistakes of the past. I suppose I got my wish, only not in Arizona but on Barsoom.

"Four years of carnage wasn't enough?" I wonder.

"You're Carter, aren't you?" challenges the man. "I thought I recognized your face. You fought for the South, Cap'n Carter, how can you say such a thing?" His outcry is almost a primal scream, mingling grief and rage. I've heard it's like before. "But I suppose I shouldn't be surprised, since you fight alongside monsters. You talk about blood; I say Lee's surrender made that sacrifice all for nothing. With these weapons, we can take back all we've lost. We can break the back of the Union."

Tars Tarkas holds his prisoner facing us, which means he cannot see the man's face. However, his touch is surprisingly sensitive, and he can feel the intensity of the man's passion reflected through the warmth of his flesh and the beat of his heart. It is a challenge he cannot help but respond to, by baring his lesser fangs, fearsome in their own right, and letting loose what is for him a gentle growl. For me, it sounds much like a steam engine rumbling past along the railroad.

None of my human companions say a word; I suspect they're still too busy trying to come to terms with Tars Tarkas and by extension with Dejah Thoris and myself. I am a known quantity, a veteran of the war, known to many in this country. All had presumed, because of her red skin, that my wife was of the Indian race. Now, seeing Tars Tarkas, seeing our familiarity with him, things no longer seem so certain. Are we friends, are we allies, or simply a different kind of enemy?

As these thoughts cross my mind, Tars Tarkas hands over the prisoner's radium rifle to me.

"Take a look at this," he suggests dryly.

Automatically, I check the gun—and receive some unpleasant surprises. The weapon is brand-new and in excellent condition. But none of the components are of Barsoomian origin. Though the design is of Barsoom, the rifle itself is of the Earth.

The rifle stock is mounted to an extended barrel, crafting a weapon easily as long as I stand tall; the stock is wood, the gun's body a metal that is more than forged iron. Whoever made this has been tinkering with the elements, to come up with something far stronger than the alloys we are used to.

Barsoom's radium rifles are much the same in basic design. One size is suitable for that planet's human inhabitants, the .other—*very* much larger—is built to fit Tars Tarkas's race. As I hold it, I find myself thinking once more of the cave, and the stories that fill these mountains, combined with the millennial lifespan of Barsoomians.

"This is something new," notes Cochise, who's stepped up for a closer look at the weapon; even in these deep shadows, he can see the differences between this rifle and those in use throughout the Southwest.

"You have no idea," I tell him softly. I think of the countless battles fought in the recent war and imagine the dreadful carnage if the combatants had been armed with these radium rifles. It's but the smallest leap of horror to bring to life their presence here on the frontier. Both sides would suffer, to a degree never before imagined on this world.

"The rounds it fired"—this from the General—"they exploded on impact." He doesn't need to say more; the evidence of its power is spread all around us.

"I'm not sure of the projectiles themselves," I respond, "or of the rifle, but back home, our version of this same weapon has a range of better than three miles."

"A shooter can't see that far," scoffs Jeffords.

"I can," notes Tars Tarkas from above our heads. "And the weapons utilized by John Carter and Dejah Thoris employ telescopic sights. They are deadly to better than a mile."

I can see in his eyes that Cochise's thoughts follow a similar path and also his determination that if we have such a weapon, his people must possess the same. It would be that or annihilation.

I brandish the rifle. "This should not be here."

He quirks an eye in silent question: *If not here, where, then?*

"This weapon may have been constructed here but its origins are in the home of Tars Tarkas and my wife." At that point, Dejah Thoris interrupts, in speech and manner every inch a Princess, daughter of a King, granddaughter of an Emperor, assessing a threat and coming to the only rational response.

"Whoever brought the design here," she states firmly to us all, including the prisoner, but mostly to Tars Tarkas and myself, "whoever constructed this, must be caught and the weapons destroyed. By this action he has forfeited his own right to life itself. If not, this world will suffer unbearable consequences."

I think of the reluctance I felt as we approached the cave and wonder if this is the reason? Somehow, had my mind caught wind of this menace and slowed my pace so that I might confront it? Perhaps it is easy to scoff but I have encountered stranger things in my life.

I look at the prisoner and speak softly: "Tell me about the rifle."

"You seem familiar enough with it already—how is that, by the way?"

"Where'd you get it?"

He fixes his mouth closed.

From behind, Tars Tarkas takes hold of him by the ears with his upper hands and utters a burbling growl that chills even my blood, and I've heard such a horrific noise before. The Jeddak of Thark opens his mouth wide, upper fangs touching the crest of his captive's skull while their great lower counterparts stroke up both sides of the man's face. At the same time, the hands that hold him make certain he can neither move his head nor close his eyes.

I hear gasps from my terrestrial companions. They can't help themselves; one effortless bite and the prisoner will quite literally lose his head.

"Think again," I suggest, "and think *very* carefully. You may not get a chance to reconsider."

"I'm not afraid to die." Bold words, but his tone belies them. He's trying to hold tight to his courage but he's fast approaching his limits.

There is a sweeping movement to my left and the sound of tearing cloth, echoed by a gasp as the tip of Cochise's knife slits open the man's shirt from waist to shoulder.

"Then I will make sure you do so screaming," he says simply. There is no mercy on his face or in his voice. "A little fire to warm both flesh and ground, a little blood to mark the way; I promise you will not have long to wait before the ants come. They will eat you alive and we will leave your bones as warning to those who would threaten the Chiricahua."

The prisoner cries out to the General. "You're an officer, and a Christian," he exclaims desperately. "You can't let this happen!"

"You slaughtered these people without a second thought" is Howard's reply, with a wave of his arm at the fallen braves. "No doubt you'd have done the same to us. I can do nothing, boy; your own actions have condemned you."

This is my great flaw as a leader of men: There are things I will not do, even though my intellect tells me they are necessary. I will kill, when necessary, without a second thought; I will fight to the fullest limit of my being. But I cannot bring myself to torture.

Cochise is made of far sterner stuff. Our captive can see that in his eyes and the stance of his body, as he has no doubt heard of, and even seen, the depredations of the Apache in the years before the recent truce. He knows the Chiricahua is not bluffing.

Tars Tarkas shifts his jaws, just a little, allowing the fangs to make their marks on both the man's cheeks. The trickle of blood is slight but it turns out to be more than enough to make up the man's mind.

He tells us of a trader, a man named Tyson Dane, whom he describes as being more a part of these ancient hills than the Apaches themselves. His presumption is that Dane is some sort of mountain man, a white man, albeit one whose skin has been deeply shaded by a lifetime's exposure to the sun. To him, the man is a paradox: possessing an air of refinement that bespeaks culture and education found in the cities back east, but also as formidable a hunter as the Apaches, moving through these mountains like a phantom.

I say nothing, but simply listen, and build a picture of this new adversary within my head. Our captive has no idea of a natural Barsoomian lifespan; he assumes that Dane's age is comparable to Cochise's. I find myself looking back across the ages. He could have been here near a thousand years. But until the Europeans arrived and began to spread across the continent, he was denied the mobility of horses and access to industrial technology. With the advances of recent generations, the so-called industrial revolution that has reshaped the face of England and of the Northern states, it must have become increasingly easier to adapt Martian designs to this world. Having waited patiently and worked so hard, he is poised to reap the profit of his enterprise.

I look to Dejah Thoris, and see the same thoughts running across her face. Whether this Red Martian first came here by accident, as I did to Barsoom, or whether his exile here was part of a grander plan, he and his weapons must not stay. The fragile peace slowly knitting together North and South, Indians and black, and white, will be ripped apart as first one, then the other, seeks the upper hand. I cannot predict if the bloody wounds that rent my nation and my species will ever fully heal, but if Barsoom's weapons come into play, even the possibility will forever be lost. It will be like so much salt rubbed deep into the wounds. A healing will not, cannot occur; the wound will simply fester and quite likely prove mortal. The dreams of her founders, of men like Jefferson and Adams and Franklin and Washington, all their prodigious hopes, will be forever lost.

How long, I wonder, before radium rifles are followed by Barsoomian fliers? Even a steamer will take weeks to cross the Atlantic. In the air, such a journey would be reduced to mere days. In my mind, I see a squadron—a veritable fleet—of such war craft descending on the great cities of Europe.

My companions are no fools: Cochise is ruler of his people and Howard a general officer. Whatever Howard personally thinks of these weapons, the decision of what to do with them rests, not with him, but with the President. Is that something I dare trust to Ulysses Grant? By the same token, Cochise no doubt thinks that possession of such weapons by the whites will mean the doom of his own people, that their only hope for survival is to possess them for themselves.

There are no options. The genie is out of its bottle, true, but it is still in its infancy. Both power and influence are limited. Dane is waiting for news of the outcome of this first expedition before making his next move. He doesn't know his customers have been stopped. If we can get to him, *he* can be stopped.

And then we'll have to deal with our friends, praying that they'll understand why we steal this path to the future away from them.

"John Carter," Tars Tarkas calls out to me, in the language of the Tharks, "what are you thinking?"

"Just remembering," I tell him, speaking slowly, *sadly*, for the memories are not pleasant, "Gettysburg. It was a battle," I explain, "between two great armies. Tens of thousands fought, and far too many—died. Imagine, my friend, if we'd possessed weapons such as these."

I look up at him and I know there is a great and uncharacteristic sadness in my eyes. "We cannot let that happen." I turn toward the others—Cochise and Tom and the General—my voice turning rough with passion as I continue in English now with a resolute intensity. "I will not let that happen. Whoever this Dane is, I intend to find him. We shall put an end to this."

"And the rifles?" This comes from the General.

The answer, to his surprise, comes from my wife. She faces him with Tars Tarkas at her back, presenting herself with all the majesty and power inherent in this representative of the ruling family of Helium. "General Howard, the weapons and any construction facilities and the plans that created them, must be destroyed. Along with anyone who knows how to recreate them."

"That's a harsh judgment, Madam, and perhaps one that is not yours to make."

"Better a few now than countless innocents later." The passion and power of her words are such that Howard has no choice but to take them at face value. To that end, the presence of Tars Tarkas proves of inestimable value.

"I suspect this Dane person likely keeps his secrets very close to his chest," I note. "Deal with him, we'll very likely deal with the threat."

With a shallow nod of approval, Cochise pulls a blade from his belt and steps toward our prisoner, his intent plain.

The prisoner does not say a word; he no doubt expected this from the start.

"Cochise," I call, "no!" Even as I cry out to him, I realize that both he and Dejah Thoris are far more merciless than I. "That won't be necessary, not with him. He may know how to shoot the rifle but I very much suspect he has no useful knowledge of how to make its key components. Leave him live—for the time being. We can always revisit our decision later."

"You assume this Dane person is truly the one you seek"—again, from the General.

I shrug. "We have to start somewhere."

"I can summon troops."

At these words, Cochise bridles, relaxing only slightly as I shake my head. "For the moment, we can afford neither cavalry nor Apaches; it's best to press on as we are."

"Just the five of us, John?" This, from Jeffords, with a touch of amusement.

"Trust us, Tom Jeffords," says Dejah Thoris, "we can handle things."

The General eyes Tars Tarkas. "Of that, my dear, I have no doubt." He's getting used to the Thark but he's still far from comfortable. I know how he feels—but then, I'd been on Barsoom, surrounded by hundreds of them.

"We will likely have to ride hard," the chief tells us, although his words are directed at Tars Tarkas. "But we have no mount that can carry you."

"Don't worry about me" is the Barsoomian's response. I've seen my friend move through these mountains; chances are he'll arrive first at our destination. "I'll look after our prisoner, as well. He can travel with me. He'll be no trouble," he assures us.

"Try to get more information," I tell him.

"I'm sure we'll have the most delightful conversations," says my friend with a Thark's terrifying smile. "He can tell me all his secrets." The prisoner visibly blanches.

As we prepare to leave, I finally find a private moment for my wife. It turns out she's read my mind. Even as I make my move, I feel her arms wrap themselves around my body, one hand behind my neck to firmly press my lips down to meet hers. It is a kiss that leaves us both breathless.

"Now I know why we are here," she notes as our faces move just a little apart. She does not release me, however, nor I, her. I say nothing, I simply wait for her to finish her thought.

"Whoever this Dane is, he threatens the future of this world. As fate brought you to us—and to me—so now it brings us here to thwart his ambitions."

"I don't know where the future will take us, or how this will end," I say, then turn my gaze toward our two friends and the General. "We have been through so much together. I don't want this to end badly, nor do I wish to do them harm." But I also know I will do whatever I have to, to preserve the future of two worlds, the one where I was born, and the other I have come to love.

"If we face it together, my Prince, the rest"—my beloved pauses a moment, and smiles—"will take care of itself."

Her tone is joking, but mine in response is surprisingly serious. "I swear, Dejah, with all my heart and all my soul, I'll find a way to bring you safely home."

The look in her eyes tells me she accepts my pledge at full value but her words take us in a different direction entirely. "I do not doubt that for an instant, John Carter. I will always have faith in you, as my champion and my love. And because of that faith, know that wherever we are, so long as we are together, that will be our home. I miss my father and my mother and my grandfather and my people—but what truly matters in the end is that we are together."

She turns her face toward Tars Tarkas.

"Mind you, while we may be content, we'll have to find a way back for Tars Tarkas. Sola must miss him terribly." Her reference is to the Thark's daughter, who dwells in Dejah Thoris's household.

Then, at the last, my warrior wife turns her eyes back to

me. "Now, beloved," she says with a tone that sets my blood aflame, "let us stop this war and teach this Dane wretch the error of his ways."

And with that, the Princess of Mars, the cavalry captain, the emerald-skinned lord of the Tharks, the one-armed general, the chief of the Chiricahua Apache, and his best friend charge forth—to save this world that was once my home from a ghost of ancient Barsoom.

Edgar Rice Burroughs possessed a powerfully fecund imagination. When he first dreamed up Barsoom, a dying world full of airships, abandoned cities, and many-limbed foes, he was just getting started. The later Barsoom novel *The Master Mind of Mars* deals with the mad scientist Ras Thavas, who transfers brains into genetically engineered bodies. Burroughs also wrote books that weren't part of the main Barsoom sequence, such as *The Moon Maid*, in which a crew of Earthmen led by a man named Julian travel to the moon and do battle with Va-gas (horselike creatures who can wield weapons with their forelimbs and who have human faces) and Kalkars (evil humanoids). In its sequel *The Moon Men*, the leader of the Kalkars, Orthis, launches an invasion of earth. (The series was initially conceived as an attack on Soviet Communism, but Burroughs was forced to change the villains from Russians to Moon Men at the insistence of his publishers.) Burroughs also wrote a series about Pellucidar, the land inside the Earth. In these stories, the Earth is hollow and contains a second sun at its center, so that the inside surface experiences eternal daylight. The sole exception is The Land of Awful Shadow, a region where the light of the inner sun is blotted out by a single geostationary moon. Burroughs created all these strange lands and peoples, and many more besides. Our next tale pays tribute to the majestic sweep of Burroughs's imagination.

THE JASOOM PROJECT

BY S. M. STIRLING

PART I
THE WARLORD

elium awoke. The swift dawn of Mars was over, and all across the city homes were lowering themselves from their nighttime height to street level. The blaze of radium lights faded from palace and tower, giving way to the sparkle of sunlight from jewel and carved stone, the tossing of foliage blossom in gardens and parks. The smooth quiet rush of the ground-fliers through the air fifty or sixty feet above the broad moss-paved thoroughfares sent a subdued whirring sound through the thin, cool air.

Crowds thronged the streets, emerging from the underground stations of the pneumatic transport system; riders on thoat-back slid along with the smooth rippling gait of their eight-legged mounts; fliers swarmed through the skies over all, from small one-man types through gorgeously appointed yachts to the huge craft of commerce and war that carried thousands from city to city throughout the planet.

Most of the crowds were the native Red Men and Women of Helium, a handsome folk with skins of a burnished reddish-brown and hair of raven black. But this was the most cosmopolitan of Barsoom's cities, and there were towering four-armed Green warriors from the allied horde of the Tharks turning their impassive tusked faces about, men yellow-skinned and vastly bearded from the domed cities of the Arctic wastes, black sharp-featured First Born, even a scattering of no-longer-Holy Therns with their pale skins and blond wigs.

And in a high garden on a flange of the immense scarlet five-thousand-foot tower that dominated the city of Greater Helium two men stood and watched the unique panorama. The tower was more singular in that its golden twin in Lesser Helium was still not fully rebuilt after the terrible storm that had toppled it many years ago; from here you could see men and machines swarming about it, doll-tiny in the distance southward where the sister-city lay.

They leaned on a balustrade of carved stone and looked out past the city to the green strips of farmland that bordered the two great canals that met here. John Carter's face was grim.

"I think that the politicians on Earth . . . Jasoom . . . have grown even more feebleminded, cowardly, and corrupt than they were when I lived there more than a century and a half ago. Which is no mean feat! To abandon the attempt to establish travel between our worlds after only one failure. And that due to sabotage, not any fault in the ship!"

Prince Jalvar grinned at him. "You mean that there, at least, Jasoom is more advanced than Barsoom, great-grandsire?" he said. "In the production of great swordsmen like yourself, and poor statesmen like the ones you are damning so harshly?"

"And about equal in the production of young scamps like you," the warlord of Mars said, smiling back.

"I wonder who I derive this quality of scampishness from?" the prince said. "Which of my distinguished ancestors provided it?"

John Carter laughed aloud. "Anyone would know your line of descent through Llana," he said. "Even if it were not visible in your face. Though if you are handsome, that is the legacy of the incomparable Dejah Thoris and your own mother."

In truth they were both men who might attract a second glance, even among the comely folk of Helium. The warlord looked to be a man in the prime of his strength, with a regular square-jawed face and a build like a hunting cat, long in the limbs, broad-shouldered, and narrow in the waist. His eyes were an odd gray color and his skin a suntanned white as pale as a Thern's, but his close-cropped hair was as raven-black as any of the Red race who dominated Barsoom.

Prince Jalvar Pan was the other man's height almost to an inch and of similar build, but his hair was lighter, a dark-brown color, and his skin of a similar hue, with only a trace of burnished red-brown that gave it a hue almost like bronze. His mother was John Carter's granddaughter Llana of Gathol, but his father was Pan Dan Chee, a warrior of the Orovars—the fair-haired, white-skinned race that had ruled Barsoom when it was young and oceans rolled where only ochre moss and savage Green Men roamed now, and who had been thought extinct until the last lost colony of them in the dead city of Horz had been discovered.

Both wore the harness of warriors, supple tooled-leather straps that carried shortsword, longsword, dagger, and pistol, and beside those, the metal of their rank—gold and silver and platinum carved and inlaid with the strange, lustrous jewels of Barsoom in the insignia of Helium and Gathol and the sigils of their princely houses.

"Still," John Carter said, turning again to watch the

pageant of Helium's awakening. "I would have enjoyed seeing men from Earth visit."

Jalvar nodded eagerly. All Barsoom—or at least the civilized parts—had been agog with the news that the Jasoomians, after forty years of two-way communication, had at last launched their ship of space. John Carter had been instrumental in establishing that communication, and in encouraging the launching of the first unsuccessful Martian ship.

But he felt its loss very keenly, Jalvar knew. *John Carter would; he has ever hated to send men into peril he did not share.*

"And now the loss of the *Barsoom* on its maiden voyage toward us," the warlord said. "Some malign curse seems to operate to keep the worlds apart."

"But that need not be, my great-grandsire!" Jalvar said eagerly.

"Ah," John Carter replied. "I think I see what you have in mind, my reckless descendant."

"You would have done the same at . . . well, you know what I mean."

The warlord shook his head ruefully. "I was never your age. I have always been as I am now—on Earth, they would say a man of thirty years. I remember no youth, no childhood, no origin. Only the life of a fighting man. Virginia I called my home, and I fought for it in the War of Secession, but I remember it when it was only a wilderness, and I set foot on it from the little ship *Susan Constant* with the first Englishmen to settle there. I remember fighting England's battles; the Armada, at Flodden Field . . . and more, back further, further. It fades into dreams. . . ."

"But age has not made you cautious," Jalvar said. "Nor would you be happy if your descendants were."

John Carter laughed and clapped a hand on the other man's shoulder.

"No. So yes, I will speak with the Jeddak. Even with

the second and third atmosphere plants under construction, funds can be found in these times of peace and prosperity. And I suppose you will have the support of your mother's father?"

Jalvar signed assent. "Gathol is rich, but it does not have the scientific resources of Helium, or the shipyards," he said.

"Five brave men died in our last attempt," John Carter said grimly. "Do you think you can do better?"

"With the advances the Jasoomians made in *their* ship, yes. Your son Prince Carthoris thinks so as well."

The Warlord's agreement held a pardonable pride; Carthoris was a notable inventor in the aeronautical field, developer of the directional compass and several other major improvements in the long-static technology of flight. Some said he was the greatest designer of fliers since the discovery of the gravity-canceling Eighth Ray, nearly a thousand years ago.

"And," Jalvar said, "I have thought of one thing that we did *not* consider in our last attempt."

That was tactful; it meant something that John Carter and the savants of Helium had not taken into account.

"You have demonstrated many times the marvelous strength your Jasoomian origins give you," Jalvar went on.

"If I had not, I'd have died on the point of a Thark lance about five minutes after I arrived here," John Carter said reminiscently.

I hope I don't dwell on the past as much when I'm five hundred years old, Jalvar thought.

Of course, though his natural span would be a thousand or so, he was unlikely to reach it. Death by natural causes was not all that common on Barsoom even today.

"But the reverse is also true," he said aloud. "On Jasoom, we Barsoomians will have to contend with a gravity three times that to which our muscles are accustomed. Ordinary men would be cripples; I doubt a Green Man like my friend Tars Sojat could even rise to his feet."

"All fourteen feet of him," the warlord said. "That is a serious problem. Unless you intend your visit to Jasoom to be spent in a hospital bed, and to leave Tars Sojat at home . . . which, if I know the grandson of Tars Tarkas, would be a foolhardy thing to do."

Jalvar shuddered. Being a paralytic cripple was not what he had in mind when the phrase *great adventure* crossed before his inward eye. And he could not ask Tars Sojat to remain behind; that was unthinkable.

John Carter frowned. "It is a fortunate coincidence that you mention this now, my descendant. But there have been many such in my life. . . . News has recently come to the Jeddak and myself of a plot against me and the royal house of Helium; a strange plot, and one that has a bearing on your plans. Like many such, it begins in Zodanga. . . ."

He explained, and Jalvar's eyes lit. "I had thought of Ras Thavas, but . . . do you really think he would lend himself to such treachery and treason?"

"Perhaps not treason," John Carter said. "But there is evidence that he is indeed creating hormads again, artificial men."

"Monsters, hideous and deformed." Jalvar shuddered. "Ulysses Paxton, your compatriot, had his brain transplanted to the body of one such. That makes him a braver man than I! I had thought Ras Thavas a reformed man, or at least a chastened one."

"We are not certain if he is truly involved; or if he is, whether he is a free agent or a captive. But it is of the first importance if he is. For we have information that the hormads he can now create are *not* monsters. They have the full semblance of humanity. Indeed, they can be made to resemble any individual as closely as a twin."

"Ah!" the prince of Gathol said. "But not *being* human,

perhaps Ras Thavas feels he can return to his old brain-transplanting tricks without breaking his oath to kidnap no more subjects for such experimentation."

"Yes, he was not called the Master Mind of Mars without reason. But the hormads are still of monstrous *strength*."

Jalvar laughed aloud. "Strength enough to survive under Jasoom's greater gravity!"

"Yes. And strength enough to be matchless warriors, able to carve their way through far superior numbers. You see why Helium cannot let such wizardry fall into the hands of enemies of the peace of Barsoom."

"And if we find Ras Thavas and free him . . . then this work of his genius will be the missing piece needed to make our expedition to Jasoom a success."

"In times past I would have investigated this myself, but alas the days when John Carter could disguise himself as the wandering panthan Dotar Sojat with a little dye for his skin are long past."

Jalvar nodded; John Carter's adventures in that role were legendary . . . which meant that any enemy would be on guard for precisely such a mercenary.

"Whereas I am little known in Helium and its dependencies; Gathol is far, and traffic thence still light," Jalvar said. "And if I disguise my appearance, few would think to link the Prince of Gathol to a soldier of fortune."

"Exactly. Will you accept this mission?

"Need you ask?" Jalvar said. "I would accept it gladly as my duty to you; and now I have a doubled reason."

"I knew the answer, but I *did* need to ask; this is not something that can be ordered."

"And the ship itself, the *Jasoom*?" Jalvar said. "I do not ask that any great effort be made until I have solved this problem, only that preliminary design and research is begun."

"It shall be," John Carter said, taking the younger man's

hand and placing the other on his shoulder. "Kaor, Jalvar Pan, and fortune go with you."

"Kaor, Warlord!"

The younger man saluted and leapt to the deck of the little one-man flier that drifted at chest-height near a mooring stanchion of wrought bronze and crystal. The propeller whirred into life, and a moment later he was lost in the thronging air traffic over Helium.

"And how I wish I was going in your place," the warlord murmured.

PART II
A TAVERN IN ZODANGA

Jalvar Pan did not like Zodanga. Few who hadn't been born there did. The city had never really recovered from its long-ago sack by the Green allies of the warlord, and its history since as a satellite of Helium had not been a happy one. At the sixth zode—he noted that it would be one o'clock in the afternoon in the odd twelve-based Jasoomian system, to which he must accustom himself—the street was still half-deserted. Only an occasional ground-flier went by overhead, and much of such traffic as there was went by on foot or thoat-back, or in vehicles pulled by zitidars.

Every fourth or fifth building was still scorched rubble thinly overgrown with scarlet or ochre weeds, and those that had been repaired often had a sleazy, run-down look to them, modern patches over the carvings of antiquity, with gaps where metal and ornament had been wrenched away. The mossy sward of the roadway was patchy and unkempt.

Jalvar had disguised himself; black hair-dye and a minor treatment for his half-Orovar skin rendered him indistinguishable from most, and he wore the plain harness of a panthan, a wandering mercenary.

Unfortunately, there was no way to disguise the fact that Tars Sojat was fourteen feet tall, green, tusked, and four-armed. Green men were not popular anywhere on Barsoom except among their own hordes, but here they were viciously hated still; Jalvar could tell that from the glances he saw, and the hands fingering sword-hilts and pistol-butts. Before the sack, Zodanga had made a policy of destroying the hidden incubators that held the eggs of the Green hordes in an attempt to wipe out the nomads altogether.

Neither party had forgotten.

"And I was hoping that my height would help disguise me," Tars Sojat said mordantly.

Jalvar suppressed a chuckle; his friend *was* short . . . for a Thark. He was still more than twice the height of an ordinary man, of course.

Tars Sojat met the eyes of one passerby until the man looked away and strode on, scowling; probably that was partly for fear of what the Heliumitic garrison would probably do, partly for fear of what the local Jed's men might do, and more particularly of what *Sojat* would most certainly do if annoyed. The Green Man had several perfectly legitimate dried severed hands of former enemies hanging from his leathers, in the fashion of his folk. Jalvar kept his eyes on the numbers, and guided them into a particular eating-house.

The sign over the circular door read: HOME OF THE FIGHTING POTATO.

Like most of the city outside the palace district, the eating-house had seen better days; there was a perceptible odor of frying food as they entered, which was appetizing enough in itself but should never have escaped the cooking machinery. They seated themselves, Sojat on the floor with his lower set of elbows on the table.

Jalvar pressed the buttons set into the polished but battered and nicked skeel table. Nothing happened. Jalvar pressed again, harder. A snort of contemptuous laughter came from one of the nearby tables, and the young prince looked over.

"It's been a while since the automatic systems worked in The Fighting Potato," the man there said; he was scar-faced and there seemed to be a disquieting grin lurking somewhere under his impassive face. "Not from Zodanga, are you, friend?"

In fact, that blow across the cheek should have taken his eye. But he has two, Jalvar noted with a thrill. *Perhaps we are near to what we seek.*

"No," Jalvar said aloud. "I and my companion are pan-thans, seeking an employer for our swords; I am named Gor Kova, and I am from Manator."

"Manator!" the man said; the city was notorious for iso-lationism and a chess fetish. "I cannot recall ever seeing a man from Manator here."

Jalvar shrugged. "Many of us have to seek our fortunes, since the accursed Heliumites attacked the city and set the usurper from Manatos on the throne, may their first ances-tors spurn them. Their heel lies heavy on us yet."

The man's eyes slitted, and he smiled with an unpleas-ant expression.

"You are not alone in feeling so about the men of Helium and their precious warlord," he said.

Then his gaze shifted to Sojat. "We don't see many Green Men here either," he added.

Tars Sojat shrugged elaborately in the manner of his race, four palms turned upward.

"I am of the Horde of Torquas," he said. "Or I was. Tars Sojat is my name. Now I wander, and fight."

The Zodangan grunted; that remote dead city had given its name, like many others, to a tribal confederation of Green Men who used it as headquarters in their nomadic wanderings. The Horde of Torquas had *not* been one of the alliance that supported the warlord's sack of Zodanga, either; that was why the two friends had selected it as Sojat's putative nation.

"Kaor, Gor Kova, Tars Sojat," the man said. "I am Dur Sivas. Also a . . . panthan."

Torquas had the added advantage of being very, very far away. Green panthans were rare but not unknown; every now and then some warrior would break one of the innumerable taboos with which the hordes were bound, and less commonly would escape immediate death. For that matter, *panthan* was a profession anyone whose past didn't bear close scrutiny could claim.

Assassins often did, for instance. Or rebels.

"How does one get food here, then?" Jalvar asked. "If the system no longer works."

"You shout," the stranger said succinctly, and did.

A woman who might have been comely if her face and one arm had not been disfigured by terrible burn scars came out from the rear of the establishment. At the sight of Tars Sojat she gave a little shriek and began to back away, but Dur Sivas growled an order and she left to return with a heavy platter.

"Eat, my friends," the Zodangan said, and tossed a coin down on the table; the woman snatched it up and fled. "Let me greet fellow-panthans by treating them to a meal. Do not mind her; she has been strange in the head since the Sack."

"Thank you," Jalvar said. "Our swords are sharp, but our purses are light, just now."

The food was a little odd; round slabs of grilled ground thoat meat between pieces of bread, mixed with strong-tasting herbs, and with a mound of deep-fried usa slices on the side. Jalvar looked at it dubiously; the usa, the starchy root that was the staple of Barsoomian military rations, was rarely served elsewhere except in the homes of the poor.

It was hot and surprisingly good prepared thus, especially with salt and a dab of the spicy red sauce that accompanied it.

"That is a *Paxton*," Dur Sivas said. "A Jasoomian dish."

"Jasoomian!" Jalvar said, startled.

Would a panthan from Manator know that Ulysses Paxton was also Vad Varo and came from Jasoom before he became assistant to Ras Thavas and then a prince of Duhor?

"Yes. Another of that cursed pasty Thern-colored breed has set himself up over good Red Barsoomians, in the city of Duhor. But I will grant him that these *Paxtons* are a worthwhile innovation."

They were; Jalvar ate two, and Sojat put away a dozen. Green men ate hugely when they could, for hunger was a common companion on their treks across the dead sea bottoms in search of pasture for their thoats and zitidars. When they were at ease over their wine the Zodangan leaned back.

"You are in need of employment?" he said. "And by that, I do not mean sitting in a barracks and polishing your gear."

Jalvar scowled; Sojat let a hand drop to the hilt of one of his array of weapons.

"We are panthans," Jalvar said coldly. "If we were afraid of a little risk, we would have found another way to earn our livings. And few jeds or Jeddaks hire panthans for garrison work; they use their own subjects for that. We follow the scent of war."

"Good," the Zodangan said. "Then let us go—"

A woman screamed from among the kitchens, more in alarm and anger than pain, and then there was a man's bellow of agony. A warrior wearing the metal of the Zodangan city watch stumbled through the open doorway the woman had used, his hands pressed to his face and boiling oil and blood leaking out between them. Dur Sivas's longsword sprang into his hand; he leapt forward with astonishing agility and thrust in a single flickering movement that drove the slender point under one arm and deep into the watchman's body. The corpse collapsed backward into the passageway still twitching and jerking; the lights went dark, and there was a confused flicker of steel.

"Surrender in the name of the Jed!" a man shouted. "We have this place surrounded!"

Jalvar's longsword was in his hand as well. He leapt ahead and crossed blades with the next man forward. Fighting reflex moved his blade as it slithered and crashed against the Zodangan warrior's. Only flickers of light came from behind the front door, barely enough to gleam on the razor-honed blades and darting points; it was like fencing in a closet, with only instinct to guide a yard of swift death.

This is a brave man, Jalvar thought regretfully; he was also upholding lawful authority. *But no more than middling with the blade. And it is important the conspirators believe me.*

His point ripped into the other's sword arm; blood spurted blackly. The blade fell from his hand, but his other groped for his shortsword. Jalvar lunged and ran him through the shoulder, the narrow blade of his longsword bending as the unbreakable point grated on bone. The Zodangan fell back with a cry of rage, and there was a scrimmage as other hands sought to haul him out of the way and crowd forward.

"Follow me!" Sivas barked, adding to the confusion with a murderous thrust, as quick as a striking banth. "Those are the Watch, Zodangan calots who serve the Heliumites for scraps."

Jalvar darted a look aside as he and Dur Sivas backed swiftly, shoulder to shoulder. Tars Sojat was fighting in the outer doorway; it was broader than the narrow door to the kitchens, but then again there was a great deal more of him to fill it—he had had to stoop a little to enter.

Just now he beat the blade out of a Watchman's hand with a smashing chop that tore it free by main force, grabbed him by a strap of his harness with his upper left hand, hoisted him high, punched him economically in groin and face with the left and right lower fists, and threw the man into the faces of his comrades with a bellow of laughter that bared the long fighting tusks in his lower jaw.

"Tars Sojat! Come!" Jalvar shouted, and the Thark backed three long strides, turned and ran.

Dur Sivas dashed down a corridor with the two comrades at his back; he grabbed a lever and threw it. Behind them a heavy door slammed home. Seconds later they could hear the pounding of sword-hilts on metal; then the bark of a pistol, and screaming curses as an officer rebuked the luckless and reckless man who'd fired a bullet in those confined quarters.

"Aluminum-steel from a wrecked battleship we found," Sivas said, with a snicker in his tone; it was too dark to see more than a gleam of teeth. "We who are loyal to the true Zodanga, the Zodanga that was, knew we might have to abandon this place swiftly with the Watch on our heels. They will not break through quickly; that slab is stronger than the stone of the wall. Come!"

It was very dark, but experienced warriors were prepared for such things. At the end of the passageway Sivas threw up his hand and peered outward through an eyehole.

"The calots are all around us. Doubtless they are on the roof as well—a pity, there were two good scout fliers there. Well, to have forethought is to be forearmed."

"We should move if you know somewhere to go," Jalvar said. "They can bring up a powered cutter and break through the door. Through the wall, if necessary. Or explosives. And I presume you have just hired us."

"Yes, we can use men like you! And the calots will curse the intellects of their first ancestors if they try to blow their way through. Quiet now. It will be *unfortunate* if I do this in the wrong order and it has been some time since I practiced. Yes, here it is—"

He pressed a carving in the wall in a particular rhythm. The stone was old, but something went *click* behind it. Noiselessly a section of the worn stone floor drew back, revealing a ladder leading downward. A waft of noisome dank air came upward.

"This leads to the sewers, and there are connections to the pits beneath the palace that the puppet Jed's calots think were stopped. Quickly, quickly!"

They sheathed their swords and scrambled downward. The tunnel beneath had a dark trickle down its center; there were radium maintenance lights, but it had been a very long time since anyone maintained them. Only one in four or five was still lit, shining dimly through dust and dirt. The ceiling was high enough that Jalvar could have walked upright, but he stooped anyway. Sojat bent forward and loped along on his legs and the long middle set of limbs, his long limber neck letting him see easily forward and the high tubular ears on the top of his head cocked forward.

"Quickly!" Sivas said again, and he picked up the pace into a slow run, one hand stretched out to touch the wall.

Then as they came to a T-shaped junction: "Right here."

They turned, and then the earth shook. Jalvar lurched forward with a stifled yell, caching his shoulder a painful thump against a metal bracket in the stone wall. Sound roared past, so loud he felt it as a thudding in his chest rather than a sound. Dust was all around them, smoking out of the junctions in the ancient stone, chokingly thick. Sojat had braced himself against the tunnel walls with all six of his limbs. Jalvar picked himself up and shook his head, wiping blood away from his nose and mouth with the back of his hand.

Sivas switched on a personal light; it underlit his face in a way that made it even more sinister than the blood, scars, and evil smile would have done otherwise.

"This is safe now," he said, waving the hand-light. "Come! We need not run, but should not waste time either. The Watch-calots will be out in force."

"What happened?"

"That battleship we found had full racks. That was a two-thousand pound flier bomb, hooked to a timing device. I activated it as we fled. The Heliumites manufacture good explosives; it was still as potent as the day the casing was filled."

Jalvar flushed and clapped his hand to his sword-hilt. A two-thousand-pounder would have obliterated half the block.

"What of the woman?" he growled.

Sivas turned and stared at him. "My daughter was a Zodangan patriot too. And had much to avenge. Come, there is a safe passage to a flier landing stage not far from here. You two are the last recruits we need."

PART III
THE TONOOLIAN
MARSHES

"**A**lready I feel several varieties of mold and fungus growing upon me," Tars Sojat said, looking down past the rail of the *Air Princess*.

The Tonoolian Marshes stretched beneath them, livid green only slightly tinted with ochre. Jalvar pitched his voice to be inaudible beyond his friend's ears, which was easy enough here at the stern of the flier with the whirr of the propellers beneath them:

"The question is, does Ras Thavas lair here, and has he gone back to his old tricks?"

"Does the calot not return to its regurgitations?" Tars Sojat said. "More to the point, *who are those men riding malagors toward us?*"

Green Men had better eyesight—as one might expect, given the size and placement of their eyes. He pointed over the stern rail. Jalvar swore and swung up his optic.

"Sivas!" he shouted over his shoulder, pitching his voice to cut through the thrum of cloven air. "Malagors to the rear!"

The *Air Princess* was a small vessel only about a hundred sofads long, ex-military of some sort, perhaps a light transport or patroler, and Jalvar thought it had been Heliumitic once. The thirty men aboard were far more crew than needed to fly it, and left everyone a little crowded. Heads turned, and curses raged as the giant malagor birds and their riders came into view. They were high in the west, diving out of the sun on the reverse of the flier's eastward course;

there was little chance of dodging them, the more so as the *Air Princess* was old and could make only about half the speed of modern craft.

"I see them," the Zodangan called. "Battle stations!"

Men ran to the guns; the ship had bow and stern chasers in open mounts with shields, and four lighter rapid-fire pieces with a pair to each side. All of the gun crews were Sivas's Zodangans, not the score of panthans who made up the rest of the ship's complement, or cargo. Jalvar felt useless, but underneath it was relief that he need not kill men doing their duty in the air patrols the warlord had established in this lawless region.

Others of the crew were handing out rifles, but the chance of hitting a man riding a malagor, or the giant bird itself, were very low. Tars Sojat felt no such compunctions, or limitations.

"What use is this toy?" he said throwing the weapon aside—and over the rail—in disgust. "You Red slugs can't shoot, and even if you could, this piece of zitidar excrement would be a waste of skill. Get me a real rifle!"

One of the Zodangans looked questioningly at Sivas, and the commander tossed his head impatiently as he worked the helm and controls. The flier came about and accelerated as the man dashed down a companionway into the shallow hull of the flier.

Just then the bow-chaser fired with a sharp *crack* and a flash of light. The tube of the cannon recoiled with a smooth yielding stroke against the hydraulic compensators, and the breech opened with a clang. Far off amid the approaching riding-birds a tiny flick of white light and puff of smoke showed where the radium contents of the shell exploded, driving fragments of aluminum steel into the air in a sphere about it.

Useless, Jalvar thought. *You could hit a* flier *at that range, perhaps, but Malagors? Only by accident.*

Another clang as the loaders rammed a shell home and secured the breech. The gunner worked the screws with his hands while he peered through the sights, and the weapon swung smoothly; then there was a *crack* as he pushed the firing contact. A few seconds later the bows of the *Air Princess* rose as Sivas worked the controls, shifting her buoyancy and sloping her course upward. The lighter flanking guns were firing, a rapid *pom-pom-pom* sound, and one malagor and its rider plummeted toward the ground in several pieces.

The rest were swinging wide, preparing to come alongside. The flier's crew were firing their rifles now, to as little effect as Jalvar had expected; he clipped his to a ring in the rail and drew his longsword instead.

Then the crewman came back up the stairway from the interior, carrying a rifle—but one such as the Green Men used, twelve feet long and fitted with a complex wireless sight, with a drum containing a hundred rounds of explosive bullets.

The red iris of Sojat's eyes glinted. "A Thark rifle," he said. "Where did you get it?"

"Dead Thark," the Zodangan grunted.

"They are dirty ulsios and lick the feet of Helium," Sojat said, checking the action. "But they make good weapons."

He waited a moment with the long rifle in his upper pair of hands, showing the bases of his tusks in a smile as the crew of the *Air Princess* gradually ceased their futile efforts. Then he threw it to his shoulder and began firing, a steady metronomic *crack . . . crack . . . crack* as the long slender barrel made its minute adjustments.

Not every round struck; the deck of the flier was moving, after all, and Tars Sojat was using an unfamiliar weapon that had probably lain untouched for years or decades. But every second or third shot did find its mark; the Green hordes had been known to bring down battleships that unwisely strayed into rifle range. The long, cruelly beaked heads of the malagors began to explode as the bullets struck and the sun reached the radium bursting charges of the projectiles. One after another fluttered helplessly down toward the surface of the marsh . . . and the hungry mouths that waited below it.

"Brave men," Jalvar said, as the last of them burst through the wall of bullets and swept down on the flier's deck.

"Death to the Heliumites!" a Zodangan snarled; in fact the men were local auxiliaries, but he wasn't inclined to fine distinctions.

There was a *boom* as a malagor braked itself by slapping its huge wings forward against the air. Jalvar dodged beneath the strike of the hooked beak and slashed, feeling muscle and bone part beneath his keen blade; the bird was too big and too tenacious of life to risk a thrust. The acrid scent of blood filled the air as its head fell to one side, three-quarters cut through. For a moment its thrashing was nearly as dangerous as the living thing had been, and then it toppled over the side to fall down through the air like a whirling leaf.

The rider freed his harness from the saddle snaps and jumped free at the last moment. Two panthans sprang toward him, but Jalvar shouted them back: "He is mine!"

A smile lit the face of the rider. "You are an honorable man," he said, panting. "It will be a pity to kill you."

With the last word he launched himself behind his point in a running thrust. Jalvar beat it aside and cut at his leg as he passed. That clashed on a parry, and then they were face-to-face, blades weaving a net of steel between them. It ended in seconds, as such affairs usually did. The patroller's foot slipped on the malagor blood that coated the worn skeel planks of the deck, and he was off balance for an instant.

Jalvar's blade snapped out and ripped into his forearm. The other man's blade clanged to the deck.

"Surrender!" Jalvar said, point to throat. "And your life will be spared."

"Never!" the man said. "You bandits will all die, and soon!"

He turned on the last word and dove over the rail. Jalvar winced, but one of the Zodangans laughed and clapped him on the shoulder. Sivas called from the controls: "Good sword! And your Green friend is a valuable man to have in a fight as well. You are worth your pay and loyal to your oaths, panthans!"

The *Air Princess* curved downward under his hands, toward a low ridge of dark rock that rose out of the marshes. The hum of the propellers sank to a low throbbing moan as the ship slowed and sank almost to the green-scummed surface of the swamp, the tips of its rudders making little wakes in the thick liquid and letting off a noxious smell of decaying vegetation. The smell and the thick wetness of the air were strange and disagreeable.

The cliff loomed closer, closer . . .

And then a section of it vanished. Jalvar blinked; one instant it was pitted, weathered rock much like that to either side—

Wait, the Gatholite prince thought. *It is* identical *to the rock to the right there. A false image. They indeed have some capable scientist laboring for them!*

Now there was a large cave. The flier eased its way inside, and there was a moment of darkness as the shield blinked back into existence behind them. Then radium lights shone, sparkling on jewel-like flecks in the rock. Within there was a huge arched ceiling of natural rock, and a rank-smelling lake beneath it; to either side the hand of man showed, in great docks and basins that had probably stood ready since this was the last shore of one of Barsoom's dying seas. Only a few of them were occupied, by a curious collection of fliers.

Apart from a few one-man scouts, the fliers all looked to be old—well maintained, but nothing that had come out of the shipyards since Llana of Gathol was young.

Still, this is a dangerous little fleet, he thought. *Enough to carry several thousand men; enough for a damaging raid.*

Ruthless men could do appalling harm with even a few cruisers, if they did not care where their bombs landed. The Zodangan conspirators had shown that in their own city. How much more heedless would they be among their enemies?

Sivas came down to stand beside him and Tars Sojat in the bows. "Soon you will see all the secrets of the cause in which you have enlisted," he said.

"Is that wise?" Jalvar said; a panthan would ask.

"Very," Sivas said.

His hands touched the shoulders of the two friends. There was a slight sting. Blackness fell.

Jalvar woke and turned his head; it was the only part of his body not strapped down to the cold surface of a marble slab. His eyes tracked across an arched ceiling carved from rock, past enigmatic machines and devices and shelves loaded with instruments and bottles of chemicals that gave the air a sharp metallic scent that crinkled his nostrils.

He found himself looking at his own body on a wheeled metal gurney only an arm's-length away. The top of his head was covered in bandages, and a monster bent over it.

Then the monster turned its head, and as real wakefulness returned, Jalvar saw that it was only a man; a young-looking man, as such things went on Barsoom, with a complex apparatus of lenses worn over his eyes that made his skull seem grotesquely large for a moment. Beneath it was a strikingly handsome face, and below that was a Red Man's body, in superb condition but a little gaunt.

"Ras Thavas!" Jalvar blurted; he had seen the eccentric scientist more than once, before he dropped out of common knowledge again.

The Master Mind of Mars was at his side in an instant, a hand over his mouth.

"You do not know me, Prince of Gathol!" Ras Thavas hissed, looking over his shoulder. "For your life you do not know me, before these madmen!" Then, louder: "This one is ready! Remove the old body for storage!"

Slaves came and wheeled Jalvar's body—*my body!* Jalvar thought with horror—away.

Sivas came into view, standing at the base of the table. Jalvar did not recognize him at first; the facial scar was missing, and the man's skin was smooth and unmarked. Barsoomians did not show age until they reached nearly the end of their thousand-year span, but they did accumulate damage. A warrior could become more scar than skin, in time.

Something had removed Sivas's scars. Jalvar looked down frantically; by craning his neck he could see his left hand. The fingers moved when he commanded them, everything seemed normal . . . except that the little divot that a shortsword had taken out of his second fingertip was gone. Sheer willpower forced back a scream, and Sivas nodded respectfully.

"Do not worry, Gor Kova," he said. "Already you show less fear than most who are surprised so."

It took an instant for Jalvar to remember his own alias; fortunately the stare of horror at his hand covered the lapse.

"Do not *worry*?" he said, with a rage that was entirely believable because it was quite genuine.

"Nothing has been done to you that has not been done to me also," he said. "To me and my men."

"You *chose* this! I did not!"

Sivas laughed. "Let us see if you will curse me when you discover what has been done," he said. "You are a warrior, and you will find your new body marvelously suited to your trade. And if you do not wish to keep it . . . well, when this enterprise of ours is over, you may have the old one back. And rich rewards besides. Now, if you are released, will you be sensible?"

There were two men behind Sivas with their hands on the hilts of their swords. Sullenly, Jalvar nodded.

Ras Thavas signaled to his slave assistants. They came forward and pulled the sheet off Jalvar and unbuckled the straps; as he had expected, his body was naked. It was also the reddish tawny color of a Red Man; he strongly suspected he had Thavas to thank for that. He felt normal; better than usual, in fact—rested and alert, though a little hungry. He pushed himself up . . .

And went soaring several feet into the air. With a shout of alarm he grabbed for the surface of the table and glared around him. An attempt to walk had him bouncing around like a struck handball rebounding from a goal disk. Sivas chuckled again.

"You do not know your own strength," he said. "Come, these men will help you out of these narrow quarters."

The warriors took their hands from their swords and instead each gripped Jalvar by the upper arm. It proved humiliatingly necessary, as his body tried to skip upward with every pace.

"Make less effort!" Sivas said. "Imagine that you weigh only as much as a child newly hatched!"

Jalvar tried that, and gradually the grip on his arms slackened. They traveled down a corridor cut through the reddish sandstone that was everywhere about, and into a great natural cave hundreds of sofads across and nearly a hundred high, brilliantly lit. The floor was sand, and men were practicing at arms—the air was full of the clash of swords and the cries of the warriors.

"Watch," Sivas said, before Jalvar could speak.

Sivas turned and ran, bounding, then leapt. Jalvar's eyes went wide as the Zodangan soared fully thirty sofads into the air, five times his own height. That was like nothing the Gatholian prince had ever seen, save by—

"The warlord!" he blurted, when Sivas bounced back. "You have duplicated the strength of John Carter!"

"And Paxton," Sivas agreed. "Or rather, Ras Thavas has, once suitably . . . encouraged. He has done as much before."

Inwardly the shock was fading, and he bubbled with delight. *I have penetrated the conspiracy. And if . . . admittedly a large if . . . we foil it and escape, we have solved the problem of existence on Jasoom!*

Jalvar looked down at his body. Save for the color of his skin, it was as like his own as two coins, except that it was himself as he had been when only a decade or two from the egg.

"I have heard of Ras Thavas's synthetic men, the hormads," he said, though Thavas's synthetic men had been grotesque monsters, misshapen and twisted. Jalvar looked over his body again. Perfect and spotless . . .

"As you can see, his art has improved," Sivas said. "You were unconscious for many months, while your new body was prepared. It has more advantages than mere strength. Observe this."

He turned and signed to one of his men. Grinning, the warrior drew his longsword and lunged. The sharp blade transfixed Sivas just below the ribs for an instant, and Jalvar bit off a started exclamation of horror and alarm. The wound bled, but not very much; Sivas coughed, spat out a clot, and straightened.

"The brains of the new hormads are still not of the first

order, but since we use the bodies only after human brains have been transplanted to them, that is of little importance. What *is* important is that these bodies—Ras Thavas has long explanations of how he takes the template from within our own cells and modifies it—are inhumanly strong, and just as important, inhumanly resistant to damage. Only the destruction of the brain or the total removal of a vital organ can kill them. They heal with great speed too. A force of such men can cut their way through the guards and eliminate our enemies!"

He wheeled, straightening and drawing his own sword, thrusting it into the air: "Death to John Carter! Death to the warlord!

And then, from a thousand throats came the roaring reply: *"DEATH TO THE WARLORD! DEATH TO JOHN CARTER!"*

PART IV
THE MASTER MIND

Ras Thavas's quarters were segregated from those of the core of Sivas's Zodangan diehards, and those in turn from the panthans who made up the bulk of the hidden force. A month's time was enough for Jalvar and Tars Sojat—who had been also been transplanted into an improved hormad version of his original body—to learn the layout of the cave complex; it was like a large set of interconnected buildings carved from a ridge of solid rock. They had learned the guard routines as well, and also to fully master their new bodies and their strengths and weaknesses.

Mostly the former, he thought idly. *But by my first ancestor, how*

I eat now! Like a starving banth! I suppose the strength and rapid heal-ing must be paid for somehow.

Now Jalvar crept through the darkness outside the gate they had forced, with only the pale light of one hurtling moon to show the way. They were committed to trigger-ing the beacon and calling the warlord's forces now, with a dead man in their wake, and he felt the freedom that comes with casting yourself headlong into action. Their feet moved through the mud and shallow water of the swamp, ooze flowing up through their toes; it was an unfamiliar and unpleasant sensation, as was the abundance of insects. So was the constant dank smell.

"If this is what Barsoom was like when water was abun-dant, I will cease to complain of its present state," Sojat grumbled very quietly.

Then they were on dry land again, and ahead loomed the nearly vertical surface of this side of the rocky ridge that contained the insurgent base. It might have been carved and planed smooth, long ago—hundreds of thousands of years ago by the Orovars, his father's people. Erosion was swifter here in this last sad remnant of Barsoom's oceans than in most, and this wasn't very hard stone, nothing like the imperishable granites and almost metallic basalts from which the dead cities were built.

Now it just looked very steep. So steep that nobody in his right mind would try to climb it, and so high to the single slit window near the top that even their Jasoomian-style muscles wouldn't take them halfway to the top. Jalvar grinned. He'd been called light-minded as a youth, but nobody had ever said he wasn't imaginative.

About thirty sofads up there was a small ledge where a section of rock had scaled away long ago; you could still see the rubble below. They'd both noted it during a training march not long ago, just after they'd figured out where Ras Thavas's quarters were. Before they came here it would have been completely out of reach to either of them, without a ladder or steel pegs to drive into cracks in the rock. Now . . .

"I go first as we planned, my brother," Sojat said.

He backed up, crouched, and ran forward with the slithering speed of a charging banth, both his legs and the longer middle pair of limbs driving him forward. Then he leapt. It was astonishing to see the great body soar so, but even then only the fingers of his upper hands went over the edge. They clamped down, and then he was holding with both hands and his chin. Javlar held his breath as Sojat lay still for an instant, then swung sharply to one side. That might tear his hands loose . . . but it didn't, not quite, and his left middle hand went on the stone as well. Then the right, and soon he was standing on the ledge with his back to the rock, testing the footing. He grinned, an alarming sight even at that range, and his mobile stalklike ears cocked forward. Then he bent his knees slightly and braced both pairs of hands together, all four palms linked low before him.

Jalvar backed up himself, carefully testing the ground with his eyes and with questing bare feet as well; they wouldn't have more than one chance. He also checked that his weapons were securely strapped and fastened in at least two places to the links and buckles on his harness. Like all warriors of noble birth he had trained in running, leaping, and gymnastics virtually since he hatched. And since Gathol was a state of many herdsmen, he'd also practiced tricks like jumping on and off the back of a galloping thoat. The past few months had been spent getting used to his new thews. Even so . . .

Even so, it must be done, he thought, and crouched into a runner's starting position. Then he was bounding forward, faster and faster, and then coming down, the muscles in his thighs coiling like springs, and a tearing effort and a *huff* of utter effort as he leapt—

Soaring through the night. Drawing his legs up again as he flew, the glint of Sojat's tusks as the Thark adjusted his position. Suddenly shockingly close, the stone wall coming at him, and then he was hanging, poised his own height above Sojat's head, the great mobile eyes tracking him as he fell forward.

Smack.

His feet struck his friend's four crossed palms. The Thark uncoiled like a catapult, all the force of his fourteen sofads of height behind the throw, and the strength of arms reinforced by Ras Thavas's scientific wizardry. Jalvar put everything he had into the leap as well. Now he shot upward like the shell from a flier's cannon; he hoped he wouldn't have the same splintering impact, spilling blood and bone and guts instead of explosive radium. His quickened healing wouldn't help an iota if he left his brains spattered over the rock like a bowl of porridge. Darkened stone rushed past him, and then the thick metal grille over the narrow window.

Too high! he thought urgently.

The lip of the ridge flashed past, and for a moment he was hanging in the air beside it. The startled face of a sentry gaped at him, and then he was falling. His hands flashed out and gripped the grille.

And it broke, the six thumb-thick bars set into the stone along the top snapping like so many dried reeds. Three of the ones below broke as well, and the others began to bend. Jalvar yelled in alarm as the twisting metal bit into his left hand—there was no need for secrecy now.

The sentry leaned over the top of the cliff twenty sofads up, leveling a rifle. The muzzle flash left a strobing image in Jalvar's vision, but the man missed—like most Red Men he was a terrible shot, and it was a difficult target in the dark and aiming almost vertically downward.

Jalvar drew his pistol as he hung from the slowly bending grille and fired back; since the other man had used a firearm first, it was permissible for him to shoot. The weapon kicked against his hand, and almost in the same instant the sentry bent double and fell forward, turning over and over as he pitched down the face of the cliff.

Jalvar Pan was a *very* good shot. Gatholians often were, since they spent much time managing their herds in the wild. And despite being the greatest swordsman on two worlds, John Carter had insisted on such training for all his descendants; evidently it was a custom in Virginia, the kingdom on Jasoom where he had lived before his mysterious transplanting to Barsoom. Jalvar blessed the long hours of tedious practice most nobles considered a waste of time that might be spent with the sword.

Another sentry leaned over the cliff edge. Below Jalvar, the Thark rifle barked, and the man's head vanished in a spray that would have been red in daylight and was black beneath the light of Thuria. Jalvar ignored it; anyone who showed himself along the edge was going to die, and that was all that he needed to know. Instead he holstered his pistol and began to draw his dagger, to hammer through the glass of the window.

It opened instead, and a hand extended through. Jalvar grabbed the man's wrist just as the last of the grillwork parted with a short unmusical *tung*. The grille spun away and clattered on the broken rock below. Jalvar was drawn upward by the man's strong arm; he was young and handsome, but there was something very old and very cold behind his eyes.

"What has taken you so long?" Ras Thavas grumbled. "Yes, yes, of course I weakened the grille. Did they think that mere metal bars would confine the greatest intellect of Barsoom when he had access to laboratory acids?"

By my first ancestor, he probably is the greatest intellect on

Barsoom. But he will never be famed for his charm or humility.

Jalvar fastened the rope coiled over his shoulder to a wall bracket and tossed it out. It was the thin, unbreakably strong type used for boarding actions in the air. Seconds later Tars Sojat was swarming up it, even as rifles barked from the cliff above. He pushed his own weapon through and then followed it inside.

"They should have thrown rocks at me," he sneered, stretching; the ceiling was just high enough for him. "That would have been more dangerous."

"Quick!" Jalvar said, turning to Ras Thavas. "You have the device?"

"Of course," the scientist said. "I detected and removed it during my preliminary examination of you. Unfortunately I have not yet broken the code."

He produced a cylinder the size of his thumb. Jalvar seized it, unscrewed the top, and then shone his belt light into the tiny pinhole opening in a series of precisely modulated clicks.

"Now we wait," he said.

"Now they will come to kill us," Tars Sojat said cheerfully, hefting his rifle. "But we shall be well avenged."

"How far away is the warlord's fleet?" Ras Thavas asked in alarm.

"That depends on how far they tracked us when we left Zodanga," Jalvar said cheerfully, tucking the beacon into a pouch. "And how long they maintained a strong patrol. If they came close, and remained in strength, we have a chance. If not . . ."

He shrugged and slapped Sojat on one of his shoulders. "As my bloodthirsty friend here said. Now, show us the layout before the guards come. And tell me: Can your helpers be trusted?"

◆ ◆ ◆

"You are relying on this bandit scum to act honorably," Tars Sojat grumbled a xat later.

"No, I am merely hoping that they are," Jalvar said. "Also that when they learn the truth they will find it too unsatisfying to merely shoot us. They will want to feel us die upon their steel."

"Or possibly take us prisoner and torture us for a cycle or so," Sojat said with gloomy relish; Tharks were perhaps a little less given to that themselves these days, but for most Green Men torturing prisoners was one of life's main amusements. "Our rapid healing would give them *weeks* of laughter."

Ras Thavas's quarters were well-appointed; there were half a dozen rooms, besides the kitchens and servant's quarters, all carved from the living rock and the walls covered in rich hangings, where they weren't a scatter of books and instruments. Thavas swore that his slaves were loyal; two of them were keeping watch on the window. This entranceway led to doors made of double-leaved skeel.

"They do not need me anymore," Ras Thavas said. "They will not attempt to break down the doors, they will merely use an explosive device. What a tragedy, if my intellect were lost to Barsoom!"

Ras Thavas had already lived more than a thousand years; he remembered the launching of the first flier. His current body was not the one which had broken his egg so long ago, though it was distinctly odd to think of the Master Mind of Mars as a merry, playful hatchling in any case.

"So," Jalvar said, laying his hand on the locking device. "We must persuade them otherwise."

Jalvar thrust the door open and ducked. Two bullets slammed into the wood, splintering it but not penetrating; skeel was *hard*. Then he thrust out his hand from behind the protection, with his sword in it.

One more shot barked, and then a furious argument broke out below, voices raised. Jalvar caught *calot of a spy deserves no consideration* and *honor demands*. Then he stepped out onto the narrow landing. The stair below was narrow too, a tunnel full of furious faces and barred steel.

Sivas stood at the head of his men. "Gor Kova, you calot! How much did the Heliumites pay you?" he growled.

Nobody violated the Barsoomian honor code by shooting down a man armed with a sword; he had earned that much, at least for a moment, by showing himself where they *could* shoot him down.

"Nothing," he replied proudly. "My name is not Gor Kova, any more than you were called Dur Sivas by your parents. I am Jalvar Pan, son of Llana of Gathol and Pan Dan Chee the Orovar, a Prince of Gathol and great-grandson of John Carter, Warlord of Mars!"

A howl of rage went up from the assembled insurgents; he thought he saw looks of alarm exchanged farther back, among the panthans. His companion stuck his head around the door and leered, an alarmingly effective expression for a Green Man with shining white tusks and red-pupiled eyes.

"And I am Tars Sojat of the Thark horde, grandson of Tars Tarkas, destroyer of Zodanga, you ruin-haunting, incubator-destroying ulsios," he added. "Do you have any families here I might slaughter after we kill you all?"

Sivas's face lost its usual cunning. Instead it twisted in a scream of unbearable hatred. He bounded up the stairs with his longsword in his hand.

"For Zodanga! Death to them! Death, *death!*" he screamed.

Steel clashed; there was only room for one, and no room for fancy footwork at all. Jalvar and Sivas stood within arm's reach of each other, Sivas on the lower step, and point and edge wove a deadly tapestry between them. Sivas was confident as well as mad with rage; he had beaten Jalvar nine times in ten when they sparred.

Within seconds both men were bleeding from minor wounds. Sivas's men raved behind him, giving him no room to retreat—not that he had shown the slightest desire to do so.

Jalvar used a daringly minimal parry that rang the Zodangan's sword upward just a hair from the line of its thrust and counterthrust in turn.

The narrow point speared through Dur Sivas's eye and stopped only when it punched into the rear of his skull; even the Master Mind's perfectly engineered hormad body could do nothing to save him from such a blow.

I let *you win those sparring matches,* Jalvar thought. *Farewell, Dur Sivas. You were a brave man, if an evil one, and you deserved a warrior's death.*

Jalvar raised his sword in salute and then stood, motionless except for a slight fighting smile, blood dripping from his blade and arm as the corpse of their leader tumbled backward.

There was a moment of silence, and then a scream from below: "The Heliumites! The warlord's fleet! *John Carter is come!*"

The air split with the rumble of bombs and the whirring of the great propellers of the battleships of Helium.

PART V
JASOOM (ABOVE EARTH)

Jalvar Pan woke eagerly, even when the grogginess of cold sleep still held his mind a little. The long voyage between the worlds was over, and soon he would be the first Barsoomian—or mostly Barsoomian—ever to set foot on the soil of Jasoom, of Earth.

He tossed off the restorative drink before he noticed the grim looks on the faces of those around him.

"Prince Jalvar, you must come to the bridge immediately," Tars Sojat said.

He nodded; whatever he needed to know would be best seen there. The corridors were more active than he had seen them since they rose from the shipyard at Helium; the whole crew would be awake now, of course. More sober looks greeted him on the bridge; even so, for a moment he lost himself in the sight of Jasoom turning like a great blue-and-white shield through the viewports that wrapped around half of the semicircular compartment. Then he swung himself into the commander's chair. A circular screen lit, and a familiar Jasoomian face confronted him.

"Admiral Julian!" Jalvar said.

The face of the commander of the Peace Fleet of the Anglo-American Co-dominium was that of a man in his middle years by the fleeting standards of Earth, hard and competent, but there was a haunted look to his eyes. The bustle of a warship's bridge showed behind him, and on a bulkhead two crossed flags, one starry, the other made up of overlapping crosses.

"Prince Jalvar. I wish I could greet you in the name of the peoples of Earth, but instead I must warn you to turn back."

"We cannot," Jalvar Pan said. "We need to recharge our tanks of the Ninth Ray; the reserve is not enough to allow us to return to Barsoom."

Julian's face grew still more grim. "Earth is under attack."

"The whole of Jasoom? But under attack from where—ah!"

Jalvar had studied Jasoom closely, of course. Its single huge moon was hollow, and inhabited by several intelligent species, one of them very similar to Barsoomian and Jasoomian humans. For that matter, Barsoom's main moon,

Thuvia, was also peopled; John Carter had traveled there.

And it was on Jasoom's moon—Luna, they call it—that the ship called the Barsoom *that they tried to send to us was wrecked. Deliberately wrecked; but I thought that the man who did so perished there!*

Julian followed his swift thoughts. "The traitor Orthis has not wasted the last twenty years; and he was always a brilliant engineer. Mad with a spirit of revenge, he has armed the inhabitants of the hollow interior of our moon, the savage Kalkars and Va-gas, and a great fleet has attacked us in the past few days. Even now transports are landing millions of them, burning and killing and destroying, and Orthis's perverted genius has equipped them with terrible weapons. Earth is helpless before them; this fleet is its only armed force, and it is intended to put down bandits, not fight wars. We have been too long at peace. I blame myself for leaving Orthis alive when the *Barsoom* left the moon to return to Earth."

"Blame those leaders who would not let you build more ships of space," Jalvar said.

"I do, prince," Julian said, and smiled with a warrior's grim cheer. "But they are mostly dead now, and those who aren't will be shortly."

Jalvar nodded respectfully. "I would join your fight," he said. "But the *Jasoom* is an exploratory vessel, not a warship. We have only a few light guns and torpedoes."

"I thank you for your offer. I would advise you to return to Mars immediately, but . . ."

But we need to refurbish, resupply, and take on more Ninth Ray. We were counting on the aid of Earth's shipyards and factories. Now . . .

"I can only advise you to make for the estate of an old friend of the family," Julian said.

He transmitted coordinates in the Earthly system of longitude and latitude, then bade a curt good-bye; Jalvar could hear him beginning to give orders even as the screen blanked.

"Well, it seems we'll be landing in the middle of a war," Jalvar said.

Tars Sojat patted his sword-hilt and barked the cruel laughter of the Green hordes.

"What a pity! Who is this friend that Jalvar sends us to?"

"I know the name," Jalvar said. "John Carter told me of him; the kinsman of the warlord's here on Jasoom who wrote the tale of his adventures on Barsoom, and who he visited, also told this man's story. *Burroughs*, was that the name? His was a strange tale—he was raised in the wilderness, by creatures not unlike our great white apes—and the man is a mighty warrior."

Tars Sojat frowned. "Are not these Jasoomians short-lived? That was several of their lifetimes ago."

"Most of them are. Not all. John Carter is one, and evidently this man is another. He has many names. *Tarzan* is one of them."

PART VI
BRITISH EAST AFRICA

The *Jasoom*'s great length pressed its landing struts into the tawny grass of the pasture; it had crushed a few odd-looking flat-topped trees. Not far away was a lake of water confined by a dam, bordered with more trees. A neat village of cottages lay beyond it, and beyond that a sprawling red-tiled mansion surrounded by very beautiful gardens, obviously the estate of a nobleman despite all the differences of detail. Surrounding all were tilled fields of unfamiliar crops, and others where odd-looking four-limbed beasts grazed. It was a lush landscape by Barsoomian standards, and not far distant loomed a primeval forest such as the red planet had not known for over a million years.

Only in the Valley Dor, at the end of the River Iss, is there anything like this. Yet their Earth has so much of it!

Prince Jalvar Pan felt the heavy tug of Jasoom's gravity holding him as he strode down the landing ramp, but his hormad body made nothing of it—he was as nimble now as he had been in his normal existence on Barsoom.

The air was thicker than normal, but not impossibly so—this was a high plateau, six thousand sofads above the level of Jasoom's impossibly abundant seas. It smelled pleasantly of growth and greenness, and a little less so of burning from the wrecked Kalkar battleship that burned some distance to the westward, sending a plume of black smoke into the odd blue sky.

"Kaor!" Jalvar said to the master of the estate.

"Welcome," the man said in English. Jalvar spoke it himself, and all the *Jasoom*'s crew had learned a fair amount.

"And thank you of disposing of *that*," the man said, nodding toward the smoke-plume.

"They did not anticipate our shielded torpedoes," Jalvar said. "The Flying Death, we call it; invented by Phor Tak of Jahar. Not sporting, but they fired on us without warning."

"The Kalkars are dull-witted enough. But that does not matter; there are more than enough of them, well-armed, and we have little to resist them with. Nairobi has already fallen, I hear."

The man spoke sternly, but without fear. He was Jalvar's height, six foot two in the Earthly measurement system. Apart from that he looked not unlike John Carter, with dark hair—worn to the shoulders of his Jasoomian garments—and gray eyes. A great scar crossed his forehead, and others showed on his face and hands; he smiled slightly as he greeted Tars Sojat with calm friendliness, weird though the Green Man must appear to an Earthling. His grip was strong and precisely judged, and he moved like a hunting banth.

This is a warrior, Jalvar decided. *Despite what Admiral Julian has said of Earth's decadence.*

Several young men of the same stamp stood behind the man, and their women; one was strikingly lovely, with long blond hair, but cradled a rifle with casual ease. The troop behind them all looked formidable as well, and half-familiar to Barsoomian eyes. They were black of skin and sharply handsome of feature like the First Born nation of Barsoom, and wearing little but loincloths and feather headdresses that made them seem more homelike still. They were heavily armed as well, with long spears as well as firearms, and they looked at the Barsoomians and their great ship with alert interest.

"My Waziri warriors," the Earthman confirmed, indicating them. "I have kept up the old ways with them, and the authorities winked at it, since I am their chief and responsible for public order in this district. Now that may save us, or at least let us sell our lives dearly."

Jalvar nodded. "I and my crew are at your disposal. The *Jasoom* cannot leave atmosphere again without extensive refitting, but we can sail anywhere on this world, if you know of a place of refuge. We can take several hundred, at a pinch, Lord . . ."

"Forgive me, Prince Jalvar," the man said. "I am John Clayton, Lord Greystoke. My wife, Lady Jane, my son, Korak . . . there will be time later, I hope."

A black warrior came up, trotting easily despite the sweat that poured from his face.

"Tarzan!" he said, addressing the tall gray-eyed man, and then more in a language that Jalvar had not studied.

276

Greystoke's face turned more grim still. "But your ship may yet save us all. A column of Kalkars and Va-Gas approaches, with ground fighting machines in support."

Jalvar felt a keen stab of interest. "Admiral Julian thought that the Kalkars would overrun the earth."

"The surface of the Earth, yes," Lord John said. "But the Moon is not the only hollow globe. Earth also has a land within it, one I have visited before. Let me tell you of a place called Pellucidar. . . ."

The opening section of *A Princess of Mars* includes a note from the author Edgar Rice Burroughs explaining the circumstances by which he obtained the manuscript. He relates that since childhood he has known "Uncle Jack," i.e., Captain John Carter, and recalls with fondness the way that the man was equally at ease playing with the children or galloping a horse. According to Burroughs, Carter seldom spoke of the days he'd spent prospecting for gold in the Arizona hills, and sometimes a look of the most intense sadness and longing would pass across his face, and Burroughs once saw him staring up at the night sky and raising his arms as if in supplication. Burroughs also remarks that in all the years he knew John Carter the man never aged a day. Carter identified Burroughs as his heir, and left behind very specific instructions for the disposition of his body after death—that is, that he be placed in a special tomb of his own devising, one that was well ventilated and which could be opened, curiously enough, from the inside. Burroughs states that he received the manuscript for *A Princess of Mars* in a sealed envelope, with instructions not to reveal its contents until twenty-one years had passed. Our next tale also opens with an author's note explaining the provenance of a peculiar manuscript, albeit one that casts a distinctly different light on the events described by John Carter.

COMING OF AGE ON BARSOOM

BY CATHERYNNE M. VALENTE

To the Reader of this Work:

In submitting to you the strange soliloquy of Falm Rojut, Jeddak of Hanar Su, I feel it necessary to add a few remarks.

This manuscript came into my possession through several twists and turns of coincidence. I had struck up a correspondence with a librarian in Chicago due to our mutual interest in archival issues relating to the early pulp authors. In the basement of her library my friend had discovered an astonishing number of books, magazines, periodicals, pamphlets, and other paper materials dating from the infancy of science fiction. One could hardly have stumbled onto a cave full of golden cups and sapphire crowns and come away with more awe and delight than that librarian felt, walking up the metal staircase and out of that dusty industrial cellar. Obviously, the new collection belonged to the library proper, but some of the documents proved to be of little value even to the most dedicated soul, being either undecipherable or in such a pitiable state that even scanning into the digital collection might be the death of the poor things. Among the latter were several manuscripts that we both suspected belonged to Edgar Rice Burroughs, whose margins contained some scribbles in his handwriting or which bore one of his pseudonyms. Among those lay one peculiar collection of pages—I couldn't in fairness call it a book. My friend informed me of it: that it was mixed in with a number of ERB's papers, that it was not in English or any dialect she recognized, and that it was short but not in too bad a state of rot. Would I like to come to Chicago and see what I could make of it? (My librarian friend was aware that I made a great study of ancient languages when I was younger, and if my vocabularies are not what they once were, I can still fake my conjugations with the best of them.)

I put aside the novel I had been working on and went west, meeting my friend in person and having a wonderful dinner downtown before happily ensconcing myself in one of the private study rooms of the library. Unfortunately, the document was far beyond the abilities of a lapsed classicist—I actually laughed when I saw it: five pages, inked on both sides, covered in hieroglyphics and ideograms I could not begin to guess at. I could not even say what language they might be, or what region of the world might have influenced the rounded, complex characters. I handled the pages carefully, examined them as best I could, but honestly, I am only human, and I hadn't even finished my doctorate.

As is my habit, I posted a description of my Chicago adventure to my blog and thought little more of it. ERB is not my favorite of science fiction's grandfathers, after all. Yet I found I could not forget the graceful, bulbous hieroglyphs. They floated in my dreams, huge and green, like living things, promising illumination to a more determined scholar. Having always been prone to insomnia I found I could scarcely sleep for a moment without those phantasms appearing behind my closed eyes and waking me with a start—soon I simply ceased to sleep at all.

In the midst of this misery an e-mail arrived in my inbox, bearing the subject heading: Emergency Translation

Services, Available Day and Night. Even if it were spam, I was curious (and possibly desperate, certainly exhausted) enough to open the message. I reproduce it here verbatim:

> Having read of your linguistic troubles we wish to offer a cipher which we believe will offer some succor. Please do not ask us where we discovered such a valuable piece of information. We could not possibly share our sources. Really, it is beyond our morality to betray such confidences. Well, perhaps your insistence has swayed us. While traveling in Arizona we chanced upon an old woman whose costume was decorated with bones and skulls in a quite unsettling way, selling charms and trinkets, bits of silver and turquoise such as are common in the Southwest. Our sister enjoys silver and we purchased several bangles, a large red stone pendant, and two rings. Much later our sister informed us that the pendant proved to be a kind of locket, and within a carefully folded piece of parchment bore strange marks and a kind of code. Upon examination we of course immediately recognized the handwriting of Edgar Rice Burroughs, may he rest in peace and all sovereignty, and felt certain the paper was a Rosetta Stone for the purpose of translating Tharkian to English and vice versa. We are happy to offer these services to you free of charge, as a fellow traveler and believer. Signed, ----

At the time, I could not say what belief I was meant to have in common with my strange and earnest translators, but I accepted their offer and, cipher in hand, I made the following translation of the (incomplete, as I came to understand) document, a scanned copy of which my librarian friend was kind enough to send me. I possess no originals of the following, and as to my linguistic benefactors I have only guesses and wild speculation, as I have heard nothing further from them, even after the publication of Falm Rojut's strange words.

Yours very sincerely,
Catherynne M. Valente

✦ ◈ ✦

A CHILD OF THARK

BY FALM ROJUT, JEDDAK OF HANAR SU
TRANSLATED BY CATHERYNNE M. VALENTE

Inside the egg I could taste the sun. It was dry and dusty and soft, like sweet ash. I sucked on the sun and the sun was a yolk and it passed into me and out of me and the world was my egg and I was my egg and I was the world. I was somewhat aware of other eggs, other worlds, rustling around me, their occasional dreaming movements filling the world that was me and the yolk and the sun and the egg with a gentle kind of music. I was content in the egg, and from the sunny ashy yolk I drew both the strength of my six limbs and the greening shade of my skin, but also a sure knowledge of my heart, and a purpose that tasted thick like blood and thick like fat and thick like the weight of a mate held with the second pair of arms.

John Carter could never understand us. He never slept in the egg.

When the egg cracks, it hurts, somewhere in the bones; the vibration is so awful and loud you think you will snap, that there was no strength after all, that you are not ready—oh, you are not ready! Being born is like dying and no one wants to die. When I think back on it now I imagine that the egg was my first opponent, that it, too, wanted to live, and so did I, and only one of us could go on. I was Jeddak of the egg before I was Jeddak of Hanar Su, and the light of my victory blinded me, the light of the sun glancing off the shards of the defeated egg like last weeping cries. Ropy remnants of yolk clung to my tusks and I tasted them, the last golden aching sweetness of my life, for nothing in this world tastes quite of that ashen, delicate purpose rushing through every limb. I blinked in the new light. All around me my brothers and sisters stretched their green bodies for the joy of it, the first expression of might and power and gods.

We were so strong. We were so beautiful.

Before us stood a long line of enormous gorgeous gods. Our mothers and fathers, their arms outstretched to us—and to remember this pains my chest—my whole life spooling out in a line and my people standing guard, standing sentinel on that line, willing me to survive and live and thrive, and all of them loving me equally, caring nothing for who laid my egg, only that I was theirs, profoundly and completely. I was their family and their future, all of us were. And we ran to them, to our lives, on legs muscled already and twitching to move, just to move over that red moss, into those green arms.

The human John Carter who came to Barsoom like a storm cloud passing back and forth over the sun, over our strength and our purpose, witnessed the generation after mine performing that first radiant dance. He was horrified. He said we had no good qualities because we could not know who our parents were. Because our families did not look like his. Because it seemed to him nothing but random

chance who caught up which child into their arms.

I am an old man now. I have forgiven him, in the end. He could not help it. What did he look like to us? A bald, white ape, with his terrifying leaps, ready and able and happy to kill us all. And to him we looked like monsters.

But I have learned to write in the old way so you may understand me. It seems to me that writing in this fashion is a very slow and inefficient way to accomplish what the Green Men do with a glance and a thought: that glimmering net of shared experience and memory that is our collective heartspace. I write and you read and it is almost as though we stand on a broad red plain together while the moons set and the thoats warble at the stars.

That gauntlet is not merely a tangle of green arms. It is a mesh of thoughts and passions snapping like ropes of light cut in half, waiting for one of us to catch the frayed end and connect, knot ourselves together. They call to us, the mothers and fathers, they say: Be my child. Be my future. Battle me with your laughter and pinching and sneaking out to hunt the banth when you are not nearly ready, fight me with your every breath, your every kiss, while I struggle to make you grown and you struggle to die as quickly as possible, and then when I am grown old take my metal and my name and go on while I recede.

I admit it looks careless, as though children do not matter to us, much more than a sleeping fur. But the human John Carter could not truly enter the heartspace. He was certain he could, that he could read our thoughts with perfect correctness, but you cannot be part of a herd and yet stand outside it. We could not read his thoughts, and so in the shimmering crosshatch of our communal dreaming, he was a terrible blank space, a void, and in his eavesdropping he only ever heard a garbled fraction of what passed between the Green Men. Yet what he heard, miserably diminished, he repeated as though total truth, and in the end this was what drove me from Thark to find my own community, a place where the Earthman had not yet told us what we were with his tiny nose in the air.

I asked him once what he had been doing just before he came to Barsoom. He answered that he had killed a great number of Indians, which were like the Red Men, but of Earth.

Why? I asked him. What had they done to you? Did you take their places in their tribe, their metal and their name, their wives and their retinue, their responsibility to guide their people and help them survive the winter? You must be a great Jeddak of these Apache, if you killed so many.

No, the rules of battle are different on Earth. I simply left them, and came here. As to what they had done to me, they were my enemy, and had killed my friend.

Was not your friend their enemy, if you were theirs? Was not killing him their duty?

And John Carter did not answer me but went about his business with his wicked war-princess. But I was baffled—he called us barbaric and yet he left those people without their warriors and took up no position among them, did not replace their strength with strength, their valor with valor? What kind of a man was he?

What would he do to us, if we became his enemy?

I remember the day his war-princess Dejah Thoris spoke to us with her honeyed words, coaxing us to join her people in amity and fellowship, to unite Barsoom and be clasped to her bosom. I was but young and yet I recall the black boom of hate and anger that sizzled through the heartspace, and how when Tars Tarkas stood to join her we felt such betrayal. The Red Men killed our children! In war they sought out the incubators and smashed the eggs, they wiped out whole communities, reducing the Green Men inexorably toward extinction. Never once had a Red Man deigned to take the place of one he killed, they only moved on, to destroy more babies and mock us as animals. No wonder the human John Carter found such brotherhood with them.

Why should we have joined with her? Because she was beautiful? Because she had a sweet voice? I could not mate with her. I found her upsetting and confusing to look upon—worse to listen to. While reclining on our silks and furs she claimed we had no art or industry! I kept staring at the silk she lay on. Where did she think it came from? That my mother spun it out of her posterior? She was cruel and would not even try to learn to speak our language, to enter the heartspace—for that is to become vulnerable, to become raw, to join with us, in something deeper and more terrifying than fellowship or amity which may be broken. Even when we battle for supremacy—and why should we not? Barsoom is dying, and every drop of water or scrap of food is a battle, a battle we know we will one day lose. Only the very strongest can push us one year further, one measly decade or century on through this hard world. How we would like to love the weak as well as the strong. How we would like to mate whenever we wished or give preference to our own blood and work for its supremacy. We cannot afford to. We reign in our instincts so that the Green Men should live, not merely one Green Man. Such a thing is the luxury of men like the Earthman John Carter and his impossibly rich and hospitable world. I cannot imagine a place where only one species rules all. What ease he must have had. Why did he ever land upon us with both his feet?

I do not like him, I said to my mother Sikuva. He humiliated Tars Tarkas! He made him say he learned friendship from that skinny Earthman! The heartspace is bigger than what he calls friendship and has more teeth, too. Why does he think he is better than us? Without us he would have starved to death!

Hush, my little spear-head, my mother said. When you are grown, you may fight him if you dislike him. Bide your time.

I have felt sorry for Tars Tarkas and his child Sola in my time. I imagine their gentle and loving feelings are a comfort to them, for they could not engage fully with the heartspace. Something was broken in them, and we could see them in the crosshatch only as shadows, vague and hazy. They expressed in the outside world the precious love and adoration and communal feeling that we keep inside, for it would surely be used against us by the other folk of Barsoom, who think so little of us, who break our eggs and dance in the ruined yolk. Poor Sarkoja tried to keep Tars Tarkas and his woman from passing on their unfit blood to a child, but she could not, she was not vigilant enough. I felt sorry for him then, when he piled up the human John Carter with praise, and we burned with anger, for he preened with his war-princess and was made sure of his superiority. We lost face, and could not get it back. We would be ruled by a crippled Tharkian, and even a decadent tyrant was better than one who could not see the world inside us except through a dark glass.

And so I grew to adulthood. I made myself strong, so that one day I could kill the Earthman John Carter and take his metal. I wanted things to be as they were, before he came. I wanted to dream in the heartspace and hunt game and ride the thoats without having to call them good and pretty for a half hour before I could feed myself—for I was always starving. There is never enough on Barsoom. You are never full, unless you are the Earthman John Carter. Unless you are a Red Man licking the yolk off your fingers.

My anger sustained me, it filled out my muscles where meat and bone could not. How dare he? How dare he drive off Sarkoja when she did little more than pinch and bite a woman who had felt no sorrow while her people destroyed us? How dare he kill our chieftains and take position among us? He had no respect, as he had none for the Apaches he spoke of. I roamed the high hills and wrestled both the great white ape and the banth, and bested them both, for I was becoming great in the fullness of my youth, and I feared nothing except the reedy voice of the Earthman John Carter telling us once more that we were brutes and should follow his lead. I walked alone, I took myself from the heartspace and it grieved me like a blow to the skull, but it was worth it, it was enough, to end the Earthman John Carter and bring my people home once more.

And yet the very day when I resolved that I had achieved my true self, and all my green limbs were hard and hot, when I was ready—oh, I was ready!—I went down into Thark with a blaze in my eyes and a blaze in my heartspace as Falm Rojut returned to the glittering crosshatching of thoughtlines like an inrushing of air and flame. The young ones shrank back from the brightness of Falm Rojut. But Sola herself told me with a haughty smile that the Earthman John Carter had gone, back into the heavens, and was beyond my reach. Sola could not see the blue fire in my heartspace, how I hated her: collaborator and traitor, who gave succor to murderers and would go unpunished. Though the Earthman John Carter had gone, he would never truly be gone. He had put his foot down upon Barsoom and everything around that footprint had begun to die. I could not stay in Thark, which was the center of his rot. I could not look Sola in the eye each day while she preened and smirked and giggled with Tars Tarkas about their friend and how glorious would be the day when he returned. I was a child of Thark—I wanted only to live and hunt and mate and see my people thrive. Instead I could not even take the metal of the interloper, could not even try.

Much later, my rage quieted to a banked ember floating

like a red planet in the heartspace. I challenged the old Jeddak of Hanar Su far over the plains, and she was grateful to lay down the burden of her long life under my blade. I watched my wife lay her eggs. I guarded them from the Red Men and owned several thoats and calots who did their work well. I heard that the Earthman John Carter returned some ten years hence, but by that time I had a community to think of, and I led them deep into the mountains, to be safe from him, from his pride, from his ignorance.

But then, that lonely day when I was so ready to destroy him, when I was so strong, when the sun spilled over my green skin like yolk, I only turned my head to the sky where, somewhere, I knew he hid from me. And I laughed—a long, terrible, awful laugh.

Our laughter was never mirth. It is our greatest grief and mourning, our agony and regret for how things must be on this difficult, painful world, our wishing fate could have gone another way, our crying out for the cruelty and unfair asymmetry of the life that owns us.

It was always our weeping.

◆ ◆ ◆

Barsoom is a highly martial place. Visitors would be well advised to get their hands on a sword and learn how to use it, not only because the environment is generally violent and lawless, but also because virtually all Barsoomian societies assign status based on battle prowess. In fact, among the Green Men you haven't even earned the right to a last name until you've slain a local chieftain. Visitors to Barsoom are faced with a dizzying array of unfamiliar ranks and titles, the highest of which are the Jeddaks (emperors) and jeds (kings). You can also expect to see plenty of military officers—jedwars (warlords), odwars (generals), dwars (captains), and padwars (lieutenants). The stories of Edgar Rice Burroughs mainly focus on Jeddaks such as John Carter and Tars Tarkas or princesses such as Dejah Thoris and Tara, but of course we can't forget that characters of a more humble station have adventures that are just as memorable, as our final tale amply demonstrates. This story shows us a distant future in which John Carter is poised to finally bring an end to the endless cycles of warfare that have rocked Barsoom. Don't worry though . . . peace hasn't come quite yet, and there's more than enough action here to satisfy even the most hardened Barsoomian warrior.

◆ ◆ ◆

THE DEATH SONG
OF DWAR GUNTHA

BY JONATHAN MABERRY

◆ ◆ 1 ◆ ◆

My name is Jeks Toron, last padwar of the Free Riders, and personal aide to Dwar Guntha. When he dies, however he dies, I pray I will go with him into the realm of legends and that our song will be sung in Helium for a thousand thousand years.

That is not a heroic boast—I won't fall upon my sword at the death of my captain; but I have been in a hundred battles with him, and we have grown old together . . . and war is not an old man's game. For odwars and jedwars, perhaps, but not for fighting men.

Dwar Guntha? Ah, now there is a fighting man. Was he not with John Carter when the Warlord raided the fortress of Issus? Aye, he was there, leading the mutiny of loyal Heliumites against the madness of Zat Arras. He was a man at arms in the palace when Carter was named Jeddak of Jeddaks—Warlord of all Barsoom. And in the years that followed, how many times did Guntha ride out at the head of the Warlord's

Riders? Look closely at Dwar Guntha's face and chest, and in the countless overlapping scars you'll see a map of history, a full account of the wars and battles, rescues, and skirmishes.

Now, though . . . ?

John Carter himself is old. His children and grandchildren, and grandchildren of his grandchildren are old. We Red Men of Helium are long-lived, but that old witch time, as they say, catches up to everyone. Guntha's right arm is not what it was, and I admit that I am slower on the draw, less sure on the cut, and less dexterous in the riposte than once I was. Even the heroes' songs for which I and my family have been famous these many generations have become echoes of old tales retold. In these days of peace there are few opportunities for songmakers to tell of great and heroic deeds; just as there are few opportunities for warriors to pass into song in a moment of glorious battle.

It seems to me, and to Guntha, that we live in an age of city men. City men, or, perhaps "civilized" men, seek deaths in bed, just as our great grandfathers once sought that long, last journey down the River Iss.

We spoke of such things, did Dwar Guntha and I, as we sat before a fire, warming our hands on the blaze and our stomachs with red wine. The moons chased each other through the heavens, leaving in their wakes a billion swirling stars. Tomorrow might be our last day, and so many days lay behind us. It sat heavily upon Dwar Guntha that our last great song may already have been sung.

I caught him looking into the flames with a distance at odds with the hawk sharpness he usually displayed.

"What is it?" I asked, and he was a long time answering.

Instead of speaking, he straightened, set aside his cup, and drew his sword from its sheath of cured banth hide. Guntha regarded the blade for a moment, turning it this way and that, studying the play of reflected firelight on the oiled steel. Then with a sigh he handed it to me.

"Look at it, Jeks," he said heavily. "This is my third sword. When I was a lad and wearing a fighting man's rig for the first time I carried my father's sword. A clunky chopper of Panarian make. My father was a palace guard, you know. Served fifty years and never drew his weapon in anger. First time I used the sword in a real battle I notched the blade on a Tharkian collar. Second time I used it, the blade snapped. When Zat Arras fitted out the fleet to pursue John Carter after he'd returned from Valley Dor, Kantos Kan himself gave him a better sword. Good man, that. He was everything Zat Arras was not, and the sword he gave was a Helium blade. Light and strong and already blooded. It had belonged to a padwar friend of his who died nobly but had no heirs. I used that blade for over twenty years, Jeks. It tasted the blood of Green Men and Black Men, of Plant Men and White Apes. And, aye, it drank the blood of Red Men, too."

He sighed and reached for his cup.

"But I lost it when my scouting party was taken prisoner in that skirmish down south. Now, why do I tell you, Jeks? That's where we met, wasn't it? In the slave pits of An-Kar-Dool. Remember how we broke out? Clawing stones from the floor of our cell and tunneling inch by inch under the wall? Running naked into the forests, wasted by starvation, filthy and unarmed."

I smiled and nodded. "We were armed when we returned."

Guntha smiled too, and nodded at the blade. "That was the first time I used that sword. I took it from the ice pirate who sold us into slavery. I snuck into his tent and strangled him with a lute string, and for a time I thought I would throw this sword away as soon as its immediate work was done."

"That would have been a shame," I said as I hefted the

sword, letting the weight of the blade guide the turn and fall and recovery of my fist on my wrist. The balance was superb, and the blade flashed fire as it cut circles in the air.

"And so it would," he agreed, and his smile faded away by slow degrees. "Yet look at it, Jeks. See the nicks and notches that have cut so deep that no smith can sharpen them out? And along the bloodgutter, see the pits? Shake it, you can feel the softness of the tang, and if you listen close you can hear it cry out in weary protest. I heard it crack yesterday when we fell upon the garrison that was fleeing this fort. Hearing it crack was like hearing my own heart break."

I lowered the sword and looked at him. Firelight danced in his eyes, but otherwise his face might have been the death mask of some ancient hero.

"I know of fifty songs in which your sword is named, Guntha," said I. "And twice a dozen names it has been given. Horok the Breaker. Lightning Sword of the East. Pirate's Bane and Thark's Friend. Those songs will still be sung when the moons are dust."

"Perhaps. They are old songs, written when each morning brought the clash of steel upon steel. What do we hear each morning now? Birdsong." He grunted in disgust. "Call me superstitious, Jeks, or call me an old fool, but I believe that my sword has sung its last songs."

"There is still tomorrow. The pirates will come and try to take this fort back from us."

"No," he said, "they *will* take it back, and they will slaughter us to a man and bury our bodies in some forgotten valley. No one will see us die and no one will write our last song."

"A death in battle is a death in battle," I observed, but he shook his head.

"You quote your own songs, Jeks," he said, "and when you wrote it you were quoting me."

"Ah," I said, remembering.

"Tomorrow is death," said Guntha, "but not a warrior's death. We will try and hold the walls and they will wear us down and root us out like lice. Extermination is not a way for a warrior to end his own song. There are too few of us to make a stand, and all of us are old. Where once we were the elite, the right hand of John Carter, now we are a company of dotards. An inconvenience to a dishonorable enemy."

"No—" I began but he cut me off with a shake of the head.

"We've known each other too long and too well for us to tell lies in the dark. The sun has set on more than this fortress, Jeks, and I am content with that." He paused. "Well . . . almost content. I am not a hero. I'm a simple fighting man and perhaps I should show more humility. I have been given a thousand battles. It is gluttony to crave one more."

Again I made to speak and again he shook his head. "Let me ramble, Jeks. Let me draw this poison out of my spirit." He sipped wine and I refilled both of our cups. "I have always been a fighting man. Always. I could never have done temple duty like my father. Standing in all that finery during endless ceremonies while my sword rusted in its sheath for want of a good blooding? No . . . that was never for me. Perhaps I am less . . . civilized than my father. Perhaps I belong to an older age of the world when warriors lived life to its fullest and died before they got old."

"You've fought in more battles than anyone I've ever heard of," I said. "Perhaps more than the great Tars Tarkas or the Warlord himself. You've *been* in most of their battles, and a hundred beside."

"And what is the result, Jeks? The world has grown quiet, there are no new songs. The Warlord has tamed Barsoom. He's broken the Assassins Guild and exposed the corruption of the nobles in the courts of Helium, made allies of the Tharks and Okarians; overthrew the Kaldanes, driven out most of the pirates except these last desert scum, and brought peace to the warring kingdoms."

"And *you* were there for much of that, Guntha. This very sword sang its song in the greatest battles of all time."

"Ah, friend Jeks, you miss my point," he said. He sipped his wine and shook his head. "It is *because* of all those battles, it is *because* of all the good that has been done with sword and gun and airship that I sit here, old and disgruntled and . . . yes . . . drunk. It is because of the quiet of peace that I feel so cheated."

"Cheated?"

"By myself. By our success. I never wanted to die the way my father did—an old man drooling down my chest while his great-great-grandchild swaddled him in diapers. Nor would I want to live on in 'retirement,'" he said, wincing at the word, "while my sword hangs above a hearth, a relic whose use is forgotten and whose voice is stilled."

We sat there, both of us staring into the fire.

I took a breath and held out his sword. He looked at it the way a man might regard a friend who has betrayed him.

"Better I should break it over a rock than let it fail in a pointless battle."

"Take it, Guntha," I said softly. "I believe it still has one song left to sing."

His hand was reluctant, but finally he did take it back and slid it with a soft rasp into its sheath.

"What song is left to old men, Jeks?"

"Tomorrow."

He shook his head. "You weren't listening. Tomorrow is a slaughter and nothing more. We will rise and put on our weapons and gear, and then we will die. No one will write that song. No victory will be won. It will be a minor defeat in a war that will pass us by. We are small and peripheral to it, as old men are often peripheral things. No, Jeks, though we may wet our blades in the dawn's red glow, there is nothing. . . ." His voice trailed off and stopped. Guntha drew a breath and straightened his back, staring down in his cup for long moments as logs crackled and hissed in the fire. "Gods," he said softly, "listen to me. I am an old woman. The wine has had the better of me. Forget I spoke."

"Do you say so?" I asked, cocking my head at him.

He forced a smile onto his seamed face. "Surely you can't take my ramblings seriously, old friend. Nor hold them against me after we've drained our cups how many times? Who am I, after all? Not an odwar or a Jeddak. A dwar I am and a dwar shall I die—though . . ." He paused and looked around at the men who slept under rough blankets on the wooden walkway behind the parapets of the small stone fort. "Truly, for a warrior what greater honor is there than to have been the captain of men such as these? Surely none of *my* songs would have ever been sung had it not been for the company of such as they."

"One might say so of all heroes, Guntha," I pointed out. I took the wineskin and filled our cups.

"Not so. John Carter needs no company of men to help him. Even old, he is stronger than the strongest."

"He is not of this world," I reminded him. "Besides . . . how many times has he been captured during his adventures? How many times has his salvation relied on others? On warriors? Even on women and men from other races? The great Tars Tarkas has saved his life a dozen times."

"Just as John Carter saved his," Guntha fired back.

"Which only makes my point. What man is a hero without another warrior or ally at his back?"

"Like you and me," conceded Guntha, then gave another nod to the sleeping soldiers. "And these creaky old rogues."

"Just so. And it is because men need other men in order

to live long enough to *become* heroes that I am able to write songs. Otherwise . . . no one would be alive to tell me the tales that *become* my songs."

"And I thought your lot made it all up," Guntha said, though I knew he was joking.

"We . . . *embellish*, to be sure," I said unabashedly. "All heroes are handsome, all princesses beautiful, all dangers fell, all escapes narrow, and all victories legendary. You, for example, are taller, slimmer, and better-looking in my songs."

We laughed and toasted that.

"But see here," Guntha said, warming to the discourse, "surely there is another kind of hero in songs. The hero whose tale is sung over his grave."

"Ah, you speak of the tragic hero who dies at the moment of his fame. Is it a death song you crave now, Guntha? Since when do you like sad songs?"

"Not all death songs are sad. Some are glorious, and many are rallying cries."

"They are all sad," I said.

Guntha shook his head. "Not to the fallen. Such songs are not melancholy, Jeks. Such songs are perhaps the truest hero's tale for they capture the warrior at the peak of his glory, with no postscript to tell of the dreary and ordinary days that followed. There are many who would agree that a hero should never outlive his own song. I know I would have no regrets."

"I would have one," I said.

"Eh?"

"If you were to die in such a glorious battle, you know that I would be by your side. Our men, too. We would all go down together, our blood filling the inkwells of the songmakers."

"So what is your regret?"

I smiled. "I am just arrogant enough to want to outlive our deaths so that *I* would be the one to write that song."

Guntha laughed long and loud. Some of the sleeping

men muttered and pulled their blankets over their heads.

"By Iss, Jeks, you'll have to teach your ghost the art of crafting songs."

We laughed, but less so this time, and then we lapsed into a long silence. Guntha and I looked out beyond the battlements of our stolen outpost, past the glow of torches, into the velvety blackness of the night. The moons were down now and starlight was painted on the silks of ten thousand banners and a hundred thousand tents. Cookfires glowed like a mirror of the constellations above. Guntha went and leaned on the wall and I with him, and we stared at the last army of the Pirates of Barsoom. Three hundred thousand foot soldiers and a cavalry of five thousand mounted knights.

Resting now, waiting for dawn.

It was a nice joke to call them pirate scum and a rabble army, but the truth was there before us. It was one of the greatest armies ever assembled, and it marched on Helium and the lands of the Warlord. Would our lands go down in flames? We told ourselves "no." We had learned long ago to believe that John Carter, Jeddak of Jeddaks, would find a way to rally and respond and soak the dead soil of Barsoom in the blood of even so vast an army.

I knew that this was the core of Guntha's despair. He wanted to be there, he wanted to be with the Warlord when the true battle came. Even though he believed that his next battle would be his last, he wanted that battle to matter, to mean something. To be legendary.

We were a nuisance who took this fortress by luck and audacity, but as Guntha said, we would be swatted before the sun was above the horizon. We would not see the Warlord's fleet of airships fill the skies from horizon to horizon. We would not be there when the last—truly the last—great battle of our age was fought. We would already be dead. Forgotten, buried in the rubble of a fort that still stood only because it was inconvenient to take it from us in the dark. There would be no moment to shine, no glory, no notice. There would only be death and then a slide into nothingness as memories of us were overlaid by the songs that would be written about the real battle.

"Perhaps the Warlord will come with the dawn," I said. "The messengers we sent were well-mounted."

He gave another weary shake. "No. They would need to fly on wings to have reached even the most distant outposts. Had we an airship . . . but, no. John Carter will come, and he will come in all his might and wrath, but our song, my friend, will have ended long before."

"You would never have made a songmaker," I said. "You don't know how to write an ending to your own tale."

"Ha," he laughed, "and that is what I've been trying to tell you all evening."

Guntha woke me at the blackest hour of night. Only cold starlight washed down upon him as he crouched over me. For my part I came awake from a dream of battle.

"What is it?" I cried. "Are we beset?"

My sword was half-drawn from its sheath when he caught my wrist. "No, sheath your sword, my friend," said he. "Just listen to me for a moment and then I'll let you rest."

"Speak, then," I said quietly, mindful of the men who slept around us.

"What I said earlier . . . they were weak words from an old tongue, and I ask that you forgive them."

"There is nothing to forgive."

"Forget them, then. I spoke from old age and regret, but

as I lay upon my blanket I thought better of my words, and of my life. To blazes with death songs and glory, and to Iss with the ego of someone to whom the gods have granted a thousand graces. I said that I was a dwar and by heaven I will die as one. Not as a hero in some grand song, but a simple man doing a simple job for which he is well-suited. A loyal soldier for whom his daily service to his lord is both his purpose and his reward." He took a breath. "I have had my day, and there need be no more songs for me. None to write and none to sing. Not for me, Jeks, and not for us. The song is over. All that remains is to do one last day's honest work and then I shall lay me down with a will, content that I have not betrayed the trust placed upon me."

I was tempted in my weariness to make light of so bold a speech at such an unlikely hour, but the starlight glittered in his eyes like splinters of sword steel. And all the shadows resculpted his face so that as he turned this way and that he was two different men. Or perhaps two different versions of Dwar Guntha. When he turned to the right it seemed to me that I looked upon a much younger man–the young dwar I met in the dungeons so many years ago; and when he turned to the other side, the blue-white starlight painted his face into a mask like unto a funeral mask of some ancient king. Neither aspect betrayed even a whisper of the doubt or weakness that had been in his voice scant hours before.

I sat up and put my hand on his shoulder. "Dwar Guntha," I said, "you would have made quite a singer of songs."

He chuckled. "Don't mock me. It's just that I had second thoughts after I lay down."

"Tell me."

"If we are to die tomorrow–or, today, as I perceive that dawn is not many hours away–then at least let us satisfy ourselves to usefulness."

"I don't follow."

"What would you rather do, Jeks? Be an insect to be smoked out of the cracks in these ancient walls and ground underfoot . . . or die as a fighting man?"

"You ask a question to which we both know the answer. The latter, always."

"Then when the sun ignites the morning, let us not wait for death behind these walls. Let us ride out instead."

I smiled. "Ride out?"

"Aye! A charge. We might make the upland cleft, where the slopes narrow before they spill out onto the great plains. It's a bottleneck and we could fill it. With our thoats, we could make a wall of spears." Guntha slapped his thigh. "By the gods I would bear death's ungentle touch, but I will not—*cannot*—bear it without blood upon my steel. Even if my blade breaks on iron circlet or skull beneath, then let it break thus, red to the hilt."

"Ride out?" I asked again. "Sixteen against one hundred thousand?"

"Better than sixteen quivering behind battlements they don't have the numbers to defend."

"We wouldn't last a minute."

"And, *ah!*—what a minute it would be."

"No songs," I said.

"No songs," he agreed. "The only song that need be written today is that of John Carter, Jeddak of Jeddaks, as he fills the sky with ships and rains fury down upon this pirate scum. This is it, you know. This is the last battle. Even if we survived tomorrow—and there is scant chance of that—war is over for our generation. Once this army is crushed, then there will be peace on Barsoom. Peace! And it was our swords, Jeks, that helped to bring about such a glorious and blessed and thoroughly depressing turn of events. No . . . let us ride out to our doom and the dooms of those who first oppose us. The Free Riders of Helium, sailing to paradise on a river of pirate blood."

I laughed. "A singer of songs, indeed!"

We smiled at each other then. Dawn was coming and we both knew that only one last sleep awaited us now.

"I'll go wake the others," said I. "I think they will be pleased!"

And so they were.

Dawn did indeed come early, and with it the silver voices of a thousand trumpets. My head ached with the hot hammers of the wine-devils, but I was in my battle harness before the pale sunlight clawed its way over the horizon. Before the first echo of the trumpets had yet had time to reach the distant mountains and come back to us, we swung open the gates to the outpost and the Free Riders rode out into the dawn.

Such a sight it must have been, could I have but seen it from a lofty perch. Sixteen men in heavy armor from another age. Spears and lances, war hammers and swords, polished and glittering.

The pirates scrambled to meet us, the pike men and foot soldiers grabbing up pieces of armor even as they counted our numbers and laughed. Had I any thoughts of surviving the day, I, too, might have laughed; but I knew a great secret that they did not. We were sufficient to our purpose: plenty enough men to die.

We raced to the upland cleft, which was a natural fissure in the red rock through which only half a dozen horses could pass at once. The footing was bad and you needed a trailwise thoat to navigate it at the best of times. All other passes were much stepped or littered with boulders, which forced the army to funnel into the pass. Hence the reason they had stopped for the night. We did not flatter ourselves that that great monster of an army had paused for us.

Dwar Guntha rode before the company, his ancient sword held high.

A dwar from the pirates cupped hands around his mouth and bade Dwar Guntha to surrender.

"Surrender, old man! Beg for your life and my Jeddak may spare it!" he taunted.

Guntha never stopped smiling, even as he hefted his spear and threw it with great power and accuracy into the throat of the pirate dwar.

"There is our surrender," Dwar Guntha cried aloud. "We will write our names in the book of death with pirate blood. Have at you bastards, and may the desert demons feast upon your cowardly bones!"

The pirates stared at the body of their fallen captain for a long moment, and then with a great roar like a storming sea, they swept toward us.

We formed ranks and drew into the cleft and only when the first wave of them rushed up the hill at us, we charged out to meet them. Spears flashed like summer thunder and the air was filled with a treasure house of bright red rubies.

Ah, the killing.

Guntha and I fought side by side, our thoats rearing and slashing with steel-shod feet. The enemy was so determined to run us down that they sent lancers and foot soldiers in rather than archers. After all, who were we but a few old men on old horses?

It was an arrogance that cost them dearly. And yes, it would have made a glorious song. A battle song. A death song that would be remembered long after our bones were dust. Alas.

Each of the Riders was a veteran of countless battles. Old maybe, but deft and clever and ruthless. They laughed as they fought, delighting in the expressions of shock on the faces of much younger men who learned too little and too late that wisdom and experience often trumps youth and vigor. They came at us in that narrow defile and we took them, shouting our ancient songs of war as the blood ran like a brook around our ankles.

But there were one hundred thousand of them. Though they sent not a single man who could stand before the least of us, they had men to spare and no sword arm can fight without fatigue forever.

I saw Kinto Kan fall, his body feathered with arrows but his own quiver empty and the dead heaped around him—two score and six to be his slaves in death. Ben Bendark, known as Thark-killer before the Warlord forged the alliance, swung his war axe, that great cleaver of a hundred tavern songs, and the head of a pirate jed flew from his shoulders. I never saw where it landed. Bendark gave a wild cry of red triumph even as spears pierced his chest and stilled his mighty heart. He fell next to his brother, Gan, who smiled even in death, his mighty hands clenched forever around the shattered throats of the men who killed him.

Hadro Henkin, the sword dancer from Gathol, leapt and turned and cut men from the saddle and slipped between spears and left a path of ruin behind him. He made it nearly to the chariot of the Jeddak himself before a dozen spearmen converged and brought him down. His best friend, Zeth Hondat, screamed like a banth and threw himself at the spearmen, cutting them down one-two-three-four. Seven fell before the Jeddak raised a huge curved sword and cut Zeth nearly in twain.

These things I saw and more. The waves of pirates were

as limitless as the dunes of a desert. An ocean of spears and swords, but Dwar Guntha had chosen our spot well and we held the high ground while they were forced into a narrow killing chute. We slaughtered five times our number. Ten times. *More*. And still they came. As I parried and thrust, cut and slashed, I could not help but compose our song in my head. Despite the melancholy musings of last night, this was a glorious end. This was such an end that perhaps the pirates themselves would write the song. Not a hero's lament or stirring death song, but a tale of desert demons who it took an army to overthrow. We would be the monsters to frighten children on dark nights, and that would please Dwar Guntha. It was a way to strike once more into the heart of our enemy.

In a moment's brief reprieve I called to him. Guntha bled from a dozen cuts and leaned heavily on his saddle horn.

"What a song!" I cried.

"Sing it with your blade," he laughed, and they were on us again.

Then I saw three things occur in close succession, and what a wonder they were to behold.

First, I saw the fresh wave of pirates swarm toward us. These were burly men, not the foot soldiers or light skirmishers; these were the cream of their cavalry on fresh thoats, led by the fierce Jeddak in his war chariot. Dwar Guntha reared up on his thoat, the reins flying free, a spear in one hand and his ancient sword in the other. With a cry so fierce and powerful that it momentarily stilled the war shouts of the pirates, Guntha thrust the spear deep into the roaring mouth of the chariot's lead thoat, and as the beast fell the chariot tilted forward to offer the Jeddak up to Guntha's sword. The blade caught red sunlight and then flashed down, cleaving gold circlet and black skull even as the Jeddak thrust his own great blade forward into Dwar

Guntha's chest. Guntha's blade snapped as he predicted it would, but only on a killing stroke. His last, and a masterful one it was. The pirates could never reckon this day's victory without counting a terrible cost.

Dwar Guntha fell, and that was the second thing I saw. He fell and as he did so the entire battle seemed to freeze into a shocked moment. The pirates recoiled as if the sight of a hero's fall and their own champion's death stole the heart from them.

And then I turned to see the third thing, and I knew then why the entire army of pirates has stalled in this moment.

The sky was full of ships.

Hundreds of them. Thousands. The great combined host of Helium and the Tharks, together in a fleet such as no man has seen in the skies of Barsoom in fifty thousand years. I do not know how our scout reached the capital in time. Perhaps he found a patrol in their airship and flew like a demon wind to spread the news and sound the alert. I will never know, and do not care. John Carter had come, and that was all that mattered. He had come . . . and with the greatest force of arms this world could yet muster. Here, to this barren place by a forgotten outpost. Here to fight the last battle. Whoever won this war would rule Barsoom forever.

John Carter, Warlord of Warlords, grown wise in his years, knew this and he brought such a force that the pirates howled in fear.

But . . . ah, they did not throw down their weapons.

I will honor them enough to say that, and to say that they made a fight of it that *will* make songs worth singing.

Yet, my heart was lifted as I looked up and saw a fleet so vast that it darkened the skies.

Or . . . was it my eyes that grew dark?

I felt a burning pain and looked down to see the glittering length of a sword moving through me below my heart.

I laughed my warrior's laugh and I slew my slayer even as the air erupted with the barrage of ten thousand airships firing all at once.

And the voice of the singer faded, even to his own ears.

* * 4 * *

I t was a cold night in Helium. The moons were like chips of ice in the black forever that stretched above the royal palace.

John Carter drew his cloak more tightly around him. He was still a tall man, still strong, though great age had slimmed him. Slender and hard as a sword blade.

He leaned a shoulder against a pillar and looked out over the city. Even this late there was the sound of music and laughter. The sounds of peace. How long had it been thus, he mused. So many nights of so many years without the clang of steel on steel? He sighed, content that his people lived without fear, and yet secretly craving those old days when he and Tars Tarkas rode out to face monsters and madmen and hordes of bloodthirsty enemies.

Those were memories of a different world than this.

He heard a sound behind him and saw Kestos, the singer, gathering up his scrolls after a night of composing songs for a pending festival. When the young man noticed Carter watching, he bowed.

"My prince," he said nervously, "I did not mean to disturb you. . . . I'm just leaving–"

Carter waved it off. "No. Tarry a moment, Kestos. Tarry and entertain an old man. Sing me a song."

"Of what would you have me sing, my prince? Of the spring harvest? Of the dance of the moons above–"

"No. Gods, no. Kestos, sing me one of the old songs. Sing me a song of heroes and battle."

"I . . . know but a few, my prince. I can sing of your victory over the—"

"No. I know my own songs. Sing to me the death song of Dwar Guntha. That's a good tale for a night like this."

The young man looked embarrassed. "My prince, I am sorry . . . but I don't know that song."

Carter turned and studied him. "Ah . . . you are so young. To not know the great songs is so sad."

"I . . . I'm sorry . . ."

Carter smiled. "No. Sit, young Kestos and I will sing you the song. Learn it. Remember it, and sing it often. Some songs should never be forgotten."

And as the moons sailed through the black ocean of the sky, John Carter, Warlord of all Barsoom, sang of the last charge of the great Free Riders.

And such a tale it was. All of the heroes were tall and handsome, all of the enemies were vile and dangerous, and each of the heroes slew a hundred and then died gloriously upon a mountain of their foes.

Or, so it goes in the song.

APPENDIX

A Barsoomian Gazetteer, or, Who's Who and What's What on Mars

BY RICHARD A. LUPOFF

APT

A six-limbed creature found near the North Pole of Mars. Its white color permits it to blend in with ice or snow. Its most notable feature is its eyes, which are faceted like those of an Earthly house fly. Each facet can be opened or closed independently. Because of its six limbs, the apt is in all likelihood evolutionarily related to both the white apes and the Green Men of Mars.

ASSASSINS GUILD

A professional society of Martian trained killers-for-hire, roughly comparable to the Earthly Mafia or Yakuza.

ATMOSPHERE PLANT

Because the Martian atmosphere has slowly leaked away into space, it is necessary for the Barsoomians to create a constant supply of new, breathable air. They built the great atmosphere plant, a huge, thick-walled building that concentrates the sun's rays to produce this air supply. The atmosphere plant is fully automated, but when its failure threatens the end of all life on Mars, John Carter must make his way into its interior to repair the damage. However, the atmosphere plant is fitted with extensive, automated defenses designed to protect it from sabotage or direct attack. John Carter must find a way to evade or detect these protective devices before he can perform repairs.

BANTH

Sometimes known as the "Martian lion," the banth is a large, dangerous carnivore. It is largely hairless except for a thick ruff similar to that of the male terrestrial lion. Banths live and hunt in packs. Their multiple rows of razor-sharp, daggerlike teeth can make quick work of their prey. Some Barsoomians have succeeded in at least partially domesticating banths and use them to torture and even murder prisoners. One thinks of the practice in Imperial Rome of disposing of victims by "throwing them to the lions."

BLUE BELLY

A soldier of the Union (Northern) army during the American Civil War. Origin uncertain, but the term probably refers to the blue uniforms worn by most Union soldiers; most Southern soldiers wore gray uniforms.

CALOT

A Martian animal roughly comparable to the Earthly dog. Calots are huge, fierce beasts capable of terrible destruction. They have ten short legs and are immensely powerful.

CARTHORIS

The son of John Carter and Dejah Thoris. Within ten years Carthoris has grown to become a courageous explorer. While on an exploration flight to the Valley Dor, Carthoris crashlands and is captured by the Therns and imprisoned in the City of Omean. There he is reunited with his father, who has first returned to Earth, then again to Barsoom. Eventually Carthoris marries the lovely Thuvia, a princess of the City of Ptarth, where Thuvia's father, Thuvan Dihn, is Jeddak.

COCHISE

An important chief or "nantan" of the Chiricahua Apaches (1805–1874). Cochise led his people in resisting the encroachment of white soldiers and settlers on their land in the American Southwest. He was especially embittered when his father-in-law, Mangas Coloradas, who had been invited to a supposedly peaceful conference with white military officers, was instead arrested and imprisoned. Cochise then decided that the white Americans had no sense of honor. He was a brilliant military strategist and inspiring leader of his people. In later years he negotiated a treaty with the army, represented by General Oliver Howard. Cochise's one white friend of many years' standing was Tom Jeffords, who helped to negotiate the treaty. Edgar Rice Burroughs held Native Americans in high esteem, especially members of the Apache Nation, as shown in his novels *The War Chief* and *Apache Devil*. Cochise meets up with John Carter in Chris Claremont's story "The Ghost That Haunts the Superstition Mountains" in this anthology.

DEJAH THORIS

A beautiful Red Martian Princess, described by John Carter as "incomparable." She is from the great Martian city of Helium, descended from Jeddaks, the rulers of the Martian tribes. In appearance she is totally human, with a perfect red complexion. However, like all members of her race, she was hatched from an egg and will lay eggs from which her children will be hatched. In time she marries John Carter and they have a son and daughter, and grandchildren. The egg-laying gene inherited from Dejah Thoris seems to be dominant over John Carter's live-bearing heredity, as all of their descendents are egg-layers, not live-bearers.

DWAR

A military rank, equivalent to a captain. [See **Military Titles**]

EDGAR RICE BURROUGHS

Of course we know of Mr. Burroughs (born 1875, died 1950) as one of the most famous and successful authors of his time. In addition to John Carter and the wonderful Barsoom novels, Burroughs was the creator of the even more famous Tarzan of the Apes, about whom he wrote some two dozen books. Burroughs also wrote other science fiction novels, westerns, detective stories, and realistic fiction. He also put himself into a number of his books as a character. In this form he was born in 1855 and was related to his "Uncle Jack"–John Carter. This fictional Edgar Rice Burroughs lived a very long life and aged slowly. Even so, the last time he met John Carter during one of Carter's visits to Earth, Burroughs mentions that he is now an old man while John Carter still appears to be thirty years old.

EIGHTH AND NINTH RAYS

Much Barsoomian science and technology is based on the study of natural rays emanating from the sun. Two vitally important solar rays, unknown to terrestrial science but understood and utilized on Barsoom, are the Eighth and Ninth Rays. The Eighth Ray provides propulsion for Martian fliers. It can be accumulated and held in tanks rather as electrical energy is held in storage batteries on Earth. Edgar Rice Burroughs's father owned a factory where storage batteries were built. The Ninth Ray is even more important, as it is the primary power source of the Barsoomian atmosphere plant.

ERSITE

A kind of stone found on Barsoom.

FLIERS

A major form of transportation and of combat on Mars is the flier. These aircraft come in many sizes and models, ranging from one-person transports to great cargo craft and aerial battleships. They are powered either by radium engines or by the magnetic field of the planet itself. They are also fitted with propellers to help them move through the air. A similar device, fitted with gigantic wheels, is sometimes used for ground transportation but the aerial models are dominant.

GAHAN OF GATHOL

The Jed of Gathol, Gahan met Tara, daughter of John Carter and Dejah Thoris, at a palace party in Helium. So smitten was he with Tara's beauty that he tried to make love to her, following which she leaves angrily in her personal flier. The flier is caught in a Martian windstorm (an event that in recent years has been proven actually to occur on Mars). Gahan pursues Tara to the city of Bantoom where they encounter Ghek the Kaldane and Luud, the King of the Kaldanes. Another flight ensues, and Gahan engages in a deadly game of Jetan in the city of Manator, finally winning the freedom—and the love—of Tara. After they marry they have a daughter, Llana of Gathol.

GREEN MEN (GREEN MARTIANS)

Unlike many other Martians [See **Races of Barsoom**], the Green Martians are a completely different species. They grow as tall as fifteen feet, are hairless, have huge tusks rising from the corners of their mouths, and have six limbs. When they wish to run as fast as possible they use four limbs as legs, rather in the fashion of Earthly centaurs. At other times they stand upright on their two hindmost legs and use four limbs as arms. The Green Men rule the dead sea-beds of Barsoom. When

John Carter first arrives on Barsoom he is imprisoned by a horde of Green Men, eventually befriending several of their leaders. There are many tribes or "hordes" of these beings, the most important being the Tharks and Warhoons. Some historians of science fiction have suggested that the famous "little green men" of pulp fiction were inspired by Edgar Rice Burroughs's description of the Green Men of Barsoom. However, Burroughs's Green Men are hardly little—they can stand as tall as fifteen feet.

HAAD

[See **Units of Measurement**]

HASTOR

One of the lesser cities of the Heliumite Empire.

HELIUM

Actually two cities located some seventy-five miles apart, Helium is the center and pinnacle of Martian civilization. Each of the two cities is surmounted by a great tower a mile high. The Heliumites are a cultured, technologically advanced people. Helium is ruled by a jeddak, Tardos Mors, grandfather of Dejah Thoris.

HORMAD

A genetically engineered synthetic body, into which brains are transplanted. [See **Ras Thavas**]

HORZ

A very ancient Martian city, once a great center of technology, learning, and culture. It now stands mostly in ruins, but is still occupied by white Orovars. The Orovars live in the supposedly impregnable Citadel of Horz. They are extremely hostile to outsiders, and kill anyone who wanders into their city.

ISSUS

The alleged Goddess of Death and of Life Eternal, Issus is an amazingly old woman even by the lengthy Barsoomian life-span. Barsoomians often reach the age of 1,000 but Issus is 5,000 years old! She ruled as Queen of the First Born [See **Races of Barsoom**], exploiting credulous Martians for her own power and enrichment. She was served by a constantly replenished supply of beautiful female slaves. She would typically use her slaves for a year, then have them thrown to the white apes to be killed. She was eventually overthrown by an invading force of Tharks and killed by her own disappointed followers.

JASOOM

This is the Barsoomian name for Earth, just as Mars is our name for Barsoom. If John Carter's travel to Barsoom involved crossing not merely millions of miles but also millions of years, then the Barsoomian astronomers of ancient times might have observed the Earth before the appearance of the first humans: a world teeming with huge creatures, steaming jungles, flying reptiles, insects the size of helicopters, aquatic behemoths compared to which modern whales would be the size of minnows, and monsters seen today only in the reconstructions of paleontologists.

JED

A military rank, equivalent to a chieftain or minor king. [See **Military Titles**]

JEDDAK

A military rank, equivalent to a great king or emperor. [See **Military Titles**]

JEDDAK OF JEDDAKS (WARLORD OF MARS)

Designation bestowed upon John Carter. [See **Military Titles**]

JEDDARA

A military rank, equivalent to queen or empress. [See **Military Titles**]

JEDWAR

A military rank, equivalent to a general of generals, or a warlord. [See **Military Titles**]

JETAN

A popular game on Barsoom, often referred to as "Martian chess." It is played on a board of one hundred squares. The front row of "chess men," instead of pawns, are thoats and panthans. The back row, instead of being rooks, knights, bishops, king, and queen, are warriors, padwars, dwars, fliers, chiefs, and princesses. While most Martians play the game on convenient boards with beautifully carved pieces—John Carter is known to carry a miniature Jetan set with him—in the city of Manator the game is played on a giant field by live "pieces." In Manator, when a piece seeks to "take" another, they actually fight to the death.

JOHN CARTER

A captain in the Confederate Army. After the American Civil War (1860–1865) he made his way westward. Trapped in a cave by fierce Indian warriors, he was miraculously transported to Barsoom (Mars). He appears to be thirty years old, but in fact has lived for centuries, always appearing to be of the same age, and always a skilled swordsman and courageous warrior. In any situation, no matter how hopeless the odds, he fights on, uttering his personal motto, "I still live." Because Mars is a smaller planet than Earth and has lighter gravity, John Carter is capable of leaping to great heights and performing other amazing feats. Upon arriving on Mars, John Carter is a stranger in a strange land, but becomes a Jeddak (warlord) and eventually the Jeddak of Jeddaks, in effect, the emperor of an entire planet.

JOHNNY REB

A slang name for a soldier of the Confederate (Southern) army during the American Civil War. The term referred to the fact that the eleven Confederate States were in a state of rebellion against the United States.

JULIAN

The Earthman hero of *The Moon Maid*, who travels to the moon to do battle with the Va-gas and Kalkars. [See **Moon Maid, The**]

KALDANES

These are surely the strangest of all Martian creatures. Really little more than a brilliant brain housed in a soft skull, Kaldanes also possess clawlike organs through which they can attach themselves to creatures called Rykors. Rykors look very much like normal human beings, but instead of having heads, their necks end in a set of openings through which Kaldanes insert their claws, thereby forming a double creature.

KALKARS

An evil humanoid race that lives inside Earth's moon, alongside the Va-gas. [See **Moon Maid, The**]

KANTOS KAN

A Red Martian, Kantos Kan was a padwar in the aerial navy of the City of Helium. Involved in a war between Helium and Warhoon, Kantos Kan was captured and imprisoned along with John Carter. The two men, one of Earth and one of Mars, became close friends. They managed to escape their prison together, and remained friends for many years, Kantos Kan rising through the ranks of Helium's navy.

KAOR

The most common form of Martian greeting. Although roughly translated as "Hello," the Martian word is sometimes used in a very emphatic, emotional manner. While uncounted different languages have developed on Earth, several hundred of which are still in use, there is apparently a single language used throughout Barsoom. Perhaps "Barsoomian" is the only language that ever developed on Mars and spread through the entire planet, or perhaps many languages were invented separately and merged into Barsoomian.

KARAD

[See **Units of Measurement**]

KORUS, LOST SEA OF

While not truly lost, Korus has shrunk since ancient times. It remains above ground at the South Pole of Mars, directly over the Sea of Omean. This very peculiar configuration is unique on Barsoom, and as far as is known, is unlike any other body or water on Mars or Earth.

LLANA OF GATHOL

The granddaughter of John Carter and Dejah Thoris, daughter of Tara of Helium and Gahan of Gathol. This young woman's beauty attracted an eager suitor named Hin Abtol, a Jeddak of the Panars. Alas, Llana doesn't care for Hin Abtol, but he won't take no for an answer so he kidnaps her. Llana is rescued by her grandfather, John Carter, and the warrior Pan Dan Chee, only to become involved in a battle, get captured and rescued again and again, for a total of at least five breathtaking imprisonments and rescues. Llana's adventures are described to Edgar Rice Burroughs by John Carter in person, when Burroughs as an elderly man is living in Hawaii and John Carter returns to Earth for one of his periodic visits.

LOTHARIANS

Once a great seafaring people, the Lotharians retreated to a beautiful, peaceful valley when the great oceans of Mars dried up. They enjoy a very lengthy lifespan and have great mental powers including the ability to create food so real that it is nourishing and weapons so effective they can kill their enemies. However, with the passage of many centuries, all female Lotharians have died, leaving an all-male society that is doomed to disappear when its present members reach the end of their lives. The lovely Thuvia becomes a prisoner of the Lotharians, but is rescued by Carthoris, son of John Carter and Dejah Thoris, and eventually becomes Carthoris's bride.

MALAGORS

The combination of Barsoom's light gravity and that planet's thin atmosphere would have a questionable influence on the evolution of flying creatures. The Malagor was a huge bird, capable of flight probably as a result of its light weight, achieved in part by the development of hollow bones like those of Earthly birds, and its huge wings. After a lengthy period of extinction, the Malagor was restored to the Barsoomian biosphere by the brilliant scientist Ras Thavas, again, as Earthly scientists hope someday to re-create extinct species by cloning preserved DNA.

MANATOR

An ancient city of Barsoom, surrounded by such rough, inhospitable terrain that it has had little or no contact with the rest of Martian civilization for many centuries. However, the game of Jetan is of such ancient origins that it is known in Manator where it is played on a gigantic board with live "pieces." Criminals in Manator are sentenced to become Jetan pieces for anywhere from one to ten games, and when a Jetan piece is "taken" in Manator, this means that he has literally had to fight for his life—and lost. [See **Jetan**]

MANTALIA

A Martian plant that can thrive with almost no water, thus giving it a high survival value on the very dry surface of the planet. The mantalia produces a flavorful and nourishing sap, rather like maple syrup, but more milky in appearance, and is highly prized as a source of sustenance.

MATAI SHANG

High priest of the Holy Therns, his own title being Holy Hekkador. He was the brother of the high priestess Issus. When the false religion of the Therns was exposed and its corrupt leaders exposed, Matai Shang succeeded in kidnapping Dejah Thoris of Helium and Thuvia of Ptarth and fleeing to remote cities where he felt he could still exert his authority. John Carter eventually rescued Matai Shang's captives.

MILITARY TITLES

The political structure of Mars is fairly primitive, a combination of military hierarchy and royal dynasties. The military ranks of jedwar (general of generals, or warlord), odwar (general), dwar (captain), and padwar (lieutenant) all have rough equivalents in Earthly armies. They are probably based on Edgar Rice Burroughs's experience as a soldier in the cavalry of the United States Army. Panthans are mercenaries. Jeds are chieftans or minor kings. Jeddaks are great kings or emperors. Jeddaras are queens or empresses. Princesses, however, are referred to simply as princesses. The ultimate title on Mars was won by John Carter, and was rendered as either Jeddak of Jeddaks or simply, the Warlord of Mars.

MOON MAID, THE

While not exactly part of the Barsoom series, *The Moon Maid* is connected nonetheless. According to this novel, which is regarded by some critics as one of Edgar Rice Burroughs's very best efforts, the events begin in the year 2024, although they are told to Burroughs in 1967, then transmitted telepathically by the author to his more youthful self for publication in 1923. In the novel, a spaceship is built on Earth in 1924. It is named the *Barsoom* and sets out for Mars, but instead crash-lands on the moon, which turns out to be hollow and inhabited. Survivors of the crash encounter a number of species and nations, most notably the Kalkars, who eventually conquer the Earth, leading to a rebellion. The Moon Maid of the title is the beautiful Nah-ee-lah. The Earth hero, Julian, rescues her from assorted perils.

MOONS OF MARS

Earthly astronomers call the two moons of Mars Phobos and Deimos. Barsoomians refer to them as Thuria (Phobos) and Cluros (Deimos). Thuria is the larger of the two; it is inhabited and its natives call it Ladan. Strangely, when anyone travels to Thuria from Barsoom, the traveler shrinks to a proportionate size, so that Thuria seems to be a full-sized planet. As far as is known, Barsoom's smaller moon, Cluros, is uninhabited.

NINTH RAY

[See **Eighth and Ninth Rays**]

ODWAR

A military rank, equivalent to a general. [See **Military Titles**]

OLIVER HOWARD

An American general. [See **Cochise**]

OROVARS (WHITE MARTIANS)

These were one of the ancient human races of Barsoom. As long as a million years ago, they were a great seafaring people, sailing the oceans of the planet and trading with many other peoples. Over the passage of hundreds of thousands of years, as the great seas and oceans of Mars dried up, the Orovars built and rebuilt their cities to remain on the edges of these bodies of water, but eventually there was so little water left on Mars that the Orovars were faced with disaster. Their civilization in shambles, they were conquered by the six-limbed Green Martians. However, the Orovars survived to combine with other Martian races—the black and yellow humans—to create the modern White Martians, the Therns and Lotharians.

ORTHIS

The leader of the Kalkars. [See **Moon Maid, The**]

PADWAR

A military rank, equivalent to lieutenant. [See **Military Titles**]

PAN DAN CHEE

An Orovar (White Martian) and, a warrior of the City of Horz. Captured by a band of Green Martians, Pan Dan Chee is rescued by John Carter, who offers to return with him to Horz. However, the policy of this city is extremely hostile to visitors (to say the least!) and both John Carter and Pan Dan Chee are condemned to death. After much derring-do they escape, but Pan Dan Chee has by now seen a miniature carving of John Carter's granddaughter, Llana, and fallen hopelessly in love with her. Although at first reluctant to do so, Llana eventually accepts Pan Dan Chee as a suitor.

PANTHAN

A mercenary. [See **Military Titles**]

PELLUCIDAR

While not directly connected with the Barsoom stories, the Pellucidar books played an important role in the works of

Edgar Rice Burroughs. The basic idea behind these stories is that the Earth is not a solid sphere like a billiard ball, but is hollow like a tennis ball. Its interior is warmed and lighted by a miniature sun which shines in the very center of the world, creating eternal daylight for the dwellers on the inner surface of the Earth. Edgar Rice Burroughs called this inner world Pellucidar. The novels set in this world were popular. The most famous of them, *Tarzan at the Earth's Core*, tells the story of Burroughs's most famous adventure hero traveling to Pellucidar on a zeppelin that navigates a great opening at the North Pole. Burroughs utilized a similar theme in his novel *The Moon Maid*.

PLANT MEN

These are truly horrible beings, very likely the inspiration for some of the monsters found in the stories of horror writer H. P. Lovecraft, an early admirer of Burroughs. The plant men are ten to twelve feet tall, hairless, and blue in color except for long, thick, black hair on their heads. They have no mouths but obtain nourishment through their hands. They have only one eye, a dreadful white orb. They are fierce fighters, hopping over their opponents to gain advantage in battle. They dwell in the Valley Dor near Barsoom's South Pole.

RACES OF BARSOOM

Unlike Earth, where there is only one surviving human species, the ancient Neanderthal and other relatives having disappeared thousands of years ago, Barsoom has at least four "human" species. There are true humans of various colors—red, white (Orovars), yellow (Okarians), black (First Born)—identical to Earth humans except for the fact that they lay eggs rather bearing their children alive. There are also the great, six-limbed Green Martians (i.e., Tharks and Warhoons), the Rykors and Kaldanes, and the strange, terrifying plant men.

RADIUM RIFLES

Because the Martian civilization is ancient, many inventions developed long ago survive into the present. These include radium rifles. These are not ray-guns of the type featured in other science fiction stories of Burroughs's era. Rather, they fire bullets tipped with explosive radium pellets, in effect tiny atomic bombs. However, most Martians consider these unsuitable, and instead prefer to fight with swords.

RAS THAVAS

A mad scientist who transfers brains into genetically engineered synthetic bodies called hormads.

RED MEN

The ancient "human races" of Mars were divided by skin color into white, black, and yellow. Over many millennia these races amalgamated, resulting in the dominant Barsoomian race of John Carter's time. They are a beautiful people with smooth skin and glossy black hair. They are identical to terrestrial humans, save for laying eggs rather than bearing their young alive. Small enclaves of the white, black, and yellow Martian races do survive to modern times. There are also other non-human peoples on Mars, most notably the six-limbed Green Men and the cyclopean plant men.

RIVER ISS

This is the largest surviving body of water on Mars, which was once a warm planet with abundant water and a rich atmosphere. For many years, Edgar Rice Burroughs's description of the ancient Mars was considered sheer imagination, but recent discoveries indicate that this description is remarkably accurate. There is overwhelming evidence that Mars once had seas and mighty rivers, the dried beds of which have been explored by orbiting satellites and robotic landers. Maybe John Carter traveled not only through space from Jasoom to Barsoom, but through time as well, from the Earthly year 1866 to the Mars of long, long ago.

RYKORS

[See **Kaldanes**]

SARKOJA

A very old Green Martian woman, member of Tars Tarkas's tribe or horde. She was treacherous by nature and wildly jealous of John Carter and Dejah Thoris, attempting to lead them into traps and bring about their doom. When her schemes were uncovered, she sought to escape justice by embarking on the pilgrimage on the River Iss, almost certainly to meet a suitably unpleasant demise at the hands of the white apes or Holy Therns.

SKEEL

A hardwood found on Barsoom.

SOLA

Upon his arrival on Mars, John Carter became a prisoner of the Green Men horde led by Tars Tarkas. Injured and imprisoned, John Carter might well have died, but Sola was possessed of an empathetic and caring nature, a great rarity among Green Martians. She nursed John Carter back to health and tutored him in the ways of Barsoom. Her parentage was at first unknown, but eventually it was revealed that she was the daughter of Tars Tarkas.

TAL

A unit of time. The Martian equivalent of a second.

TARA OF HELIUM

Daughter of John Carter and Dejah Thoris and sister of

Carthoris. Beautiful but vain, she is courted by Gahan of Gathol and flees Helium in her personal flier. After a series of breathtaking perils, imprisonments, and rescues, she agrees to marry Gahan and eventually becomes the mother of Llana of Gathol.

TARS TARKAS

A Green Martian warrior. At first, Tars Tarkas believes that John Carter intends to destroy the eggs of the Tharks, Tars Tarkas's tribe or "horde." Eventually they become close friends and comrades in arms.

TARZAN (A.K.A. JOHN CLAYTON, LORD GREYSTOKE, WAZIRI)

Tarzan, most famous of Edgar Rice Burroughs's creations, is still one of the world's most widely recognized fictitious figures, along with Sherlock Holmes and Superman. Burroughs liked to spin connections between his fictitious worlds, for instance sending Tarzan to Pellucidar in one novel [See **Moon Maid, The**]. Many enthusiastic readers and not a few writers have expressed the wish that Tarzan would travel to Mars and meet John Carter—a "superhero team-up" for the ages! Unless a previously lost manuscript should be discovered, however, it appears that Burroughs never wrote such a story, although several other authors have attempted it, including some in this anthology.

TELEPATHY

When John Carter first arrived on Mars, he discovered that Barsoomians were able to read one another's minds. This would obviate the need for a spoken language, but they have one nonetheless. Perhaps the spoken language evolved before the telepathic power, and spoken Barsoomian will someday cease to be used, but for the time being the Martians can communicate in either manner, just as people on Earth can communicate by spoken words, hand signals, computer links, or other means. At any rate, while John Carter (and later Ulysses Paxton) could read the minds of Martians, the Martians could not read the minds of their visitors from Earth, which motivated John Carter and Ulysses Paxton to learn to speak Barsoomian.

THARKS

A tribe of Green Men. [See **Green Men**]

THERNS

The ancient Martians were divided into races or tribes of different colors [See **Races of Barsoom**]. The Therns are the remnants of the White Martian race. They live in the Mountains of Otz and the Valley Dor. This region is reached by pilgrims traveling on the River Iss, the largest river on Mars. The Holy Therns spread the religious belief that pilgrims on the River Iss reach a land of eternal bliss, but in fact they are either enslaved or devoured by the Therns. All male Therns are bald but wear blond wigs.

THOAT

Although sometimes described as the "Martian horse," the thoat bears little resemblance to Earthly equines. Its most obvious features are its size—as tall as ten feet—and its eight legs, four on each side of its body. This would indicate that thoats are not closely related to either four-limbed or six-limbed species on Mars. They may actually have evolved from the eight-limbed cephalopods that swam in the warm, nurturing waters of Mars millions of years ago! By the time of John Carter's arrival on Mars, the thoat has been domesticated and even bred into several subspecies. The most common are used as transportation. They are controlled by their riders through telepathic commands.

THURIA

The Barsoomian name for Mars's moon Phobos. [See **Moons of Mars**]

THUVIA

Having embarked on the pilgrimage down the River Iss at an age much younger than most Martians, Thuvia of Ptarth became a slave to the Holy Therns. While thus imprisoned she encountered a fellow prisoner, none other than John Carter, with whom she managed to escape from the Therns. Following a series of exciting adventures, she became the bride of Carthoris, son of John Carter and Dejah Thoris.

TOM JEFFORDS

An agent authorized to interact with the Native American tribes on behalf of the U.S. government during the Apache wars of the nineteenth century. [See **Cochise**]

TOONOLIAN MARSHES

While ancient Barsoom was covered with huge seas and oceans, little surface water remains due to eons of evaporation and loss of water vapor. Several bodies of water do still survive, such as the River Iss and the Sea of Omean. The Toonolian Marshes are not so much a body of water as an area of swamps, ponds, mud, and quicksand. There are two city-states in this region, Toonol and Phundahl, hostile to each other. A third city, ancient Morbus, was restored by the scientist Ras Thavas but was destroyed again. The marshes are inhabited by dangerous reptilian and insect life, as well as primitive bands of humans.

TUR

While Edgar Rice Burroughs never criticized sincerely religious people, he was an opponent of religious hypocrites and of anti-scientific, anti-intellectual fundamentalists. His satire of their attitudes and abuses were expressed in his description of the cult of Tur. This was the official religion of the City of Phundahl (note the pun), where the *Turgan* or sacred book of Tur is considered the ultimate source of truth. There are many idols and temples of Tur, and great theological debates are held over the meaning of the holy phrase, "Tur is Tur." The racketeering practices of the priesthood of Phundahl, headed by the Jeddak Dar Hajus, were eventually revealed by the heroic Earthman Ulysses Paxton.

ULSIO

The so-called "Martian rat," found most often in the dungeons of prisons on Barsoom. Hairless and repulsive, as large as a medium-sized dog, the ulsio has six legs, thereby suggesting that it is evolutionarily related to the white apes and Green Men of Mars. The ulsio has razor-sharp teeth and is extremely dangerous, although in combat it tends to be sly and cowardly rather than courageous.

ULYSSES PAXTON

An officer in the American Expeditionary Force fighting in France during the First World War, Ulysses Paxton was severely wounded. He had read of the wonderful adventures of John Carter on Barsoom, and discovered that he had the same power to travel to cross the millions of miles separating Earth from Mars. On Mars, Paxton fell in love with the beautiful Valla Dia, princess of the City of Duhor. However, Valla Dia had been the unwilling subject of a surgical procedure, and her skull now housed the brain of the hideous and cruel Xaxa of Phundahl, while Valla Dia's brain was in Xaxa's body. Ulysses Paxton brought about the restoration of Valla Dia's brain to her own skull. They were then married and Paxton became a noble citizen of Duhor.

UNDER THE MOONS OF MARS

This was the original title of the first John Carter novel by Edgar Rice Burroughs. The author submitted the story to *All-Story* magazine under the byline "Normal Bean." The story was accepted and published as a serial between February and July, 1912, with the author's byline changed to "Norman Bean." The first book edition was published in 1917 under the more familiar name *A Princess of Mars*, with the author's name, Edgar Rice Burroughs.

UNITS OF MEASUREMENT

Barsoomians divide the circle into 360 karads, just as Earthly mathematicians and cartographers divide the circle into 360 degrees. At the Barsoomian equator, one karad is the equivalent of 100 haads, the haad being the Martian equivalent of a terrestrial mile. However, the actual circumference of Mars is approximately 13,300 miles. Dividing this distance by 36,000 haads, gives an actual value of the Martian haad of roughly .37 miles. As one moves away from the equator toward either the North or South Pole of Mars, the circumference grows progressively smaller, as does the karad. At the poles the karad would have a theoretical value of zero.

USA

A starchy root. A staple of Barsoomian military rations, rarely served elsewhere except in the homes of the poor.

VA-GAS

Horselike creatures with human faces who can wield weapons with their forelimbs. They live on the inner surface of the moon, along with the Kalkars. [See **Moon Maid, The**]

VALLEY DOR

When Martians sense that they are approaching the end of life (those not previously killed in the seemingly ceaseless wars of

Barsoom) they make a pilgrimage down the River Iss to the Valley Dor, a sort of Martian version of heaven located near the South Pole of their planet. To reach this valley, they must travel through an icy region not unlike the ice fields near the North and South Poles of Earth. Surrounded by a towering mountain range, the Valley Dor is indeed a lovely place, a sort of lush oasis. However, it is inhabited by the terrible plant men who capture the pilgrims and deliver them to the white Therns, who use them as breeding stock for slaves and for food.

WARHOON

A tribe of Green Men [See **Green Men**]

WHITE APES

Fierce creatures standing as tall as fifteen feet, with dead white skins and white hair. They have six limbs, like the Green Martians, and are thus more correctly regarded as relatives of the six-limbed Tharks, Warhoons, and other green hexapods than of Barsoom's true humans. They are social creatures, living in groups, and are intelligent enough to make and use simple tools. They are almost certainly the "missing link" or transitional species from which the Green Martians evolved.

WOOLA

A calot assigned to guard John Carter early in Carter's adventures on Mars. Later, Woola is attacked by white apes and very nearly killed. He is rescued by John Carter and nursed back to health, forming a close bond of loyalty, friendship and affection as a result.

ZITIDAR

A large, dinosaur-like animal. These creatures have been domesticated for many years and are used by Martians to draw freight wagons or drays.

ZODANGA

A large and powerful city, at one time second only to Helium in wealth and influence on Barsoom. There was a serious rivalry between the two cities, until a military confrontation led to the subjugation of Zodanga and its incorporation into the Empire of Helium. During the grand showdown between the two cities, the incomparable Dejah Thoris was kidnapped by Sab Than, son of the Zodangan Jeddak, Than Kosis. To rescue Dejah Thoris, John Carter and his friend Kantos Kan, an naval officer of Helium, disguised themselves and enlisted in the navy of Zodanga.

ZODE

A unit of time. The Barsoomian equivalent of an hour.

ABOUT THE CONTRIBUTORS

JOHN JOSEPH ADAMS

John Joseph Adams (johnjosephadams.com) is the bestselling editor of many anthologies, such as *Wastelands*, *The Living Dead*, *The Living Dead 2*, *By Blood We Live*, *Federations*, *The Improbable Adventures of Sherlock Holmes*, *Brave New Worlds*, *The Way of the Wizard*, and *Lightspeed: Year One*. BarnesandNoble.com named him "the reigning king of the anthology world," and his books have been named to numerous best-of-the-year lists. He is also the editor of *Lightspeed* magazine and is the cohost of io9's *The Geek's Guide to the Galaxy* podcast. Forthcoming anthologies include *The Mad Scientist's Guide to World Domination* and *Armored*. He has been nominated for the World Fantasy Award and the Hugo Award.

DAREN BADER

For the past seventeen years, Daren has been an art director for the video game and entertainment industry, working with a large variety of companies, including Disney, Nintendo, and Capcom. Currently he is the Senior Art Director for Rockstar San Diego where he recently finished art direction for the critically-acclaimed *Red Dead Redemption*. On the weekends, Daren is a freelance illustrator for various trading card games such as *Magic: The Gathering* and *World of Warcraft*, amassing well over two hundred cards in the field. He has also done the occasional book cover, including a series of covers for fan-favorite R. A. Salvatore. Daren lives in northern San Diego with his wife and son.

JEREMY BASTIAN

Jeremy Bastian lives with his wife, Emily, and their menagerie of livestock and poultry in Plymouth, Michigan. He has lived in Michigan all his life minus the two years he spent attending the Art Institute of Pittsburgh. He is currently working on his creator-owned comic *Cursed Pirate Girl* for Olympian Publishing and has had work published through Dark Horse and Archaia comics. His love of an antique world of illustration has warped his artistic integrity into a slow-paced battle against a minimalistic streamlined world. He revels in the most microscopic detail and challenges himself with every page to dig even deeper into the bizarre abyss of his imagination.

PETER S. BEAGLE

Peter S. Beagle was born in 1939 and raised in the Bronx. Thanks to classics like *The Last Unicorn*, *A Fine and Private Place*, and "Two Hearts," he is a living fantasy icon. He also wrote the episode "Sarek" for Star Trek: The Next Generation and the animated *Lord of the Rings*. His nonfiction book *I See By My Outfit* is considered a classic of American travel writing, and he is also a gifted poet, lyricist, and singer/songwriter. He currently makes his home in Oakland, California.

Peter has vivid memories of entertaining himself during slow elementary school classes by writing original adventures of the Lone Ranger, the Shadow, and different characters created by Edgar Rice Burroughs. Getting invited to contribute to this anthology felt, he says, "like a golden ticket back to my childhood."

TOBIAS S. BUCKELL

Tobias S. Buckell is a Caribbean born SF/F author and *New York Times* bestseller who now lives in Ohio. He is the author of *Crystal Rain*, *Ragamuffin*, *Sly Mongoose*, *Halo: The Cole Protocol*, and over forty short stories in various magazines and anthologies. His next novel, *Arctic Rising*, is due out sometime soon from Tor, and he's working on his next book. Find him at tobiasbuckell.com.

JEFF CARLISLE

Jeff Carlisle is a graduate of the prestigious Columbus College of Art and Design. A year or so after graduating, Jeff submitted art to the *Star Wars* fan site TheForce.net, which resulted in a dedicated fan art gallery there. In the year 2000 he met acclaimed fantasy artist and children's book author Tony DiTerlizzi. DiTerlizzi encouraged Jeff to "get in the game," which led Jeff to the 2000 GenCon game fair, and his first industry job: drawing starships, droids, and aliens for *Star Wars Gamer* magazine. After six years of freelance illustration and concept design, Jeff has worked with a number of clients, including: Alderac Entertainment Group (AEG), COSI Studios, Decipher, Goodman Games/Sword and Sorcery, Green Ronin Publishing, Lucasfilm Ltd., Paizo Publishing, Poop House Reilly, Presto Studios/Microsoft Game Studios, The Scarefactory, Inc., Topps, and Wizards of the Coast. Jeff currently lives in Columbus, with his wife, Lisa, and their white hellcat, Snow.

MIKE CAVALLARO

Mike Cavallaro is originally from New Jersey, where he attended the Joe Kubert School of Cartoon and Graphic Art. He began working in the New York comics and animation industries in the early 1990s. His clients include Valiant Comics, DC Comics, Marvel Comics, Image Comics, BOOM! Studios, First Second Books, IDW Publishing, MTV Animation, Warner Brothers Animation, Cartoon Network, and others. Mike is a member of the online webcomics collective, ACT-I-VATE.com, where he contributes free weekly webcomics, including the superhero-sci-fi epic, *LOVIATHAN*, and the true-life historic memoir, *Parade (with fireworks)*. Other graphic novels include *The Life and Times of Savior 28*, a collaboration with writer J. M. DeMatteis, and *Foiled*, the first graphic novel by legendary author Jane Yolen. Mike is a member of the National Cartoonists Society and a founding member of Deep 6 Studios in Brooklyn, where he currently resides.

CHRIS CLAREMONT

Chris Claremont is best known for his award-winning, ground-breaking work on Marvel Comics' *The Uncanny X-Men* series. Chris's work has served as the foundation material for the X-Men movies, including *X-Men: First Class* and the forthcoming second *Wolverine* movie. Chris is currently putting the finishing touches on a young adult novel, *Wild Blood*; working on an adult novel, *The Winter King*; and a screenplay, *Hunter's Moon*.

MOLLY CRABAPPLE

Artist and comics creator Molly Crabapple has been called "a downtown phenomenon" by *The New York Times* and "*the* artist of our time" by comedian Margaret Cho, using her hyper-detailed Victorian pen for graphic novels, giant nightclub murals, and for clients like D.C. Comics, Marvel Comics, SXSW, Red Bull, and the *Wall Street Journal*. She is the creator of *The Puppet Makers* (D.C. Comics) and *Straw House* (First Second Books).

TOM DALY

Both Tom Daly and the modern maraschino cherry hail from the same beautiful small town in the heart of Oregon's Willamette Valley. Both ventured out of the valley, Mr. Daly going on to New York to study art, and the cherry going on to pretty much every bar on the planet. Mr. Daly has been making drawings for books, magazines, and comics since graduating from Parsons School of Design, way back in the twentieth century. When not drawing, Mr. Daly enjoys playing in the park with his sons, reading, long walks, and writing about himself in the third person. Mr. Daly lives in New York City. More of his work can be seen at TomDalyArt.com.

THEODORA GOSS

Theodora Goss was born in Hungary and spent her childhood in various European countries before her family moved to the United States. Although she grew up on the classics of English literature, her writing has been influenced by an Eastern European literary tradition in which the boundaries between realism and the fantastic are often ambiguous. Her publications include the short story collection *In the Forest of Forgetting* (2006); *Interfictions* (2007), a short story anthology coedited with Delia Sherman; and *Voices from Fairyland* (2008), a poetry anthology with critical essays and a selection of her own poems. She has been a finalist for the Nebula, Crawford, and Mythopoeic Awards, as well as on the Tiptree Award Honor List, and has won the World Fantasy and Rhysling Awards.

AUSTIN GROSSMAN

Austin Grossman is a video game design consultant and a doctoral candidate in English Literature at the University of California at Berkeley. He is the author of the novel, *Soon I Will Be Invincible*. His second novel, *You*, is forthcoming from Mulholland Books in 2012, and his short fiction is also slated to appear in John Joseph Adams's anthology *The Mad Scientist's Guide to World Domination*.

MEINERT HANSEN

Meinert has a long list of credits in film, television, and games. He has worked in animation, visual effects, and production design, in both traditional and digital media. He worked as production illustrator and concept artist on *The Mummy: Tomb of the Dragon Emperor, Leatherheads, The Spiderwick Chronicles,* and *300*. As a visual effects concept artist and matte painter, he worked on such films as *Silent Hill*, *Across the Universe*, and *Stranger Than Fiction*. Meinert also worked as an art director on the computer game Myst: Revelation. His television credits include *The Secret Adventures of Jules Verne*, *Inside the Space Station*, and *Alien Planet*. As an animation director, Meinert's credits include *Bad Dog*, *Bob Morane*, and his own cartoon short for Hanna-Barbera, *The Adventures of Captain Buzz Cheeply*. He is currently the senior concept artist at Warner Bros. Games in Montreal.

MICHAEL WM KALUTA

Michael Wm Kaluta began his career in comic book illustration, working for Charlton Comics, DC Comics, Marvel Comics, and some smaller firms. He later illustrated for science fiction magazines such as *Amazing Stories* and *Fantastic Stories*. During his early professional years, he was knee-deep in art for the Mystery comics—*House of Mystery*, *House of Secrets*, and the like—and began doing covers for both *Detective Comics* and *Batman*. In 1973 he illustrated the DC Comics revival of *The Shadow*. Along with various Shadow projects through the years, his career highlights include: the comic book adaptation of Edgar Rice Burroughs's *Carson of Venus* for DC Comics, the art for the 1994 J. R. R. Tolkien calendar, illustrating two Robert E. Howard books (*The Lost Valley of Iskander* and *The Swords of Shahrazar*), and his dream project, illustrating Thea von Harbou's *Metropolis*, the novelization of Fritz Lang's famous silent science fiction film. The pinnacle of his science fiction/adventure/comics efforts is the ongoing comic *Starstruck*.

DAVID BARR KIRTLEY

David Barr Kirtley's short fiction appears in books such as *New Voices in Science Fiction*, *Fantasy: The Best of the Year*, *The Dragon Done It*, *The Living Dead*, and *The Way of the Wizard*, and in magazines such as *Realms of Fantasy*, *Weird Tales*, *Intergalactic Medicine Show*, and *Lightspeed*. He's the cohost (along with John Joseph Adams) of *The Geek's Guide to the Galaxy* podcast on io9, for which he's interviewed dozens of authors and scientists, including George R. R. Martin, Orson Scott Card, Robert Kirkman, and Neil deGrasse Tyson. He holds an MFA in fiction and screenwriting from the University of Southern California, and for the past eight summers has taught at the Pittsburgh-area Alpha Young Writers Workshop. He lives in New York.

JOE R. LANSDALE

Joe R. Lansdale is the author of over thirty-five novels and twenty short story collections. He is also an editor and coeditor of several anthologies of fiction and nonfiction. He has sold numerous screenplays and comics. He has received the Edgar Award, seven Bram Stoker Awards, the British Fantasy Award, and numerous others. Two of his stories, "Bubba Ho-Tep" and "Incident On and Off a Mountain Road" have been filmed. He writes regularly for *The Texas Observer* and is Writer in Residence at Stephen F. Austin State University. He is also a member of The Texas Institute of Letters.

RICHARD A. LUPOFF

Richard A. Lupoff first discovered the works of Edgar Rice Burroughs at the age of nine when he came across a copy of *Tarzan and the Ant-Men*. That was all it took, although it was many years before he found himself, at Canaveral Press in New York, working with the previously unpublished manuscripts of the famous author. After editing *Tarzan and the Madman*, *Tarzan and the Castaways*, *Tales of Three Planets*, and *John Carter of Mars*, Lupoff wrote two of the earliest and most important books about ERB–*Edgar Rice Burroughs: Master of Adventure* and *Barsoom: Edgar Rice Burroughs and the Martian Vision*–as well as editing and publishing *The Reader's Guide to Barsoom and Amtor*. Lupoff has written many novels and short stories. His recent books include *The Emerald Cat Killer, Rookie Blues, Killer's Dozen,* and the trilogy *Terrors, Visions,* and *Dreams.*

JONATHAN MABERRY

Jonathan Maberry is a *New York Times* bestselling author, multiple Bram Stoker Award winner, and comic book writer. His novels include *Rot & Ruin, Dead of Night, Patient Zero, Dust & Decay, The King of Plagues, Ghost Road Blues, Dead Man's Song, Bad Moon Rising,* and *The Wolfman.* His nonfiction books include *They Bite, Zombie CSU, Wanted Undead or Alive, Vampire Universe,* and *The Cryptopedia.* He is the cofounder of the Liars Club and founder of the Writers Coffeehouse. Jonathan is also a career martial artist specializing in Jujutsu and Kenjutsu, and has worked as a bodyguard and chief-instructor for a company that provided advanced defense workshops to all aspects of law enforcement including SWAT. In 2004, he was inducted into the Martial Arts Hall of Fame. Visit him online at jonathanmaberry.com.

GREGORY MANCHESS

Creating a moment that communicates emotionally with the viewer is the essence of Gregory Manchess's artwork. He combined his love for fine art and science fiction and began his freelance career painting for *OMNI* magazine. His versatility and broad range of interests allowed him to cross over to mainstream illustration. There he was able to expand his work to include covers for *Time, Atlantic Monthly, National Geographic*; spreads for *Playboy, Rolling Stone, Newsweek,* and *Smithsonian*; and numerous book covers, including sixty covers for Louis L'Amour. He is one of a few illustrators to have a painting on the cover of *National Geographic* magazine. Widely awarded within the industry, Manchess exhibits frequently at the Society of Illustrators in New York, where he won the coveted Hamilton King Award. He painted the Oregon coast for the 2009 Oregon Statehood Stamp for the USPS, and a 2011 portrait stamp of Mark Twain.

Gregory is included in Walt Reed's latest edition of *The Illustrator in America, 1860–2000.*

L. E. MODESITT, JR.

L. E. Modesitt, Jr., is the author of more than sixty science fiction and fantasy novels, including the Saga of Recluce, the Corean Chronicles, and the Spellsong Cycle, a number of short stories and technical and economic articles. He has the unusual distinction of never having been nominated for a SF/F award, despite numerous starred reviews in many review publications, and five nominations and two awards from romance-oriented reviewers even if in only one of his books did he even write a semi-graphic sensual scene. His novels have been translated into German, Polish, Dutch, Czech, Russian, Bulgarian, French, Spanish, Italian, Hebrew, and Swedish. He has been a U.S. Navy pilot; a market research analyst; a real estate agent; director of research for a political campaign; legislative assistant and staff director for U.S. Congressmen; Director of Legislation and Congressional Relations for the U.S. Environmental Protection Agency; a consultant on environmental, regulatory, and communications issues. His first story was published in *Analog* in 1973, and his latest book is *Princeps* (Tor, November 2011), the fifth book of The Imager Portfolio.

GARTH NIX

Garth Nix was born in 1963 in Melbourne, Australia. A full-time writer since 2001, he has worked as a literary agent, marketing consultant, book editor, book publicist, book sales representative, bookseller, and as a part-time soldier in the Australian Army Reserve. Garth's books include the award-winning fantasy novels *Sabriel, Lirael,* and *Abhorsen*; and the cult favorite young adult SF novel *Shade's Children.* His fantasy novels for children include *The Ragwitch*; the six books of The Seventh Tower sequence, and The Keys to the Kingdom series. His most recent book is *Troubletwisters*, cowritten with Sean Williams. More than five million copies of his books have been sold around the world, his books have appeared on the bestseller lists of *The New York Times*, *Publishers Weekly*, *The Guardian*, and *The Australian*, and his work has been translated into thirty-eight languages. He lives in a Sydney beach suburb with his wife and two children.

JOHN PICACIO

John Picacio is one of the most prolific American cover artists for science fiction, fantasy, and horror of the last ten years. His body of work includes covers for books by Dan Simmons, Harlan Ellison, Robert Silverberg, L. E. Modesitt, Jr., Mark Chadbourn, Ian McDonald, Joe R. Lansdale, Jeffrey Ford, Frederik Pohl, James Tiptree, Jr., and many, many more. He has produced acclaimed artwork for franchises such as *Star Trek* and the *X-Men*, as well as major epics such as George R. R. Martin's A Song of Ice and Fire and Michael Moorcock's Elric saga. Accolades include the World Fantasy Award, the Locus Award, four Chesley Awards, and two International Horror Guild Awards, two *Asimov's* Poll Awards for Best Cover Art, and seven Hugo Award nominations in the Best Professional Artist category. His website is www.johnpicacio.com.

TAMORA PIERCE

Tamora Pierce is a *New York Times* and *Wall Street Journal* bestselling author and has written over two dozen fantasy novels for teenagers. *Tortall and Other Lands: A Collection of Tales*, her most recent book, was published in February of 2011. Tammy was born in South Connellsville, Pennsylvania into a long, proud line of hillbillies. While her family didn't have much money, they did have plenty of books, and books continue to be the main yardstick by which she measures true wealth.

Crediting her fans with her success, Tammy loves the chance to go on tour and thank them in person. "Struggling along as a kid and even through my twenties, it's the kind of life I dreamed of but never believed I would get. And I never take it for granted." She hopes her books inspire her readers with the feeling that they, too, can do anything if they want it badly enough.

Tammy now lives in Syracuse with her beloved Spouse-Creature Tim Liebe, and their numerous cats, two parakeets, and whatever freeloading wildlife takes up residence in their backyard.

MISAKO ROCKS!

Misako Rocks! is a Japanese graphic novelist from New York City. Her first break came when *The Onion* decided to use her illustrations for their now famous "Savage Love" column, which runs every week. Shortly thereafter, Misako scored a two-book deal with Hyperion, a three-book deal with Henry Holt, and a writing gig for *Archie* comics. Recently Misako published a Japanese children's book, *Kodomo Eigojuku*, with Japanese publisher Meijishoin. Also, she is now running a monthly comic column in *Aera English Magazine* in Japan.

S. M. STIRLING

S. M. Stirling was born in France in 1953, to Canadian parents—although his mother was born in England and grew up in Peru. After that he lived in Europe, Canada, Africa, and the U.S., and visited several other continents. He graduated from law school in Canada but had his dorsal fin surgically removed, and published his first novel (*Snowbrother*) in 1984, going full-time as a writer in 1988, the year of his marriage to Janet Moore of Milford, Massachusetts, who he met, wooed, and proposed to at successive World Fantasy Conventions. In 1995 he suddenly realized that he could live anywhere and they decamped from Toronto, that large, cold, gray city on Lake Ontario, and moved to Santa Fe, New Mexico. He became an American citizen in 2004. His latest books are *The Council of Shadows* (May 2011) and *The Tears of the Sun* (Sept. 2011), from Roc/Penguin. His hobbies mostly involve reading—history, anthropology, archaeology, and travel, besides fiction—but he also cooks and bakes for fun and food. For twenty years he also pursued the martial arts, until hyperextension injuries convinced him he was in danger of becoming the most deadly cripple in human history. Currently he lives with Janet and the compulsory authorial cats.

JOE SUTPHIN

Illustrator and designer Joe Sutphin has been drawing creatures and creating stories about them since he was very young. He spends as much time as possible in nature observing and picking up little critters to draw in his sketchbook. He is an avid collector of kids' books and possibly addicted to black licorice and root beer. Joe does not live on the Red Planet, but he does live in a big red barn along with his family in Carroll, Ohio. You can visit him at joesutphin.com.

CATHERYNNE M. VALENTE

Born in the Pacific Northwest in 1979, Catherynne M. Valente is the author of over a dozen works of fiction and poetry, including *Palimpsest*, the Orphan's Tales series, *Deathless*, and the Andre Norton Award-winning, crowdfunded phenomenon *The Girl Who Circumnavigated Fairyland in a Ship of Her Own Making*. She also is the winner of the Tiptree Award, the Mythopoeic Award, the Rhysling Award, and the Million Writers Award. She has been nominated for the Pushcart Prize, the Spectrum Awards, and was a finalist for the World Fantasy Award in 2007 and 2009. She lives on an island off the coast of Maine with her partner and two dogs.

GENEVIEVE VALENTINE

Genevieve Valentine's first novel, *Mechanique: a Tale of the Circus Tresaulti*, was published by Prime Books in 2011. Her short fiction has appeared in *Running with the Pack*, *The Living Dead 2*, *The Way of the Wizard*, *Teeth*, *Clarkesworld*, *Strange Horizons*, *Escape Pod*, and more. Her appetite for bad movies is insatiable, a tragedy she tracks on her blog at genevievevalentine.com.

CHARLES VESS

Charles Vess was born in 1951 in Lynchburg, Virginia. His award-winning work has graced the covers and interior pages of many comic books from publishers including Marvel (*Spider-Man*, *Raven Banner*) and DC (*Books of Magic*, *Swamp Thing*, *Sandman*). His recent work is found more in book illustration, such as *The Ladies of Grace Adieu*, *The Green Man: Tales from the Mythic Forest*, *A Circle of Cats*, and *Peter Pan*. Charles's awards include the Inkpot Award, three World Fantasy Awards, the Mythopoeic Fantasy Award, two Spectrum Annual Awards—a Gold and a Silver—two Chesley Awards, a Locus Award for Best Artist, and two Will Eisner Comic Industry Awards. Charles's most recent publications include two *New York Times* bestselling picture books penned by Neil Gaiman, *Blueberry Girl* and *Instructions*. He has resided on a small farm in Washington County, Virginia, since 1991, and works from his studio, Green Man Press, in Abingdon. For visual treats and updates, visit his website: greenmanpress.com.

ROBIN WASSERMAN

Robin Wasserman is the author of several books for children and young adults, including *The Book of Blood and Shadow*, *Hacking Harvard*, and the Cold Awakening Trilogy (*Frozen*, *Shattered*, and *Torn*). She lives and writes in Brooklyn, New York, and is impatiently awaiting the day she wakes up on Mars.

CHRISSIE ZULLO

Chrissie Zullo is an artist and illustrator best known for her cover work on DC/Vertigo's Eisner-nominated *Cinderella: From Fabletown with Love* and *Cinderella: Fables are Forever*. She has also done work for Topp's *Star Wars* trading cards, a variant cover for *Hack/Slash*, and interior work on DC/Vertigo's *Madame Xanadu* and *Fables*. She is currently working on interior work for the upcoming *Womanthology* comic book. Her work has been featured twice in *Spectrum: The Best in Contemporary Fantastic Art*. Chrissie currently resides in New York City, a city quite far from Barsoom. Her weekly progress in art can be found at her blog: chrissiez.blogspot.com.

ACKNOWLEDGMENTS

Many thanks to the following:

Edgar Rice Burroughs for creating this wonderful world and peopling it with these incredible characters, and for firing the imagination of the generations of science fiction writers who have followed in his footsteps.

David Gale at Simon & Schuster for publishing this anthology, and to him and his assistant, Navah Wolfe, for shepherding the book through the publication process. Jenica Nasworthy for her copyediting prowess, Lizzy Bromley and Tom Daly for their work designing the book, and Michelle Kratz for guiding the book through production.

A special thank-you to Tony DiTerlizzi, for helping us connect with several of our artists even though, in the end, he couldn't participate himself.

My agent, Joe Monti, for finding a good home for this project, and for the incredible amount of support he's provided since taking me on as a client—he's gone above and beyond the call of duty. To any writers reading this: You'd be lucky to have Joe in your corner.

Gordon Van Gelder, who, like John Carter, is immortal and forever young. Or maybe he just seems that way because he's so full of wisdom and has taught me so much. Truly, he is the Jeddak of Editors.

David Barr Kirtley for his assistance wrangling the header notes, and for our continuing friendship.

Richard A. Lupoff for writing the wonderful gazetteer found in this volume, and for being a vast font of knowledge of all things Barsoomian.

My amazing wife, Christie Yant, for all her love and support and for hugging me while I write this. Also, for the chicken chili, which doesn't really have anything to do with this book, but is so good that it really deserves acknowledgment.

My mom for her endless enthusiasm for all my new projects.

My dear friends Robert Bland, Desirina Boskovich, Christopher M. Cevasco, Douglas E. Cohen, Jordan Hamessley, Andrea Kail, and Matt London for enduring endless conversations about possible anthology projects and hearing me go on at length about Barsoom while I was working on this one.

The readers and reviewers who loved my other anthologies, making it possible for me to do more.

And last, but certainly not least: a big thanks to all of the authors and artists who appear in this anthology.